The Shadow Follows

DAVID MEDALIE

PICADOR AFRICA

First published 2006 by Picador Africa
an imprint of Pan Macmillan South Africa
P O Box 411717, Craighall, Johannesburg 2024
www.picadorafrica.co.za

ISBN-13: 9781770100145
ISBN-10: 1770100148

Edited by Alex Dodd
Typeset in 11 on 14pt Palatino by The Setting Stick
Cover design: Donald Hill of Studio 5

Printed and bound by Pinetown Printers

For my family: Sheila, Joe, Jalene, Aurelle,
Miriam, Gloria, Melanie, Stephen, Shirley,
Ory and Rose

And my second family: Adrienne, Merle,
Daniel, Adam, Laurie, Jocelyn, Charles, Jake,
Noah, Martin, Audrey, Emma, Jeanne, Oliver
and Joseph

Perhaps all our loves are merely hints and symbols; vagabond-language scrawled on gate-posts and paving-stones along the weary road that others have tramped before us; perhaps you and I are types and this sadness which sometimes falls between us springs from disappointment in our search, each straining through and beyond the other, snatching a glimpse now and then of the shadow which turns the corner always a pace or two ahead of us.

Evelyn Waugh, *Brideshead Revisited*

We cast a shadow on something wherever we stand, and it is no good moving from place to place to save things; because the shadow always follows.

E. M. Forster, *A Room with a View*

For thou shalt see the land afar off...

Deuteronomy, Chapter 32, verse 52

1   *Blood*

GRIEF HAS A trajectory, which has been published and is available for instruction: there is denial, there is anger; at the end there is acceptance, after which you may take your grief and lay it away.

Deanna couldn't remember what the sequence of grief was supposed to look like – what came first, what followed. And she was convinced that, whatever the sequence was, it didn't correspond with what she was experiencing, for she'd begun with misanthropy; and that, surely, wasn't on the list?

Misanthropy was a curious impulse, especially for one in her profession. She was supposed to heal people and alleviate their suffering, but she felt now that she could quite blithely consign them all to medieval agony. Beneath her antipathy she felt the tug of fear. Why were people so frightened of ghosts and vampires and corpses that refused to lie still? There was no reason to be afraid of any of these ghouls, so timid – docile, even – beneath their extravagant menace. The truly fearful object was the unremarkable person who sat next to you at the movies and annoyed you by scratching noisily in a box as he excavated his popcorn. For even if you glared at him or shrank away from him and surrendered to him the elbow rest, there was no escaping him. He breathed over you. He coughed over you. He sneezed over you. He had been to the toilet and had not washed his hands (very few men did: not even one in five, according to studies). He was not innocent of drops of urine and faecal particles. There were bacteria under his fingernails, which were too long. He was shedding bits of skin, which meant that he would be with you for quite some time. There was more than a faint possibility that you would even ingest some of him before you went to bed that night.

He seemed innocuous enough: he ate his mound of popcorn (which never came to an end), and watched the American movie with as much absorption as if he had never in all his life seen a car chase or an unscathed hero or a happy ending. But he *was* a threat, a grave threat. For there was no getting away from him – from his imperviousness, his proximity, his droppings, his sheddings, his germs, his power to infect you; his blood. More than anything, it was his blood.

The wind, which had been blowing on and off all day, was dying down with the onset of twilight. Deanna began to shiver, but couldn't bring herself to go inside and get a jersey. She sat on a bench in the garden and the anger that blood had provoked threatened to overwhelm her. Blood: so thick, so copious, so indiscreet, so overbearing. Why must they make their blood everyone else's problem? Why, oh why, could they not keep their blood to themselves?

Aunt Maisie had never trusted Richard. She would not now say, 'I told you so,' but she would think it. She would show that she was thinking it. She was not a person who hid her feelings. She'd been suspicious of Richard even before she met him. 'Tell me about his family,' she had said, and Deanna told her as much about his parents as she thought was wise, adding that he was an only child; then, almost hoping that her aunt wouldn't hear, she muttered that he was adopted. But Aunt Maisie heard only too well. She stiffened. She put down her cup and saucer and waved in the air a block of shortbread which she had been about to put in her mouth. Deanna knew what was coming: blood.

Aunt Maisie was obsessed with blood. Not the spectacular kind, which didn't interest her: she never watched anything violent or gory on TV and, although she liked to read murder mysteries, they had to be in the bloodless, intellectual tradition, where the victim was unlikable, mourned by no one, and the discovery of the corpse, lying demurely in the drawing-room or smoking-room, caused only mild consternation. No, it was blood in all its genetic eloquence that engrossed Aunt Maisie – blood that confessed its origins and hinted darkly at its destinations. For her, blood was proscriptive, unyielding, unforgiving. Blood was a ringmaster who cracked his whip and life itself, however much it snarled and put its ears back, still had to jump through the hoops and do his bidding.

'There's bad blood there,' Aunt Maisie would say; and that meant that there could be no appeal, no mitigating circumstances. If there were illness in the family, every generation would have to succumb. ('There's bad blood in that family,' she said once. 'Even the new-born babies suffer from gout.') Similarly, if there had been insanity, schizophrenia, drug addiction, alcoholism, adultery, a pregnancy at fifteen, a fondness for frequenting racecourses or even a tendency to embezzle other people's trust funds, the same principle would apply: bad blood coursed in the veins and bad blood must out. Blood was where it all started; and, for Aunt Maisie, that was where it ended. She was entirely indifferent to the claims of Nurture, but Nature was everything to her. Nurture was a cardboard house into which people fled in their desperate search for refuge, but Nature would invariably come along and huff and puff and blow their house down. 'Do you want to know the secret to a long and healthy life?' she was fond of asking. 'It's quite simple, really.' She would pause for effect. *'Choose your parents very carefully.'*

The fact that Richard was adopted was, therefore, to Aunt Maisie an obstacle that could not be surmounted. When she ascertained that he didn't even know who his biological parents were, her alarm intensified. Richard's blood was a blank. It peered out at the world as from behind a one-way mirror. It saw but it could not be seen; it knew but it could not be known. And whether, from that vantage-point, it smiled as sweetly as butterscotch or grinned with fiendish design, no one could say. Deanna hoped that once Aunt Maisie had met Richard, she would feel easier in her mind and allow herself to be happy for her beloved niece. But it made no difference at all – in fact, her suspicions grew. 'Yes, he's charming,' she conceded. 'Very good manners. Impeccable. Yes, he's soft on the eye, no doubt about that. But that's all on the surface. It's what's inside that matters and that's what we know nothing about. You know what I mean? It's much too risky.'

Deanna thought she would keep all this from Richard. But one day, not long before their wedding, he said, 'I don't think your aunt likes me very much.'

'It's not that,' Deanna said. 'She doesn't trust you – that's all.' She told him why.

Richard was incredulous; then he began to laugh. 'You mean to tell me that nothing I do is going to make any difference? Your aunt is never going to like me because I don't know who my real parents were?'

'I'm afraid so.'

'My blood is a mystery?'

'Your blood is a mystery.'

'And that's a problem?'

'That's a *big* problem.'

'But I've never heard anything so absurd. It sounds like a line from Oscar Wilde – you know, that terrifying woman, Lady something-or-other. What does she say? She won't allow the young man to marry her daughter until he finds his parents.'

'You mean Lady Bracknell. She says something like, "I strongly advise you, Mr Worthing, to acquire at least one parent of either sex before the season is over."'

'Yes, that's right. I must read it again.'

Deanna joined in the laughter, but she felt some disquiet, which she hid from him. It was important to her that Aunt Maisie approved of Richard. She didn't want her to withhold her blessing, however illogical her reason, however eccentric (*batty* was the word Richard used) she was. Richard shouldn't be condemned simply because there had been no exegesis of his blood.

Later that evening the wind rose again. The roof creaked and a branch scratched against the bathroom window. Deanna caught the melancholy of the wind, but she couldn't reconcile what she felt with the forlornness it bore. Her sorrow was so keen and the season's so sluggish. She wanted gales, floods and heat waves – something that strained at the leash and bit as soon as it was released. But it was the wrong time of year for that. In August the wind on the highveld is soulful with dust and desiccated grass. Trying to bring news of spring, it succeeds only in telling tales of matted winter. It pants like an arthritic dog. It is beset by seizures that come upon it unexpectedly: effete little whirlwinds which chase their own tails.

A farmer told Deanna once that if there were no wind in August, there would be no spring rains in October. 'Seasons must be what they're supposed to be,' he said. 'Winter must be cold, summer must be hot and rainy, the wind must blow in August. Otherwise the whole year will be wrong.' She thought now of what he had said. It was intriguing to think that seasons could be unseasonal – or insufficiently seasonal. People would relish and be grateful for a mild winter; a still August, free of this scratchy wind, would be welcomed. But if there were drought in the summer, then the mildness of the winter and the stillness of the early spring would be too great a price to pay. Once the circle is bent at one point, can it correct itself at another – or must it remain lopsided? Can a misshapen season ever be repaired?

A virus has no purpose and no capacity for malignancy. It may do harm, but it means no harm. Rationally, Deanna knew that. But in another part of her mind, the virus had a plan of action and a mind to malice. There it was a spy, a traitor, a psychopath, a serial killer, a Trojan Horse. With an effort of the will, she could suppress temporarily the images that emanated from that part of her mind. But when she did so, she found it difficult to know how to react to what had happened to her. An enemy in her blood, an old-fashioned despot, an unrelenting taskmaster – that was something she could understand, even as she feared it. But how does one respond to an insensate danger?

The banality of the incident that had brought this upon her struck her again and again. It belonged with the accidents of ordinary life: the dented bumpers, the shards of broken glass, the forgotten appointments, slips of the mind and of the fingers. When she had to inform her patients of an unfavourable diagnosis, she drew her words and advice from that same discourse of the everyday. And when she told Neil what had happened, she tried her best to speak in the same matter-of-fact way.

'But how could such a thing happen?' he demanded. 'I can't believe what you're telling me.'

'These accidents are more common than people realise,' she said. 'They happen all the time. I had given a patient an injection and was withdrawing the needle. He was confused and thrashing around, and the next thing he knocked my hand and I stabbed myself in the thumb with the needle.'

'And he was HIV-positive?'

'Yes, he was.'

'And now? Are you infected too?'

'It's most unlikely that I am. Infections from this kind of injury – we call it a needle-stick injury – are very rare. About three out of every thousand. It depends on the size of the needle, the depth of the penetration, and so on. But we have to take precautions.'

'What precautions? What are you going to do?' Neil's questions had an aggressive edge to them, but Deanna maintained the same cool tone. His reaction was a familiar one: the relatives of people who were ill were often more accusatory or emotional when they heard bad news than the patients themselves.

'I'll have to take medication for about four weeks. I've already started taking it. It's called PEP – Post-Exposure Prophylaxis.'

'And then?'

'We test the blood. And keep testing it. All going well, it will test negative.'

She regarded her dispassionate words as if from a distance. They had been to obedience school and, when they had to perform, how well they did their job! But making them prevail in her own mind was another matter. What had occurred was a mishap, just a mishap, but it strained to be more than that. It wanted, above all, to become a metaphor. And she didn't know if it would be possible to thwart that impulse. She held onto the triteness of the incident as tightly as she could. But her misanthropy, she knew, was one of the signs that her grasp wasn't as secure as it should be. And what would happen if she failed? What if she had already failed? What was being prepared for her even now in the domain of dreams and of darkness?

The conversation with Neil had taken place several days ago and there had been no word from him since. She tried to phone him, but with no success. Where *was* he? She was growing tired of making excuses for him. She knew that he was worried and distressed. But of what use is a concern that is not demonstrated? The truth was that he was neglecting her. He was the one person she wanted to hear from; one of the very few she could exempt from her moroseness and misanthropy. From whom else could she expect support? (They had decided not to tell Aunt Maisie what had happened.) But there was no sign of him.

She was swallowing more headache pills when the telephone rang. She thought it had to be Neil at last; possibly even a contrite Neil. Instead, it was Richard.

'Oh, it's you,' she said.

'I'm just calling to find out how you're feeling,' he said.

'Lousy.'

'What sort of lousy?'

'Straight-out-of-the-textbook lousy. Headache. Nausea. Diarrhoea. Fatigue. Insomnia. A charming ensemble.'

'Anything I can do?'

'No thank you. It's kind of you.'

'Well, I'm concerned about you. So's Neil.'

'*Neil*? When did you hear from him?'

'He phoned me this morning.'

'I can't believe my ears. He's been avoiding me like the plague. He hasn't called or been to see me since I told him what happened. I get no support from him – nothing. And yet he phones you!'

'He probably doesn't know how to express his concern. But he's very worried, of course.'

'It amuses me that you two still keep in touch.'

'Deanna, you know he doesn't want to take sides.'

'This doesn't sound like not taking sides. It sounds like taking sides with *you*. And he's *my* brother, not yours!'

'Well, that's between you and him. I just wanted to find out how you are and see if there's anything I can do. Some shopping, maybe?'

'No thank you, I'm fine.'

'Are you sure?'

'Quite sure.'

'It's a genuine offer. Even estranged husbands have their uses, you know.'

'I'm sure they do. But really, I'll be okay. Thanks for the call. And when you speak to my flesh and blood, you can tell him that his solicitude is overwhelming.'

Richard didn't respond to her last comment. He said good-bye and rang off. Deanna lay down on the bed. She was feeling dizzy. She thought of what Richard had said: *even estranged husbands have their uses*. He had offered to do some shopping for her. That was thoughtful of him. It was more than her brother had done. Why then did she feel annoyed by the gesture? Why couldn't she permit the good intention, even if she'd declined the offer itself? This bitterness troubled her. It was like biting into a fruit and discovering, too late, that it is rotten inside; no amount of spitting and rinsing can wash the knowledge, the soft dismay, out of one's mouth.

She wondered if she should make herself something to eat. It seemed like too much trouble. And she wasn't hungry. She might not be able to keep it down anyway. Even when she wasn't feeling nauseous, she felt no inclination, since Richard had moved out, to prepare food. She knew that people who live alone tend to neglect their nutritional needs. Was she now joining their ranks? They eat take-aways and too many cheese sandwiches. They think vaguely of meat and three veggies but end up with scrambled eggs on toast instead. They buy pizza slices and eat some of them and leave the rest for tomorrow. They are disgusted the next morning by the leftovers. Cold pizza makes them feel sad about their lives and a little ashamed. The truth is that they don't make proper meals because they don't consider themselves worth the effort. They succumb to a notion of their own meagreness. They can't feed themselves without feeding their solitude and so they begrudge themselves anything that takes time and care to prepare.

As Richard grew older, the identity of his birth mother became more and more important to him. Curiosity gave way to a stabbing need to find out who she was – who *he* was. But there was very little to go on. He knew that he had been born in 1964, on Boxing Day, in the Countess of Athlone Home. The Home was then an institution for young white unmarried mothers. They wished to keep their pregnancies secret. When they began to 'show', as it was called, they moved into the Home and remained there until they gave birth. In most cases, they gave their babies up for adoption before returning to their lives. The circumstances surrounding Richard's birth, however, were rather different. A woman in the very last stages of pregnancy arrived alone in a taxi, carrying one small suitcase, and admitted herself. It was the afternoon of 24 December 1964. She gave her name as Rena Niemandt, her address as 27 Low Street, Springs, her age as twenty-nine and her next-of-kin as her mother, Mrs J.A. Niemandt of the same address. She had no identity documents, but said that her mother would be coming to visit her after Christmas and would bring whatever the Home required. The Matron was very strict and would usually have insisted that she produce these documents, but it was almost Christmas Eve and she decided to admit the woman and get what they needed from her after Christmas. When questioned further, the woman said she was unmarried and indicated that she wished her child to be given up for adoption.

Two days later her waters broke and she went into labour. Richard was born in the early evening of 26 December. The birth was uncomplicated and the baby was big and strong, weighing just over eight pounds. The mother said she had no desire to see the infant, although she asked whether it was a boy or a girl. Just before midnight, a nurse looked in on the woman, who was sitting up in bed. She assured the nurse that she was fine and asked for something to drink. At 4am, the nurse looked in again. The bed was empty. She was gone.

No one ever saw her again. When they tried to trace her, they found that the address she had filled in did not exist and it soon became clear that the names she had given for herself and her mother were fabricated too. Richard was adopted by Jock and Elaine Slater and the identity of his birth mother was declared an unsolvable mystery.

But in his mind he couldn't let the matter rest. He would not. This mysterious person was tied to him in the closest way possible: through blood. If she remained unknown, then a part of him would remain forever unknown too. Blood should reveal, not conceal. It should unmask, declare, attest. It should bear witness. In recent months his preoccupation with his origins turned suddenly into a determination to make every effort to find his biological mother. Until she was found, he would continue to be oppressed by questions to which he could find no answer. And his blood would remain hidden to himself, a stranger dwelling permanently in his own house – a stranger with an occluded face.

To most people the years as they went by were kind or not kind; in Aunt Maisie's case, they seemed too frightened even to approach. Tall, big-boned, chain-smoking, gruff-voiced, judgemental and irrepressible, she oversaw the passing of the decades like a haughty bird, perched high up, full of contempt for the puny lives of those so far beneath it.

Even mortality she did not find particularly daunting, for she'd decided long ago that she was fully entitled to extreme longevity. It was a right that she had every intention of claiming. Her grandmother had lived to 102, her mother to 91, her father to 93 and her aunt to 98. It was clear to her that genetically she was destined to outlive most (if not all) of her contemporaries. Her blood had decided before she was born that she would live a very long time and, that decision having been made for her, all that was left was to take care that she didn't do something careless, like stepping in front of a bus. Smoking was not a danger she felt she needed to avoid. When Deanna, still a medical student and full of proselytising zeal, tried to tell her about the dangers of smoking (she even offered to show her a photograph of a diseased lung), her aunt waved the advice and the photograph away. 'If it shortens my life,' she said, 'then I'll go at 95 instead of 99. I'm willing to sacrifice those four years. After all, 95 is still a decent age.'

Aunt Maisie was an avid reader of the newspaper – or, rather, of parts of it. She immediately discarded the sports section, the business pages and anything that had to do with motorcars, fashion, spirituality (New Age or otherwise), dating, courtship, dieting and advice on how to achieve better orgasms. She perused the rest dutifully, sighing loudly or clicking her tongue as she did so. What she read most carefully, however, poring over it as if it were an ancient manuscript that had come recently to light and which only she could decipher, was the part of the classified section which she always referred to as the *Hatched, Matched and Dispatched*. It was her Bible, her Koran, her *Bhagavad-Gita*, her Key to All Mythologies. It was much more to her than pages of announcements (in very small print) about the lives of other people – somehow it had become an oblique commentary on her own life. Deanna and Neil had learned long ago that they had no need even to glance at that section, for Aunt Maisie would always keep them informed of its activities. Despite the circumscribed life that she led in her Killarney flat, she seemed to know everybody in Johannesburg and scrutinised the *Hatched, Matched and Dispatched* with proprietary zeal as if the newspaper maintained it chiefly to keep her informed of the life events of her acquaintances.

In addition, she used the information gleaned there to confirm her in her devout beliefs about blood and its dictates. 'Twins,' she said one day after the *Hatched* column had been carefully explored. 'A boy and a girl. Yes, there are a lot of twins in that family. They were bound to have some in this generation too. But they'll have to watch their cholesterol very carefully. The parents should get them into the habit of drinking low-fat milk from the start.'

'People can have twins these days for different reasons,' Deanna ventured to say. 'Nowadays many couples have treatment for infertility, and that sometimes produces multiple births – even triplets.'

'Infertility!' Aunt Maisie shook her head. 'Let me tell you, there's no infertility in that family! They all breed like rabbits. The husbands only have to *look* at their wives and they fall pregnant.'

She also studied the insertions for every whiff of hypocrisy. When she detected it, she was outraged, as if someone had dared to sully the testamentary purity of her *Hatched, Matched and Dispatched* with false professions. 'Look at this!' she would say. 'His sister barely spoke to him for years. They quarrelled over their father's will. There was no love lost there, I can tell you. Now he's died and she puts *beloved brother, deeply mourned and sadly missed* and all that sort of thing. It's enough to make me puke – and to make him turn in his freshly-dug grave!'

On another occasion she reported that a woman, recently divorced, had placed an insertion in response to the death of her ex-husband. *Some bonds are never severed*, the woman had written. Aunt Maisie regarded this as an act of deliberate effrontery. 'What a cheek! She says some bonds are never severed, but she's just succeeded in severing quite a few – you know what I mean?'

She liked tributes to the Dispatched to be full and generous, although she despised sentimentality. The best elegists, she declared, were the Greeks and the Lebanese. The Jews rated high on her list too (Aunt Maisie had had a Jewish father and, although she was not Jewish herself, had a special interest in the Jewish community). However, she felt that the Jews sometimes went too far: every acquaintance and every distant relative, it seemed, felt the need to place an insertion. When the time came for her to die, she didn't want someone who had once nodded to her from across the street to proclaim inconsolable grief.

The worst contributors to this section, she declared, were those whom she called the 'Wasps'. 'You know who I mean,' she said. 'They live in the mink-and-manure belt and are always going to gymkhanas and having parties where there is too much to drink and too little to eat. And they have double-barrelled names and small, yappy dogs.' Their insertions she deemed terse, ungenerous and, worst of all, uninformative. 'From Priscilla,' she read and shook her head in despair. 'What's the use of that? Who *is* Priscilla? The mother, the sister, the daughter or the woman who shoes the horses?'

In the absence of any information about Richard's blood, Aunt Maisie rapidly construed a history of her own devising. He came, she decided, from a long line of good-looking, ingratiating, dissolute charmers who preyed on women. They lost their looks, turned to drink and gambling, had everything they owned repossessed by the sheriff of the court, and died young and overweight in shabby hotels. Their corpses were judged by morticians to be at least twenty years older than they actually were. Deanna, futile as she knew the effort to be, had pointed out repeatedly that Richard drank nothing except a glass of wine with his meal, never gambled and was in no apparent danger of losing his looks. Predictably, it made not the slightest difference. 'I'm perfectly aware of that,' said Aunt Maisie. 'I'm not a fool. But blood has its own rules and follows its own path – you know what I mean? The details may vary but the pattern never does. The beginning and the destination are the same.'

When sleep will not come, there is nothing you can do about it. Sleep is not summoned or seduced; it can't be bullied out of its grot. Deanna felt exhausted, but lay awake for hours. Eventually she got out of bed and walked in the dark to the kitchen to get something to drink. Her headache had returned – she would need to take more painkillers. In the passage she felt something silky under her bare foot and bent to pick it up. It was a feather. She grimaced and went to wash her feet. Percy had killed and eaten another bird. In the morning she would have to scoop up the feathers and, no doubt, there would also be entrails to remove and blood stains in the pile of the carpet. It was a regular occurrence.

She remembered how intrigued Richard had been by her cat when they first lived together. His father was allergic to cats and he had little knowledge of them. He thought that they wouldn't appeal to him or he to them; he thought, as many people did, that they were perverse and proud. When Percy jumped into his lap or climbed onto his shoulders, he was taken aback at first, then delighted.

'Why do people have the idea that they're aloof?' he asked.

'Because they compare them with dogs. They express affection differently.'

He rubbed Percy's ears and scratched her under the chin. 'Women like cats,' he said.

'Well, in my experience they tend to have strong feelings about them, but not necessarily of a positive sort. They either love them or hate them.'

'You've always loved them?'

'Oh, yes. For many reasons. One is that they're never blasé, never jaded. A cat without its curiosity would be like a giraffe without a neck. Or a shark without teeth. The ancient Egyptians worshipped them, you know.'

'Yes, I know. By the way, why did you call her Percy? She's a girl.'

'It's short for Persephone. I found her outside my doorstep one cold July night. She rose up towards me, as I always say, out of darkness and winter.'

When Deanna finally fell asleep, she had one of those brimming, importunate dreams that had so often disturbed her sleep and unsettled her waking hours when she was younger, but which had become less and less frequent as she grew older. She dreamed that she had been invited back to her old primary school to speak to the children. She arrived at the school wearing her white coat and a stethoscope around her neck. The school seemed deserted at first: the sports fields lay silent beneath the winter sun and her footsteps echoed hollowly in the dark corridors. But then Miss Lloyd, who'd taught her when she was in Grade Two, came forward to greet her. Deanna felt puzzled as she shook her hand, for wasn't Miss Lloyd dead? Someone, she seemed to remember, had insisted that she was dead. Yet here she was, exactly the same: her grey hair still tied back in a bun, and her big, crooked toes looking, as always, squashed and uncomfortable in the white sandals which she always wore, even in winter.

'The children are looking forward to meeting you,' she said as she ushered Deanna into a classroom. 'They're so excited, the little dears.'

Deanna wanted to stop her, to explain that she didn't know what she was expected to talk about, but there was no opportunity for that. They entered the classroom. It was so bright and cheery that her anxiety receded. The walls were painted duckling yellow and were almost covered by drawings done by the children – all depicting parks, swings and picnics. About a dozen children were sitting on the floor. They stared at her impassively.

'Children,' said Miss Lloyd, clapping her hands, 'please pay attention.' The children remained silent and motionless. 'This is Dr Deanna Lewis. She was also in Grade Two. She has come to answer all your questions.' She looked expectantly at Deanna.

'Thank you, Miss Lloyd,' said Deanna. 'I'm not sure what you would like to hear, but I thought I would tell you about my work as a doctor and maybe we can chat about how we stay healthy by eating the right food and doing exercise and getting lots of sleep.'

'They were hoping you would talk to them about diseases that afflict the very young,' said Miss Lloyd, 'and inform them of the latest research.'

'Well, there's chicken pox...' began Deanna, but she was interrupted by a little blond-haired girl with a round white face like a complacent marshmallow, who tugged at her sleeve.

'Hypertension,' she said. 'I suffer from hypertension.'

'Well, that's *most* unusual,' said Deanna. 'At your age, that's very rare. Do they know...'

Again the child interrupted her. 'My Mommy gives me pills,' she said. 'Beta-blockers. She gives me beta-blockers every morning and evening. And I'm on a low salt diet.'

'No crisps for you,' said a little boy, putting out his tongue at her.

Deanna scarcely knew how to respond. 'Well, that is the conventional treatment. I hope it's sorted out the problem,' she said lamely.

A dark-haired boy put up his hand. 'Doctor, what is the best treatment for haemorrhoids?'

'Oh, I don't think you have to worry about that,' said Deanna. 'Not at your stage in life.'

'But I've got haemorrhoids!' His voice rose and it sounded as if he were about to burst into tears.

'There are various lotions,' Deanna said hastily. 'And suppositories. In severe cases, surgery is recommended.'

'But I don't *want* surgery!'

Much to Deanna's relief, Miss Lloyd interposed. 'What the children really want to know about,' she said, smiling benignly, 'is the movement of blood in the body.'

'Well, *that* I can tell you about. That's no problem at all. You see, boys and girls, the heart…'

This time it was Miss Lloyd who interrupted her. 'No, no,' she said. 'That's not what I had in mind. Children, tell Dr Lewis how we do things here.'

'*Show, don't tell,*' the children chanted dutifully. '*Show, don't tell. Show, don't tell.*'

Deanna was about to retort that she had no way of demonstrating the circulation of blood in the human body in a Grade Two classroom when she saw that Miss Lloyd was pointing at something in the corner of the room. It was a big red curved tube, made out of something that looked like fibreglass. It was almost as high as the ceiling, with a cavernous opening at the base. How odd that she had not noticed it before!

'You see,' said Miss Lloyd, 'we have built our own gigantic blood vessel. We'll all climb inside with you and then you can show us how the heart distributes blood around the body.'

The children, unbidden, got up and formed a queue at the mouth of the blood vessel. They looked expectantly at Deanna. The hypertensive little girl was sucking a lollipop. Deanna walked to the front of the queue. As she did so, she glanced at the drawings pasted on the walls and wondered why they had seemed so bucolic to her at first. She saw now that there were dark smudges all over them and, in one of the picnic scenes, a family was dismembering a teddy-bear and serving it up as a meal.

The children and Miss Lloyd followed Deanna into the big tube.

They all managed to fit in, but with difficulty. It was stifling inside. The blood vessel was dimly lit with a single red light bulb and Deanna's voice echoed as if in a cave as she tried to explain to the children the difference between systolic and diastolic. 'Where we are walking now the blood should be gushing,' she said. 'This is like a dry river-bed. You have to imagine the blood pouring down here.'

'The children are afraid of blood,' said Miss Lloyd. 'They get very upset when they cut themselves or scrape their knees. I've been trying to explain to them that there's nothing to be afraid of, but they don't believe me. That's why I invited you here today.'

'Miss Lloyd is quite right,' Deanna said. 'Children, you should listen to what your teacher tells you. Blood is good, not bad. We need it. If we didn't have blood, we would all be dead.' (She was about to say 'as dead as Miss Lloyd', for she still had a vague but persistent impression that Miss Lloyd had been reported dead, but she stopped herself.) She paused and the children gathered around her. She felt as if she were pointing out a noteworthy sight to a group of tourists. 'Blood brings us into life,' she told the children. 'And it keeps us alive.'

They were climbing up a steep incline now, nearing the top of the tube. Suddenly the children stopped and stared ahead of them. Deanna saw that they were not alone in the tunnel. The figure of a man lounged against the wall of the blood vessel. He was dressed most curiously: his left side in red and the right in white. And when they drew closer, they saw that there was a division of another sort too. His left side was strikingly beautiful, the hair thick and glossy, the skin warm with a sanguinary glow, the lips full and red over the fine white teeth. But the other side was gaunt and livid, the skull bare, the skin mottled with patches of yellow and white, the teeth stained and broken. The children shrank back, but Deanna felt unable to move. The man approached her. She saw that where the face was beautiful, the eye was imperious and scornful, but where the face was hideous, the eye was forlorn and kind.

The children were running away now, down the red gullet of the blood vessel. There was no sign of Miss Lloyd. Only one little boy remained, a pale, wistful-looking child whom Deanna had not noticed before. A mark like a red flower crept across his brow. She took his hand and led him slowly towards the entrance which framed the end of the tunnel like a horseshoe of light.

Deanna switched on the light to see what time it was. It was a quarter to three. She sighed. Would she ever get back to sleep? And if she did, would there be more unnerving dreams like that? How eerie it was to have gone back to school. And there was Miss Lloyd, who had, of course, been dead for many years; even in the dream she had dimly known that. Those crooked toes protruding from the white sandals: what odd things one remembered!

She made herself a cup of tea and rummaged in her bookcase. She found *The Rivals* and took the well-thumbed book and the tea to bed with her. She skimmed through the play, reading only Mrs Malaprop's speeches, smiling to herself as she had done so often before. The phrases were as familiar to her as rhymes from her childhood:

my affluence over my niece is very small
he is the very pine-apple of politeness
she's as headstrong as an allegory on the banks of Nile

What upside-down joy they communicated; what pleasure there was in the placing of their misplacing! Here, only here, was the wrong word right, the wrong note sonorous.

To her surprise, she felt quite soon the tug of sleepiness. Perhaps, she thought, the best way to be spared unpleasant dreams is to think benign thoughts before crossing over into sleep. Perhaps it was time to let go, for a little while, of the anger and the bitterness and the fear. Perhaps she needed to let herself enter a world which has what this messy one of ours lacks: internal logic. Surprisingly, she found it quite easy to do. She went to sleep conjuring up scenes in which pineapples were studiously polite and allegories sunbathed ostentatiously on the banks of the Nile.

2 Frogs

IN THE HOUSE in which Richard grew up it was always Sunday afternoon. The rooms were quiet, sombre, sleepy, as if they had been swathed in cotton-wool. The ticking of the grandfather clock and the clack of footsteps across the parquet floors seemed to come from far away, to be receding always. The silence was as thick as gristle.

Richard was brought there when he was three days old. He arrived so suddenly that no preparations had been made for him, and, there being no cot for him to sleep in, he lay for the first few days in a desk drawer which had been emptied and lined with a blanket. In the years that followed, he felt that the house was never more than distantly tolerant of him. It was too stiff to bend in welcome. It watched, unblinking, as his boyhood and adolescence sped past.

From the outside, it was an unremarkable house – one of those old Greenside clinkers that were built when the sun was not in fashion. Since it faced the wrong way, it was always dark inside: cool in summer, bitterly cold in winter. Large trees on either side made it even darker and colder.

It smelled of wood, of leather, of old books. This was Jock's house, no matter who else lived there. It was like a dog with only one master. There were things which belonged to Elaine, but there was no trace of her personality. The only exception was a portrait which hung above the fireplace. An artist friend had sketched her before she married Jock, had captured in the coquettish toss of the head and the directness of the gaze something that was now gone for ever, that survived only in the frame. Elaine, as she grew older and dimmer, made an anachronism of her own portrait.

Richard found her sitting in the lounge, reading the Sunday newspapers. 'What a lovely surprise!' she called. He bent over her to kiss her. 'Your father is having his nap.'

'I'll see him when he gets up.'

Elaine smiled at him. She had the kind of smile that reveals the gums as well as the teeth. 'You look well,' she said.

'I feel well.' He knew that she meant he was bearing up.

'How is Deanna?'

'She's taking a lot of strain.'

'Have you seen her?'

'No. I've spoken to her on the phone. She doesn't want to see me.'

'It's easy to blame others when things go wrong,' Elaine said. His parents had sided with him immediately; it amazed him how swift and urgent their solidarity had been. Yet he had not asked for it.

'What's that supposed to mean? Isn't she entitled to feel angry?'

'She also has to assume responsibility. Both parties must share the blame when a relationship runs into difficulties.'

Richard snorted.

'Well, what do you want me to say? Should I put all the blame on you?'

'Why not?'

'I'm sorry. I can't do that. It's not fair to you.'

'You mean you can't bear to think less of your son. You don't want him to sink, even a little, in your estimation.'

His mother did not answer. Indeed, there was no answer to make, for what he proposed was impossible – he knew it as soon as he had uttered the words. She was as unlikely to condemn him as to disown him. She had been loyal to his father through everything; she would be loyal to him too. Nothing could prise away her mistletoe love.

'Will you stay for supper? I'll make omelettes and toast.'

'No thank you. I'm meeting Neil for supper.'

'Neil? Do you still see him?'

'Why not? He's my friend.' Elaine looked puzzled. It was clear that she expected Neil to side with his sister, just as she had sided with her son. She could not conceive of a less chauvinistic affection than her own.

'He's a strange boy,' she said after a pause.

'What's strange about him? And he's not a boy, Mom – he's twenty nine!'

'Is he really?'

'You know that he's been trying…he's been helping me.' Richard had not kept from his parents his desire to locate his biological family. They assured him that they understood the impulse and supported him, but he had not believed them for a moment. He knew that they were dismayed and felt threatened, but were too ashamed of their feelings ever to admit it.

'I don't see what it has to do with him. It's not his business.'

'He's become interested in it. He says it makes him feel like a detective. I like sharing it with him.'

'Some people don't have enough to keep them busy in their own lives.'

Richard didn't reply. There was seldom any use in arguing with his mother. It wasn't that she was stubborn – in fact, especially where his father was concerned, she was almost always compliant. It was that she simply effaced what she didn't wish to hear. She dismissed his remonstrances as a dog's ear twitches away flies. Instead he smiled at her and, in the seeping twilight, she smiled back. She looked small and fragile. For decades people had felt sorry for her. They had pitied her for the shadows which those events of so many years ago had cast upon her. They had done so without knowing whether she deserved or desired their pity.

Richard looked about him as the room darkened. The lights, when they were switched on, would be inadequate. He'd always felt, as a child, that he was straining his eyes when he read. The globes always seemed too small, the lampshades too voluminous. In every room there were unlit corners. And the garden at night was darkened by tall trees and vast black shrubs that the moonlight couldn't penetrate. During that summer of his sixteenth year, the worst year of his life, he'd felt as if they were hiding in their own house. He would lie in bed at night, hearing only the sporadic muttering of the frogs which gathered around the pond in their neighbour's garden. It wasn't a companionable undertone; it wasn't a rich chuckle. The frogs called as if from the depths of a wet, squatting degradation. It was the loneliest and most desolate sound in the world. The frogs, he felt certain, spoke only to those who had, like himself, been cast out by shame and secrecy and lay now beyond the threshold.

There were many different theories afterwards about that dismally unsuccessful crime. Those two young men – Anthony Eric Strauss and Wayne Steven Meyer, both aged twenty – what had they really hoped to accomplish? What had prompted them? It was known that Wayne Meyer had been reading about the Glazer kidnapping and he confessed that he had been excited by it and had spoken about it to Anthony Strauss. Kidnapping had seemed to them so exotic, so rare a crime. Societies specialise in varieties of crime just as they have their own cuisine. In South Africa the diet of theft, housebreaking and quotidian killings would not excite the palate of the crime connoisseur. Even family murders – caviar or quails' eggs elsewhere – are here as unremarkable as fish and chips. But kidnapping! That was something different. In those days there were very few kidnappings. It hadn't yet taken on. There was no indigenous tradition of kidnapping. It was an acquired taste and the taste hadn't been acquired. The Glazer kidnapping stood almost alone, a freak of felony. Perhaps, one theory went, Anthony and Wayne believed that they could succeed where the notorious kidnappers of Mrs Glazer and her son had failed. But that theory left a number of questions unanswered. The two young men came from relatively affluent homes: they did not seem to be desperate for money. There was no evidence of a drug habit, which would have explained such reckless behaviour. And there was another question which was even more difficult to answer: even if there had been a desire to commit a crime for money or for its own sake, that still did not account for the choice of victim. It did not explain why they chose the prime minister's grandson. To many, this suggested a political motive. But there wasn't much to go on. Both young men were Wits students. Anthony was found to have a NUSAS membership, but he wasn't, it seemed, very active in the organisation. A copy of Steve Biko's *I Write What I Like* was found in Wayne's bedroom. That was all. But for some it was enough.

The prime minister's daughter lived in a double-storey house set in an acre and a half of garden in Waterkloof, Pretoria. Anthony and Wayne gained entry to the house by cutting the telephone wires earlier that morning and then pretending to be technicians sent to repair the fault. The prime minister's son-in-law wasn't at home. His wife was upstairs in her bedroom, nursing a migraine. The child, aged two, was downstairs with his nanny. Nothing could have been easier. But everything went wrong;

catastrophically wrong. Anthony and Wayne promised the nanny that they would not hurt her if she kept quiet: they were simply going to tie her up. They expected her to subside into quivering acquiescence. They expected fear to silence her. But they were astonished to find that their muttered injunctions, stern yet gentle, had quite the opposite effect. The nanny began to throw herself about as if they'd already begun to strangle her. She knocked over a vase, which shattered on the tiled floor. She produced a keening sound which grew louder and louder: a cry so overwhelming it seemed to surge beyond her own predicament and resonate with a cosmic anguish. Nothing could silence her or subdue her thrashing movements. When they seized her and tried to gag her, she fought as if for her life and in her wail she seemed to give voice to the grief of every surprised and waylaid soul. Wayne and Anthony gave up trying to restrain her and grabbed the little boy. But by then the prime minister's daughter had descended and saw what was happening; what is more, she had an opportunity to see quite clearly (and to identify subsequently) both the would-be kidnappers. They rushed outside with the child, but the iron gates were closed and they could not get them open. They tried to crash through them, but they wouldn't yield. They left the child sobbing on the paved driveway, still clutching a toy truck, and abandoned their vehicle (an old Peugeot which Anthony's parents had bought him for his eighteenth birthday). They leaped over the wall and ran down the street.

It wasn't their ineptitude which the more conservative newspapers dwelt upon in the days that followed. It was the fact that a brazen attempt had been made to kidnap the prime minister's grandson. These publications did not doubt for a moment that the foiled kidnapping was politically motivated. They speculated that the release of political prisoners would have been demanded instead of a ransom. The little blond boy was depicted as everything that was precious, innocent and vulnerable, the nanny as that loyal kind of family retainer who will lay down her life for her charge. The crime had left a moral stink which, until the culprits had been apprehended, would affront the nostrils of every law-abiding citizen. A furious hunt for the two men was soon under way.

Anthony Eric Strauss and Wayne Steven Meyer could not have imagined that their bungled attempt would have produced such a frenzy. What were they to do? They must have seen that whatever their intention had been, the incident had assumed a terrible course of its own; they must have realised, too, that the desire for revenge in certain quarters would be boundless and the hunt indefatigable. Anthony's uncle was an accountant, an influential and respected man. They decided to appeal to him for help.

The attempted kidnapping had taken place on a Wednesday afternoon. The two young men came to the uncle's house just before eleven o'clock on the Thursday evening. The house was in darkness when they approached. They rang the doorbell and the uncle himself came to the door. He saw immediately that something was wrong and led them to his study. They didn't see Anthony's aunt and cousin who were, presumably, asleep. Wayne and Anthony hadn't slept for almost forty-eight hours; nor had they eaten anything. Anthony couldn't stop trembling, even though it was a warm summer night. Wayne kept swallowing and rubbing his eyes. They were a pitiable sight. They told Anthony's uncle what they had done; whether they told him also what their intention had been is not known. The uncle listened gravely and without comment. When they finished their story, he did not condemn them or scold them. Instead he asked them what they expected him to do. They begged him to help them get onto a plane bound for London. They wanted to go into exile. They felt confident that the British authorities wouldn't extradite them to face the wrath of the South African government and the police. But they could not do it without his help. They didn't even have the money to buy the tickets. Wayne began to weep. Anthony averted his eyes and stared at the carpet. They told him that they would be indebted to him for the rest of their lives. The uncle sat silently for a minute or two. Still he did not condemn or rebuke them. When he spoke at last he told them that he would do his best to help. He had contacts, he said. They had better go to sleep in the spare room. He would telephone his contacts at first light. They went off to an exhausted sleep.

What did the uncle think as he sat alone in the dark house? Did he know from the first what he was going to do? Did he weigh up the alternatives? Did he think with compassion of his sister's son and the other young man? Did he think with compassion of his sister and brother-in-law? Did he resolve to try to help the young men and consider the best way of getting them out of the country? And then, as the darkness began to spawn the hours between three o'clock and dawn – those hours which are its coldest, most silent children – did he harden his heart and change his mind?

At 5am he put through a call. He did not identify himself. He told the police that the would-be kidnappers of the prime minister's grandchild were in his home. He gave the address. By the time Richard woke up, his cousin and his cousin's friend had already been removed from the house.

A few months later, Richard, aged almost sixteen, had a fight with another boy on the rugby field. Richard was bigger and stronger and won quite easily. The boy, who was called James Pilkington, was released to a torn shirt and a bloody nose. He had always disliked Richard and had been taunting him; he had not expected Richard (who had ignored his taunts in the past) to turn suddenly on him.

'I'll get you for this,' he said. 'I'll get you, Richard Slater, if it's the last thing I do!'

'I'm not scared of you,' said Richard. But something made him uneasy. He knew he could always beat Pilkington in a fight; there was no anxiety from that source. But he didn't know what else he might do. Several weeks went by and nothing happened. Richard's sense of foreboding began to abate. He stopped worrying about it. But then Pilkington struck; and it was much, much worse than Richard had imagined.

They were doing English Orals. The teacher, Mrs Cooper, had told them that they could choose their own topics. The class had already heard speeches on such subjects as *Watergate: the Downfall of a President*; *Why the Bantustans Are Not Viable*; *The Life and Death of Elvis Presley*; *How Sport Builds Character*; *Why We Should Resist Peer Pressure*; *Antarctica: the Unknown Continent*; *Why I Don't Want to Remain in South Africa after I Matriculate* (ostensibly a criticism of apartheid and conscription, but consisting largely of an idyllic depiction of Australia); and several talks inspired by the writings of

Kahlil Gibran (then very popular amongst Richard's classmates) in which the lines *Your children are not your children./ They are the sons and daughters of Life's longing for itself./ They come through you but not from you,/ And though they are with you they belong not to you* were invariably quoted. Richard hadn't yet been called upon to deliver his, but he had rehearsed it and felt quite proud of it. It was called *Medicine: The Noble Profession* and it began with a brief history of important medical discoveries – Hippocrates, the Curies, Pasteur, Bright, Fleming, Salk and so on – and ended with an account of why he wished to be a doctor. There was even some humour in it as he anticipated having to force himself to overcome his revulsion and dissect frogs and cadavers; but he ended by declaring that this unpleasant ordeal would be a small price to pay if it meant that he could be admitted to The Noble Profession. He had the speech open on his desk and, as he listened to the others, he stole glances at it to reassure himself that he knew it by heart.

It was James Pilkington, however, who was called upon next. He stood at the front of the class, cleared his throat and said, 'The topic of my speech is: *Famous South African Crimes*'. He read his speech from a pile of stiff yellow cards which he held before him. 'There have been many fascinating and unusual crimes in South Africa,' he began. Then he described several of them. The class grew fascinated. They knew about politically-motivated crimes, but they had no idea that there had been so many juicy non-political crimes in South Africa. Pilkington found himself in the unaccustomed position of being the stoker of other people's imaginations as he presented scenes that could not but enthral. The class saw Daisy de Melker stirring strychnine into her husband's Epsom salts; they saw Bubbles Schroeder lying dead in the Birdhaven plantation with bits of clay in her throat (a crime that had never been solved); they saw the body of Mrs Susan Cohen, bludgeoned to death by her own husband in the library of Southcape, her luxury Constantia home; they saw the hands that were held over Mrs Etty Glazer's eyes so that she could not see where the kidnappers were taking her and her 22-month-old son.

As he spoke, significant glances were exchanged by his classmates. This meant that they suspected – in fact, they felt certain – that James Pilkington had not written his speech. It smacked of parental assistance. Despite the contempt which such a suspicion ought to have aroused (and which they sought to express by means of raised eyebrows and rolled eyes) they found that they were enjoying it thoroughly. Pilkington had an appreciative audience. His talk was a great success.

'In recent months, another crime has taken place which can be added to these,' he went on. 'It is a very different kind of crime. But, like the others which I have described, it will be remembered for many years to come.' He paused and looked at his classmates. 'I call this one *The Attempted Kidnapping of the Prime Minister's Grandson*'.

Richard felt his heart beginning to pound. His tongue was suddenly dry and furry in his mouth. He looked at Mrs Cooper, but her head was turned away. He wanted to call out to her, to say, 'Stop this! You can't let this happen!' Surely she would not permit James Pilkington to exact this terrible revenge? Surely she would not condone this public humiliation of one of her pupils? But Mrs Cooper said nothing and Pilkington continued.

Whatever others may have surmised, he was in no doubt as to the motive for the crime and the intentions of the two young men. He stated with conviction that the difference between this crime and the others he'd mentioned was that this one was politically motivated. He sketched a portrait of two idealistic young men, determined to take their stand, to find a way of drawing attention to the injustices which they could no longer tolerate. That, he said more than once, was what lay at 'the heart of it all'. The words 'apartheid regime' featured prominently in his talk. James Pilkington – whose parents employed four servants and who'd been known to declare that black people were too immature politically to be given the vote – became in that moment a fiery radical. He described how the plan was hatched, how the two men gained entry into the mansion in Waterkloof, Pretoria of Mr and Mrs van Wyk, daughter and son-in-law of the prime minister, how everything went wrong when they were unable to subdue the nanny, Mrs Rosie Mthimkulu, whom in their scrupulousness and fair-mindedness they didn't wish to hurt or traumatise more than was necessary: she was, after all, one of the oppressed. He described the abandonment of the plan and their flight. 'Then,' he said, pausing for effect, 'the full force of the apartheid regime descended upon the two young men.'

Richard kept his eyes down. He felt certain they were all looking at him, but he didn't want to meet their gazes. Why, oh why, did the bell not ring? It was a double period, he recalled, but even so they must be well into the second forty-five minutes by now. Why did nothing come to his aid? Why did the teacher not intervene, why was there not a bomb scare, a fire, an earthquake – some kindly natural disaster which, in destroying the school, would claim only two casualties: James Pilkington and Mrs Cooper? Why was there nothing to relieve his humiliation, his rage?

Pilkington continued. He was getting to the best part and his nasal voice began to soar. He described the terror of the two young men, Anthony Eric Strauss and Wayne Steven Meyer, who were being hunted down as if they were murderers or assassins; as if they were Harris, Pratt and Tsafendas all rolled into one. As brave and heroic as they were, how frightened they must have been as they faced the full repercussions of what they had done. They had wanted to shake things up; but now that things were shaken, they must have felt like hunted animals.

'Then an idea came to them. Anthony Strauss's uncle, Mr Jock Slater, was a prominent man, a well-known accountant, and Anthony was a particular favourite of his...'

Richard wanted to shout, to make him stop. He wanted to say that Anthony was *not* a particular favourite of his father's – Jock had never treated him with anything more than a remote kindliness. He wanted to dispute what Pilkington was saying; to contest his right to say these things. He wanted to fight back, as he had done on the rugby field. But he could not. Never in his life had he felt so helpless. Never had he felt so great a desire to kill. He felt that he could at that moment have extirpated without compunction every slimy, treacherous creature that had ever lived. And when they were all gone, this remorseless nasal voice – which nothing and no one would silence – would at last also be still.

In the midst of his anger, he felt his eyes prick with tears. And then he knew that he couldn't remain in his seat. He could not weep in front of the class. And he could not sit there and listen to the details of the arrest: Jock's telephone call, his accompanying the young men to the police station, his visit to the home of his sister and brother-in-law to break the news to them, his offer (which they declined) to post bail. He could not listen to the details of the trial, the evidence that was led, the two witnesses who were called – Mrs Hannelie van Wyk and Mrs Rosie Mthimkulu. He could not hear how the photograph of the little boy, Arnoldus Pieter van Wyk – commonly known as Noldie – appeared repeatedly in the conservative newspapers, as if to illustrate again and again the smallness, the smilingness, the blondness of that which they had sought to seize. He did not want to hear of the eleven-year sentence which had been handed down, of the outrage which this harsh sentence provoked in some quarters and the satisfaction which it brought in others. Most of all, he did not want to hear what everyone already knew: that it was only Wayne Steven Meyer who received this sentence. He did not want to know what words James Pilkington would use when he described to the class how his cousin Anthony had hanged himself in a deserted gym two days before the sentencing; how the groundsman had found the body and called the police.

Richard got up suddenly, knocking his desk over in front of him. When the loud crash subsided, the room was completely silent. Looking at no one, his face burning, he strode through the door.

The next morning, Richard told his mother that he felt ill. On the following day he informed her that he was much sicker. In this way, he managed to stay away from school for four days. He lay in bed, imagining that the silence of the house was water and that he was a solitary fish in a fish-tank. From time to time diffident little noises broke the profundity of the quiet: he heard the vacuum-cleaner being used in another room and the distant hum of cars driving past in the street outside. It seemed odd to him that dust or crumbs on the carpet should prompt even this modest frenzy of the vacuum-cleaner. And as for those cars in the street: were there really people who wanted to travel somewhere – who wanted it so badly that they clambered into a car and switched on the engine? It seemed incredible. Why did anyone bother? It was so much easier to lie back, to let his body relax, to empty his mind and see what vapours of insignificance drifted into it. At night he lay on his bed and stared at the ceiling. He did not read. He did not listen to the music which he and his friends played over and over again in their bedrooms and at parties – *Bohemian Rhapsody* and *I'm Just a Sweet Transvestite* and *Oh, What a Night!* He did not want anything that reminded him of his classmates or of school. He lay in the darkness and breathed in the smell of the gardenia outside his window.

He tried to think of random, pointless things: he wanted no logic, no connection, no causes, no results. He thought about cabbages and kings; he considered earnestly why the sea is boiling hot and whether pigs have wings. He mulled over imponderables. He let his mind hop. For some reason the words quoted in several of the Orals – *Your children are not your children* – came into his thoughts and he found himself repeating them like an incantation. They had a compelling rhythm, but what were they trying to say? His classmates must have felt drawn to the phrase or it would not have cropped up in so many of the speeches, but what did it *mean*? Whose children were they if they were not their parents'? He had been told, as soon as he was old enough to understand, that he was adopted and that no one knew who his biological parents were. Now he thought about them again. What were they like? Would he feel a kinship with them if he found them? Why had he been given up? And where was he conceived? He thought of various scenarios. It seemed most likely to him that he originated foetally from an encounter in an old Volkswagen Beetle, parked under a willow tree next to a dam on a Saturday night. In the distance there would be light and music and raised voices and laughter, but in the confines of the Beetle there would be only the hot and cramped business of his conception.

He wondered why Jock and Elaine had adopted him. After all, they had been married for seventeen years before he was born. What made people want children? He thought about Mrs Cooper and wondered whether she had any children. If she had, she had never spoken of them. He tried to think of Mrs Cooper having sex (Richard spent a lot of time imagining various people having sex), Mrs Cooper pregnant, Mrs Cooper giving birth. He saw the nurses leaning over her, drawing her wispy grey hair aside and bathing her wrinkled brow as she strained and gasped and laboured to push an impossibly large, abrasive baby out of a very small opening. Then he thought about James Pilkington. He imagined the shock and dismay of Mr and Mrs Pilkington when, instead of the demure offspring (resembling themselves) which they had been anticipating, there appeared instead a red, resentful creature which emitted a thin and reproachful shriek when it was slapped and which glared at the other infants in the ward, suspecting them of wanting a share in its mother's breast. Mrs Pilkington could not have brought herself to breast-feed such a child: she would have turned her head away and, in a tone of sad mortification, would have requested that milk formula be prepared.

Could parents disown their children? And could children disown their parents? (*Your children are not your children.*) The shame and embarrassment he had had to experience because of what his father had done enraged him. He did not understand why Jock had telephoned the police – for all he knew, it had been the right thing to do – but he resented the way in which the consequences of this had spilled over into his own life. What had he to do with the prime minister's grandchild? And though he was very sad about it, truly sad, he had also to ask: what had he to do with a lonely, deserted gym and a body hanging in the darkness? It should never have become his problem. It should have stayed in that dark and obdurate corner of the world which even the turning of the earth on its axis could not expose to the light.

After the fourth day, his mother said that he had to go back to school. He seemed much better now and he was missing too much work. He had not told her what had happened, so she had no inkling of the dread that he felt. However, when he got to school, no one referred to what had happened – not even James Pilkington. In fact, many of his classmates greeted him with more warmth than usual, reserving a seat for him in the assembly and buying food for him from the tuck-shop. The English Orals were over, but a special opportunity was made for him to speak: five minutes were set aside for him at the beginning of a class on *Macbeth*. Although he hadn't intended to read even a phrase of his speech, only to hold it in his hands for reassurance, he now abandoned that plan and read it out in a flat and languid voice, not once raising his eyes from the paper. 'I think you will make a very fine doctor, Richard,' said Mrs Cooper when he finished. He looked at her but didn't reply.

Several years later, when Richard was in his fifth year of medical school, he bumped into Mrs Cooper in a shopping mall. He and Deanna had just got engaged after going out for four years (they had met over the dissecting table) and life was good. Seeing her brought back unpleasant memories, but the sensation was also liberating, for he felt certain that he would never again be as helpless as he'd then been. At that stage in his life, graduating from childhood and adolescence seemed to him to be the first and most empowering of journeys.

They exchanged pleasantries. Mrs Cooper asked how his studies were going; he told her that he was engaged; she offered him warmest congratulations. Then she paused, and he felt that she wanted to say something. He knew what it was. 'Richard,' she said, 'I know there's no use raking up the past, but I've always meant to say how sorry I am about what happened that day during English Orals. I kept meaning to tell you that, but the right opportunity never seemed to come along.'

'That's all right,' said Richard. 'Don't worry about it. As you say, it's in the past.' This gesture, too, was empowering. And how sweet and salty was this power – to be an adult, to negotiate, to forgive.

'But I do feel that I need to apologise. It's something that has weighed on my mind for so many years. I should have stopped James Pilkington when he began to speak about that case. I should have told him – oh, I don't know – that his speech was too long and that it was time to give someone else a chance. But I didn't react quickly enough and then I didn't know how to stop it. It was very remiss of me. I feel ashamed and I want to ask your forgiveness.'

'I won't pretend that I wasn't very angry at the time,' said Richard, 'but I have no anger left. Really.'

'You have no idea how much that means to me,' she said. 'One of the things I hated most was that I felt like such a *coward* – especially when you had the courage to get up and walk out.'

'Oh, that wasn't courage,' he said, laughing. How delightful this was; there was no end to what magnanimity could do! A creature lay beneath his boot, cast down in abasement. He had the power to crush it. But he had also the power to spare it, to step over it, to let its ineffectual life persist. 'I was about to burst into tears,' he said. 'That's why I ran out of the classroom.'

Richard glanced at his watch. 'Have you spoken to him again?' he asked. 'You know, about selling the house.'

'Oh, there's no use.' Elaine sighed and scratched the side of her nose. 'He'll never move. You know what he's like.'

'But why will he not listen to reason? He knows how dangerous it is. You just have to read the newspaper – elderly people are murdered every day in this city. In their own homes. And you don't even have proper burglar bars on the windows!'

'There's no use shouting at me,' Elaine said. 'I've told you that I would be prepared to move – even though I've spent all my married life in this house. But your father is adamant that he's not going, so what am I supposed to do? I'm not moving to a retirement village without him.'

'He's so stubborn!'

'That he is. That he has always been.' She spoke as if she were describing an unalterable law of the universe rather than a streak of temperament.

'And so selfish!'

She didn't reply. Stubbornness in Jock she was prepared to concede; selfishness she was not. Her protectiveness infuriated Richard. But what was the point of being angry? That was how it had always been. There were no new emotions in that house: only old feelings played over and over again in the groove of years, muffled by the silence.

'He hates change – you know that.'

'Yes, I know. But that's not the point. I'm the one who has to worry about you all the time.'

'That's kind of you, my boy,' said a voice from the doorway. 'But there's really no need.' Jock stood there, his tall frame outlined against the passage light. Neither of them had heard him walk towards the lounge. He'd moved as silently as always. As the years passed he walked more slowly, but no less quietly. He came closer and shook Richard's hand. As a boy, Richard had been amazed to see fathers and sons hugging one another; sometimes they even kissed! He and his father always shook hands. It was the only kind of physical contact there had ever been between them, and he couldn't imagine any other.

Jock was very tall: well over six feet. His face was so long and angular that his round, podgy nose looked incongruous amidst the slope of the features. 'I've got film star looks,' he always used to declare; and, when people looked puzzled, he would point to his nose and say, 'Look at my Karl Malden nose.' Then he would wait for the laughter; but, as the years went by, his joke tended to be met instead by a vague smile: few nowadays knew who Karl Malden was or what his nose looked like.

'It's good to see you,' he said. 'Your mother and I don't have the pleasure of your company very much these days.'

'I've been rather preoccupied,' said Richard. 'As you know. But let's not change the subject. You heard what I was saying. You know as well as I do that you cannot go on living here like this. Times have changed. Johannesburg has become a violent place. It's not the same as when you bought the house in the 1940s.'

'It was 1947,' said Elaine. 'The same week that the Royal family came to South Africa.'

'I know that,' said Richard impatiently. Elaine, a fervent royalist, had been repeating that bit of information all his life.

'I appreciate your concern,' said Jock. 'I really do. I know that you have our interests at heart. But you've spoken about this before. Deanna has also spoken to us about it. Your mother and I don't want to move. It's as simple as that. We've lived here all our married life. We are considering having burglar bars put in' – Richard looked up in surprise; this was a major concession – 'but we don't want an alarm.'

'No, I couldn't bear one of those,' said Elaine.

'Well, burglar bars are better than nothing,' said Richard.

'But please stop nagging us,' Jock went on. 'It doesn't achieve anything. In the end, it's our decision.'

Richard didn't reply. The discussion was ending where all their family discussions ended.

Elaine got up from her chair. 'Are you sure you won't stay for supper?' she asked. 'I know you're meeting Neil, but you can still have a quick bite with us. Come, let me make you an omelette. Tomato and cheese? Mushrooms and cheese?'

Richard and his father spoke only once about what happened the night the two young men came to the house. A few months after the Pilkington incident – about which nothing was ever said to Elaine and Jock – Richard remarked one day on the fact that he never saw his Uncle Harold, Aunt Dorothy and cousin Tessa any more. No response was made to this comment, but later he was summoned to Jock's study.

His father was pacing up and down. 'Listen here,' he said abruptly. 'I don't want you to speak of what happened. Or even refer to it. It upsets your mother. We won't be seeing your uncle and aunt any more. Let's leave it at that.'

'But...' Richard struggled to find the right words. 'But how can we never see them again? Aunt Dorothy is your sister. And they're my only uncle and aunt. Tessa and Anthony are...I mean, Tessa is the only cousin I have.'

'Sometimes things happen, Richard. Circumstances change, people quarrel. Of course, it's very upsetting for everyone concerned, but that's how it is. You just have to accept it and move on.'

'But why? Why won't they see us? Do they blame us for what happened to Anthony? That's not fair. I mean, you didn't intend...'

Instead of replying, Jock walked to the window and gazed out of it. For a long time, he didn't speak. When he turned around, he looked into his son's eyes. 'Anarchy,' he said. 'Richard, listen to me carefully. Do you know what anarchy is?'

'No, not really. At least, I think...'

'Don't think. Look it up. Read about it. Make sure that you know exactly what it is. And when you know what it is, remember what I am saying to you now: the greatest irresponsibility we can ever indulge in – as individuals and as a society – is anarchy. Especially when things are less than perfect, when a society is still trying to find its feet, that is when anarchy is the greatest threat. That is when we need most to be on our guard. Anything that is gained through anarchy is not worth having.'

'But what does that have to do with Anthony? Or with Aunt Dorothy and Uncle Harold?'

'It has everything to do with them. Go and read. Go and work it out. You have been blessed with brains, Richard. Use them. And remember what I have told you. No one is free when anarchy prevails. No one.'

Richard felt baffled, but he did as he was told. A few days later, when Jock was driving him to school, he said, 'I've been reading about anarchy. But I still don't quite see...'

Jock shook his head. He was clearly in no mood to revive the former conversation. Instead, he said, 'Son, I've been giving the matter some thought. It's understandable that you're distressed by what has happened. It occurs to me that it may be wrong of us to deprive you of an association with your uncle and aunt and cousin. After all, we're such a small family. I think that if you telephone them and ask to see them, they're unlikely to object. If you wish to spend a day or even a weekend with them every so often, your mother and I won't stand in your way.'

Richard thanked him, but did not take advantage of the offer. Something – pride? shyness? shame? – prevented him. Dorothy and Harold Strauss sent him a birthday card every year until he was nineteen; then no more cards came. On two occasions a gift (in both cases an item of clothing) arrived for him from Tessa. He always wrote back, thanking them. But then all contact ceased.

The attempted kidnapping of the prime minister's grandson was never mentioned again in that house, not even obliquely. Even when reference was made to it in the newspapers or on the television, Richard said nothing. In the months that followed the incident, he spent more and more time alone in his room. Sometimes he listened to music. At other times he lay on his bed and read, or slept, or listened to the faint sounds of the garden that came in through the open window. He indulged in fantasies in which he discovered that his real parents were jet-setting millionaires who, in remorse at having given him up, endowed him with all that contrition could devise: a Caribbean island of his own. And they left him there to discover its delights: white beaches, surfing, catamarans and yachts, topless girls with long blond hair.

All his fantasies were of lordship: in all of them he gave orders and they were carried out. But in reality he was cowed, not only adopted by his parents, but fostered by the life they all led in that discreet, murmuring house. Although his heart was never docile, he had learned to conduct himself like a slave. And he didn't know the extent of it.

In Johannesburg restaurants come and go, come and go. New ones open and the little flame of their entrepreneurial ambition flickers: will they succeed or not? Diners may decide that there is too much chilli on the menu, too many spices ('Cajun? I thought that went out of fashion years ago.') They may feel there is too much couscous, an excess of eggplant, not enough drizzling of this or sprinkling of that. The portions may be considered too big ('Honestly, I didn't know whether to eat it or climb it!') or too small ('They can keep their miserable *nouvelle cuisine* – I don't want to have to stop at McDonald's on the way home because I'm still hungry.') Much depends on the chicken salad, on which Chinese noodles perch like a beehive hairstyle: will it become legendary or be superseded by other chicken salads?

Some of the little fires go out at once. Others grow suddenly to a conflagration of Northern Suburbs approval. Bookings at the newly favoured restaurant have to be made weeks in advance; those who manage to get in are triumphant, those who can't are aggrieved. ('Why don't they enlarge it and have more tables? It's ridiculously small. And why do they have to be so rude? He said, "Nothing until October!" and slammed the phone down on me.') And then, as suddenly, the fire dies down, threatens to go out. The owners discover that there is nothing as fickle as the Johannesburg diners whom they had learned to treat with such hauteur. Now there is no problem at all getting in: you can turn up at eight o'clock on a Saturday night and ask for a table and they will say 'choose whichever one you like'. But those who do go feel uncomfortable: the place is too empty (patrons feel obliged to tip more than ten per cent, as if to compensate for the empty tables), the manager and the waiters too eager to please; in restaurants, as in lovers, desperation is a turn-off. People stop going. The place folds. A new one opens. 'The chicken salad,' people say. 'I can't tell you how delicious it is. It's served with big chunks of avocado and a mustard dressing. You *have* to order their chicken salad.'

Richard and Neil decided to try a new restaurant, specialising in South African food. It was called *Renaissance*. A dark and narrow passage, opening out as if into a cave, formed the entrance to the restaurant. There was a distant sound of drums which grew louder as they were led to their table and seated. The colour scheme was ochre and copper. On the wall behind them were large, black-and-white photographs of the Big Five, a secretary bird, a blue crane, a protea and three shots of Nelson Mandela: in the first he was a young man in a boxing ring, in the second a much older man, walking out of the Victor Verster Prison and raising his fist in the air, his former wife at his side; and in the third he was being embraced by Oprah Winfrey. There was also a photograph of a rugby ball soaring over the posts. This bore a caption which read: *Joel Stransky's drop-kick in the closing minutes of the game. South Africa wins the World Cup: 1995.*

The menu included pap-and-wors, braised kudu steaks, tripe, bobotie, sosaties and kebabs, morogo, waterblommetjiebredie, biltong omelettes, kingklip, yellowtail, kabeljou, stumpnose, cutlets of Karoo lamb, T-Bone steaks with monkey-gland sauce and mopane worms (SQ). The dessert offerings included melktert and koeksisters.

'Quite a choice,' murmured Richard. 'How adventurous should we be?' They studied the menu in silence.

Neil was the first to look up. 'When is the appointment with Mrs Curtis?' he asked.

'In two week's time,' said Richard. 'The twelfth. It's a Friday.'

'What time and where?'

'11 o'clock. She suggests we meet at the Countess of Athlone Home. Isn't it odd? That's where I was born.'

Neil made a note in his diary and said, 'I'll be there. I know where it is.'

'Thank you,' said Richard.

They ordered drinks. 'I've got a good feeling about this woman,' Neil said at last. 'I mean, she does this for a living – helping people like you trace their biological families. She's found long-lost relatives in New Zealand, Canada, all over the world.'

When the drinks came, they clinked glasses. 'Here's to knowing who I really am,' said Richard.

'To knowing who you really are.'

'Now: to change the subject. Deanna's feeling hurt because you haven't contacted her. She feels you haven't been supportive. What's going on? Why don't you do your bit?'

Neil tried to look down at the menu, but Richard had a way of staring at you, of locking your gaze onto his, which made it impossible to look away. 'I'll phone her tomorrow,' said Neil. 'Don't worry about it.' He had a thin face and sharp features. The receding of his hair-line (which began shortly after his twenty-first birthday) made his face look even more angular.

'I don't want to interfere…' Richard began.

'Good idea. Don't interfere.'

'I still care about Deanna,' said Richard, ignoring the comment. 'You know she's going through a very difficult time right now. She needs you.'

'I said I'll phone her tomorrow. Let's talk about something else.'

'All right. I won't nag.' Richard sighed. 'It's good to sit and relax. I've just been to see my parents. My father is being his usual stubborn self – it's absolutely maddening. It's so dangerous for them to carry on living there in that big old house, but he won't even consider moving. It's not as if I'm trying to get them to go into an old-aged home! They could have a lovely little cottage in a retirement village, with twenty-four-hour security.'

'But you can't force them to go if they don't want to.'

'I know, but I have to try. If something happened to them and I hadn't even tried to persuade them, I would never forgive myself. Deanna also spoke to them about it, but with the same result. It's not my mother – she says she'd be willing to go. It's my father. And he's the most obstinate man in the world. Once he makes up his mind, there's nothing that will make him give way.'

The waiter reappeared and they studied the menu again. Both, after much deliberation, chose kingklip. 'We're not being very daring,' said Richard. 'You can get kingklip anywhere. We really are food nerds. At *Renaissance* we should be having something like tripe.'

'No way,' said Neil, shuddering. 'I'm as patriotic as the next man, but when it comes to tripe I draw the line. I don't care how indigenous it is. I wouldn't eat frogs' legs in France either. How can you eat tripe without thinking about what it is and what it used to do? And can it ever really be clean?'

'But are your objections really logical, dear brother-in-law? Once you're consuming a part of an animal's corpse, what difference does it make which part you're eating? Why is a haunch or a forequarter less objectionable than a tongue or brains or intestines or testicles?'

'You're probably right, but I'll stick to steak and chops, chicken breasts and drumsticks and things like that, thank you very much.'

'Sheryl's a vegan,' said Richard. 'She won't eat any animal products.'

'Who's Sheryl?'

'The woman I've been seeing. I told you about her.'

'You didn't. You told me about someone called Hayley.'

'Hayley? No, no – that's over. You're a bit out of touch. Anyway, you'll meet Sheryl. You'll like her. She's got a great sense of humour.'

Neil made no response. The waiter bent over them to exchange their meat knives for fish knives. Richard, clearing his throat, said, 'Neil, I don't know where this thing with Deanna is going. It looks like the marriage may be coming to an end. If it does, I hope it won't mean the end of our friendship too.'

'It certainly won't,' said Neil. 'You don't have to worry. Our friendship is solid.'

'Thank you. That means a lot to me. I thought it's what you would say, but I wanted the reassurance.' Richard gazed at him meditatively. Then suddenly he smiled. 'But there *is* someone who must be thrilled about the break-up,' he said. 'How jubilant Aunt Maisie must be! Those sweet, sweet words: *I told you so.* How she must be relishing them!'

'Well, she's upset on Deanna's behalf,' said Neil. 'I wouldn't say she's jubilant. But, as you might expect, she has been saying, "No one would listen to me."' He spoke more deeply to imitate Aunt Maisie's husky, pack-a-day-for-thirty-years voice. '"You have to know what's in the genes. He was adopted: we knew nothing about him. You must never be taken in by good looks." She's been saying that to anyone who'll listen.'

'I can imagine,' said Richard. 'Ah, the dark horse turns out to have been very dark indeed. The prince regresses and shows himself to be a frog after all – and covered with warts at that.'

'Don't pay any attention to her,' said Neil, noting the change in tone. 'Don't let her upset you. She's an old woman with eccentric ideas. And she has no one to worry about except Deanna and me.'

It was chilly when they left the restaurant. Richard and Neil hugged each other, as they always did, and then ran to their cars to escape the cold night air. The jasmine had begun to flower; but the nights were still biting. It was evident that spring was preparing to speak, but winter still lingered, a frog in the throat of the changing season. When spring finally found its voice, however, nothing would be able to silence it, for it had the cycle of the turning year on its side; and cycles are always unrelenting.

3   Lice

NEIL HAD DEVELOPED a habit of listening to certain radio stations which weren't really to his taste. He wasn't sure what drew him to them, but supposed that he tuned in for the same reason that people used to wear hair-shirts: to subject himself to the torment of irritation, to purify something within himself. Inclined to solitude and words carefully selected, he found himself listening to talk shows (thus inviting into his home people whom he would never invite into his home), muzak and the babble of radio stations incessantly advertising themselves. This was the white noise of his otherwise hushed existence.

High on the list of these invited tortures was a local radio station called Radio Frangipani. Neil listened to it while driving to the appointment with Richard and Mrs Curtis. The late-morning slot was hosted every morning, Monday to Friday, by a woman called Helena Verster. She was easy to listen to: she had a soft-serve ice-cream sort of voice. She assumed an intimate relationship with each of her listeners and presented the light music on offer as though the lyrics offered great wisdom, as though there were a life lesson sprouting from each popular melody.

'Now, listeners,' she was saying as Neil switched the radio on, 'whatever you do, make sure that you don't ever find yourself in the situation described in this next song. I must say, I really can't think of anything worse. Avoid it at all costs. Take it from me, it can only bring terrible unhappiness. Here on Radio Frangipani, 91.8, the Home of Highveld Harmony, we bring you Mary MacGregor with her song *Torn Between Two Lovers*.'

Neil had dialled Richard's number on the previous evening to confirm their appointment with Mrs Curtis. When a woman answered the phone, he put the receiver down without saying anything. He didn't want to speak to Sheryl – or had Sheryl already made way for someone else? Whoever it was, he didn't feel inclined to ask for Richard or leave a message.

The spring sunshine was mild and warm; the very light seemed clean, as if it had been washed as it made its slow south-bound passage. But somehow, even in its freshness, there was the hint of something old and vestigial. It is no wonder, thought Neil, that this time of the year has attracted so many clichés – but how is one to look past them all in order to know this particular spring in its own time and on its own terms? New-born as this one was, there were many blighted seasons that had laid their eggs deep within it and, as it gave birth to itself, it engendered them also.

Neil stopped at a traffic light and was approached by a man who waved a piece of cardboard at him. He dutifully read the words which were scrawled on the placard:

NO MONEY
FIVE CHILDREN TO FEED
PLEESE HELP
GOD WILL BLESS YOU
I DONT DO CRIME.

He brought out his wallet, which made the man hasten towards him eagerly, but then he found, to his dismay, that he had no coins at all. He wasn't inclined to give him a ten rand note. 'I've got no coins today', he said. 'I'm sorry. I'll give you something next time I come this way. I promise.'

The man said, 'Please. Just one rand. I'm hungry.'

'I don't have coins,' Neil protested. 'I really don't. It's the truth.' To his relief, the traffic light turned green and he was able to drive away.

The song had ended. After a commercial break – which included an advertisement for unit trusts followed by one for a remedy for vaginal thrush – Helena Verster was back. 'Take it from me,' she was saying, 'our lives would be meaningless if we had no one to love. Love is what makes it all worthwhile. But we're not born with an understanding of what love entails. We have to learn how to love. We have to walk that path. But we all do, sooner or later. Radio Frangipani, 91.8, the Home of Highveld Harmony, brings you Foreigner with *I Want to Know What Love Is.*'

Neil cursed himself for having brought out his wallet and disappointing the beggar. Perhaps he should have given him the ten rand after all – but if he gave out ten rand notes to every beggar at every traffic light in Johannesburg, he would soon be a beggar himself. Still, he must remember to give that particular one several coins next time – three or four rand instead of the usual two. What a joy it must be to live in a city not infested with beggars! Here there was no getting away from them. And yet, he thought, berating himself, if they had nothing to eat, why should they not beg? It was better that they beg than turn to crime. And if poverty were rife, why should it hide itself away simply to ease his discomfort? An empty stomach has no inclination for euphemisms. And he – he who had been put out to find that his wallet held only notes – what entitlement had he to euphemisms of any kind?

Once, when he and Deanna were having tea with Aunt Maisie, the New South Africa cropped up in the conversation. Deanna declared that it would take a long time for South Africa to become a normal society, the most progressive constitution in the world notwithstanding, but their aunt was convinced that much had already changed. 'For a start, the beggars aren't all black any more,' she said. 'There are white beggars now wherever you look. Lots of them. And many black people drive smart cars. Black people driving BMWs and white people begging at robots. If *that's* not the sign of a normal society, then I'd like to know what is!'

'It's not going to be easy, Dr Slater,' said Mrs Curtis. 'I won't lie to you and pretend that it will be a simple matter to find your birth mother.'

'I'm well aware of the difficulties,' said Richard. 'That's why I've come to you. I don't know where else to turn.'

Mrs Curtis had worked as a social worker for many years, specialising in adoption cases. Since her retirement, she kept an office in the Countess of Athlone Home, where she used to work, and from it she ran a little business called *Relative Success*, helping people to trace lost family members. More often than not, she was called upon to reunite those who had been adopted with their biological families: mothers, fathers, siblings. Sometimes it was the mothers (less often the fathers) who approached her, asking her to help them find children whom they had given up for adoption years ago; sometimes – as in Richard's case – it was the child who had been adopted, now an adult, who initiated the search.

'It's something I just have to do,' said Richard. 'I feel as if something will always be missing in my life if I don't find some answers.'

'This is the thing, you see,' said Mrs Curtis. 'I quite understand. Most of the people who come to me feel the same way.'

Neil had always been fascinated by verbal quirks. It intrigued him that people uttered little phrases without even being aware that they were doing so. It was almost as if these sayings had grown on them, had attached themselves, and now they could not speak without producing them. They meant nothing, these word hiccups – or, if they did have a meaning, it must be something other than what it seemed to be. Aunt Maisie, for instance, always said, 'You know what I mean?' And yet no one was blunter, more direct, less likely to be misunderstood than Aunt Maisie. People knew only too well what she meant. And Helena Verster kept saying, 'Take it from me', but from whom else could one take it, seeing as she had sole command of her listeners' attention? And now here was Beryl Curtis and hers was the best of all: 'This is the thing, you see,' she kept saying. Oh, how delicious it was! Neil showed no sign of his delight, but he beamed inside. Mrs Curtis spoke rapidly, her words falling over themselves to get out; but every so often she would pause, look at Neil and Richard and then out it would come: 'This is the thing, you see.'

The Edwardian grandeur of the Home, built high up on a ridge, overlooking some of the oldest and most opulent suburbs of the city, was undiminished: there were still the heavy wooden doors and the long dark passageways, the big, generous bay windows, the high ceilings, the pervasive smell of wood polish. It had not altered much in appearance since Richard was born there in 1964. Its function, however, had changed dramatically. Young unmarried white mothers did not come here any more. In fact, no mothers of any sort came here now. The Home had become a nursery and the rooms were filled with babies, all of them black. As Mrs Curtis guided Neil and Richard to a small office where the interview was to be held, they looked through the door of one of the nurseries and saw rows of babies, some sleeping quietly, some making fidgety little movements. They could hear a baby crying in another room, a thin cry which went on and on and yet seemed to have no shrillness in it, no vehemence and no anger.

'Where do all these babies come from?' Neil asked.

'Many of them were abandoned,' said Mrs Curtis. 'People bring them here and leave them on the doorstep. Or they leave them in hospitals. Or in public toilets. Or on rubbish heaps. Even on pavements on cold winter nights. Scores of new ones arrive here every month.'

'But what will happen to them?'

'We hope that people will adopt them. But the majority remain in institutions. We can't find enough adoptive parents for them. Not even for the HIV-negative ones.'

Richard said, 'And white babies? I take it that the situation is quite different for them?'

'Oh, yes. They're in great demand. There's a long waiting list for white babies.'

'It's terrible,' said Neil, peering into another room. 'I had no idea there were so many unwanted children.'

Throughout the interview, they could hear the wailing baby. It cried as if it had no hope of ever being consoled, as if it would weep without pause from birth to death. And yet it was such nonsense to think that way: there were people here who cared for it, who would continue to do so. One shouldn't read an existential crisis into a baby's cry. But still Neil could not get out of his mind the long row of babies, lying like larva in the spring sunshine. And, although he knew the baby cried because it was hungry or had stomach cramps, it was tempting to think that its unimpassioned wail really did have cosmic overtones. For coming into this place was like wandering unwittingly into a ghastly allegory of unwanted and unpremeditated life: could there be anything that illustrated more powerfully an existential helplessness than these infants, found in toilets and on rubbish heaps, abandoned into thankless birth? Children who are found in that way are supposed to be special: foundlings, saviours in the making, Moses in the bulrushes; but there was no mystique about these children. They were simply what was not wanted: the ants at the picnic, the lice in the hair, the mosquitoes in the dark; the small, vexatious, inconsequential life.

'The biggest problem,' Beryl Curtis was saying, 'is, of course, that your birth mother gave false information when she was admitted here – false name, false address. *Niemandt*, as you probably know, means "no one" in Afrikaans. A person who gives "no one" as her name clearly does not want to be identified or found.'

'And as far as you know, no one has tried to trace a baby born on that day in this institution?' Richard spoke calmly, as if he were making routine enquiries. There was nothing in the way he asked the question that revealed how important this information was to him. There are mysteries that are alluring because they remain unsolved, that should not be explicated lest all the enchantment and the romance be lost along with the secret. But Richard's was not one of these. It held no compensations. It was not its own justification. It was an obstacle in his life, which, as it loomed larger and larger over the years, had held him back. It was something that crawled on the very skin of his soul, that made him burn with frustration. There was nothing that would give him relief from it except knowledge.

'I've managed to get hold of a nurse who used to work here,' said Mrs Curtis. 'Fortunately, she does remember your mother. Thousands of young women passed through here, but your mother stands out in her memory because everyone was stunned by her disappearance. Only a few hours after she had given birth, she crept out of her room and vanished into the night.'

'What does she say about her?'

'She says that she was very different from the other mothers. For a start, she was much older. She gave her age on the form as twenty-nine and the nurse says that that was probably right – she may even have been older than that. And she says' – here Mrs Curtis smiled kindly at Richard – 'she says that she was very beautiful. She had dark hair and a very pale skin. She says that if you saw only her face, you would never have imagined that she was to give birth in less than forty-eight hours.'

'I see.' Richard sat quietly, taking it in. 'It's very little to go on.'

'This is the thing, you see. Normally we have some solid information from the forms that the birth mothers fill in. But here is a woman who did not want to be traced. Ever. Even if we found her, it's a possibility that she would not want to meet you. You need to prepare yourself for that scenario.'

'Let's deal with that when we reach that point,' said Richard. '*If we ever get there.*'

'Try not to feel too discouraged, Dr Slater. I've had what looked like hopeless cases before, and yet I've found the lost relatives. Sometimes it's taken me years, but I never give up. The case stays on my files until it's solved. I never close it. My business isn't called *Relative Success* for nothing.'

It occurred to Neil that Richard had been abandoned too – not, admittedly, on a rubbish heap or in a toilet, but, still, it was an abandonment. It must be very difficult to recover from that. More than ever before, he understood why this quest had become so important – such an obsession – to Richard. Of course, the difference between the child left here in 1964 and the babies who lay here now was that there had been no difficulty in finding a childless couple to adopt the unknown woman's baby. Neil knew that Richard's relationship with his parents was strained, but he knew also that they had given him everything of the best, they had educated him and – in their own rather stiff way – they had loved him.

'Perhaps your brother has some questions he would like to ask?' Mrs Curtis turned to Neil.

'Brother-in-law,' he corrected. 'No, I don't think so. Well, except to ask what we do next? Where do we go from here?'

'The first thing for me to do is to place adverts in newspapers, giving as many details as possible of the circumstances of the baby's birth (I won't reveal your name, Dr Slater, don't worry) and appealing for anyone who knows anything about it to come forward with the information and to contact me. Let's see what comes of that. If it doesn't work, we broaden the search.'

They all stood up and shook hands. 'I'll be in touch, Dr Slater,' Mrs Curtis called out. 'Think positively!'

'Will do,' said Richard, turning to wave to her.

They blinked when they stepped out of the dark corridor and into the bright sunshine. 'I feel a bit overwhelmed,' said Richard.

'She knows what she's doing,' said Neil. 'You just have to be patient.'

'I suppose so. Thanks for your support – as always. Have you got time for a quick lunch? I don't have any appointments until two o'clock.'

'No, I wish I could. Sorry. I've got to rush off to therapy.'

'Ah, yes,' said Richard. 'Therapy. I'd really like to know what goes on there!'

Neil smiled. Richard had been teasing him about it since he started therapy a few months ago. 'Not much,' he said. 'There's no great mystery. I talk about my problems. The therapist listens and makes a few remarks, and then throws me out and sends me a hefty bill.'

'There must be more to it than that. And what do you talk *about*? That's what I'd like to know.'

'This and that. Nothing that would satisfy your curiosity.'

'Ever talk about me?' Richard smiled mischievously. His low-spiritedness seemed to have vanished completely.

'I talk about my problems.'

'Well, that rules me out. I know I'm not one of *those*.'

Helena Verster was introducing a new song as Neil switched on the car radio. 'The world is a very unequal place,' she was saying. 'Some have so much that they don't know what to do with it, while others have nothing at all. Will the problem ever be solved? Perhaps not. But the good news, listeners, is that there's always love. Take it from me, love is the great equaliser. That's because you don't have to be rich to give love or to receive it. Here, especially for you, from the Home of Highveld Harmony, Radio Frangipani, 91.8, is Air Supply with *Making Love Out Of Nothing At All*.'

Love. Love. Love. Love. Love. Neil was struck by the fact that every song he had heard that morning had the word 'love' (or a variant thereof) in the title. And what was the object of this love? In as much as he could tell, it was a monster, a grotesque compound of youth and maturity: old enough to betray lovers with pathological regularity, yet too young to dress itself; old enough to play sexual games, but not yet toilet-trained; old enough to have mauled many hearts, yet still needing to be fed every two hours. This swaddled god of love, who rules the airwaves, was a creature called Baby.

Baby, I'm A-Want You, Baby I'm A-Need You
Baby Love, My Baby Love

My Baby Just Cares For Me
When My Baby, When My Baby Smiles At Me
Ooh, Baby, I Love Your Way
Baby, You Can Drive My Car

He glanced at his watch. He switched off the radio, clicked the steering lock in place and clamped the gear lock. He took the radio out of its bracket and locked it in the boot of his car. It was time for therapy.

Zelda and Issy Langman owned a string of butcheries in the Free State. In the late 1970s they sold the butcheries and their house in Bloemfontein and retired to the Cape. They bought the penthouse of a tall block of flats in Sea Point. It had two balconies: from the one they could see the Atlantic Ocean and from the other Lion's Head. They called their balconies 'sea view' and 'mountain view' respectively. Zelda and Issy had nothing when they married, but their years of dogged work in the meat industry brought them prosperity. When they moved into their flat, they felt – although neither of them had even seen the sea until they were well into their twenties – as if they had come home. They enjoyed watching the sea, and its restlessness made no impact upon them, for they had at last found ease. They felt safe, high up in their nest of glass and cream blinds and fresh white paint, far away from the drab grasslands of the Free State and all the weary work of the butcheries.

On a Saturday morning in December 1980 someone rang their doorbell. Zelda was writing a letter to her daughter in London. Issy was reading the newspaper in the kitchen and eating a late breakfast. It was a hot, bright morning. The most timid of breezes ruffled the blinds. A woman stood on their doorstep. Zelda said afterwards that she was in her late thirties and that she had short blond hair. She was wearing a white cotton dress and gold sandals. Her legs were tanned and shapely. Issy didn't remember what she was wearing, but said she was attractive. He thought she was about twenty-five.

'Don't be ridiculous, Issy,' said his wife, rolling her eyes. 'She was *much* more than twenty-five.' She turned to the reporters.

'Don't write down what he says,' she commanded. 'What does he know about such things?'

The woman was well-spoken and very polite. She apologised for disturbing them. She assured them that she was not selling anything. She knew it was audacious of her to ask this of complete strangers, but what she really wanted was to have a look at their home. She was considering buying a flat in the building when one became available and wanted to see what they looked like. She would take only a few minutes of their time. She didn't introduce herself.

Zelda and Issy ushered her in and assured her that it was no trouble at all; she could spend as much time as she liked looking around. They were flattered by her interest and her enthusiastic praise of their beautiful flat. No, they were not in the habit of inviting people whom they did not know into their home, they assured the reporters and the police; but they felt that she was a decent woman who wouldn't steal the jewellery when their backs were turned. They showed her the kitchen, the bathrooms, the bedrooms. They explained that they had retiled the kitchen and painted the entire flat. 'It was a sort of muddy green,' Zelda said. 'We couldn't possibly leave it like that.' They explained that they had also replaced the curtains with blinds.

The woman commended the changes they had made and said it had given her some good ideas – she too would renovate before she moved in. 'Everything looks so fresh and clean,' she said. 'It's really lovely.'

Zelda and Issy liked her. They took her onto the balcony – 'mountain view, not sea view,' Zelda interjected – and they admired the view together.

'You *are* lucky to live here,' the woman said. At that point, the telephone rang. Issy went to answer it. The woman put her hand on Zelda's arm – her nails were not painted, but they were beautifully manicured – and asked if she could have a glass of water. Her hand was steady, strong, surprisingly cool.

Zelda spent some time in the kitchen, struggling to get the ice-cubes loose – 'Issy usually does it, but he was on the telephone' – and preparing the glass of water, which she carried out on a tray. She came out onto the balcony, but there was no one there. She presumed that the woman was looking over the flat again and set off in pursuit of her, but she was nowhere to be found. Issy finished speaking on the telephone and came to help her. They searched every room and called out, but the woman had vanished. Could she have let herself out of the front door? She must have done so, but they had not heard the door opening and closing. And how odd that she had crept out without thanking them and saying good-bye! 'Aren't people strange?' Zelda said to Issy. 'Aren't they too peculiar for words? I hope she didn't steal anything.'

They lived so far up that the noise from the busy street below seldom reached them. But the woman's visit had made them feel uneasy and when they heard what sounded like shouting or screaming, they went onto the balcony and looked down. Directly below them, facing the main road, was an old house, now converted into a fashionable fish restaurant. On the roof of the house was something which shone white. They saw it and then they knew at once. The woman's body was lying on the roof, but part of it hung over the edge. 'Oh, my God,' Zelda said, turning to Issy. 'She jumped. That woman jumped. From *our* balcony.' She felt the prick of tears in her eyes. 'Oh, how terrible. I can't bear it. It's too awful.' She dabbed at her eyes. Issy shook his head disconsolately and went to phone the police.

Deanna and Neil were watching TV in their hotel room. Neil was seven years old and Deanna was eleven. It was their second visit to Cape Town. Their father had gone to visit an old school friend of his and their mother was out shopping. 'I won't be long,' she called out as she left. They heard the ambulance sirens in the street outside, but thought little of it. They quarrelled over which channel to watch and ate potato crisps. The morning passed uneventfully, for the event which claimed the life of their mother (thirty-nine years old) did not intrude upon it. It was several hours later that they heard.

Years later, Neil attended a dinner party where the conversation turned to suicide. Different ways of taking one's life were discussed and there was some debate about whether it was an act of courage or of cowardice. Neil did not venture an opinion. Then one woman said, 'I have an incredible story to tell you. It happened years ago. My mother's cousins were living in Sea Point in a penthouse flat. It was about fifteen floors up. Overlooking the main road – what's it called? Well, never mind. Anyway, a woman turned up one day at their door – a complete stranger – and asked if she could have a look round. She said she wanted to buy a flat in the building. And do you know what she did? She walked through the flat, admired it and then jumped off the balcony!'

'No,' someone said. 'I don't believe it. It must be one of those urban legends.'

'I promise you it's true! I'm telling you, my mother's cousins owned the flat.'

'But can you imagine how they must have felt?' interjected someone else. 'A person you've never seen before comes into the flat, you show her round, and then SPLAT – out the window she goes.'

'Perhaps they blamed themselves? Perhaps they berated themselves? "I *told* you that horrible brown wallpaper was depressing. But you wouldn't listen, would you? A woman comes to see the flat, takes one look at it and jumps out the window! She wasn't feeling suicidal until she saw the colour scheme."'

The laughter round the table rose. Others began to chip in:

'If she didn't like the lounge suite, she could have just said so. Was it really necessary for her to kill herself over it?'

'Our guests come in through the door but they leave by the window.'

'Boy oh boy, are we in need of Feng Shui!'

'You're very quiet,' the woman sitting next to Neil said to him. 'Don't you approve?'

'Of what?'

Perhaps you think suicide is not something to laugh about?'

'Not at all,' said Neil. 'Laughter is undoubtedly the most appropriate response to suicide. Won't you pass me the pickled cucumbers?'

Neil was a therapy agnostic. He was beginning to understand the ritual and to grow accustomed to the strange little priest who presided. But he had not been converted – perhaps he never would be. And he had not witnessed any miracles, although others spoke of them: the man who had lost his way, went down a dark path and found a light at the end of it, a lamp that lit the road behind him and, in doing so, showed him something of what lay ahead; the spiritually destitute woman who stumbled and fell and in her abasement reached out and beheld before her a nugget of pure self-knowledge. Neil had heard of these things, but he could not bring himself to believe in their immanence – certainly not as a creed which he could adapt for his own purposes. He didn't look forward to therapy; and when it was over he was left with a sense of release in which there was also a trace of resentment. But, for all that, there was something that made him persevere, that made him cling to the faint hope that it would bring him what he needed: a way out of the impasse of himself, a journey to a land where he could meet himself as if he were being introduced to someone new and exciting.

The room in which therapy was offered was curiously subterranean. It was a flatlet tucked like a black pouch beneath the therapist's house. One reached it by walking around the house and through the garden, which was now full of peach blossoms and butterflies; but Neil had to turn his back on all that as he descended a flight of stairs, knocked on a wooden door, and was admitted into a dark little room which looked the same throughout the year. The only thing that ever changed was that during the winter an oil heater burned and, when the winter was over, the heater stood unused next to a small bookcase.

It wasn't unfitting that the custodian of this seasonless place, this cave which grew colder and warmer but remained otherwise unaltered, was a gnome. He had a big head, a goatee, a short, thick body and deft white hands. Throughout the winter he'd worn corduroy trousers and jerseys, but now he was dressed in navy pants and a white shirt. The gnome was called Farrell. He was the therapist.

He sat in one black chair; Neil, facing him, sat in another. Behind Neil there was a wall clock which he couldn't see. This always bothered him. It meant that, unless he looked repeatedly at his watch, which seemed rude, he never knew how much time he had left and when the fifty minutes which had been allotted to him would be over. But Farrell always knew: he had the clock before him at all times. Neil felt that this arrangement placed him at a serious disadvantage. He wanted to be able to wind things up, to end on a high note, to round off his thoughts (not merely finish them), to say, 'Well, that's all for this week, thank you for listening,' but he never could do that; instead, he had to wait until he was interrupted and told that there was no more time. He didn't feel that what he had to say should be terminated so abruptly – even a doctor would say, 'Okay, you can get dressed again' – but there was nothing he could do about it.

When he first began therapy, he used to ask Farrell how he was and Farrell always said, 'Very well, thank you.' But then Neil stopped asking. There was no point to it. Farrell was never going to tell him how he was. His entire family (if he had one) and all his friends (those gnomes and trolls with whom he shared his subterranean life) could have been wiped out that week and he would still say, 'Very well, thank you.' So Neil would just say 'hi' and make his way towards his black chair while Farrell slid onto the other and blinked and moved his goatee up and down. Then there would be a long pause. It made Neil feel as if it were his responsibility to close the silence. He resented having to perform, to leap through the hoop of disclosure like a trained seal. But then he would tell himself sternly that what happened in that room *was* his responsibility; that he had to use what was on offer and, in doing so, make it possible for Farrell to do his job. Even agnostics must look for God. So he would clear his throat and begin to speak.

'What did he say to that?' Farrell asked.

'He said, "Oh well, at least I'm not one of your problems," or something like that. He was just making small talk. He was thinking about the meeting we'd had and how difficult it's going to be to find his mother. He's not really interested in what goes on in my therapy sessions.'

'You didn't feel you could say something?'

'What? What could I say? I couldn't say, "Actually, you *are* one of my problems."'

'Why not?'

'I just couldn't.'

'You're anxious that he'll realise what's going on?'

'Yes.'

'And you're not ready for that?'

'No.'

'You're afraid to tell him?'

'I – I don't know if I'm afraid. I'm not ready, that's all.'

'But what kind of a friendship is it if you can't be honest with him?'

Neil looked at the bookcase. He had thought, when he first began therapy, that the books would tell him something about Farrell. But they did not. There were a few biographies, novels (nothing unusual – Leon Uris, James Michener, that sort of thing), a few books on photography (did that mean Farrell was interested in photography?) and two coffee-table books: *The Fairest Cape* and *Johannesburg: From Mining Camp to Metropolis*. There were no books on psychology. Was this banal selection an indication of Farrell's extra-therapeutic preoccupations, or were these the books he left here precisely because they did not interest him? Did you have to go into the house and look at the bookcases there to know what his passions really were? And what would you find there? Cookery books? Books on how to build model aeroplanes? *Therapy Without Tears*? *Pavlov's Dogs and Other Animals*? Did the books in the therapy room reveal or hide the real Farrell?

Neil's curiosity was of a very mild sort. It didn't matter greatly to him that, as the months passed, he grew no nearer to knowing anything about Farrell. He wasn't intrigued by him. He didn't care what he did when he wasn't sitting opposite him in his black chair. He didn't even care to know what Farrell's orientation as a therapist was – whether, for instance, he was a Freudian, a neo-Freudian, a quasi-Freudian, a lapsed Freudian, an anti-Freudian or a non-Freudian. Of what significance are the views of a man who won't even tell you how he is?

Neil answered the question slowly. 'What kind of friendship is it? As you well know, it's a very unsatisfactory sort of friendship. I'm in love with my oh-so-straight brother-in-law and he isn't even aware of it. And I'm angry with my sister, which I have no right to be, because she has not been able to save her marriage and that threatens my relationship with him, makes me afraid that he'll slip out of my life. I'd rather see him under false pretences than not at all. I'm helping him to find his biological parents so that I have an excuse to see him more often. Pathetic, isn't it?'

'I don't think it's pathetic,' said Farrell. 'We are often inclined to be hard on ourselves, but these are very common human feelings.' One little white hand fluttered for a second and then was still. Outside there was the sound of a lawnmower starting up, followed by the derisive cackle of a grey lourie: *go 'way, go 'way, go 'way.*

'Certainly, it is a very difficult situation,' Farrell continued. 'And it's making you unhappy. And present unhappinesses have a way of bringing back past sadnesses.'

'Making me unhappy? Yes. It's making me unhappy. He haunts me.'

'You're suffering from unrequited affections.'

'Unrequited affections,' repeated Neil in a dull voice. What a strange phrase it was, what a strange concept – 'unrequited affections'. It sounded quaint, old-fashioned, almost chivalric. It sounded like something that people didn't get any more, like smallpox. It had the ring of a euphemism, an unctuous word that had to take the place of one too ugly to be used. And in any case his affections were not really unrequited, although they were certainly not being requited in the way that he would have liked. If 'unrequited affections' didn't quite capture what he felt, then what was the malady that afflicted him? He was suffering from something that was as red as a welt, as hot as an infected wound; something that made him burn and itch, that made his own skin loathsome to him. 'Don't scratch,' his father used to say, when he complained that he had been bitten by mosquitoes and was suffering from what they used to call 'itchy bites' – 'don't scratch, you'll only make it worse.'

He didn't know what words he should use to describe the house of his grief, to take him and Farrell beyond the façade of sadness and show the grim emptiness of the rooms that lay behind it: the dust that settled everywhere, the paint that flaked, the floorboards that swelled. Wasn't that what therapy was about – finding a way to speak the words of sorrow? But what could he say?

'I'm suffering…' he said and stopped. He tried again. 'I'm suffering from desire.'

As he drove home, Neil reflected that there had been no explicit mention this time in his therapy session of his mother's suicide.

But it had been referred to, of course: *present unhappinesses have a way of bringing back past sadnesses.* He could suppress the event all he liked in his daily life, but Farrell would always make sure that it loomed large in therapy. Everything seemed to come back to that – even the way he felt about Richard.

Neil felt deflated, short-changed by everything and everyone. He had handed in such a large, such a shiny, such a promise-laden note, and a few dull coins were all that had been returned to him. (He thought again of the beggar at the traffic light: he *must* remember to give him an extra coin next time.) And to whom could he complain about being short-changed? Even Farrell, whose attention he paid for, watched the clock surreptitiously and kicked him out after exactly fifty minutes.

'The time has come to bid you farewell,' Helena Verster was saying. 'What a delightful morning it has been! What good company you all are! We have time for one more song before I hand over to my colleague. You know, listeners, our natural resources are being depleted. Soon there will be no oil left, no coal, no fish in the oceans. But take it from me, there is one thing that is never used up and that is love. Love is never depleted, it just grows and grows. It's a cornucopia that is available to us all. We should all go out and drink from the well that never runs dry. And here on Radio Frangipani, 91.8, the Home of Highveld Harmony, is that wonderful Barry White composition, the theme song to the album whose title says it all: *Love Unlimited.*'

4 Flies

'FLIES,' SAID Aunt Maisie. 'They're dying like flies. And the government does nothing about it, of course. Absolutely nothing. You'd think they'd look after their own people – you know what I mean? But they don't. It's quite scandalous.'

Deanna and Neil glanced at each other. Neil winked. Aunt Maisie had cast-iron opinions about everything. What other people thought merely washed up against the rock of her convictions, floundered there and was sucked away again, leaving her unmoved. When views were expressed which did not concur with hers, she brushed them away impatiently. And such was the force of her personality that these irksome notions usually settled elsewhere and did not bother her again. Whatever else changed, she (and her opinions) did not.

Deanna and Neil were having tea with her on a Saturday afternoon. They both made a point of seeing her regularly. They had scarcely known her before their mother died, but now they could not imagine life without her. She was an eccentric: not a harmless one, not invariably an endearing one, but always colourful in her abrasive way. 'Why did you never get married, Aunt Maisie?' Neil asked her once when he was a little boy.

'All the young men got killed in the war,' she replied. 'There was no one left for me to marry.'

'The Second World War?'

'The Boer War.'

Neil thought about this for a while. Eventually he said, 'But you weren't *born* when the Boer War was on.'

'I don't suppose I was,' she said. 'Well, then – no wonder I didn't get married. I was waiting for the soldiers to come back from the wrong war.'

Deanna and Neil would report to her on what had happened in their lives since their last visit and she would fill them in on whom she had seen and what she had read. In particular, she would make known what her forays into the *Hatched, Matched and Dispatched*, that tumultuous world of ceaseless begetting, betrothal and bereavement, had brought to light.

Aunt Maisie's flat was decorated, rather surprisingly, in understated colours: beige, grey and cream. It was as if her personality, so vivid and overpowering – clothed, as it were, in clouds of magenta – needed a respite from itself and that was what the soft hues of her home supplied. The spring sunlight that came in through the windows was bright but diffident, still too new a visitor from the Tropic of Cancer to be quite at home.

Bertha came in bearing tea, shortbread (Aunt Maisie's favourite) and sponge cake. She had greeted Deanna and Neil at the door when they arrived and now nodded at them again as she set down the tray and left the room. 'Thanks, Bee-Bee,' they said.

'Thank you, Miss Bertha,' said Aunt Maisie.

'That's okay, Miss Maisie,' she replied.

Bertha had been employed by Aunt Maisie for over twenty years. Their relationship was full of convoluted tensions and power struggles, all of which would have been amusing to Neil and Deanna had they not had to listen for so many years to drawn-out complaints from both women. In some ways theirs was the customary maid-and-madam relationship, but in other ways it was not: they lived their lives, for the most part, within a stereotype as confining and archaic as a corset, but every so often they would wriggle out of it – and that was when they became really interesting. Their hostilities largely took the form of a Cold War, but heated skirmishes were not uncommon.

On the very day that Bertha was first employed, there had been a brief struggle over names – one that anticipated the many, many battles that the next two decades would bring. Aunt Maisie said she didn't want to be called 'Miss Lewis'. And she couldn't bear the idea of being called 'Madam'. 'You can call me Maisie,' she said. 'Just Maisie. That's my name and I'm happy with it.'

This was unconventional – almost unheard of at the time. Maisie's friends would have frowned upon it. Bertha, too, frowned upon it. It was much too iconoclastic for her. She was no doormat, but her subversions were stealthy. She didn't approve of conduct that flouted the conventions so openly. 'I'll call you Miss Maisie,' she said.

'No. You'll call me Maisie,' ordered Aunt Maisie.

'Miss Maisie,' countered Bertha.

'Maisie,' repeated Aunt Maisie.

'Miss Maisie,' said the intransigent Bertha, beginning to sulk. Aunt Maisie did not know it then, but Bertha was very good at sulking. It was her way of dealing with all forms of opposition. She was a servant and could be given orders, but when the sulking set in it meant that that part of her which was not a servant was asserting itself with all the grandiloquence a sullen silence could muster. And Aunt Maisie recognised this, even on that first day. It was the first time these two strong personalities took the measure of each other. What started off as a stalemate became a significant victory for Bertha. Aunt Maisie yielded. But she still had one last weapon. 'If you call me Miss Maisie,' she said, 'I will call you Miss Bertha.'

'All right,' said Bertha. She did not gloat; instead, she looked down and fingered her Church of Zion badge. She knew that she had won, but she knew also that Aunt Maisie did not like losing and that it wouldn't happen often. And so that was what they remained to each other as the years passed – 'Miss Maisie' and 'Miss Bertha'. 'It's quite ridiculous,' people said. 'It's like something out of *Gone with the Wind*. Don't they know how risible it is?' But what was ludicrous to others was to Maisie and Bertha a sombre compromise, a pact forged when iron first met iron and one implacable will had had to give way to another.

Neil and Deanna, however, called Bertha 'Bee-Bee'. They were watching her bake a cake one afternoon a few months after their mother's death – Aunt Maisie 'lent' her to them for a few days every week as part of her project to provide support to the bereft household of her brother and his children. Bertha was not particularly motherly (she had no children of her own, although she had an enormous extended family), not indulgent, not tender; but they found her presence reassuring nonetheless. They liked people who didn't treat them as if they had fallen ill or regressed to a pre-school age simply because their mother had jumped off a building while they were on holiday in Cape Town. Bertha gave them the spoon to lick.

'What's your surname?' Neil asked suddenly.

'Nyathi,' she replied.

The children repeated it slowly. They liked the sound of it. 'N-ya-thi.'

'What language is that?' Neil asked.

'Zulu.'

'And what does it mean?'

'Buffalo.'

'Buffalo?' They looked at each other and then shrieked with delight. 'Is that *really* what it means?'

Bertha glared at them. She couldn't understand why they found it so amusing. 'That is my name,' she said curtly. 'What's wrong with it?'

'Bertha Buffalo,' the children chanted. 'B-B. Bertha Buffalo. B-B.' Like most children, they were in love with alliteration, with the sounds that language makes when you tickle it on the tummy and it begins to squirm. And so on that day she became Bee-Bee; and they called her by no other name, even when they were adults.

'What news of You-Know-Who?' Aunt Maisie suddenly demanded. She adamantly refused, since the separation, to call Richard by his name. He was now always referred to as 'You-Know-Who'. The blank of his blood had always meant that, for Aunt Maisie, his identity was at best tenuous; but now he had lost his name too. It was as if he were in danger of being effaced entirely. But she still wanted to talk about him. And so did Bertha. She always greeted visitors, even Neil and Deanna, rather coldly when they arrived – they were used to it by now and expected no effusiveness – but she would warm up considerably before they left. Neil would undoubtedly be dragged into the kitchen (she considered it indelicate to question Deanna) and news of 'Dr Richard', as she called him, would be demanded.

'You should ask Neil, Aunt Maisie,' said Deanna. 'He sees more of him than I do.'

Aunt Maisie turned her inquisitorial gaze onto Neil. 'I don't see that much of him,' he protested. 'I went with him the other day to meet a woman who's going to help him find his biological family. But it's not going to be easy. His mother gave a false name when she abandoned him at the Home, so there's very little to go on.' Aunt Maisie flicked her cigarette ash into the ashtray with a vehemence that suggested that she, too, would be tempted to abandon such a baby. 'And the Slaters never made any efforts to find out,' Neil went on. 'The less they knew, the happier they were.'

Aunt Maisie gave a snort that would have alarmed a matador. She had never liked Richard's parents and, since his separation from Deanna, had become even more scathing in her denunciation of them. 'If blood could be undone,' she said, '*if* it could – which it can't – those two certainly would not be the ones to undo it. What a family he ended up in!' She spoke as if Richard had chosen his adoptive parents rather than the other way around.

'They loved him as best they could,' said Deanna, not sure why she felt the need to defend them. 'And Elaine's not so bad. She's quite harmless, really. Jock is very difficult, I admit.'

'She's under her husband's thumb,' retorted Aunt Maisie. 'She hasn't got a mind of her own. Let me tell you, such people are *never* harmless.' She lit another cigarette and fixed Deanna with a look that in its time had quelled traffic cops, plumbers, post office officials, supermarket managers and motor mechanics. 'Now tell me,' she said, 'are you going to divorce him or not? Let's have no more beating about the bush. After all, he was unfaithful to you. '

'Did you read an article about AIDS in the newspaper, Aunt Maisie?' asked Neil. 'Is that why you said that people were dying like flies?' Deanna looked at him with gratitude. But it was no use, of course: Aunt Maisie was not to be deflected from her line of enquiry by such ploys.

'Don't change the subject!' she ordered. Then, turning to Deanna, she said, 'Well?'

Had anyone else asked such intrusive questions, Deanna would have been indignant. As it was, she felt no anger at all. Aunt Maisie always behaved as if she were the Queen of Hearts at the croquet game. She was frequently in danger of becoming a caricature of herself, but she never quite spilled over into absurdity. She was bossy and interfering, but not malicious. And her rough devotion to them over so many years had earned her the right to ask whatever she liked. Aunt Maisie was loyal; and loyalty does confer entitlement. Deanna knew that she, too, was fiercely loyal. Perhaps it was because she had tried for so long to be loyal to her mother, to the memory of the mother, who – whichever way one looked at it – had not been loyal to her? Neil had angered and disappointed her with his lack of support since the separation, but now, as she looked at him, she felt a surge of tenderness. He looked thin. His fingers were long and pale. His trousers were a little too short and revealed too much sock, a sight which, for a moment, filled her with pathos. 'We have been through so much,' she thought. 'We are going through so much now.' And she knew it was as true of Neil as it was of her, although his pain was closed to her.

Turning to Aunt Maisie, she said, 'I'm not ready to make decisions.' There was much that her aunt did not know. She was still unaware of the needle-stick injury and the PEP. She did not even know much about the marital problems. She could not be blamed for her ignorance: she was simply not the kind of woman in whom one readily confided.

Later on, Bertha cornered Neil in the kitchen, as he knew she would. Dr Richard, he informed her, was fine. He told her that Richard had sent special regards to her (this was a lie). Bertha adored Richard and always defended him stoutly, which was another source of tension between her and Aunt Maisie. No, he said emphatically, Deanna and Richard were not trying to patch things. It was possible that they never would. Bertha should not get her hopes up. 'But why?' demanded Bertha. 'They must fix it!'

'Bee-Bee,' said Neil, 'maybe there are things in life that can't be fixed? Maybe this is one of them?'

Bertha shook her head firmly. Neil may as well have been speaking a language that she did not understand. She had no interest in generalisations, hypothetical situations or rhetorical questions. She was steeped in a pragmatism so deep that the current of it bore her whole life along.

'I want to ask you something,' Archie said to the woman in white.

'Yes? What is it?' She was carrying a tray out of the room and seemed impatient.

'Did I remarry?'

'Did you *what*?'

'Did I remarry? You know, did I have a second wife?'

'No,' the woman replied. She walked out of the room. Archie

felt dissatisfied. He did not know whether or not to believe her. She seemed sure of her facts, but there was something brusque about her which made him feel as if she were brushing him off. He had a vague feeling that he did have a second wife. But if so, who was she? And what had happened to her? He did not seem to have any wife at all now. And why would the woman in white lie to him? What was she trying to hide? Perhaps – the answer came to him suddenly – perhaps she was involved in a plot to steal his money? That must be it. That was why she seemed so shifty. That was why she seemed so anxious to get away from him. Although the thought of losing his money distressed him, his awareness of the threat made him feel much happier. It was better to know what one was up against. They all wanted to steal his money. He had no friends in this place, not one. He looked around the room. People were sitting in armchairs, talking or snoozing. Some watched the TV, which featured an infomercial that said everyone could have 'firmer buns' with a minimum of effort. *Call NOW!* it urged. *Call NOW!*

In the rose garden outside the window the first blooms of the season were visible: buds of salmon and pink and yellow were beginning to open. 'Just Joey,' Archie said to himself, looking at them. Wasn't there a rose called Just Joey? What colour was it? Or was Just Joey a racehorse which had won the July Handicap years ago? Once he had dreamed that a particular horse would win the July Handicap. In the morning he rushed off to put money on it, although everyone scoffed at him. It won the race and he won forty pounds, which was a lot of money in those days. What was it called? Elizabeth of Glamis? Sea Cottage? Or were those also the names of roses?

This perplexity notwithstanding, Archie felt quite cheerful. He had been in poor spirits since he woke up, but now he was elated because the realisation that everyone was after his money explained so much that was otherwise confusing to him. It dissolved so many mysteries. It made him less fearful of the thoughts that flitted through his mind. 'I've got flies in my head,' he said to everyone. 'They buzz around. And I chase them. I try to catch them, but they're always too quick for me.'

'Use insecticide,' someone said to him once.

'I can't,' Archie replied sadly. 'Not in my own head.'

An elderly man with a red face and a bulbous nose came and sat next to him. 'Lovely morning, isn't it?' Archie said, smiling. The man muttered something and turned away. 'Tobruk?' said Archie. 'Did you say you fought at Tobruk?' There was no reply. He longed for the man to repeat himself. He thought he had said, 'I fought at Tobruk.' But it could have been, 'I'm reading a good book,' or even, 'I'm learning to cook.' Archie hoped it was the first. He had also fought in the war and liked to share reminiscences. 'So many fell during the Desert Campaign,' he said. 'We got rid of Rommel, but at a great price.' The man muttered something again. 'I beg your pardon?' said Archie. He wished his companion would articulate more clearly. Why did people mumble so? Even on the TV they spoke so badly that he could barely understand what they were saying. It sounded as if the man had said, 'We got him – the Desert Fox,' but he wasn't sure. 'Yes,' he said, shaking his head. 'We got him eventually. But what a price we paid!'

This florid-faced man was all right, he decided. He was the only one who wasn't after his money. Old comrades of the desert they were, old soldiers, old survivors. They would stick together. 'Did you also recite a poem when you were in the army?' he asked. 'You know, the one about the camel and the sphinx?' The man made no reply. Archie leaned over and recited the poem:

The natural lust of the camel
Is greater than anyone thinks
When aflame with the fire
Of carnal desire
He tries to doodle the sphinx.
But the sphinx's little depression
Is filled with the sands of the Nile
Which accounts for the camel's expression
And the sphinx's inscrutable smile.

He felt triumphant when he finished reciting it. This was indeed a good morning. He hadn't thought of that poem for years, yet he had been able to recite it as if he were still in North Africa. There was nothing wrong with his memory! How many people could remember something like that more than sixty years later? But if his memory were so good, then why couldn't he remember whether he had remarried or not? He knew he'd had one wife, there was no doubt of that; but had there been a second one? Could she have made so little impression that he'd forgotten her? Would he have consented to marry someone so nondescript, such a miserable, self-effacing shadow of a woman? It seemed unlikely.

Suddenly he began to weep. He brushed away the tears, but they kept forming. Everything seemed unbearably sad to him now. That poem about the camel and the sphinx – why had they thought it so amusing at the time? Poor, poor camel. Poor, poor sphinx. So much indignity. Such great obstacles to surmount. Such a tale of being unlucky in love. It was the saddest thing he'd ever heard.

Then he saw her, coming towards him. She walked with quick, precise steps. She was as beautiful as ever; she seemed never to age. He remembered their first date. They went to the Alhambra bioscope and he bought her an ice-cream before the show. The movie starred Errol Flynn – or was it Tyrone Power? Well, one or the other. 'This is my wife,' he said to the red-faced man. 'My dear, I'd like you to meet this gentleman. His name escapes me now, but we fought together in North Africa. I recognised him immediately. He also remembers that slightly risqué poem about the camel and the sphinx.' He tapped the man, who now appeared to be asleep, on the shoulder. The red face scowled at them and then turned away.

'How do you do?' she said. 'Nice to meet you. I'm his daughter, not his wife.' She bent over and kissed Archie. 'Hello, Dad. How are you today?'

Archie found that his eyes were full of tears again. 'Deanna,' he said, holding her hand, pressing it, pleading with her. 'I've been so upset this morning. Did I remarry – after your mother died? The nurse asked me if I remarried and I didn't know what to tell her. She gave me such a funny look.'

'No, Dad. You didn't.'

Archie sat back. 'Thanks for clearing that up,' he said. 'I've got flies in my head, you know. But you always know how to get rid of them.'

'I've brought you some white chocolate,' said Deanna. 'Your favourite. And some rusks and biscuits.'

Archie made no reply. 'They want to steal my money,' he said. 'You can't imagine the trouble I'm having. I have to be on my guard every minute of the day. You had better take it with you when you go and keep it for me. They'll rob me blind here.'

'Okay,' she said. 'If you want me to.'

'And they talk such nonsense!' he went on. 'Do you know that there was someone here this morning who was insisting that Sea Cottage was the name of a rose? Have you ever heard anything so stupid? I told him straight. You would have been proud of me. I said, "Sea Cottage was a horse, you nincompoop. Roses are called Just Joey or Double Delight or Elizabeth of Glamis."'

'Quite right,' said Deanna. 'Well done.'

A fly landed on Archie's forehead. Deanna waited for him to get rid of it, but he made no effort to do so. It crawled from one side of his face to the other. Its uninterrupted progress appalled her. Living creatures, she thought, always react to flies. They twitch, they slap at them, they flick them away with their tails. It is only the dead who allow flies to settle, who open their eyes and tongues and intestines to them, who receive them so completely and with such ignominy. She leaned over and brushed the side of her father's face with her hand. 'What are you doing?' he asked, raising his own hand and rubbing his temple.

'There's a fly on you,' she said. 'I'm just chasing it away.'

'Now there are no flies on me!' he said and laughed loudly. 'Isn't that good? No flies on Archie. That's quite hilarious. And I must tell you something else that's rather funny. This man fought very bravely at Tobruk – I told you that, didn't I? – and he recited a funny little poem about a camel. I'll repeat it for you. It's a bit risqué, but I think you're old enough for it now.'

Neil finished his drink and wondered how soon he could make an escape. He shouldn't have come. He knew hardly anyone. He wasn't good at small talk and, in any case, he wasn't getting an opportunity even to be bad at it, since no one was talking to him. One group of people was standing around the bar, which was on the patio. Another group had moved towards the swimming-pool. 'Let's swim,' shouted someone.

'Are you insane?' another voice called out. 'The water will still be freezing. I make a point of never swimming before Christmas.'

'Come on, don't be a sissy!' someone else roared, but in the end no one did swim. The jocularity had a forced quality to it. There's nothing, thought Neil, as dreary as an unsuccessful party. Would it be considered rude if he left now? Perhaps he could say he was feeling ill?

Then, suddenly, he heard a voice which he knew very well. He turned around to see whom it came from, but to his surprise he couldn't see anyone he recognised, except the person who had invited him to the party in the first place, and it wasn't her. No one looked familiar at all, and yet he *knew* that voice, knew the clear, low tones. But how could he know it so well and not know to whom it belonged? And how could it emanate from a group of complete strangers?

At last he traced it to a woman who was standing near the bar. She was short and slight and wore a grey track-suit top over black jeans. Her dark hair was cropped short and she wore a stud in her nostril. Neil stared at her. It was bizarre. He was certain that he'd never seen her in his life before; but the voice was as familiar as a room he'd slept in, as a table he'd eaten at. 'Oh, that jerk,' she was saying. 'Oh, that idiot. Take it from me, that man is a complete fuckwit.' And then he knew.

Later he found himself sitting next to her at the bar. He decided to be brave and talk to her. 'You're quite different from what I imagined,' he said. 'It's strange how one forms a mental picture, based on the voice, and then the person isn't like that at all.'

'I hope I'm not a disappointment to you,' she said. Her face was oval, her eyes a dark brown.

'No. It's just that I imagined someone a bit more...a bit more conservative.'

She threw her head back and laughed. 'I like that,' she said. 'Conservative. I really like that.'

Neil put out his hand. 'I'm Neil Lewis,' he said.

'Hi. And I'm Helena Verster.'

'Yes, I know.'

They spoke for hours. Neil was overwhelmed by the discovery of what the person behind the Radio Frangipani voice was really like. He had imagined a woman in her late thirties or forties, married to a bank manager, the mother of two children, living in Linden or Blairgowrie; someone who, despite her age, wore an Alice Band in her long, straight hair, went to church on Sunday mornings, read novels which always ended happily and hung a framed copy of *Desiderata* in her toilet. Instead he found a sort of pixie, aged only twenty-seven, who had been sharing a house with some friends in Brixton since she broke up with her last girl-friend, and who said 'fuck' more often than anyone he'd ever met.

'What gave me away?' she asked.

'Well, I was certain I knew the voice from somewhere. But when you said, "take it from me," then it hit me. You say it all the time.'

'Do I?' She laughed. 'I didn't even realise it.'

'But how did you come to be employed by a station like Radio Frangipani?' Neil asked. 'It doesn't seem to be your style at all.'

'Well, a girl's gotta eat. And this girl likes prawns and langoustines.'

'But surely you don't believe in all that stuff? You know – love and schmaltz?'

'Are you out of your mind? Of course I don't. That's what my bosses want. That's what they decided I should do. They invented that persona for me. I had no say in the matter. Fucking assholes.' She looked intently at him. 'But now let me ask you something,' she said. 'I know why I do it. But why do you listen to it?'

'I'm not sure. I suppose I want to know what it is I can't bring myself to believe in. I'm like a vegetarian who peers through the window of a butchery.'

'I think this is the start of a beautiful friendship,' said Helena. 'A fucking beautiful friendship.'

Later, a little drunk, they lay on the carpet in the TV room. 'So, my new friend,' said Helena. 'Is there someone in your life?'

'No,' he said. 'Just a brother-in-law.'

'A what?' said Helena.

He told her. Helena threw her head back and laughed. 'That's not very compassionate of you,' he said.

'Fuck that!' said Helena. 'A secret crush on a straight brother-in-law. It's hilarious. Is he hot?'

'He's hot.' Despite himself, he found that he was beginning to laugh too. 'Is it really something we should be laughing about?' he asked.

'There's nothing we shouldn't laugh at, that's my philosophy. You cry when you're happy and you cry when you're sad. Everyone accepts that. Well, I think we should also be able to laugh when we're happy and laugh when we're sad.'

'Yes,' said Neil. 'There is something to what you say. Well, in that case I have two things to tell you. First, you're going to hear what I do for a living. And after that I have a little story about what happened one year when my sister and I were kids and we went to Cape Town on holiday.'

'I'm all fucking ears,' said Helena.

Percy was missing. She'd been missing before and Deanna told herself firmly not to worry: she would probably turn up soon, wailing with hunger. For all her sauntering domesticity, there was another side to Percy, dark and secret. It was, presumably, into this other life that she vanished when she was not to be found. Deanna walked around the garden just before midnight, calling Percy and shaking the bag of biscuits which were her special treat. There was no response.

She wished the cat had not chosen this very time to disappear. It unsettled her. Everything seemed to unsettle her these days. And yet she knew that she ought to be less anxious, less mournful. The clod of sorrow lodged within her should have been breaking up. When the cosmos offers us a reprieve, do we have the right to be ungrateful? The needle-stick injury had not, it seemed, harmed her. Her blood had been tested several times and the result in each case was negative. In all probability, she was out of danger. Her relief was great, but she couldn't bring herself to be jubilant. Good fortune had not remade her. A narrow escape is exactly that: narrow. She did not feel ennobled by survival.

The sky in the distance flashed white and then turned black again. Could it be lightning? The first storm of the spring? Deanna stood under a large pin-oak and waited to see if it recurred. She breathed in the night scents. The air was still, cool, sweet. The flicker of lightning came again, unmistakable this time, but no thunder followed – the storm was far away. She was struck by the silence. She knew that the garden had its own night tumult, full of small scurryings, small foragings, small murders and small feasts, but none of it reached her ears and, as she stood there, it seemed easy to believe that she was quite alone; cosmically alone.

There were things that she missed bitterly – what was the point of denying it? She missed the even breathing in the dark of the bedroom, the sight of shoes that had been kicked off and lay on the bedroom floor, the smell of aftershave and deodorant. But was this the same as longing for Richard? Or were these things not him at all, but the trace of him, the palimpsest of Richard? Was she living her own sadness, *really* living it, or was she merely a fly on the wall at the scene of her own sorrow?

She was not angry with Richard because he hadn't desired her sufficiently, because he hadn't loved her in the way she wanted to be loved (but continued to love her in another way, which made the situation much more difficult). She was not even angry with him because he had sought and found others who could satisfy him. She was angry with him for destroying the vision of togetherness that she had nurtured, the belief that you may find in another the self-reflection that returns you to yourself. Suddenly she remembered the dream she had had a few months ago, in which she had once more visited Miss Lloyd's Grade Two classroom. She saw again the man who dwelt in the blood vessel and whose face was split in two, so divided that even the eyes wore different expressions.

There was lightning again and, this time, the thunder sounded faintly. The storm was drawing closer. Another sound reached her ears. In the quiet of the night, it was discordant. At first she couldn't place it; she knew only that she resented its shrillness. And then she realised it was the telephone ringing inside the house. Who could be phoning so late? She was not on call at the hospital that weekend. She ran towards the house. As she came in through the back door, she heard a thud, followed by a plaintive sound: Percy had jumped in through the kitchen window. She stooped to scoop her up, kissed her on the top of her head and carried on running. Percy wriggled and scratched Deanna's arm. She wanted food, not fondling. Deanna threw her down and made her way to the telephone.

It was Richard. 'I'm sorry to phone so late,' he said.

'That's okay. Can I phone you back in a minute or two?' Deanna was out of breath. 'Percy has just…'

'I wanted to let you know,' he said. 'I'm sorry.' He spoke more softly than usual.

'Is there something wrong?'

'Yes. My father has had a stroke.'

'Oh shit,' she said. 'That's terrible. I'm so sorry. Is it bad?'

'I'm not sure. He's still conscious. We're waiting for them to do an MRI. '

'Where is he now? I'd like to go and see him.'

'No, don't worry, it's not necessary,' he said. 'I'll keep you posted. I'm really sorry to call at this ungodly hour.'

'Stop apologising. Tell me which hospital Jock's in. I'll go there immediately.'

Driving to the hospital, Deanna heard more thunder. She had fed Percy, thrown on a jersey, locked the house and sped to the car. Now she wondered why she had left in such haste. What difference would it make if she got there a few minutes later? None to Jock, that was for sure, whatever his condition. She knew it was not the news of his stroke that made her react like this. She was responding to the knowledge that this was what one did; she was submitting to the hallowed urgency of the call that comes late at night, to the fear of such calls that lives with us always, to the things over which we have no control and that tear so easily and so roughly through the skein of our workaday routines.

She could hear her own car changing gear as it passed through the silent streets. The roads at this hour were almost deserted. It felt as if the world were avoiding her, and rightly so: for aloneness is not just a state of being, it is also a disease which may be passed on to others and a crime which must be roundly condemned. But, oh, to be alone and not feel ashamed! To be alone and not feel like a failure! To have the power to shun rather than be shunned – the power to say, 'I won't play with you,' rather than, 'You won't play with me.' What she had now was the worst of all possible scenarios. She had to contend with being alone, but was also afflicted by people from whom she could not get away, and who had so recently even threatened her life with their blood. What an unenviable fate it was: to be alone and yet not *left* alone.

The needle-stick injury, especially now that she knew it had probably not harmed her, seemed like an inevitability, a flow of larva that had been bound to reach her sooner or later. There was no such thing as a safe passage.

Before she knew it, she was in the parking lot of the hospital.

Dorothy Strauss bumped into an acquaintance at a shopping centre. The woman, knowing of the rift in the family, suspected that she might not have heard what had happened and told her that her brother had suffered a stroke. 'Is it serious?' Dorothy asked. Her acquaintance didn't know any details. All she'd heard was that Jock had been hospitalised.

Dorothy was looking for a birthday gift for Tessa, who'd been living in London for many years. She went from shop to shop, hoping for inspiration, but none came to her. She wanted to buy her daughter something African, something she couldn't get in the U.K., but anything that resembled a curio wouldn't do: if it were aimed at the tourist market it would be most inappropriate for someone who had spent half her life in Africa. And Tessa was very quick to discern inappropriateness, in conduct and in gifts. She was a vegetarian and an animal rights activist, which ruled out bubble-wrapped biltong. It also ruled out anything made of animal hides. A South African man who knew her only slightly was once a guest in her home in Barnet. He presented her with a fly-whisk made out of a zebra's tail, thinking, no doubt, that she would be pleased to have a little bit of the bushveld in her living-room. 'I wanted to use it on him,' Tessa said. 'I wanted to beat him with it until he was black and blue. Can you imagine such an awful gift?' She threw it away as soon as her guest had left. And if one gave her a bowl or cloth or beadwork, she would be anxious to know that the people who made it were properly paid and that there was no whiff of exploitation. Tessa was so damn politically correct, thought Dorothy, gazing gloomily through the window of a curio shop at painted ostrich eggs, a brass elephant, an ivory paper-knife and a set of Liberation Struggle place mats which featured twelve portraits (from where she stood she could make out Albert Luthuli, Steve Biko, Helen Joseph and Robert Sobukwe). It was all very well having such fine compunctions – she admired Tessa for it, she really did – but sometimes it made life very difficult.

She didn't know how to react to what she had been told. When your brother has a stroke, you shouldn't hear about it from an acquaintance whom you meet by chance in a shopping-centre. The information shouldn't be slipped in between comments about the weather and the exchange rate. But how else do you receive news of a brother with whom you have had no contact for over twenty years? They lived in the same city, but they had taken great pains to avoid one another. Once, only once, a few months ago, she had had a glimpse of him. Coming out of a movie with a friend, she saw the whole family going up an escalator: Jock, Elaine, a youngish man whom she presumed to be Richard (she would certainly not have recognised him had he not been with his parents), and a woman whom she had never seen before but whom she took to be Richard's wife. She didn't want them to see her, would have been mortified if they had spotted her peering up at them; but still she could not stop herself from staring. She watched the foursome until the escalator bore them out of sight. They did not notice her.

Jock and Elaine had both aged well, she conceded. They were less altered than she would have expected. What would they have seen if they had noticed her? For a moment she looked down upon herself, saw herself as one would who had no desire to be indulgent and no inclination to make allowances. She judged herself with the judgement of unfriendly eyes. She had not aged well, she knew. She felt daily the treacheries of her body and dreaded the greater ones that were still to come. She saw her thick, mutinous legs; the walking-stick that she was now obliged to use; her hair, so thin now, but not entirely grey. She saw, spread out like a plain with no shadows, her life. She thought of Harold, who had died in 1999. She saw his tombstone. The inscription read *Beloved husband of Dorothy, father of Tessa and Anthony.* She thought of Tessa, who lived so far away. She saw Tessa and Brian's house in London, which she had visited five times, the stairs which she would now find difficult to manage, the small, neat garden, the daffodils, the hollyhocks. She thought of Anthony – most of all, of Anthony. She saw what she had never seen: the room she had never entered, the room she *knew*. She saw Anthony. He was so quiet, so still – still beyond reproach. She saw the deep shadows, the cold eerie light of the gym.

And suddenly the sight of her brother and his family filled her with rage. Irrational as it was, she felt as if the encounter had been deliberately arranged by Jock. It was as if he wanted to show her that he had come off best, that the stringent years had forgiven him, even if she hadn't, that her churning hatred had not held him back from partaking of the choicest delicacies that life had to offer. He seemed, surrounded as he was by his intact family, to rebuke her for her broken family. The power he held over her still was expressed somehow in his obliviousness. She wished, now, that he *had* seen her, even if all it meant was that he would turn to his family afterwards and say, 'Did you see? My sister has grown old and thick with bitterness.'

She decided to go home. She would look for Tessa's gift another time. She was tired; everything seemed to require more energy nowadays than she could summon. She clambered into her car, threw the groceries she had bought onto the back seat, laid her walking-stick on the passenger seat beside her and sat there for a while, breathing heavily. The steering-wheel, when she touched it, was hot from the sun. Was it still spring? Was it early summer now? Either way, the days were becoming hot. She wondered whether Jock would die. Perhaps he was dying now, while she sat here in the parking lot of the shopping centre? Perhaps he was in a coma and they were deliberating as to whether or not they should switch off the life-support system? She wondered how she would feel if he did die.

She had always imagined that, before Jock's death or her own, she would meet him again: not in overt hostility, not in reconciliation, but in a spirit of cold reckoning. She had always been convinced that she would be granted – as a meagre entitlement, a coin tossed to the penury of her suffering – an opportunity to confront him, to ask him why he had done what he had done and to tell him, sparing neither him nor herself, what the results of his actions had been for her, for Harold, for Tessa. She didn't care whether Jock apologised or not: she had no interest in his contrition. She simply wanted the opportunity to tell and be told. On TV she'd seen some of the Truth and Reconciliation Committee hearings. She'd watched with keen interest the encounters between those who had been wronged and those who had done wrong, and wondered where and how her scrap of truth would be tossed to her. The emphasis on forgiveness puzzled her. She understood that malefactors desired forgiveness. But what does it *mean* to forgive? Forgiveness, surely, is a cold, stale repast which the wronger and the wronged must swallow together. But how does one forgive when there's no hope of repair, when there's a hunger that such a food cannot satisfy? She could not imagine bestowing forgiveness. But she felt, nonetheless, especially when she saw the weeping mothers, that she too could have taken her rightful place in the queue of grief, for, even if it hadn't been entirely clear to her when Anthony died, it was evident to her now that his death was bound up with what South Africa was then, a recognition which (she was always emphatic about this) in no way exonerated what Jock had done, but was perhaps the beginning of an explanation for it. She had never actively sought the opportunity she craved, had never tried to make it happen; nonetheless, she waited for it as one waits for an event which lies in the distant future, but which is destined to occur. And now she had to face the possibility that it might not come to pass.

Two insights came to her at once. The first, surprising to her in its intensity, was that she did not want Jock to die. She couldn't bear to think that she would be cheated of what was hers, the small bequest of her long pain, the moment in which all would be told. And the second revelation was that this, however compelling it was, was quite simply the only reason she had for caring whether he lived or died. There was absolutely nothing else that made her incline one way or the other. She thought of their childhood: of how she and Jock used to play for hours in the vlei near their home until, at dusk, the mosquitoes drove them inside; of the terrible anxiety she felt when Jock's appendix burst (he was then a teenager) and his life was deemed to be in danger; of Jock's taking Harold aside the first time they met, ostensibly to give him whiskey but really to appraise him, and then, when they returned, giving her the thumbs-up behind Harold's back. How could one have such memories, inlaid by the years, and not be swayed by them? If an acquaintance – or even someone she had never met, someone she knew only by name – were ill, her concern would be greater than it was now. She was not an unfeeling person: how, then, could she regard the fact that her only sibling might die with as much indifference as if she were contemplating the death of a fly? How does something fall so low in the hierarchy of pathos? The process whereby such a decline had set in amazed her; the sheerness of the drop appalled her.

A notorious remark had once been made – many years ago, shortly before Anthony died. She had deplored it when it was uttered and she always would decry it; yet it came unbidden now to take hold of her. It had taken its time. It had waited patiently. Knowing it – *knowing* it for what it was, understanding it only too well – she could nevertheless not evict it, this slow, careful incubus. It had grown in her. It had hardened her heart. And now its moment had come. She could say it. *The prospect of my brother's death leaves me cold.*

'I hate leaving you behind,' said Barbara Lombard. She said it because it was what she felt she had to say. She was trying to close her bulging suitcase.

'I wish I was going with you.' Hannelie spoke wistfully. She sat on the bed and watched Barbara's struggle with the suitcase. 'Maybe you should sit on it?'

'No, I'm getting it closed.' Barbara was panting as she squeezed the zips closed, inch by inch.

'Don't break the zips,' said Hannelie.

'Sitting there and giving orders really doesn't help,' muttered Barbara as she closed the suitcase. 'There,' she said, standing up. 'If I've forgotten anything, I'll have to do without it. I'm certainly not opening this thing again.' She saw that Hannelie was hurt. 'Sorry,' she said, bending to kiss her. 'I didn't mean to snap.'

'That's okay.' Hannelie gave her a wan smile.

'Have you got one of your migraines coming on?'

'I think so,' said Hannelie.

Looking through the window, Barbara could see the sea. After all these years of living at the coast, she still found the sea a rather odd creature: so determined, so much effort, so much thrashing about – and to what end? Its ceaseless energy made her feel melancholic. This showed, she thought wryly, that you could take the girl out of the platteland, but you couldn't take the platteland out of the girl – even if the girl had always detested the platteland. She would have been happiest living in a lush valley or up in the mountains. Her only requirement would be that there would have to be water: fresh water, preferably running water. It was Hannelie who wanted to live by the sea, who had wanted it so badly that her wish had to be granted. The only consolation was that it was the Atlantic: if she had to live by the sea, let it at least be icy. She despised the Indian Ocean, which ran off your skin like the hot drops of someone else's perspiration, which panted after you like an obese lapdog.

'I'll be back in nine days,' she said. 'Next week Friday.'

'I know,' said Hannelie. 'I know exactly when you're coming back.' She blew her nose. 'I'm sure the exhibition will go well.'

'I hope so.' She glanced at Hannelie, who was tugging at a lock of hair near her ear – an habitual gesture. When and how had the love she felt for her turned into something else – something in which the prevailing note was tender obligation? When and how had the prospect of the years that lay ahead been traded in for the claims of the years that lay behind? When and how had her love for Hannelie grown smaller than Hannelie's love for her? Something had turned lop-sided when no one was looking, and, even when she became aware of it, she did not know how to right it. She saw it clearly enough, but did Hannelie? At times she felt certain that she did; at others she was convinced that Hannelie remained oblivious of the change.

'I always enjoy your exhibitions,' said Hannelie. 'They remind me of the one that brought us together. Do you think of it too?'

"How could I not?' There was nothing of that day she had forgotten. She had watched Hannelie for some time before Hannelie had even seen her. The exhibition was at a gallery in Pretoria in the early 1980s. The woman and the little boy had walked past her, unaware that she was the sculptor, and she had watched them pause before each piece and discuss it. She could not hear what the mother said, but she saw the boy listen earnestly to her words. They were both blond – in fact, their hair was identical in colour. She would have liked to sculpt them, to make them every bit as beautiful as they were, and then to call the sculpture *Verwoerd's Aryan Dream* or something like that. For that was how she worked during those years. Her realism was unstinting and so was her irony. And she would have been closer to the truth than she could ever have imagined, for little did she know as she gazed appreciatively at them that this young woman, looking so intently at the sculptures, was none other than the prime minister's daughter; and this serious child, who kept so close to his mother, was the little boy whom, a few years before, two men had attempted to kidnap. Without knowing it, she had got them right. But she had also got them utterly wrong.

'I'm sure Noldie will be here soon,' said Hannelie, looking at her watch. 'He knows you have to get to the airport.'

'Don't worry, Noldie is never late,' Barbara reassured her. 'There's plenty of time. I'm going to have a last cup of tea.'

The doorbell rang soon after. Noldie kissed them both. 'Let me carry the suitcase,' he said.

'Thank you,' said Barbara. 'It's very heavy.'

He grunted when he picked it up. 'You should find another way to transport your sculptures, Barbara,' he said as he carried it out of the door. 'Stuffing them in your suitcase is not the answer.'

'Very funny,' she said. Noldie waited in the car while she said goodbye to Hannelie.

'Don't worry,' he said as Barbara clambered in beside him. 'I'll look in on her whenever I can. Theresa will too. And I'll phone several times a day.' He drove very carefully, keeping to the middle lane and to the speed limit.

'Thank you. I know you will. But I can't help worrying,' said Barbara. 'I hate leaving her. But I just couldn't take her with me. You know I couldn't. It would have been a nightmare.'

'Yes, I do know. Don't worry, it'll be okay,' he replied.

Despite her misgivings, she found his words (the tone of them more than the words themselves) reassuring. There was something about him that people found reassuring. She watched him as he drove and felt, as she often did, that she liked the man he had become. She was not his mother, but she felt she was entitled, nevertheless, to be proud of him – just a little proud. She'd never wanted a child of her own, but had found herself having to be a parent to Noldie as he found himself with a sort of second mother. It was not easy for either of them. But they emerged from it – and this, she felt, *was* something to be proud of – with affection intact. As she looked at him, changing gears with his fine, slender hands, she found it difficult to reconcile this Noldie, over thirty years old now, well over six feet tall, his hair, still very blond, thinning in front, with the timid little boy who often came home from school with his face tear-stained because his classmates had teased him about the kidnapping. 'But why are you so upset?' she used to ask him. 'It doesn't matter what they say. It wasn't your fault. You didn't do anything wrong. And nobody will ever try it again, I promise you. You're safe now. Those bad men are in jail.' (They kept from him until he was a teenager the fact that one of the men had committed suicide before the trial.) But Noldie would never say why it upset him so. 'They must just shut up about it,' was all he would say. 'They must *shut up!*'

Barbara thought of Hannelie, of how she'd tried to be brave when they parted and failed dismally. It was as if only a modicum of self-assurance were available and Noldie and his mother had had to share it. As it had grown in him, it had dwindled in her. It was sometimes difficult for Barbara to believe that the Hannelie for whom small anxieties now seemed insuperable had once been so full of high disdain, so defiant, so daring. Three weeks after their meeting at the exhibition, she left her husband and moved in with Barbara. Her father, who was then still prime minister, suppressed the scandal as best he could. He told her that if she didn't return to her husband and renounce this depravity, unheard of and unprecedented in their family, he would never speak to her again. Hannelie refused. The Prime Minister never spoke to her again. Hannelie's mother would meet her daughter surreptitiously and weep over Noldie and buy him sweets.

When the old man (now retired from politics) was dying, his wife begged Hannelie to visit him. 'Not unless he asks for me,' she replied.

'He can't do that,' her mother said. 'You know what he's like. He just can't. But he wants to see you. Please, I'm begging you.'

'Not unless he asks for me,' repeated Hannelie. He did not ask. She did not see him before he died, nor did she attend the funeral. Her absence was noted in several newspaper accounts of the funeral.

Hannelie was like a lion in those days. Barbara had been in awe of her resoluteness. She was even a little afraid of her. She'd found it difficult to believe that she had the power to attract such a person, that such fierceness had been willing to come to her and be gentled. Was this the same person who clung to her now, who became anxious when she was left alone, even for a short period, who gave off that slightly fetid smell, like old cheese, that dependency always produces?

There was so much in her life, in Hannelie's, in Noldie's, that she could never have predicted; so much that she, who had lived the changes, found hard to believe. If it appeared in a novel, the readers would scoff and say it was unbelievable. But that seemed to be the strange thing about fiction, reflected Barbara (who had written a novel many years ago, failed to get it published and decided to stick to sculpture): fiction had to be life-like, it had to go to obedience school, it had to come to heel. But life did just what it liked. There was nothing more anarchic than life.

She remembered the time, a few years ago, when J. G. Strijdom's bust fell and smashed to pieces in Strijdom Square in Pretoria. She thought at the time that if she still went in for heavy realism and heavy irony (she had since developed a distaste for both), she could have done a sculpture of one of the Nationalist prime ministers – Hannelie's father, say – and then broken it deliberately and exhibited it like that. And no one would have liked it. People would have dismissed the symbolism as too contrived, too glib. They would have wanted a lighter touch. *Ozymandias*, they would have said, and yawned. *The Fall of Apartheid in the Heart of Pretoria*, they would have said, and rolled their eyes. And yet something – a heavy hand indeed – had sent the bust of Strijdom crashing down. And no one seemed to mind. Everyone accepted it. The artist who fashioned that event was about as subtle as King Kong climbing the Empire State Building. But no one objected.

As they went past Groote Schuur, the traffic grew heavy and they had to crawl along. 'Relax,' said Noldie. 'You've got plenty of time. You won't miss your plane.'

'I know,' she said. 'I'm not panicking.'

Truly, no one could have foretold what the future would bring. Take Noldie, for instance. If one wrote the story of his life, people would say the ironies were too neat, too triumphant. They would say that not even South Africa, with its special talent for extravagant ironies, could produce a tale of such gleeful, stick-your-tongue-out transformation. And yet it was so. How Hannelie's father must be turning in his grave! Like a dervish he must be, spinning madly from side to side in his subterranean outrage. For the prime minister's grandson, Arnoldus Pieter van Wyk, that cherubic little blond boy, who, after the attempted kidnapping, became an icon of the Nationalist cause, was today the son of a lesbian, the husband of a coloured woman, and an ANC member of parliament.

Neil still listened to Helena Verster's radio programme. But his knowledge of its seditiousness, of what the dulcet tones masked, made him respond to it completely differently. Helena, he now knew, was peddling wares that she had no confidence in; she was the grand merchant of ersatz love. His enjoyment was heightened by the fact that there was a special compact between them: Helena had promised him that she would lay it on even more thickly, just for him. Millions would tune in and hear the earnest credo of love; only he would hear in it the lapsed love, the apostate love, the love turned inside out.

He had the radio on at work. 'I was always taught,' Helena was saying, 'that gentlemen don't kiss and tell. They certainly shouldn't brag about their conquests. That's what my parents told me when I was growing up in Kakamas' – Neil guffawed and slapped his knees with pleasure; Helena, he knew, had lived in Johannesburg all her life – 'and that's what I still believe. Call me an old-fashioned girl if you like, but that's what I am. I'm the product of my upbringing. And take it from me, the old values are still the best. Anyway, here are two men who can't stop themselves from crowing about the fact that they've managed to seduce so many women. I find it a little distasteful. On Radio Frangipani, 91.8, the Home of Highveld Harmony, we bring you Willie Nelson and Julio Iglesias with *To All the Girls I've Loved Before*.'

Neil wondered how Helena managed to say these things without bursting into laughter. He felt certain that in her place he would start spluttering and be fired by the station managers after five minutes. Helena betrayed nothing, however; she was a professional, for all her cynicism. But how she must chortle once she was off the air! Had he not met her at the party, had they not become friends, he would not now be laughing so much that he had to gasp for breath. What she said had an added significance for them both because he knew whom it was coming from and she knew to whom it was going. The anonymity of the radio, the voice that comes from nowhere and goes nowhere, had been replaced by something they had made for each other, a whispered secret that must not be told to the grown-ups.

The telephone rang. The receptionist put the call through to Neil. It was someone who wanted to speak to Archie. 'He doesn't work here any more,' said Neil. 'He retired some years ago. This is his son. Yes, I've taken over the business from him. Perhaps I can help you?' The man enquired after Archie. 'He's all right,' said Neil, who didn't feel inclined to go into details. In response to another question he said, 'He lives in a Home. His health isn't bad. Yes, I see him quite often. Certainly, I'll be glad to give him your regards.'

He recalled guiltily, after he put the phone down, that it was more than two weeks since he had been to visit Archie. How he hated going there! But what was the use of paying a visit that would be forgotten the minute he left the room? 'Never mind that,' Deanna would say. 'He enjoys the visit while you're there. That's good enough.' She was right, of course. And she visited their father regularly. She always did the right thing. But the horror – the soporific ghastliness – of that place! What was the trendy term used these days – 'assisted living'? Their father was in an 'assisted living' facility.

His cellphone rang. It was Helena. 'Wasn't that fun?' she said. 'I hope you were listening.'

'Of course I was listening,' said Neil. 'I was laughing so much I nearly choked – especially when you told us about your childhood in Kakamas. But aren't you worried your bosses are going to realise what's going on? I don't want you to jeopardise your job.'

'Don't worry about it,' said Helena. 'They wouldn't know a parody if it bit them in the fucking derrière. Now, are we still on for tonight? What about a movie?'

'Of course we're on,' he said as the telephone on his desk began to ring. 'But I'll have to phone you back. I must take this call.'

The caller had special requirements: none of the standard designs would do. He wanted a tree made of white marble, the trunk severed to indicate a young life cut short, and angel wings sprouting from the side. 'Sir, let me make enquiries,' said Neil. 'That's very different from the standard memorials, but let me see what I can do. I'll speak to our craftsmen and ring you back later today.' In response to another question from the caller he said, 'Let me find out first if they can do it, Sir. If they can, I'll fax you a quotation.'

He could hear the receptionist's voice in the background as he replaced the receiver. '*Time Immemorial Tombstones*,' she was saying. 'How may I help you?' Her voice was thick and nasal.

Neil sat brooding and doodling on a notepad. Even the thought of seeing Helena in the evening didn't cheer him up much. He hadn't heard from Richard for days. He hadn't been to see his father. Deanna was disappointed in him. Well, so she might be – he was disappointed in himself. This was not what he had envisaged for himself. Dropping out of university and taking over his father's business were not what he had planned. And the company was called *Time Immemorial Tombstones*. And it came with an adenoidal receptionist. And they all had shares in it, even Aunt Maisie: his father had fifty per cent, Deanna and he each had twenty, and Aunt Maisie had ten. And there was a man who insisted upon a severed tree and angels' wings, carved out of white marble. And he would get it too.

Bathos is no doubt the destination of us all. But we should get there only after a long travail, a slow surrender. He had arrived there much too soon. 'Assisted living,' thought Neil. 'I could do with some of that myself.'

Deanna, sitting next to Archie on a couch, was reading bits of the newspaper to him. 'This is good. You should get into the habit of reading the newspaper every day,' said Archie. 'I read it from cover to cover from a young age and so did my sister – we even used to fight over it when it arrived. It's the best way to improve your general knowledge.'

'Aunt Maisie is still an avid reader of the newspaper,' said Deanna. 'But she doesn't read it from cover to cover.'

Archie continued as if Deanna hadn't spoken. 'If you don't keep up with current affairs, your brain turns to mush,' he said.

Deanna found it difficult to find anything suitable to read to her father. What would be the point of reading an article about AIDS orphans to him? The same was true of stories about crime in Johannesburg, suicide bombers in Israel or Iraq, famine in the Horn of Africa, massacres in central Africa, gaping holes in the ozone layer. It would upset him, and to what end? Yet it was astonishing how little there was that was unlikely to distress him. And there was another problem: his frame of reference was limited. He recalled only what had happened a long time ago. He remembered Vietnam and the assassination of Verwoerd and the moon landing and Watergate, but not much after that. He didn't know what Zimbabwe was. He thought the Nationalists were still in power in South Africa, although, interestingly, he did seem to know that Mandela had been released. It was strange how he could remember some things so well, while others were lost to him completely. He inhabited years that were long gone, but incompletely so – as if the past were a house, once grand but now decaying, and he was restricted to a very small part of it, the other rooms having been boarded up.

'Here's something interesting,' said Deanna. '*Queen Elizabeth Now World's Second-Longest Reigning Monarch.*'

'How time flies,' said Archie, shaking his head. 'It seems like it was only yesterday that the king died. Yet it must be twenty years ago at least.' Deanna began to read the article to him, but he interrupted her. 'Lung cancer,' he said. 'And he was still a relatively young man. I told Maisie not to smoke, but she always knows best. I wonder why I never see her?'

'You see her every week,' said Deanna.

'No, I don't. Don't talk nonsense. I haven't seen her in months.'

Deanna didn't try to read the rest of the article to him. She turned the page. There was an article about cloning, which interested her, but she read it to herself – there was no point in trying to share it with Archie. Then she read him a few sentences from a story about the difficulties experienced by zoologists in achieving successful artificial insemination of giant pandas. 'Strange the kinds of things they write about these days in the newspaper,' said Archie. 'Don't they realise that children read these things too?' Deanna found it intriguing that, the deterioration of his faculties notwithstanding, there was much that had remained unchanged. He had been a prude all his life and he still was. He could not talk about sex and he had a horror of scatology. He said 'sherbet' instead of 'shit', spoke of going to the lavatory for 'number one' and 'number two', and even called it 'the smallest room in the house.'

Deanna turned the page again and began to read aloud from an article about a sculptor from Cape Town whose works were being exhibited in New York. 'American art critics have been unanimous in acclaiming the work of Barbara Lombard' she read. 'Lombard enjoys a growing international reputation, although many feel that the veteran sculptor has not received the recognition she deserves in her own country.'

She saw that Archie wasn't listening. 'Have you had enough of the newspaper, Dad?' she asked. 'Would you rather have a nap?'

Archie leaned forward suddenly and grabbed her wrist. There were reddish blotches on his hand which stood out against the pallor of his skin. His hand felt papery and dry, although the grip was surprisingly strong. 'Did you take the money away?' he asked. 'I told you to. Did you? If you leave it here, they'll steal the lot. They will. And then there'll be nothing for you and your brother when I'm gone.'

'Don't worry,' she said. 'I took it all. It's perfectly safe.'

He smiled – a crafty grin that made him look like a smug gargoyle. Deanna, at that moment, found him utterly repellent. She had made a great effort, since he became ill, to love what he now was as an act of homage to what he used to be. But it seemed to her now, as he sat there, smirking like a schoolboy who has just spent hours pulling the wings off flies, making red ants and black ants fight with one another and shooting birds with a pellet-gun, that there was nothing left in him to love. What had happened to him was cruel, but what he had become was also cruel, driven as he was by the pricklings of an egotism that was small, base and fearful.

'They're going to be so frustrated when they can't find anything,' he said. 'Can you just imagine it?'

There was a sudden flash of lightning, followed by heavy thunder. The room in which they sat had suddenly turned dark. 'I'd better go, Dad,' said Deanna. 'I really don't want to get caught in the storm.' She laid her hand on his and said, 'Do you remember how frightened Mom used to be of these summer storms on the Highveld?'

He looked at her. There was a fleck of spit on the side of his mouth. 'No,' he said. 'I don't remember that. My mother was never frightened of storms.'

'Not *your* mother – *my* mother.'

He frowned and sat in silence for a moment. Then he said, 'They've no idea I smuggled the money out. I've outwitted them, that's for sure.' But the horrid grin was gone. He spoke now as if saddened by his own cunning. 'I may have flies in my head, but it doesn't mean I don't know what's going on. I'm still one step ahead.'

The retirement complex would consist, when it was completed, of several small groups of dwellings within larger clusters, a concept – according to the developers' brochure – inspired by a traditional African village. *Majuba's Haven: a Place for the Over Sixty-Fives to Come Home To*, it said. *The Peace, Tranquillity and Fellowship of Africa in the Heart of Johannesburg*. The first two sections of the complex, already completed, were called *Dingaan's Close* and *Shaka's Nest*. Elaine and Jock had bought a two-bedroomed unit in *Shaka's Nest*, which was now ready for occupation. It was about a tenth of the size of their home in Greenside, and cost them appreciably more than they got out of the sale of the house. Richard tried desperately to sound enthusiastic about it. 'It's light and airy,' he said. 'And you've even got a small garden. And a patio. We'll buy some ceramic pots for it and some new garden furniture. Best of all, there's a panic button in every room, in case you need assistance, and twenty-four-hour-a-day security, electric fences, everything.' He was about to add that there was also a frail care facility for the residents but decided that it would be more tactful to make no reference to it.

He hated the forced joviality in his voice. He hated his own crassness. Why should his parents be impressed by something that was 'light and airy' when they had lived contentedly for decades in a house that was neither light nor airy? Most of all, he hated his victory over his father. The stroke was a mild one: Jock's speech was slightly affected at first, although it soon came right, and he was a little unsteady on his feet. Physically, there had been much less damage than they had dared to hope for. But in other ways it was devastating. Jock was now afraid. He was afraid of the stroke he had already had, terrified of having another one, mortified by his own vulnerability. The very knowledge that he had been ill hung over him like an imprecation and, instead of being heartened by his excellent recovery, he brooded over what had been taken from him. Richard saw, when his father was discharged from hospital, the abject failure of Jock's attempts to be stoical and realised that his opportunity had come. He was shocked by his own ruthlessness. He simply took over. 'There's no point even arguing about it any more,' he said. 'You can't go on like this. You've been very fortunate, but a mild stroke like this is a warning. You simply have to change your lifestyle and begin to take things easy. And you must have medical attention at hand if you need it. It's not fair to expect Mom to cope on her own again if something happens.' (Jock had collapsed in the bathroom at night; Elaine, when she discovered him, had been unable to lift him.) A stiff dignity had always come effortlessly to Jock. Now he had to feign it in the face of crushing defeat. He pretended that he needed a few days to think it over. Richard went along with the pretence. Then Jock told him that 'after careful deliberation,' he'd decided to sell the house and to move to a retirement village. 'I realise that it will be for the best,' he said. 'It will give you and your mother peace of mind.'

'I feel like such a shit,' Richard said to Deanna. 'I know they're going to hate that trendy little place. It's so damn twee. And they'll be at the mercy of all sorts of busybodies, which they'll hate even more. But what can I do? An elderly couple were attacked the other day in their home just two streets away.'

'You know you've done the right thing,' said Deanna. 'You don't need me to tell you that. Just keep thinking of the old saying – "sometimes you have to be cruel to be kind."' She didn't feel as sorry for him as he wanted her to be. She resented the fact that he still used her as a moral arbiter.

'But I feel so guilty,' he said.

'Oh, I'm sure you'll get over it,' she replied.

5 Pestilence

MARIE MOXLEY hated her name. One day, she vowed, she would find another and this affliction which she bore would be no more. Marie Moxley would be no more. After all, her name had been changed once already, so why shouldn't it be changed again? Everyone thought that your name was what you were born with and spent the rest of your life growing into, but did it have to be that way? Perhaps a name could be a destination, something you travelled towards, something you aspired to; and if your life took an unexpected turn, then your name could take a new direction too. There was no reason why your name should be cast in stone – at least, not until you were dead. Film stars changed their names all the time; they were expected to, it seemed. Even one who had been born with a very glamorous-sounding name, Lucille LeSeuer, had still felt the need to change it: she became Joan Crawford.

Marie Moxley thought that if she'd been lucky enough to have been born with a name like Lucille LeSeuer, she wouldn't have changed it. She would have been proud of it. Instead she'd been born Marie van Aswegen, which was far from satisfactory. She would never get to Hollywood with a name like that! They wouldn't even know how to pronounce it. And then her father ran off and, when her mother finally managed to get a divorce, she married William Moxley, an Englishman. He adopted her and her name was changed to Marie Moxley. For five years she was Van Aswegen and for eight she had been Moxley. So, like the queens of Hollywood, her name had already been altered – but in her case it was for the worse! She couldn't go around for the rest of her days with a name like Marie Moxley! When they announced the newest Hollywood release, they simply couldn't say *Tyrone Power and Marie Moxley star in…* or *Paramount Pictures present Robert Taylor and Marie Moxley in…*She would be a laughing-stock. Was it any wonder she hated her name? Was it any wonder she hated her life?

Marie had a secret place where she used to think and read. There was an open piece of ground just below the farmhouse, hidden by a cluster of blue-gum trees. Running through this stretch of veld was a small donga. Marie used to clamber down the powdery grey walls and sit there for hours, alone with her books, her thoughts and her imperious dreams. Sometimes she found a spider there or a praying mantis. Once there was even a white cattle egret, but usually she was completely alone, protected by the walls of the donga even from the company of the wind. In this solitude she reflected that if she were ever to have a life worth living, a tolerable life, she had no choice but to remake herself. She had a dream, a Pegasus dream, of what her life could be: she saw herself vaulting over everything small and grubby, flying higher and higher until she could inhale the ether of possibility. But it wouldn't happen if she remained this dusty platteland girl who dreamed of Hollywood with the zeal of a convert but had seen only three films in all her life. Oh, *when* would Moxley take them to see a film again?

That day, as she made her way to her secluded spot, she was trying out new names. As always, she looked to Hollywood for her inspiration. She wanted someone to find her, and in that finding, to disclose her new identity to her. She wanted to be *discovered*. Lana Turner, she'd heard, had been discovered selling sodas; Carole Lombard, so the story went, had been playing baseball in the street. She wasn't sure what sodas were – were they the same as soda water? – and no one played baseball on the platteland; but still, she too could be found, yanked out of ordinariness, lifted to a plane where being called Marie Moxley would immediately be seen for the injustice and humiliation that it was. She tried out various combinations of names: she put Jean Arthur and Lana Turner together and got Jean Turner and Lana Arthur – no, that wasn't right. Joan Davis and Bette Crawford didn't appeal to her either. Then she tried Barbara Stanwyck and Carole Lombard. Carole Stanwyck? No. Barbara Lombard? Now that wasn't bad. Not bad at all. Barbara Lombard. She could live with a name like Barbara Lombard.

As she made her way to the donga, climbing carefully through the barbed-wire fence so that it wouldn't tear her clothes, the smell of death reached her nostrils. It was unmistakable. Ahead of her she saw several dark mounds. When she drew closer, she saw three of Mr de Bruyn's dairy cows. Flies had settled on their eyes, their nostrils, their protruding tongues. Their bellies were grotesquely distended. She had seen a dead cow in the same place the previous week; now there were three. Something was killing the cattle. Marie didn't pause for long; she had little interest in cattle or farming or anything that belonged to the platteland. She skipped down the incline and made her way to the donga. *Barbara Lombard* – this time she said it out loud – *Tyrone Power and Barbara Lombard star in...*It wasn't bad at all.

She had brought a book to read, but first she sat there, enjoying her seclusion, kneading the clay that lay at the bottom of the donga. She was confident that the remaking of herself was an inevitability, but one thing troubled her: what if she had no talent for acting? She already knew she couldn't sing, a failing which would limit her career; but what if she wasn't good at dramatic roles either? How then would she make her escape? Well, she would just have to work at it, that was all; surely she too could laugh and weep and be cheerful and haughty and do all the things that actresses did? In the meantime, she found that, without thinking, she'd moulded the clay into two little human figures: one male and one female. Adam and Eve. She gave the male an enormous penis and giggled. Then she crumbled them in her hand and settled down to read.

She had found in the public library a book called *Myths and Legends*. She'd read it from cover to cover, and was now going through it again, rereading the bits she liked. This was the fourth time she was reading about Pandora. There was something about the story that delighted her. She would have liked to be Pandora. Like Eve, she too was the first woman – but she was a *much* more interesting first woman than Eve! She saw herself holding the enigmatic box; she saw herself opening it slowly, wholly delighted by what emerged. She felt the power of Pandora. She was the keeper of secrets; and when she opened the box, she didn't lose her secrets. As much as she released, she still held something back. Marie saw herself holding each plague like a bird in her fist – not a terrified bird, huddling there with a beating heart, but a calm bird, awaiting its moment. And then the unfurling, the release, the

92

jubilant, defiant release. In that glorious moment, Pandora, too, was found, discovered; she shed her ordinariness; she was transformed. She outgrew the smallness of her life. Pandora did not have to wonder why the farmers' cattle died. She knew. She did not have to ask *why*, as they all did when Jannie Bosch, a boy in Marie's class, died of a burst appendix, nor did she have to be content with the reply that only God knew – a response which didn't satisfy Marie at all. Pandora knew why. She knew it all. She knew where the illness that killed the cattle came from, for it came from her. She even knew where the flies that had settled on the dead cattle came from, for they too came from her. Sorrow and death were but two sedate little birds to her, small enough to hold in the palm of her hand.

If she were Pandora, Marie thought, she would not waste death on cattle. She would use it on William Moxley. She would make sure that she never had to see his big white face again, his small red mouth; she would see to it that she never had to feel again the touch of his smooth, clammy hands with their long, pointy nails.

The radio was on when she came into the house. Her mother and stepfather were listening to it in the lounge. William Moxley was shouting. Marie paused unseen in the door and watched him as he leaped out of his chair and thrust his fist jubilantly in the air. It was a cold day, but there was a moist sheen on his face, as if he suffered from fever. 'Did you hear that?' he said to Marie's mother. 'Can you believe it? Standerton! They've lost Standerton! Smuts has lost his own seat!' He seated himself again and slapped his knee with pleasure. 'Mark my words,' he said. 'This is a day we will never forget.'

Hannelie sat on the patio in the shadow of an effusive bignonia. All about her was the brazen light of summer. A glass of lemonade and a bran muffin lay untouched by her side. She had no taste for anything. She wanted what the azure season could not give her. She wanted to die. No, that wasn't quite true. It wasn't death itself that she sought. It was the power of what it could achieve: the effects without the cause. She wanted, once and for all, to have the courage to give up, to have the burden of remonstrating with her own failure lifted from her. She wanted to make a habitation in a place that was as close as solace and yet irredeemably remote at the same time. She wanted to come to rest in sweet imprecision. Here everything was too sharp, too intense, too insistent. The heat, the light and the vivid colours were overbearing. They demanded from her what she could not supply. The bold season defeated her; the triumphant day unnerved and frightened her. And when you are afraid of a beautiful summer morning in Cape Town, a day gliding on the stream of its own satisfactions, then there is nothing that you will not fear, nothing that you can expect to prevail against. You have become too small.

In the days of her former prowess – how remote that time seemed to her now – she had not been afraid. She had feared certain possibilities, it was true. She feared for the safety of her son, especially after the would-be kidnappers had tried to seize him. She feared her own mortality, but only in the sense that she didn't want to die while Noldie was still a child and leave him to grow up without a mother. But she was not *afraid* as such; she was not abashed by life.

The conservative household in which she had grown up had instilled in her from an early age a lust for rebellion. And when the opportunity came at last to give expression to that defiance, there was no fear at all, only the taste of seditiousness, which she relished as if she had been fed on bland food all her life, and then, all at once, discovered hot mustard, ginger, anchovies, capers, blue cheese. She left more than her husband, her home, her Waterkloof life. She left her childhood, the mahogany furniture in her parents' home, the photographs of unsmiling ancestors on the walls, the white aprons of servants, the big fireplaces and the smell of polish. She left the happiest memory of her early life: on the day her father was elected prime minister, the congratulatory telegrams had lain in mounds on the floor of the entrance hall and she threw them up in the air and let them fall over her like leaves and her father, seeing her, scooped her up in his arms and they laughed together. She left the memory and the old joy that it held. She left everything that she had imagined God to be and religion in all its guises (not merely the Dutch Reformed variety), dismissing it now and from now on as a sort of higher cowardice, a refusal to countenance the abysmal fact of our cosmic aloneness. She saw then how all destinations break their promises – saw it, faced it head on and was not afraid. And now a fulsome sun and a glittering sea had the power to intimidate her. Oh, how she pined for what she had once had! How she mourned what she desperately needed now: a vision, a saving illusion of her own efficacy in the world. She had found her way too quickly out of the maze; she had left the game too soon. She couldn't get back in.

Theresa Abrahams came through the glass door, greeted Hannelie, kissed her on the cheek and sat down opposite her. She saw at once that Hannelie was having a bad day. They all knew the signs by now. There was something in her eyes, on her skin, that was unmistakable. 'Hannelie, don't you want to drink your lemonade? Don't you want this lovely muffin?' she asked, but the concern in her voice was only partly sincere. Try as she might, Theresa couldn't suppress entirely the suspicion that depression was, at least in part, self-willed and self-indulgent; that it was a cage that the prisoner had wrought for herself. She had no right to judge, she knew. She hadn't been in that position. But resolve as she might, she couldn't summon in her heart a truly generous compassion.

Hannelie shook her head. She wanted nothing to eat, nothing to drink. Her appetite was always poor when she was depressed. That showed how ill she was, thought Theresa: people who were ill never wanted to eat. Why couldn't she treat her simply as if she were ill – as if she had cancer or heart disease? But she could not. It would be much simpler if Hannelie's affliction were a physical ailment. Sympathy would then have been no problem at all. Instead, she was repelled by this malady which seemed to consume everything within reach, which asked so much of them all – Barbara, Noldie, herself – but could not be appeased by all the efforts they made.

And yet, as Noldie kept telling her, Hannelie wasn't always like this. She wished she could have known her mother-in-law when she was a force in the world, the Hannelie both Barbara and Noldie revered as if she were an heroic figure who had fallen in battle. At the same time, the assurances that Hannelie had once been so powerful disturbed her. If such a person could be reduced to this ignominy, were they not all susceptible? Could they be certain that what she was suffering from wasn't contagious, an infectious disease to which they could all fall prey? Irrational as it was, she felt sometimes that Hannelie was a danger: that she should be removed and placed in quarantine. But looking at her now, seeing how she sat there in an inert estrangement from the sun, the trumpet flowers, the glint of the blue-green sea, it struck Theresa suddenly that Hannelie was already in a sort of quarantine. And with that realisation came an impulse of compassion stronger than any she had felt before; and while it lasted it was full-hearted. But what was she to do with this sudden rush of sympathy? Those who are ill want relief, not pity. They want the pain to be taken away.

'Noldie tells me that Barbara's exhibition was such a success that there's going to be another one, this time on the West Coast,' said Theresa. 'Perhaps in San Francisco.'

'Oh, that's old news,' said Hannelie.

Theresa sighed. One of the symptoms of Hannelie's condition was an infuriating mean-spiritedness. She seemed, when it came upon her, to begrudge everyone everything that lay outside her own small ambit. She begrudged Barbara her fame and Noldie his political career. She made no effort to hide her jealousy and possessiveness and they were revealed for what they were: nasty, biting little creatures like ferrets. She made it quite clear that they were the only two people she really cared about – not even her grandchildren had any claim on her. But those two, her son and her lover, she clung to as if she suffered from a lockjaw of the spirit. She didn't want to share Barbara with her sculpture, even though that was what had brought them together in the first place. And she didn't want to share Noldie with his work, his wife, his children. 'I have so little,' her petulance seemed to imply. 'Aren't I entitled to cling onto the little that I have?'

'Is there anything you need?' asked Theresa. 'Would you like me to do some shopping for you?'

'Barbara always does that,' said Hannelie. 'And if she couldn't for any reason, I would ask Noldie.' She didn't even feign courtesy. 'I'm too ill for pretence,' she seemed to imply. 'My affliction exempts me. I can say what I like. Don't try and push in: the circle is closed.'

Theresa didn't answer. She thought of her long-dead father, of his vast tolerance which had once seemed so noble to her and which she now regarded as a reprehensible turning of the other cheek when one ought to be doing some face-slapping of one's own. 'Don't take it to heart,' he would say. 'Take it from whence it comes. The insults of the unworthy are always unworthy of your attention.' And he would dry her tears. Now she despised his passivity and was ashamed of it. She adored him for being a gentleman of the old school while scorning him for never graduating from it; yet still her first instinct when she was insulted was to take it from whence it came, to put the hurt aside and deem the assailant unworthy. This remorselessly sad woman scarcely knew what she was saying: she was ill, her spirit damaged, probably beyond repair. Compassion was the only emotion she should elicit, no matter what she said or did. Theresa heard her father's voice, felt him drying her cheeks with a white handkerchief, knew what he would be urging now; but she shoved him away as the old rebelliousness arose in her. The brief impulse of compassion towards Hannelie was gone. She was tired of making excuses for her. This woman had had nothing but privilege, power, indulgence and servants all her life. For heaven's sake, she was a prime minister's daughter! If one truly took it from whence it came, if one looked at who she was and where she came from, one would be more inclined to condemn than not. 'But she broke away from it all,' Barbara and Noldie would say. 'Look at the courage she displayed.' Theresa was tired of hearing that too. Besides, it was all gone – the courage, the iconoclasm, the defiance. All there was now was a Hannelie who seemed as dictatorial in her illness as her father, the Nationalist prime minister, had been when he was in office.

Theresa got to her feet. 'She competes with me for Noldie, but I never compete with her,' she always said to her friends. 'I don't stoop to that level.' But in her heart she longed to fight back, to put aside all considerations of the unworthiness, the puniness of the foe and let her have it. 'Barbara doesn't love you any more,' she would say. 'And Noldie gives you a dry peck on your dry cheek, but it's my bed he comes home to.'

Suddenly her father appeared to her again, like a figure in a sour little dream, impeccably dressed in a dark, double-breasted suit, his head bowed before the dusty winds of the Cape Flats. 'Goodbye, Hannelie,' she said. 'I have to go now. Look after yourself.'

'I'll meet you at *Voetstoots* at nine o'clock,' Helena said. *Voetstoots* was a new night- club in Melville. 'Don't be late,' she went on. 'I've got a few surprises in store for you.'

She and Neil had begun to spend more and more of their spare time together. Helena had met the whole family – everyone except Archie. She had even been taken on a tour of *Time Immemorial Tombstones*. Neil, however, had not yet been introduced to her family. To his surprise, Helena and Aunt Maisie had got on well. They smoked a large number of cigarettes together. 'I'm amazed,' he said to her. 'I didn't think you'd agree with a single thing she said.'

'Oh, I don't. But that doesn't matter. What I like is that you know where you stand with her. What you see is what you fucking get. That's fine by me. People like that make me feel safe. '

'But she can be so overbearing!'

'That's okay. So can I.'

The one who impressed her least was Richard. 'Oh, no,' Neil sighed. 'Please don't tell me you're going to be another of the Richard-bashers. Aren't there enough of them already?'

'I'm not trying to be a Richard-basher. I just don't want you to be hurt. Your friendship, such as it is, is unsafe. In fact, it's dangerous.'

'Oh, that's nonsense. There's no danger whatsoever. Can't you see what an interesting person he is?'

Helena didn't reply immediately. 'He's a complicated person,' she said at last. 'That's not the same as interesting. Certainly, there's more to him than meets the eye.'

'Don't you at least like what meets the eye?'

'Oh, please!' She tossed her small, dark head. 'Can't you try and be a bit more original in your tastes? The jaw so square, the eyes so blue. It's like they cloned some has-been Hollywood actor from the fucking B-list.'

'Well, *I* think he's very good-looking!' said Neil defiantly.

'I'll tell you who *is* hot,' said Helena. 'Your sister.'

'Deanna? Hot?'

'Take it from me, that's one sexy lady. Any chance of getting her over to the other side?'

'Not a hope in hell.'

'Oh, well, I suppose you can't win 'em all.'

Voetstoots was small, dark and smoky. The tables were grouped in a semi-circle around a tiny stage. 'They have live music here most nights,' said Helena as they took their seats. Neil had assumed that some of Helena's friends would join them, but none did. Helena seemed distracted and on edge: she was smoking more than usual. The music, when it began, was so loud that they couldn't hear one another and had to forgo conversation.

'I hope it's not all going to be like that,' said Neil, turning to Helena when the drums and electric guitars had at last fallen silent. But there was no one to hear what he'd said. He was alone at the table. Helena had vanished. Perhaps she'd gone to the toilet? He waited and waited, but she didn't reappear. It was most disconcerting. Should he go and look for her? Where *was* she?

A few people clapped and he turned to look at the stage. There was Helena, standing silently in the middle in a saucer of light. She was wearing what she had on before – black jeans and a white T-shirt. A man was seated at the piano.

She looked very young and very small. 'I'm Helena,' she said, 'and this is Francois at the piano. I have to tell you that it's most unlikely that I'll ever be a bride. I never wanted the dress and the cake anyway – or the groom, for that matter. But I always wanted something old, something new, something borrowed, something blue. And so that's what I'm going to share with you tonight. Let's start with something old and borrowed. It's a Rosemary Clooney number called *Mixed Emotions*.'

When she began to sing, Neil thought the sound was coming from somewhere else, from someone else. It was impossible to believe that the voice he heard now and the silky Radio Frangipani one could come from the same person. This one was husky, a little rough, full of swoops and sudden descents. It was a superb torch song voice. He was astounded.

I have mixed emotions
When it comes to loving you
I know I shouldn't like
The things you shouldn't do

But if you were perfect
It wouldn't be the same
To a tiger a tiger's
Not a tiger if he's tame

But when you're near me
I am happy just alone with you
But when you're far away from me
I'm awfully blue

You're the bitter and the sweet combined
So what am I to do?
I have mixed emotions
Over you.

The applause was enthusiastic. Neil realised that most of the people knew her, had heard her sing before. 'Now it's time for something new,' said Helena. 'You can't get a song that's newer than this, 'cause I just wrote it. It's called *Genetically Modified Lover*.' Francois leaned over the piano and the music started again.

I'm hungry for you
But I'm so afraid

If only I knew
How you were made

Are you safe for me to eat?
Can I chew your tender meat?

Can I swallow without a qualm?
Will you nourish or do harm?

Can I tuck in and have my fill?
Or will you make me gravely ill?

Are you sweetest near the bone?

The time has come to make it known:
Where did you get your muscle tone?
Were you, dear, organically grown?

   Someone whistled; people laughed and clapped. Helena's
audience could not have been more appreciative. When she spoke
again, her voice was very soft. 'No prizes for guessing what comes
next,' she said. 'Here's something blue. It's another of my own
compositions and it's called *The Road Never Travelled*. This song is
for Neil.'
   Francois bent forward but he didn't begin to play at once.
Helena stood motionless, her head bowed. At one of the tables
someone dropped a knife onto a plate; in the stillness of the room
the noise it made was as discordant as an affront. Then at last the
music started up and Helena raised her head and sang. Her voice
was even lower than before; it was soft and dark, full of caves and
tunnels, of secrets too tender to be told, too insistent to be
withheld.

Never, never seen the midnight sun
Gleaming on the Arctic snow
Never, never seen the lemmings run
Or been to an off-off Broadway show

Never, never visited St Tropez
Or Big Sur; or the Dead Sea
Don't know the way to San José
Never hugged a giant redwood tree

Possibility is a bird
Discarding one by one its plumes
Possibility is a ghost that haunts
My silent, vacant rooms

Never climbed to the top of Lion's Head
Or admired a silvery Aegean dawn
Haven't seen Shakespeare's second-best bed
The rock of Gibraltar; or Cape Horn

Never, never been to Yosemite
Or to the Wailing Wall; or to Shanghai
Never, never been to the Alps to ski
Don't know where elephants go to die

Possibility is a bird
Discarding one by one its plumes
Possibility is a ghost that haunts
My silent, vacant rooms

This time the applause was muted, diffident. Neil rubbed his eyes to get rid of two little upstart tears. One or two voices called out, 'More! Encore!', but Helena didn't oblige them. It took ages for her to make her way to their table: everyone wanted to congratulate her. When she got there, she said, 'Let's go. I've had enough of this place for one night. It's so fucking hot in here.'

'I think your fans want to talk to you,' said Neil. People were approaching their table from all directions.

'Fuck that,' she said. 'Come on, let's *go.*'

In the parking lot, standing next to Helena's battered old car, Neil said, 'You're very talented. I had no idea.'

'Thank you.'

'And I'm very moved that you dedicated that song to me.' She waved her hand dismissively, but didn't reply. 'I don't know how to respond to it,' Neil went on. 'Is it a warning? Some sort of prophecy?'

Helena turned to look at him. 'Nope,' she said. 'I don't go in for that.'

'What do you mean?'

'I sing about the here and now.' She opened the passenger door and slid along to the driver's seat – the lock on the driver's door was damaged. 'The present moment is wide enough for me,' she said, rolling down the window. She turned on the engine, which coughed as if trying to expel sputum. Helena waved and drove off. Her car moved noisily and spasmodically down the road.

'It's very difficult to refuse,' said Aunt Maisie. 'How do I tell her that she's overdoing it? I can't very well say, "You're allowed only one funeral this month, Miss Bertha: you must choose between your stepbrother's niece and your cousin's granddaughter and your sister-in-law's brother. You can't go to them all." So I bite my tongue. But it's a bit vexing, to say the least. Whenever I'm counting on her to be there, she's off to another funeral.'

'You think she's taking advantage?' asked Deanna. They were on their way to visit Archie. Aunt Maisie was behind the wheel of her ancient Volkswagen Beetle.

'Well, I know she's not inventing any of these dead family members – the woman has never told a lie in her life. And one doesn't want to seem to be lacking in compassion. But does every relative, no matter how distant, have to be present at every funeral? And do they have to spend so much money – which they can ill afford – on it? It's bad enough that all these young people are dying, that the breadwinners are dying, but then they still have to find the money to feed hordes of people. You know what I mean? I suppose they belong to funeral societies – Miss Bertha is very involved with hers – but does that cover all the costs? How do these burial societies work?' She lit a cigarette and threw the lighter back into her handbag.

'I don't know much about it,' confessed Deanna. 'Perhaps you should ask her?'

'Can't do that,' said Aunt Maisie. 'Goes all sullen. Thinks it's not a subject to discuss with white people. Thinks we treat death with a shameful lack of respect. Has the idea that we cheerfully stick the deceased in the ground – or worse, in an oven – acting with indecent haste, making no fuss at all, not even going to the trouble of slaughtering a few oxen, and then carry on as if nothing has happened.'

'And what does she say these relatives died of?'

'Oh, never what we suspect. One got a pain in her stomach, another collapsed and then was too weak to get out of bed, and so on.'

'But do you think Bee-Bee knows what AIDS is?'

'She watches the TV. She listens to the radio. She's not stupid.'

Aunt Maisie applied the brakes sharply as a speed hump came into view. 'Do these damn things have to be so high?' she complained. 'The only way you can get over some of them is by hiring a sherpa. And they call it Traffic Calming – well, it doesn't calm *me*, I can tell you!'

Deanna laughed. She and Neil had spent large chunks of their childhood in Aunt Maisie's white Beetle, of which there had been several over the years. Being driven by their aunt was always an adventure: a journey in any other vehicle seemed staid by comparison. For one thing, they knew that the trip would be peppered with invective. Aunt Maisie's father had not passed his religion on to her, but he had taught her a number of Yiddish curses – 'much better than religion,' she said, '*much* more useful' – and these she bestowed chiefly upon road hogs. The curses were all gloriously savage.

'*Zolstu farbrent veren!*' Aunt Maisie shouted one day. A motorist had failed to stop at a stop sign.

'What does that mean?' the children asked.

'It means, "May you be burned!"'

The children made her repeat it until they had learned it. When the next misdemeanour occurred, they all shouted it together: '*Zolstu farbrent veren!*'

On another occasion, a car cut in, causing Aunt Maisie to slam on the brakes. She called out, '*A chaleria af dir!*'

'What does that mean?' Neil and Deanna enquired.

'It means, "May you get cholera!"' She told them what cholera was. They memorised that one too.

When a car sped through a red light, narrowly missing them, Aunt Maisie yelled, '*A shvartze magayfa af dir!*'

The children liked the sound of that one. 'It means, "May you get the Black Death!"' their aunt explained.

'What's the Black Death?' asked Deanna.

'Bubonic plague. You can look it up.' Aunt Maisie knew how fascinated Deanna was by all things medical.

'The next time they travelled together, Deanna said, 'Bubonic plague was carried by rats – or, rather, the fleas on the rats. People were bitten by the fleas and became ill.'

'Yuck,' said Neil. Deanna ignored him.

'The first symptoms,' she went on, 'are vomiting, headache and giddiness, followed by inflamed eyes and a swollen, furry tongue. Then the buboes appear – that's the swelling of the lymph nodes. The Black Death wiped out a quarter of the population of Europe in the fourteenth century.'

'Very good,' said Aunt Maisie. 'Well researched.'

'But I don't think people get bubonic plague any more,' said Deanna. 'At least, not in this country. So I don't think it's a very useful curse.'

Aunt Maisie didn't seem to be at all disconcerted by the scarcity of bubonic plague. 'Never mind, perhaps it will come back,' she said cheerfully.

Deanna mulled this over. 'But isn't it bad to curse people?' she asked. She was then about twelve years old. She had revelled in the curses, but suddenly it struck her that they were wishing very bad things indeed on those whose conduct on the roads was reprehensible. Behind the sonorousness of the curses, the tangy sounds which one could roll around in one's mouth and savour over and over again, were destinies that were perhaps too ghastly even for those who had flagrantly disobeyed the traffic rules.

'Only if you really mean it,' said Aunt Maisie. 'Only if you say it with a heart full of hatred. You know what I mean? And we don't say it in that way, no matter how angry we are. So it's all right.'

Deanna was not convinced. 'But how can we be sure?' she asked. 'If one of these drivers fell very ill – with bubonic plague, say – and then infected other people, we wouldn't realise that we were responsible. We wouldn't know that we had started it.'

'I don't think we have that kind of power – more's the pity.'

Deanna's anxieties were not alleviated by this. She continued to chant the curses with as much gusto as ever, but a vague sense of disquiet remained with her. Once you released a curse, did you not lose control of it? Could you call it back again, or would it make its own perverse way in the world? And if widespread suffering – caused by plagues and old-fashioned diseases, thoughtlessly resurrected – afflicted the population at large, could they be traced back to her and her family? And if so, what punishment would they have to face for being the originators of so much suffering and death? Aunt Maisie said it was a pity they had so little power, but Deanna felt it must be a terrifying thing to have power; it was alarming to think that you could become powerful without even realising quite how powerful you had become. As she uttered the curses – 'A shvartze magayfa af dir!' soon became the children's favourite – she prayed she would always be too weak to make her curses prevail.

Archie called out to them as soon as they entered the lounge. 'Maisie, Deanna,' he said. 'Here I am. Come and join us. Happy New Year!'

'Lucid today,' Aunt Maisie muttered. 'What a relief.'

Archie was in excellent spirits. He was sitting on a couch between two elderly men. 'This is my sister,' he said to them. 'And this is my daughter. She's a doctor.'

'Please don't stand up,' said Deanna, but the two men got laboriously to their feet and said, 'How do you do?' and 'Happy New Year.' Everyone shook hands.

'This is Mr Hammerstein,' said Archie.

'Rogers,' said the old man.

'He's eighty-eight years old. And this…'

'Eighty-six,' said Mr Rogers, interrupting him. He smiled at Deanna. 'Your father is making me even older than I am. And I'm quite an antique as it is.'

'Forgive me,' Archie said to him. 'I seem to be afflicted by a terrible case of foot-in-mouth disease these days.'

'My dear fellow,' said Mr Rogers, 'it's quite all right. Don't give it another thought.'

Archie turned to the other man. 'This is Mr Levin. He's ninety-one.'

'Guilty as charged,' said Mr Levin, inclining his head.

'Ninety-one? There's a lot of longevity in my family too,' said Aunt Maisie, as they all sat down. 'It's in our genes.'

'So you're a doctor. We have a black doctor working here,' said Mr Levin, bending forward to speak to Deanna. 'Very nice. Maybe you know him?'

'Yes, maybe you do,' said Mr Rogers.

'She probably does,' said Archie. They all looked expectantly at Deanna.

'Well, I won't be able to say until you tell me his name,' said Deanna, beginning to feel as if she were at the Mad Hatter's Tea Party.

'Dr Moyani,' said Mr Rogers.

'No,' said Deanna. 'I don't know him.'

'He's very good,' said Mr Levin, and the other men nodded. 'Highly qualified. A real gentleman. You don't mind them when they're like that. He's the kind you could have at your own dinner table.'

'When times change,' said Mr Rogers, 'you must change with them. Otherwise you get left behind. No one can help growing old, but who wants to be a fossil?'

'Quite so,' said Mr Levin.

Deanna glanced at Aunt Maisie, who was about to light a cigarette. 'No smoking allowed in here, Maisie,' said Archie. Turning to the others, he said, 'I'm trying to get my sister to give up smoking. She knows it's not good for her, but she persists. And smoking is a particularly unattractive habit in a woman.'

'Oh, *please*,' said Aunt Maisie, throwing her cigarettes and lighter back into her handbag. 'What's it going to do to you lot if I smoke? Bring you to an early grave?'

'Some people here have bronchial problems,' said Mr Rogers. He smiled sweetly, as if explaining something to a truculent child. 'The smoke is bad for them.'

Several conversations started up at once. 'Has Neil been to see you?' Deanna asked, leaning across to her father. She noticed that the ruddiness she had been so pleased to discern on his face when they arrived had faded. His eyes looked rheumy and the pupils were very dark against the sudden pallor of his skin.

'No, not for months.'

'Perhaps he's been working very hard.'

'I'll tell you something in confidence,' said Archie. 'One day, when he's older, I'm going to hand *Time Immemorial Tombstones* over to him. I wouldn't mind retiring, I can tell you. I've worked hard all my life. I could go and settle at the coast. But only when I feel he's ready for it. He's still much too young and irresponsible.' His voice quavered as he completed the sentence; then it dropped to a whisper. Deanna had to move closer to hear what he was saying. 'I'm sorry, my dear. I know I should introduce you to these gentlemen, but for the life of me I can't remember their names. And it's embarrassing to have to ask them – after all, I dine with them every day.'

'That's okay,' she said. 'Don't worry about it, Dad. It's not important.'

'You've no idea how upsetting it is when you can't remember things like you used to. A good memory is a blessing. But when you get flies in your head, like I've got, that's a curse. A terrible curse.' Suddenly he became agitated and grabbed Deanna's wrist. 'Who did it?' he asked. 'Who did it?'

'Who did what?'

'This.' He waved his other hand, as if to indicate the room they were sitting in. 'Who did this to me? This isn't what I had in mind – for me or your mother or you kids. This isn't what I worked for all those years. Who did it?' Deanna disengaged her wrist and patted his hand. Archie went on, his voice rising. 'Things don't just happen. That's what I need to explain to you. Something always lies behind it. You should never accept a bad situation at face value. There's always a reason. You must dig until you find it.'

'I'm afraid that sometimes there *isn't* a reason, much as we would like one,' said Deanna. She looked to Aunt Maisie for help, but her aunt was talking to the two old men. 'There's a book I should get for you, Dad – I haven't read it myself, but it's got an interesting title: *Why Do Bad Things Happen to Good People?*'

'Yes, why?' Archie spoke resentfully as if it had fallen to him to untie this cosmic knot. 'Why do they? I tell you, there has to be a reason. Action and Reaction. Cause and Effect. I sit here and I think and I think until I feel as if my head is going to explode.'

'You shouldn't distress yourself about it,' said Deanna. 'People have been trying to answer these questions for thousands of years. You can't expect...'

'Let me go home,' he said, interrupting her. 'Please don't leave me here. Please. I'm begging you. This place is like a prison.'

'I can't,' she said. 'I'm sorry. I just can't.'

Aunt Maisie, who had overheard the last exchange, rose briskly to her feet. 'Deanna, it's time to go,' she said. 'We've had a lovely time with your father and his charming friends, but if I don't have a cigarette soon, I won't be fit for human company.'

'Thank you for rescuing me,' Deanna said, as they made their way to the car.

Aunt Maisie made no reply. 'This car is as hot as a furnace,' she said, unlocking the passenger door for Deanna and seating herself behind the wheel. 'Why don't they plant some trees here for shade? Honestly, it's unbearable.' As she started the engine, she said, 'I can't understand where it comes from. There was never any history of Alzheimer's or senility in our family. None. My grandmother lived to 102, as you know, and her mind was as clear as a bell until the day she died. And yet look at what has happened to my poor brother. It doesn't make any sense genetically.'

'The worst is when he starts begging me to take him away,' said Deanna. 'Like he did today. I don't know what to say to him when he does that. It makes me feel terrible.'

'I never weep,' said Aunt Maisie, 'as you know. The lachrymal ducts dried up years ago through disuse. But I must say that if I still had the capacity, there are things in life that would make me feel inclined to shed a tear or two.' She changed gears with a vigorous movement of her arm.

'What does home mean?' Tessa wondered. 'What does it really *mean*?' It was New Year's Day. Dorothy was in the kitchen, preparing lunch. She had said she didn't want any help. Tessa walked through the house, trying to look at each room as if she had never seen it before. But it was impossible: you cannot look deep into the house you were born in, grew up in, as if it were made of clear liquid; as if it were not clotted with everything that has happened. Her room was as it had been when she left home; Anthony's as it was when he died. These rooms were dusted, the carpets vacuumed, the windows cleaned. But they didn't change in any way. When she looked at Anthony's room, sadness overwhelmed her. But it was the neat, austere gravity of her own adolescent room that made her want to weep.

Pausing in the passage, she looked at the bookshelves. Every book was familiar to her. She hadn't read them all, but she knew them, knew their covers, their faded titles, the sweet old confidential smell of them. *Jock of the Bushveld* was reddish-brown, with gold lettering on the spine. *Lamb's Tales from Shakespeare* was pale blue, the letters so faded the title couldn't be made out. But she knew what it was. She had read both of these over and over. She had not read *The Forsyte Saga*, but she had always liked to see it anyway, to feel the bulk of it; the idea that there were fat books in the world had appealed to her, although she had no particular desire to read them. 'Read anything you find on any of the bookshelves,' Dorothy had told her. 'If we feel you shouldn't read it, we won't put it there.' And so she read *Lady Chatterley's Lover* and *The Well of Loneliness*. She found them both much less engrossing than she expected.

Not a single book had been moved for decades. There was a shelf above Dorothy's bed and she had seen some new titles there; but in the bookcases, the books were dusted and put back in exactly the same spot. The heavy dining-room furniture remained the same, squatting beneath the same vast, swooping chandelier. And the ficcus in the laundry-room must have grown taller over the years, but it too looked the same. The two houses which had featured most prominently in her childhood – her parents', and Uncle Jock and Aunt Elaine's – were not dissimilar, she reflected, although Dorothy and Harold's was always much brighter, much warmer, much noisier. They were both – she struggled for the word – *conservative* houses. Even though the views of the sister and brother differed radically on most matters (especially politics), even though they brought their children up differently, they had – how curious it was to see it so clearly now – created homes that were marked by the same kind of stern entropy. But perhaps that held the key to what home means: maybe it is the thing that never changes, that calls to you always with the same urgent susurration. Can you ever leave home? And can you ever return?

'Lunch is ready,' called Dorothy. 'Let's eat on the patio.' It had rained in the night and now there was a day of rich green and sunlight. A hoopoe pecked at something a short distance away from them and two mynah birds chattered angrily in a bottlebrush tree. 'I've made a light summer lunch,' said Dorothy. 'Spinach quiche and fruit salad.'

'That's great,' said Tessa. 'That's wonderful.' And of course it was – especially the fruit salad. Her mother's fruit salads were famous and for good reason. This one had paw-paw, spanspek, watermelon, gooseberries, mango, black grapes, green grapes and prickly-pear. Dorothy never put in apples and bananas – she considered them boring.

They sat silently. They both knew that a difficult conversation lay ahead and they were loath to initiate it. Finally Tessa said, 'Mom, your response to what I told you yesterday disappointed me. I thought you'd be over the moon.'

'It was a shock,' said Dorothy. 'It was the last thing I expected.' Her walking-stick, which she had balanced against her chair, clattered to the floor. 'Leave it,' she said. 'We'll pick it up later.'

'I know it came as a surprise,' said Tessa. 'But I thought it would be a pleasant one. I'd been so looking forward to telling you. And you seemed – well, almost dismayed.'

'I just don't think you've thought it through properly.' Dorothy chewed and swallowed. 'You left so many years ago. And you and Brian have made a life for yourselves in London. You struggled for so long to set yourselves up there. And now you want to give it up, uproot yourselves and the kids, and come back here.'

'Do you really think we would make a decision like this without considering it carefully? We've been talking about it for months. For years. And one of the things that pleased us most was that you would have your family living near you again, Mom. And we thought you'd be just as pleased.'

'I don't want that responsibility.' Dorothy spoke sharply. 'I don't want you to do this because of me. Your father and I grew used to being alone and I am growing used to being alone without him. You mustn't make me your reason for doing this. I won't have it.'

'That's not our reason,' said Tessa, taking care to keep sharpness out of her own voice. 'You don't have to worry about it. That's something extra, an added benefit, if you like. We aren't doing it for you. We're doing it for ourselves.'

'But why now? You didn't come back in '94, as other people did. Why now, so many years later?'

'I told you. The circumstances weren't right then.'

'And they're right now?'

'Yes.' Tessa reached over to help herself to some quiche. 'I can't tell you how this astonishes me,' she said. 'You used to say that young people shouldn't leave. You used to say they were needed here. And now I want to come home, to make a contribution, and look how you respond!'

'Come home!' Dorothy threw her head back. 'That's exactly the problem. It's *not* your home any more. You've been away so, so long. You don't know this place. You're coming back to the dream of something that's gone.'

'I'm coming back to a democratic South Africa. You know what I left.'

'Of course. But you don't understand. You have no idea how things are here now. I'm not saying it's all gloom and doom – you know I don't feel that way. But there are such, such problems. I would worry all the time about your safety – yours and Brian's and the children's. You don't know what the crime is like here. You don't know how people drive. You don't know what the AIDS crisis is doing, is going to do. You think you do, but you don't.'

'Is this what it's come to?' This time Tessa didn't keep the sharpness out of her voice. 'That fine old Black Sash liberalism? You've ended up sounding like your brother.'

Dorothy lifted a triangle of quiche onto her plate. 'Don't be ridiculous,' she said. 'My beliefs haven't changed in the least. I don't have to defend myself to anyone. After all, I stayed in the country that took both my children away from me. I just don't want you to do anything reckless. What does Brian know about South Africa? He's been here on holiday. And for your father's funeral. He doesn't realise that that's not the same as living here.'

'Brian is as keen on this as I am. He's behind it all the way.'

'But it's your idea, isn't it? Come now, be honest.'

'Yes, it is.'

'But why? Just tell me why?'

The mynah birds had fallen silent. A soft wind stirred the leaves of the trees. 'I'm tired,' said Tessa.

'Of what? Of London?'

'Of what London represents.'

'And what's that?'

'Twenty-five years of homesickness.'

'But I thought it got better over time?'

'It does. It did. But it's a chronic condition.'

'And you think this will be the cure?'

'I don't know. We'll have to see. All I know is that I'm coming home.'

Dorothy made no reply. She stirred the fruit salad with a large spoon.

Tessa drew a deep breath, put her knife and fork down and said, 'There's something else.' She tried to speak breezily, but she knew she wasn't succeeding. Her throat tightened in anticipation so the words had to be squeezed through. 'I may as well bring it up now – while we're speaking so frankly.' It hadn't been her intention to broach this with her mother: one momentous announcement was enough. She had thought she would raise it after she and Brian and the kids had made the move to South Africa. But Dorothy's response to their plans took away the desire to spare her mother the pain or herself the unpleasantness. She wouldn't put it off; on this hot, quiet New Year's day, this day of oozing summer, she would utter the rough, unwelcome words.

'Do tell,' said Dorothy, removing a grape pip from her mouth.

'When we're back in Jo'burg, when we're settled…' Tessa tried to speak calmly, but the words rushed out. 'I'm going to make contact with the Slaters. I intend to get in touch with them. All of them. First Richard, then Jock and Elaine. I've decided I want to speak to them. I *need* to speak to them.'

For a few moments Dorothy didn't speak. Then she said, 'I can't believe what I'm hearing.' Her agitation was undisguised. 'Are you trying to hurt me? What have I done to deserve this?'

'I'm not trying to hurt you. Please don't think of it that way. That's the last thing I want to do. This isn't about you. I've thought long and hard about it and I really believe it would be best – for all of us.'

Dorothy looked down at the tablecloth. A muscle twitched in her cheek; her heavy face seemed to be gathering itself in preparation for something. Then she said, 'Please do me just one favour. I'm begging you.'

'What?'

'Wait till I'm dead. Then you can do whatever you want. But please wait till I'm dead.'

'But that's exactly the point. If we wait much longer, everyone *will* be dead. Jock's had a stroke…'

'A *mild* one,' Dorothy interjected. 'I heard the other day that he's quite all right.'

'Nonetheless,' Tessa went on. 'If we don't do something soon, it will be too late.'

'Too late for what? What do you think it's going to accomplish? Do you think they're going to apologise? That they're going to make it up to us? That we're going to be one big, happy family?'

'No, of course not. It's just that – when we come back here, Brian and I and the children, we'll be making a new start. In a new country. And I don't want to be held back by these old bitternesses. I don't want to start my new life with the same old anger and hatred and pain. If you only knew how tired I am of it all.' Tessa had promised herself that she wouldn't weep, but now the tears threatened to come. She shoved them back down her throat and went on. 'I want to free myself of it. I want to do it for me – and for you. Not for them. For us.'

Dorothy stood up suddenly and groped for her walking-stick. 'Thanks for nothing,' she said. 'You've decided the time has come and so that's all there is to it. It doesn't matter to you whether I'm ready for it or not. Apparently I don't have any say in the matter.'

'But surely you've also thought of it? Don't tell me it's never crossed your mind?' Her mother didn't reply. 'Aren't you tired too?' Tessa called out. Now the tears could not be stopped. 'Don't you just want to let go? After all these years – just let go?'

'Of what? Of Anthony?'

'No. Of fighting for Anthony. Of keeping him with you in outrage instead of in love.'

When Dorothy spoke again, her voice was clipped and dry. 'I had no say when he was taken away from me,' she said. 'I was helpless. I wasn't given the chance to protect him. I wasn't consulted as to what should be done. But I won't be helpless again. No one is going to tell me what I should or shouldn't do with his memory.'

Tessa was on the verge of uttering what had remained unspoken between them for so many years. What she wanted to say was, 'Have you never asked yourself why Anthony didn't come to you and Dad for help? Why he went to Jock?' But she stopped herself: blunt as she had been today, that was a question that had to be withheld. Instead she said, 'But don't you want healing? I feel as if this bitterness is like an illness that we've all been suffering from for almost thirty years. Don't you want it to end?' She rummaged in her bag for a tissue.

'Not when it comes as an injunction. Not to please somebody else. Not because forgiveness is the flavour of the month.'

'I didn't say anything about forgiveness,' said Tessa. 'I just want to talk to them, to hear their side of the story.'

Dorothy was walking away from her, making her slow way through the patio door. She gave no indication that she'd heard Tessa's last remark. She paused and waved her walking-stick at Tessa. 'Do what you like. If you can't wait until I'm dead, then just leave me out of it. I may be a sour, bitter old woman, but at least I've kept faith. At least I still respect the past. I still cherish it.'

'No doubt,' said Tessa, raising her voice. 'But does it still cherish *you*?'

'Ask Slush to deal with it,' Susan Southern said to her secretary. 'I'm too busy to attend to it now.'

'But he's not here,' said the secretary. 'And he's not answering his cellphone. Is he still on his skiing holiday in Europe? I thought he'd be back by now.'

'He is. He got back on Sunday. Oh, all right. Put the call through.' Susan spoke crisply into the cordless telephone, walking in circles around her office as she did so. When she finished speaking, she made a few notes on a writing-pad and then sat down in front of her computer. She was slim and fit. Her hair was ash-blonde. She was over seventy years old, but very few people knew it. The offices, which were on the nineteenth floor of a gleaming block in Sandton, were all chrome, glass, deep-pile carpets and shiny pot-plants which looked artificial, but weren't: Susan had forbidden plastic plants, which she loathed. These were cleaned and had their leaves polished every fortnight by a company called *Leaf It To Us*, which specialised in the maintenance of office plants.

Susan was known as a self-made woman. And that is truly what she was, for there was very little of her that had not been deliberately (even remorselessly) made and, where necessary, remade. She was often accused of being hard, but it didn't bother her. Her identity had been forged out of a passion to be greater than she was, and if hardness was the result, then so be it: for that is what fire does.

The other accusation that was made against her was that she was cynical. There was less truth to this. Susan tended to be cynical about means, but not always about ends. She knew how much money there was in dreams and so she sold them in large numbers. She understood advertising, which is always a cynical force, and used that to her advantage. She was too successful a capitalist not to know that capitalism is, above all, a race; and if races are run, there will inevitably be winners and losers, however much you may pretend otherwise; so you'd better make sure you're one of the winners. She had come too far and seen too much to be swayed by any common illusions or inducements, including tawdry cynicism. She was immune by now to all such mundane ailments. She had been canny for too long. But what lay behind all that was something few people discerned in her: a great and embracing trust in freedom, in the act of freeing oneself, which is always preferable to being freed by someone else.

Few people in the tourist industry were as well placed as she was to benefit from the new South Africa. Her company was already established when the new dispensation came; all it needed was the favourable change in circumstances. When the country ceased to be the polecat of the world and became its Pekinese instead, Susan was more than ready to take advantage of the turn-about. She had managed to sell South Africa when it was very difficult to do so; she had no problem now, when everyone was clamouring to visit, in marketing it with gusto. Within a short time, she had transformed a successful tourist company into an empire.

Her motto was *Maximise the Positive*. 'And minimise the negative?' people asked. 'No,' she said firmly. '*Delete* the negative.' Her strategy was simple: use it all. Use the sun, the wildlife, the scenic beauty, Madiba Magic, Robben Island, the Sterkfontein Caves, the most enviable constitution in the world, the Garden Route, the Apartheid Museum, Sun City, Gold Reef City. Use it all.

Bring the Boer War enthusiasts, the find-my-roots-and-kiss-the-ground African-Americans, the ornithologists, the icthyologists, the astronomers, the palaeontologists, the gay men and women with their pink dollars, the climbers, the divers, the surfers. Bring them all.

In the 1980s, her company was called *Southern Adventures and Safaris* and the slogan was *South Africa: Come See for Yourself*. In 1990, after the ANC was unbanned and Mandela released, Susan called her team together. 'We need a new name,' she said. 'And a new slogan. Draw up a short-list of five or six, and I'll decide.' She rejected the first offerings. 'You can do better than that,' she said. 'You *will* do better than that.' The team drank more coffee, smoked more cigarettes and had more late nights. They presented her with another list of suggestions and waited nervously while she flipped through them. 'This is the one,' she said, turning to the team. 'Let's take it and run.' They hid their delight. When they were well clear of her office, they laughed and joked, the women hugged everyone and the men slapped one another on the back.

The company logo featured a small, young sun rising over Table Mountain, casting a tentative golden light over its slopes. The rays had not yet reached the foreground, where the unlit sea could only just be discerned, heaving in the darkness. The slogan read *South Africa: Land of Miracles*. And the new company name was *Promised Land Pleasure Tours*.

6 Boils

IT WAS STUFFY in the familiar little room. The two small windows were open, but there was no movement of air. It was high summer and the days were ripe and greasy. The heat brought inertia, but it was not itself inert: beneath its languor there was something that moved dyspeptically, that seethed as if its stomach were made of lava.

Farrell, perched as always on his black chair, did not seem to be affected, but Neil felt droplets of sweat forming in his armpits and trickling down his sides. He had not wished Farrell a happy New Year, nor had he asked him whether he went away during the break or stayed at home. He knew that nothing would be gained by such enquiries. Their relationship – but could one use the word 'relationship' to describe this most curious of interactions, so personal and yet so impersonal? – was not able to sustain such banal courtesies. He tried to imagine, briefly, what Farrell would look like in a swimming costume, frolicking on the beach, but he dismissed the picture after smiling at the incongruity of it. Farrell, he was beginning to realise, did not go on holiday. He did not watch movies or eat in restaurants. He had never seen the inside of a supermarket. His milk had never gone sour, his bread was never dry. He had never had a mortgage or an insurance policy. He didn't have friends or a family. He had no past and no future, no memories and no hopes, no existence beyond this room. He was defined and enclosed by the catacomb hours which he shared with Neil, with no one but Neil.

'Helena's friendship has become very important to you,' said Farrell.

'Yes,' said Neil. 'I even took her with me last week to visit my father. I never imagined going there with anyone except my sister or my aunt, but I knew it would be okay to take Helena. And it was.'

'Why is it so difficult to take people to see him?'

'I suppose I feel embarrassed. Ashamed. I know I shouldn't be, but I am.'

'Then why was it all right to take Helena? Is it because she's not judgemental?'

'Oh, she's *very* judgemental. But I don't feel intimidated by her judgements. Or afraid of them. I know she has my interests at heart, even when I don't like what she's saying.'

'For example?'

'Well, she's very anti-Richard. Or, to be more accurate, she's against the friendship. She thinks I should use the failure of his marriage to Deanna as an opportunity to ease myself out of my relationship with him – you know, stop phoning him, see him less and less, withdraw gradually.'

'What doesn't she like about it?'

'She thinks it's a dangerous friendship. That's the word she uses: *dangerous*. She thinks I'm going to be hurt, that I'm out of my depth. She says I'm not being honest with myself about it. Or with Richard. She calls it bad faith.'

'I see.'

'She says that at some level I'm still hoping that he'll come to want more than friendship from me. That I'm clinging to a notion that he'll change. In himself. And towards me.'

'Is she right?'

'Yes and no. I do know, rationally, that it's not going to happen. I know that it's a cul-de-sac. But I can't cut him out of my life, like she wants me to. I can't stop thinking about him, just like that. It's not like turning off a tap. She means well, of course, but what she wants me to do seems too drastic. I admit that as a friendship it's not very satisfying. But I feel sorry for Richard. He needs my support. He's also been through a lot. It's easy to condemn him because he was unfaithful to Deanna, but I think there's something pathological about the fact that he has so many women who come and go, come and go. In his own way, he still cares about Deanna. He cares about me.'

There was a momentary breeze, soft as forbearance. Then it was gone. Neil wiped his brow. 'And he hasn't had an easy life,' he went on. 'He's been damaged – his father is quite awful, terribly domineering and dogmatic. And he's become obsessive about finding his biological mother, but he's getting nowhere. Even the woman I told you about, from *Relative Success*, hasn't been able to make any progress. No one's replied to any of the ads she's placed in the newspapers, she's been on the trail for months and she's come up with absolutely nothing. Richard's very upset about it. But Helena says she doesn't care about him, he doesn't mean anything to her, it's me she cares about. And she says I should be protecting myself.'

There was a pause. Neil saw Farrell glancing upwards – it was clear that he was looking at the clock – and then returning his gaze and resuming his expression of dutiful attention. Ever since it had become apparent to Neil that Farrell had no life of his own, no extra-therapeutic existence whatsoever, the time constraints under which therapy was conducted were annoying him more and more. Why was Farrell so strict about time, so obedient to the dictates of the clock that only he could see? After all, what else had he to do, except wait for Neil to turn up for next week's appointment? He knew that Farrell must have other clients, but he didn't like to think about them. They had no substance: their therapy sessions were like the whispering of shadows. What they thought of as their pressing unhappiness was merely a dry shell, such as dreams discard when they flee forever. It was only he who brought real heat and urgency into this unchanging room. And why should a time limit be placed on that?

'In other words, Helena thinks it would be better to make a clean break now, however painful,' said Farrell. 'Endure the pain of severing the friendship and get it over with, get on with your life and let him get on with his.'

'Yes. That about sums it up.'

'But you can't bring yourself to do that?'

'No.'

'Because your feelings are too strong? Or because it seems like an abandonment, recalling other abandonments?'

There it was. Sooner or later, Neil knew, a reference to his mother's death would be made. For Farrell, it was like the sprinkle of salt which some cooks cannot do without: he didn't believe that the therapy dish would taste right without it. And how should his question be answered? When Neil thought of never seeing Richard again, it wasn't abandonment that came to mind; it wasn't even feelings. It was Richard's voice, his eyes, his hair, his hands – the most beautiful male hands he had ever seen. But how did one articulate that? What language is there for the body, for its beauty – or its ugliness for that matter? What is the name of either the pleasure or the pain that it brings? Where do you find the just word, the honest word, for clean, taut, shining skin? What do you call the body's betrayal, the skin that sags and dries, the sores that suppurate, the importunate pus that has waited long enough and will no longer bide its time?

Before he could answer, Farrell spoke. 'We'll have to leave it there, I'm afraid,' he said. 'Time's up.'

Hannelie was absent because they had come together to discuss her. The children were swimming: through the open window they could hear shrieks and splashing sounds. The sitting room looked out onto the front garden, which consisted mostly of lawn and shrubs. Theresa and Noldie had no interest in gardening. What they had wanted was a low-maintenance garden with a pool for the kids, and that is what they had found. Their house was a modest one for that part of Cape Town, for it was not possible to see either the sea or the mountain from it. Noldie disliked ostentatious houses, preening houses, proud houses. He remembered the one his grandparents lived in when he was a boy, the prime minister's official residence, and how small it made him feel. He never wanted to be intimidated by a house again, or to live in one that would intimidate someone else.

'Thanks for coming to see us, Barbara,' said Theresa. 'We really need to talk to you about this.'

Noldie smiled, a wan smile. He looked tired, thought Barbara. His customary calmness had a rumpled quality to it. 'We have to put our heads together,' he said. 'All of us who care about Mom. This is a very difficult situation.'

The children's voices were raised: they seemed to be quarrelling. 'I hope they're not fighting again,' said Theresa. 'They've been playing together so nicely the last few days.' No one responded. A long silence followed.

'Look,' Barbara said at last, 'I'm not sure what you want me to say. It's actually got nothing to do with me. You two have to come to a decision. No one can make it for you.'

'We know that,' Noldie said. 'But it's not true that it's got nothing to do with you, Barbara. It's got everything to do with you. If you're not going to be able to cope without us, if it's going to be too much for you, you have to say so.'

'And if I do? If I say it'll be too much for me? Then what will you do?'

'Then we won't go,' he said firmly. 'We'll say no.'

'Just like that?' said Theresa, turning to him.

'Just like that. We'll turn it down. There's no way I would ever ignore Barbara's wishes. Not after everything she's done to hold this family together.'

'Well, I'm sorry,' said Theresa. 'I cannot just accept that. Really, I can't. I won't go along with it.' She was trying to keep her voice as flat as Noldie's and Barbara's, but it slipped away from her and edged towards shrillness. 'It not as simple as you make it sound, Noldie. With all due respect, our lives can't be ruled by what Hannelie and Barbara want. They can't hold us back. I'm saying it in front of you, Barbara. I respect you too much to say things behind your back. I'm trying to be as honest as I can about this.'

'It's not a case of holding us back.' Noldie spoke patiently, softly, but Barbara could hear the weariness in his voice. 'If we go, the full weight of the responsibility falls on Barbara. And it's a huge burden, as you very well know. Is it fair to place it all on her shoulders?'

'Then…then another plan will have to be made,' said Theresa. 'If she can't cope, we'll have to consider other options.'

'You are talking about having Hannelie institutionalised,' said Barbara. She spoke matter-of-factly. 'Please say what you mean. You said you wanted to be honest. Well, spare us the euphemisms.'

'Yes. I am.' Theresa spoke defiantly. 'That is what I'm saying. I've thought for a long time that that might be the best thing. For her. For everyone. Maybe this has come at the right time. Maybe it will force us to face what has to be done.'

Noldie shook his head, but it was Barbara who spoke. 'Theresa,' she said. 'You're making assumptions. You're speaking as if I've already said that I won't be able to manage. The truth is I haven't yet replied to Noldie's question. And I haven't said that you shouldn't go. In fact, what I was going to say is that you *should* go. I won't pretend that it'll be easy for me – Hannelie will be much,

much worse if Noldie isn't here. We all know that. And of course I won't be able to go away. It'll be the end of travelling to exhibitions and so on – and you know my career is important to me. But I would do it for Noldie, because I love him. And because I think it's a tremendous honour to be appointed ambassador to the Netherlands – especially for such a young man. He shouldn't be prevented from taking it up by his mother's illness.' Still she did not raise her voice. 'But please, Theresa, don't be a hypocrite. Don't pretend to be guided by your concern for Hannelie. If you'd prefer to stick her in an institution and be rid of her, then that's fine. But don't sit here and tell us that your primary concern is her welfare. No one's fooled by that.'

Theresa had to swallow before she replied. 'That's very harsh,' she said. 'Really, I must protest. I don't think I deserve that. I've made as many sacrifices as anyone…'

'No one's saying you haven't,' said Noldie. Turning to Barbara, he said, 'Let's not fight amongst ourselves. Please. We've always stuck together.'

There were few things Theresa disliked as much as being scolded. She got up to offer Barbara and Noldie tea, hoping that the small, earnest business of enquiring, pouring and passing would enable her to pretend that she hadn't been wounded, to hide the welt that Barbara's remarks had left. But the injustice of what had been said boiled within her. She had not been remiss. She had not been inattentive. She had done nothing wrong. Nothing at all. What was being found reprehensible in her was that, try as she might, she could not love Hannelie. It was as simple as that. Was that such a terrible crime – especially when Hannelie's condition made her so unlovable? Is love then an obligation as well as an inclination? Can you be compelled to love that which repels you? She loved Noldie, she loved her children, she had loved her parents, especially her father. She had done her bit for love. She had volunteered for it when it seemed appropriate to do so; but she would not be a conscript in service of it. And in any case, if it came to harsh truths, how much did Noldie and Barbara *really* love Hannelie? She suspected that there wasn't much love for her in either of them, although they would never admit it. How much was guilt? How much was a dutiful tending of the place from which love had drained away – an expression of loyalty to what Hannelie used to be, to the woman no effort could now recover from the ruin of what she had become?

The thought that Noldie could be prevented from taking up the ambassadorship because of her mother-in-law filled her with rage. It was intolerable that Hannelie should be allowed to come between them and this opportunity. There was nothing she had that she hadn't had to struggle for, nothing that she didn't struggle for even now. Her hungry nostalgia for the home they were evicted from when she was a child, the poverty of her childhood that was like a hole that could never be filled, no matter how much she had tried later on, the quaint, tremulous dignity of her father, the black suit that grew more threadbare despite his efforts to preserve it – all these things had done their best to lay her low. They were with her still; they crouched in wait for her every day. They would be with her until she died. You can overcome them, but you can't expunge them. You can make them less loud, but you can't silence them. A doctorate in sociology, a good job at the university, a comfortable home, a husband and children she loved and who loved her – these were nothing more than gossamer victories. They were trophies made of dandelions. At any moment the battle could swing in the enemy's favour. She had to be on her guard all the time. And Hannelie was her enemy – never had that been as clear to her as it was now – just as Hannelie's father, the prime minister, had been the enemy years ago. His power had oppressed Theresa's family then, just as Hannelie's enfeeblement was oppressing her now. For there is a terrible, sucking power that comes from being needy, a power that is much harder to avoid than the boot and the baton. How curious it was that one's enemies changed, changed utterly in some instances, but the enmities did not. She had struggled, she was struggling still; yet she was expected to place above her own desires the needs of a woman who had always resented her because she didn't want to share Noldie with anyone, a Nationalist prime minister's daughter, living out her days in the cheerless draught of a cold entitlement.

'I know you don't take sugar,' she said to Barbara. 'Would you like some lemon in your tea?'

As so often happens, high summer brought drought. The skies were busy, yet moribund. There were daily thunderstorms which produced little or no rain. Drought, Richard thought, as he sat with his parents on the patio of their shiny little cottage, makes people bad-tempered. Relentlessly blue skies are dispiriting enough, but it's worse when every afternoon brings clouds which thicken and turn black and then drift away. When the sky fails to keep its promises, people always take it personally.

Jock's erstwhile hauteur had been replaced by an irritability, which, as he recovered from the stroke, grew more pronounced. Nothing anyone said or did made any difference. He could not be placated, his querulousness could not be soothed. His own skin chafed him. He wanted to blame others for what had happened to him, but he knew he couldn't exonerate himself entirely, for that would mean admitting that there had been a period in which he had been so weak and bemused that he had allowed other people to make decisions on his behalf. It would mean confessing that he had been a victim, and Jock had despised victims all his life. But, whichever way he looked at it, he had to face the fact that he had indeed been complicit in his own undoing: he had stood by and allowed his house and most of his possessions to be sold while he was bundled off to *Majuba's Haven* to play bingo and bridge, drink tea and gin-and-tonic, gossip about the other residents and smile soft, supplicating, geriatric smiles. If you lose control, he had always believed, you lose something of yourself and the one and only hope you have of recovering what has been lost lies in taking control again. There is no other solution. Being in control is the only way there is of making yourself substantial; the loss of it is smallness, humiliating smallness, followed by ebbing, fading, passivity and death.

But how was he to recover control? He could not get his house back. He supposed he could buy another one and enough furniture to fill it, but it wouldn't be the same. Besides, Elaine wouldn't want to move again. He could force her to if he were sufficiently determined – he had always been able to do that – but it would require a great deal of effort. And he would have to fight Richard, who was fortified by the belief that he had done the right thing. Jock's anger was the mark of his shame, of his defeat, but he clung to it nevertheless with all his strength. While he was angry, he still had a chance. When he gave up anger, he would be finished.

Majuba's Haven had been built so recently that the gardens were filled with immature trees and shrubs. *Dingaan's Close* and *Shaka's Nest* were now both complete and work had begun on the third section, which was called *Isandlwana Cove*. The administrators had initially declared that only indigenous plants would be permitted in the communal gardens, but when the residents realised that this meant that no roses would be planted, there was an outcry. The administrators were advised to give way – elderly people are fond of roses, they were told, especially if they can't keep pets. Eventually they relented: roses would be allowed. But that was as far as it went: there would be no daffodils, no tulips, no camellias, no azaleas, no gardenias, no Pride of India.

'From morning till night we're told what we can and can't do,' Jock complained to Elaine and Richard. It was a Saturday morning, not yet ten o'clock, and already they were uncomfortably hot. The sprinklers had been on since sunrise, as they were every day, and the lawns of *Majuba's Haven* were green; but beyond the perimeter fence everything had been burned brown and yellow by the sun. 'They treat us like children,' he went on, when there was no response. 'It's supposed to be a retirement village, not an old-aged home.'

'Well, maybe you need to get onto the residents' committee,' said Richard. 'Then you can tell others what to do.'

Jock scowled at him. He picked up a newspaper and began to flip through it. Richard dropped three more blocks of ice into his glass of fruit juice. 'How's Deanna?' asked Elaine. 'Have you seen her lately?'

'I haven't seen much of her,' he replied. 'But I bumped into her in Rosebank the other day. She was having lunch with Aunt Maisie. They didn't invite me to join them.'

'Dreadful old gorgon, that aunt of hers,' interjected Jock. 'Quite unbearable. A dried-up old maid, sitting in judgement of everybody. What gives her the right, I'd like to know?'

'She's not so bad,' said Richard. 'She's a real character. I know she doesn't like me – in fact, she's never had any time for me, from day one – but I'm fond of her all the same.' There was something in his voice which made his mother look carefully at him. Jock rustled his newspaper.

'How does Deanna seem to you?' asked Elaine.

'Okay, I guess. It's hard to say. I think she's all right.'

'And do you still see Neil?'

'Yes, from time to time.'

'That boy,' said Jock, looking up again, 'is not quite right.'

'What's that supposed to mean?' asked Richard.

'You know perfectly well what it means,' said Jock. 'He turns the other way.'

'Whichever way he turns, as you so quaintly put it,' said Richard, 'is his business and no one else's. It's not up to us…'

'Anything interesting in the paper, Jock?' asked Elaine, interrupting him. 'I haven't had a chance to read it yet.'

'Oh, yes,' said Jock, 'if you can call murder and rape interesting. And child abuse. Hijackings and cash-in-transit heists. Let me see – what else is there? Strikes. Corruption. All very interesting. There's plenty of the usual fare.'

'I don't read those reports any more,' said Elaine. 'It's just too depressing. Why subject oneself to it?'

'Doesn't leave you with much else to read,' said Jock. 'Horoscopes and weather forecasts and Hollywood gossip, that's all that's left.'

'I suppose you're right,' said Elaine. 'Perhaps it would be better to let the subscription lapse?'

'No, no,' said Jock. 'Mustn't do that. It's our duty to be good citizens and struggle through it, no matter how gloomy. Let's at least be well informed, even if around us the country is going to rack and ruin. In this miserable institution in which we've somehow landed up, our lives are over-regulated, and elsewhere there is anarchy. What a predicament!'

'At least there's good security here,' said Elaine. 'They promised us there would be, and there is. It's the most important thing these days. The guards are always on duty, they check up on everybody who comes in, and there's electric fencing, panic buttons in every room – it really gives one peace of mind.'

'I feel happier too,' said Richard. 'It's such a relief not to have to worry about you all the time.' He picked up a section of the newspaper and opened it. 'Come now, it's not *all* bad,' he said. 'Let's not exaggerate. There's something here about more plans to rejuvenate the inner city.' Jock sighed and rolled his eyes. 'And look at this,' Richard went on, 'here's something that could only happen in the new South Africa. Six new ambassadors have been appointed to represent South Africa abroad: one white, three black, one coloured and one Indian. Don't you think that's interesting?' He began to read from the article: 'Ms B. K. Mtshali appointed ambassador to Slovakia, Professor Y. Pillay appointed ambassador to Ghana, Mr A. P. van Wyk appointed ambassador to the Netherlands...'

'I feel sorry for them,' interrupted Jock.

'Why?' Richard looked up.

'Well, how are they going to do their jobs? How are they going to sell this country? That's what ambassadors are supposed to do? What on earth are they going to say?' Jock looked flushed. His cheeks were red and the veins stood out on the sides of the Karl Malden nose. He didn't look well, Richard thought, even though everyone agreed that he had made an astonishing recovery. Perhaps he should arrange for him to have more tests?

'Nonsense. There's plenty they can say,' he said. 'This country can teach the rest of the world about conflict resolution. We...'

'Do you *really* think that our conflicts have been resolved?' demanded Jock. 'Do you? Come now, son, let's be honest. As you know, if there's one thing I've got no time for, it's naïveté.'

'And if there's one thing I've got no time for, it's cheap cynicism,' said Richard.

'Please don't argue with him,' said Elaine, speaking to Richard in a low voice. 'He just gets upset and it's not good for him. In any case, you know as well as I do that no one's ever been able to make him change his mind about anything.'

'More's the pity,' muttered Richard. He got up. 'Thanks for brunch,' he said. 'I'll see you next week. Same time, same place.'

'But we may have another engagement,' said Jock. 'You'd better phone first. After all, we lead a very full life. You may find us taking part in the annual tiddlywinks championships. Or attending a lecture on arthritis. Or crocheting.'

'You won't believe it, Richard,' said Elaine, 'but last week someone gave a talk in the auditorium on "Sex for the Elderly".'

'Did you go to it?' asked Richard.

'Of course not,' said Elaine. 'Don't be silly.'

If the drought continued, water restrictions would have to be introduced. Still the clouds came, still the clouds went away, still the churlish days persisted. Richard took several showers a day, but couldn't cool down. He lay at night in a sticky pool of his own sweat. The only creatures that seemed not to be listless were the mosquitoes. February, the hottest month of all, came rushing in like a beast with smelly, blasting breath.

When there is heat and drought, it is easy to believe that someone, somewhere, is terribly angry; that some ancient, high-handed wrath is bearing down. And in the face of this castigation, Richard became angry too, angrier than he had ever been in his life. His anger boiled within him. And everything seemed to aggravate it. Visiting his parents put him in a particularly bad mood. It dismayed him that, in making such a good recovery, his father had become more unpleasant than ever and, instead of being grateful for what had been done for him, was full of resentment. It was galling that there was little or no appreciation of the good intentions that had prompted him to move his parents to the retirement village. When he came home to his rented, furnished flat, it irked him that, at this stage in his life, he should be living in a rented, furnished flat. He was angry with Beryl Curtis for failing to find his birth mother, for remaining so cheerful and optimistic, even though she had discovered nothing at all.

'Don't lose heart, Dr Slater,' she said, when they spoke on the phone. 'You must be patient. I told you it could take a long time.'

'Yes, you did. And I don't mind waiting if it's going to lead to something in the end, but what if it's all in vain? All a waste of time?'

'No, no. You mustn't think like that. As I said to you, I never give up.'

Richard was tempted to say, 'I'm sure you don't – not while I'm writing out the cheques,' but he stopped himself. Instead he said, 'So what's the next step?'

'I'm going to place more advertisements, this time in magazines as well as newspapers. I've already listed it on some internet sites that feature missing persons, but I'm going to extend that search. And perhaps we should think of putting an ad in some overseas publications as well – starting with the U.K., the U.S., Canada, Australia, New Zealand. I've interviewed several of the staff who were working at the Countess of Athlone Home at the time, and I'm trying to track down two or three more.' She paused. 'There's something else that might help.'

'What is it?'

'A reward. If you could see your way to offering a reward, Dr Slater, that might tempt someone who would otherwise not be willing to step forward. You don't have to say how much it is. Just that a reward will be paid for any information leading to the discovery of the identity of a woman who...'

'If you think it might produce results.'

'I do. I really do.'

'I suppose money always talks.'

'This is the thing, you see. It does.'

Richard told her to go ahead, but he reflected sourly that people offered rewards when they lost their pets or their jewellery. How absurd it seemed to offer a reward for a lost mother! How dreadful to be forced to do so. And suddenly, for the first time, he allowed himself to be angry, wholeheartedly and unsparingly angry, with his mother. Until now she had been too ethereal to be resented, too faceless to hate. She had been obscured by the shadows of her secrecy and her impenetrable whims. He had thought of her as a character in an old black-and-white movie. When he pictured the scene at the Home, her face was never visible, only her figure as she ascended the stairs, heavy with the last stages of her pregnancy. But he saw now that the face was turned away rather than hidden. It was turned away from the child to whom she had just given birth. He saw indifference in the closed countenance, not the challenge of an enigma. When she slipped out at night and sped away, she was not a heroine in a melodrama, she was a thief running away from the scene of the crime. And it was he who had been robbed, for she had taken from him something to which he was entitled, to which everyone was entitled. He was struck as never before by the starkness of the abandonment. He felt inclined to phone Beryl Curtis and tell her to call the whole thing off. He would say that he had decided that his mother was not worthy of the effort. But something prevented him from doing so.

Lying awake for hours in the heat, unable to fall asleep even though he had a fan next to his bed, he thought of the failure of his marriage and felt he could eventually come to terms with it. He could see himself mourning it less and moving on. But what he couldn't bear was the thought that Deanna would fade completely from his life. It had hurt him that she and Aunt Maisie had not invited him to join them when he saw them in Rosebank. That disappointment showed him again how much he needed her, how he longed still for her friendship. For he could no longer pretend, even to himself, that his love for Deanna was more than what one feels for a friend. It was not a less profound kind of love, but it was love of a different sort. She was a beautiful woman, but he had never been able to love her sexually. Her body had never engrossed or fascinated him. He had admired her beauty, but had not been haunted by it. He had tried desperately to force himself to feel something that couldn't be forced. But he saw now that, in doing so, he had been guilty of something unforgivable: perfunctory love.

And so his greatest anger he reserved for himself. He was angry with himself for getting it all wrong, for making such a mess. He had lusted after other women's bodies when he was with Deanna, and when he was with those women, it had been painfully obvious how inferior they were. He despised himself for finding these other women so compelling. He scorned himself for the power they had over him and for the power that, more often than not, he had over them. His greatest betrayal of Deanna had not been the other women, the ones she had known about and those she had known nothing of: it had been the ignobility of his desire, its truancy and base deceits. Loving her the wrong way had been worse than not loving her at all. Why was there this perversity in him that had made him treat her – and himself – so unjustly?

Long after midnight he heard thunder, but knew better than to expect rain.

Renaissance was so popular now that patrons had to reserve a table at least a week in advance, and so expensive that dishes cost more than double what Neil and Richard had paid when they first started to eat there. They decided it was time to go elsewhere. 'I heard of a good Tandoori restaurant in Westdene,' Neil said. 'It's called *The Pink Chicken*. Let's go there on Thursday. I can fetch you, if you like. Your flat is on the way. What about 7.30?'

'That's fine,' said Richard. He made a note of the arrangement, but when Thursday came he didn't look at his diary and forgot about it. It was another hot night, the air thick as if pressed into too small a space. For Richard, it had been a day of ragged disgruntlement and frustration. He phoned Michelle. 'What about a movie and a bite to eat?' he asked. 'Sorry it's so last-minute.' She accepted. He knew that they would spend the night together.

He had just emerged from the shower and was wrapping a towel around his waist when he heard the buzzer. It was Neil. Only then did he remember their plans.

'Running late?' asked Neil, when he came to the door and saw that Richard was not dressed.

'Neil, I'm sorry,' said Richard. 'I completely forgot about it. Please forgive me.'

'Well, I'm not in a rush,' said Neil. 'Get dressed. I'll wait for you.'

'No,' said Richard. 'No, we can't go to *The Pink Chicken* tonight.'

'Why not?'

'I made another arrangement. I'm going to movies and dinner with Michelle. I'm really sorry.'

'Oh,' said Neil. 'What a pity.'

'Hey, why don't you come with us? I'm sure Michelle would like to see you again.'

'I doubt that,' said Neil. 'I've never even met her. She can't possibly want to see me *again*.'

'Never met her? Are you sure? I thought you came with us the night…'

'I'm telling you, I've never met anyone called Michelle. You must be thinking of one of your other women.'

Richard looked at him, but didn't reply at once. He fetched another towel and began to dry his hair. 'Look, I can't keep apologising,' he said. 'I slipped up. I'm only human. Please come with us tonight. Let me make it up to you. Besides, you must meet Michelle. I'm sure you'll like her. And I know she'll like you.'

'No thank you,' said Neil, picking up his car keys. 'We'll have dinner another time. It's not important.'

'But I want to see you. Please don't go. I meant what I said – I really want you to meet her.'

'What for?'

'What do you mean – "what for?" I've already explained to you...'

'What's the *point* of meeting her? That's what I mean. By next week she'll be gone and there'll be another one. And then you'll be saying, "You must meet Lisa. Or Debbie. Or Andrea. The two of you will get on like a house on fire." Please, Richard, let's not do this any more. We both know what you want from these women. They don't mean anything to you and they don't mean anything to me. So just count me out – I'm not playing this game of make-believe with you any longer.'

Richard looked at him. Once more, he did not answer at once, but Neil could see in his face that he had been stung. He wished at once that he could withdraw his words. He wished he had hidden his disappointment. When Richard spoke at last, he said, 'So that's what you think, is it? You judgemental little shit. So much for being understanding. So much for being my friend through thick and thin. I make one little mistake and you turn on me.'

'I'm not turning on you. And it doesn't matter about tonight, really it doesn't. We'll reschedule. But I can't go along with the pretence any more. Friends should be honest. They should tell the truth. That's all I'm trying to do. I'm sorry if it sounded harsh.'

Richard tossed aside the towel with which he had been drying his hair. He left the room. When he came back, he was spraying deodorant under his armpits. 'Friends should be honest,' he repeated, in a low, flat voice. 'They should tell the truth. Hmm, that's very interesting. And what about you, little Neil, little brother-in-law, little friend? What about you? Are you always honest?'

'I...' Neil began. 'I don't know. I try to be.'

'Do you? How hard do you try?'

Neil felt his heartbeat quicken. There was a faint sound of

thunder, distant and lowing. 'I think I should go,' he said. 'You've got to get ready for your date. You don't want to be late. I'll phone you tomorrow and we'll make another arrangement.'

He opened the front door of the flat and was about to let himself out. Suddenly he felt himself spinning away from it and heard the door bang. Richard had moved with astonishing speed across the room to push him away from the door and slam it shut. 'You're not going anywhere,' he said. His voice was soft and cold. 'You had your chance to say what you wanted to say. But if you think you can come in here and fling those accusations at me and then run away, you've got another think coming.'

'Richard, I'm sorry,' said Neil. 'I didn't mean it…'

'Oh, but you did. You meant every word of it.'

Neil wondered if he could make another dash for the door. He suppressed the impulse, telling himself that it was ludicrous to think of running away. But Richard's frosty belligerence alarmed him. 'Let's not quarrel,' he said. 'We've managed despite everything to keep our friendship going. Let's not damage it.'

'Bit late for that.' Richard came closer towards him. 'You started this. Now I think we should have a little chat.'

'About what?'

'Oh, about friendship.' He took another step closer. 'About honesty. About secrets.'

'I don't know what you want me to say,' Neil faltered. He tried to step backwards, but found himself pressed against the couch, with Richard oppressively close to him. 'Stop this. You're scaring me.'

'No need to be scared,' said Richard. 'We're just going to have a little talk. We're going to exchange a few truths. You know what they say about truth – it liberates you. It sets you free.'

'Look, there are things we should talk about,' said Neil. 'Things we should have spoken about already. You're not wrong. I admit it. But we shouldn't do it tonight. Not while you're in this mood.'

'Oh, but I think this is a very good time.'

'What about Michelle? Won't she wonder what's happened? Hadn't you better phone her?'

'Michelle will wait,' said Richard, his eyes fixed on Neil's. 'They always do.'

Neil looked down. His heart was beating even faster. He was sweating profusely. He looked up with what he hoped was a defiant gaze. 'Okay. So what do you want to know?'

'Well,' said Richard. 'Let's see. You don't seem to have any compunction about passing judgements on my sex life, even in pouring scorn on it. So let's talk about yours. Come on.'

'You know perfectly well that I don't have anyone...' began Neil.

'Never mind that,' said Richard. 'Never mind what's not happening.' He poked Neil hard in the chest with his finger. 'Let's talk about what *is* happening. In there. Let's talk about desire.'

The word struck Neil even more forcibly than the stab in his chest had done. He remembered telling Farrell that he was suffering from desire and how pleased he had been with the formulation; how satisfying it had seemed in that context. Since then, it had become for him the word that held the key to the strongbox in which secrets were laid away. He could lock and unlock it as he chose, but only he: it was *his* word, his murmuring, talismanic word. But when Richard used it, it was hard and accusatory, something which he needed to fend off, to protect himself from.

'What do you want to know?' he asked.

'I want to know what's in there. I want the same honesty from you that you demand from me.'

Trying to keep his voice firm, he said, 'Okay. I'll tell you. Against my better judgement.' He paused, then swallowed and went on. 'What's in there is...you. I should have told you that long ago. What I feel for you is more than friendship.' Everything seemed to be pinning him to the spot in which he stood, even the scratchy heat of the room. A car hooted in the distance and, as if in response, a dog barked lethargically. Richard didn't speak.

'There you have it,' said Neil, finding the silence intolerable. 'Are you satisfied now? Is that what you wanted to hear?'

'All I want to hear is the truth. Nothing but the truth.'

'Well, now you've heard it, although this is certainly not how I meant to tell you. I hope you're pleased with yourself for forcing it out of me. Now I'm going home.'

Once more he found his way blocked. 'Not so fast,' said

Richard. There was no change in his tone. 'What you've told me is not as much of a revelation as you think. I had an idea that something of that sort was going on. I sensed it a long time ago. I was waiting for you to find the right time to tell me.'

'Well, there you are then. You knew it all along. So there's no point in continuing this unpleasant conversation.'

'Oh, but there is.' Richard stood back a little, but there was no softening in his gaze. 'You can't get away with that. That's much too easy. You've told me that I pretend to have relationships with women when all I want to do is have sex with them. You've accused me of dishonesty. You've made me feel like a sexual predator. Fine. Maybe you're right, maybe you aren't. But what about you? What do you want?'

'Nothing,' said Neil.

'Nothing? I don't believe that for a minute. You can't feel desire and yet want nothing.'

'I didn't ask to have these feelings,' said Neil. 'I wish I didn't have them. I wish we could have an uncomplicated friendship.'

'Yes, but what feelings *are* they? Be specific. Let's hear more about them. Elaborate.'

'I can't answer questions like this when you're so hostile,' said Neil. 'Please, let's not take this any further. We can have a rational discussion when…'

'I'm tired of rational discussions.' Richard rubbed his chin. 'Let me explain something to you, Neil,' he said. 'You think there's a big difference between what people desire and what they do. Well, you're wrong. Quite wrong. From desiring to doing is just a tiny little step. The doing lies in the desiring. You think you know what I'm all about and you don't approve of it. Well, I want to know now what it is that you desire. Tell me, what do I really mean to you? Spell it out. Now's your chance to be truly honest.'

'No,' said Neil. 'I'm not talking about this to you any more.' Leaping forward, he tried to run towards the door. But once more Richard was too quick for him. Neil found himself knocked off his feet, sprawled on his back on the couch. And then Richard was on top of him, straddling him. He felt the heaviness of him, he smelt soap and shampoo and deodorant on his skin. And he was trapped not only by Richard's body, but by his own fear too, which lay upon him like an added weight. The fear made him want to close his eyes. But something forced him to keep them open, to study Richard's body with an almost dispassionate curiosity. He had never noticed before that there were a few fine grey flecks in Richard's dark hair or that there were crow's feet, very faint but discernible nonetheless, around his eyes. He saw the straight line of dark hair running down his chest, from the sternum to the first peeping pubic hairs which the towel failed to hide. Two things overwhelmed him at once: the sheer, flagrant maleness of this body, expressed in every inch, every hair, every pore; and, at the same time, the terrible danger which it held. And the two things were linked: the maleness was part of the danger and the danger emanated from the maleness.

He looked at Richard's hands and noticed that, for the first time, there was no wedding band on the fourth finger of the left hand, only a pale circle of skin where the ring had been. These were the hands which he knew so well and loved so much; these were the doctor's hands, the healer's hands. And yet, at that moment, nothing frightened him more than these hands. He imagined them encircling his neck and squeezing the breath out of him. He saw quite clearly that these beautiful hands would take his life.

And at that moment what he most dreaded, what he wished so desperately to avoid, happened. He couldn't prevent it. He had an erection. Looking into Richard's eyes, he saw that he knew it too. But even that abysmal shame did not make it subside.

Richard got off him. 'There's our answer,' he said. 'Now we know. I think you'd better leave.'

Driving home, Neil wondered why stop streets and red traffic lights still made him bring the car to a halt, why he bothered to indicate when he wanted to turn left or right. What did such things matter now? His life was over. Tomorrow was a land from which he was forever barred. He had had a glimpse of it and it looked appealing, it had distinct possibilities; but he wouldn't be able to enter it. The deprivation was great – it could not be more profound. But from within the loss he was conscious of another sensation: a black, whirling freedom. The worst had happened.

There was nothing left to dread. The boil had been lanced. The abasement was complete. He could not now be threatened by it.

This reckless freedom almost made him nauseous. It was like vertigo. He forced himself to scale the heights and give himself over to dizziness. But – how curious it was! – he found that he was not alone. Someone stood there with him on the parapet, someone who offered him the companionship of the irredeemably lonely and the faith of the irretrievably lost. They gazed down together. He wept, wiping away his tears with the back of his hand. He knew who the person was. It was his mother who kept him company there, and she was with him as she had not been for decades. She loved him so. He felt her love; he was overwhelmed by it. He stood there with her, looking down and seeing scurrying life in all its pathos and remoteness. And he knew what she wanted: she wished him be one with her, to join her in what she was about to do.

As soon as Neil got home, he phoned Helena. Fortunately, she was in. He told her very briefly what had happened. 'Don't move,' she said. 'I'm coming over.' He sat and waited for her. He heard a sound, soft but disconcerting, which he couldn't identify at first. It grew louder. At last he realised that it was the pulse of raindrops falling on the roof.

When Helena arrived, she wouldn't let him speak. He wanted to tell her in more detail what had happened, to repeat everything that he and Richard had said to one another. But she shook her head and said, 'Don't talk.' She drew him into the bedroom and switched off all the lights except for one small bedside lamp.

'What are we doing?' he asked.

'We're going to sleep.'

'Yes,' he thought, as he felt his clothes being peeled off him, very gently and slowly, 'sleep is best.' A great weariness lay suddenly upon him. He climbed into the bed and lay on his side, drawing up his knees. He felt the covers being pulled over him. He couldn't see Helena, but he could hear that she was removing her own clothes. Then she climbed into the bed and lay next to him, cupping him with her body. Her skin felt surprisingly cool. In one part of his drowsy brain he thought that this was a very strange thing to do, even for Helena. In another part he sensed the wisdom of it, understood what she was telling him: skin can only be healed through skin, the remedy must come from the same place as the affront.

7 *Hail*

MARIE MOXLEY did not have to wait long before she fled her early life. She was almost seventeen when she left the home of her mother and stepfather. Her escape didn't come about because someone discovered her, as she had hoped; no one saw immanent greatness in her as she walked home from school or from the hours of reading and dreaming in her secret donga. Hollywood, alas, did not have the presence of mind to send for her. All that happened was that the Christiaan Shweizer Players came to the dorp and, four days and seven performances later, when they left, they took Marie with them. They were an itinerant theatre company who traversed the Transvaal, the Orange Free State, Northern Natal and the Northern Cape, staging their plays in almost every dorp, but avoiding Johannesburg and Pretoria. They had a repertoire of nine plays: four comedies and five melodramas. The larger the town, the longer they stayed and the more performances they put on. They needed someone to pack and unpack props, help the actors with their make-up and costumes and design and put up posters, all of which Marie was more than happy to do or to learn to do. She left her mother a brief note, telling her that she had found a job in the city and would write to her from time to time. Of course, it was a long time before she went anywhere near a city, and she soon found that the platteland was full of somnolent towns much like the one she had left behind, and that they were all surrounded by stretches of the same thorny and monotonous veld which had always seemed to close in on her like a whittling destiny; but she felt, nonetheless, that the first resolute steps had been taken on the path towards that incandescent place where her promise to herself, her dream of a grandiose self-founding, could be fulfilled.

The name Marie Moxley was discarded the day she joined the Christiaan Shweizer Players. From the first, they knew the young woman only as Barbara Lombard and they believed her to be nineteen years old. And she herself soon thought of Marie as a forlorn and dead creature, still-born within her, which had had to be removed because it was not viable but which, in being excised, made possible the birth of another. The process of dismembering her erstwhile self had not been quite as easy as she had thought it would be: surprisingly, it provoked a quick, cold little grief; but, once it was done, she set to work filling in the hollow which was all that was now left of defunct Marie.

Christiaan Shweizer was famous across the platteland. He was believed to be a noted Bavarian actor. He spoke English and Afrikaans with a thick accent. His ponderous Teutonic mien left everyone in no doubt as to his origins. He was deliciously exotic, brooding and lofty. Everyone was struck by the incongruity of having such a man in their midst. They felt honoured that he had deigned to bestow his heavy foreignness upon them. In fact, Shweizer had never been to Germany. He had never met Dietrich or Von Sternberg or Riefenstahl, although he claimed to know them all. His real name was Christoffel Niewoudt and he came from the Western Transvaal. He was born in Christiana after the Boer War and when he was a youth his family moved to Schweizer-Reneke; and so, when he needed a stage name, he thought of the towns he had grown up in and reinvented himself as Christiaan Shweizer. It gave him a curious satisfaction to think that he had found his new identity in the very world which he had scorned because it couldn't sustain his ambition.

But in the end his unprepossessing beginnings took their slow, grinding revenge on him, for Shweizer did not escape the platteland and, as time passed, it seemed less and less likely that he ever would. He never found the renown he longed for, although he had fame of a bathetic sort in the little sphere in which he condescended to move. Sometimes the troupe toured the Western Transvaal and entertained audiences in Christiana and Schweizer-Reneke, the very places he had once thought he would never see again; and, as he surveyed the audience, some of whom he recognised although they didn't recognise him, as he looked at the packed rooms, at the young men and children sitting on the floor because there were not enough chairs for everyone, as he felt the adulation of the crowd, he wondered whether he had returned to the towns of his youth as a victor, or as someone who would be reminded again and again of defeat. He had wanted to become a playwright and director of international stature. Instead he found himself putting on farces and melodramas in shabby schoolrooms and church halls. The platteland audiences were not interested in the serious plays he had written. They wanted to see again and again the old favourites (or variations thereof), to weep over weathered West Coast fishermen, old before their time, searching in vain for their drowned daughters, and to laugh uproariously at the ouderling who had to hide in a cupboard from the jealous husband.

Shweizer became a drinker, and a gloomy and methodical one at that. He never touched alcohol during the day or in the early evening, but as soon as the last curtain fell, he would settle down and drink slightly more than half a bottle of brandy. He consumed four bottles every week, never more and never less. His moroseness affected the whole company, who pretended to ignore the drinking, but who would become noticeably subdued as soon as he sat down with his bottle and glass.

Barbara did not dislike Shweizer, who was kind to her in a gruff sort of way, but she had little tolerance for his melancholy. She didn't mind in the least that he had discarded his original identity; in fact, she applauded it. It was evident to her that most people lived their lives phlegmatically, but when they at last wanted to make a change, they were distressed to find that it was too late and they were trapped. If you allow yourself to remain stuck in the groove of your beginnings, then you have no one but yourself to blame if your origins turn into your destination. Her path, she had vowed, would not be circular: it would lead in a vivid line from the wretchedness of what life handed out to the splendour of what it could be compelled to yield. She was driven by a passionate belief in the triumph of possibility over the accidents of circumstance; it was nothing short of a religion to her. In Shweizer – and this is what made her shrink from him – she had to witness the despair of one who had lost his faith. The problem was not that he wasn't what he pretended to be. It was that he hadn't been able to see the invention through. She detected subsidence in his spirit and her fanatic heart couldn't forgive that.

Fortunately, there was much to distract her. Shweizer soon realised that Barbara had an eye for décor and building sets, and he put her skills to use. The deftness of her own hands astonished her. They seemed to have plans of their own, ambitions greater than what she had devised for them. Sometimes she would gaze at them in wonder. Hands fascinated and delighted her: often she could recall people's hands better than their faces. Feet, however, she found repellent – some more so than others, but they were all ugly to her, blind as newborn mice. Hands, she felt, tell us how far we have travelled, the whole evolutionary passage is there in our hands, whereas feet remind us that we are still trying to scrape off the ancient slime and that a long ascent awaits us.

Christiaan Shweizer was at that time composing a new farce, which he called *My Vrou, Haar Man en Ek*. It featured a divorced couple who meet unexpectedly years after their marriage has ended and find that they are still attracted to one another. There was nothing original about this scenario, of course: Shweizer had lifted it from Noël Coward's *Private Lives*. As he wrote the play, he cursed himself violently for participating in the debasement of art and the platteland audiences for forcing it upon him. He knew it would be a great success. In a moment of inspiration, he gave the second husband a bad case of myopia and exploited this for as many laughs as he could wring from it. In one scene he had the unfortunate man, already being cuckolded by his wife and her first husband, mistake a carved head on a plinth for his rival and hurl abuse upon it. Shweizer discussed it with Barbara and said, 'How vould vee do zis, Barbara? Vot vould vee use?'

'I'll try and make something,' said Barbara. 'Can you get me a block of clay?'

When she had the clay, she let her hands take over. She worked for several weeks, draping a cloth over the bust when she was not busy with it so that no one could see it in its unfinished state. Out of the clay her hands drew a large, heavy-set male head. It had fleshy features and a long, trailing beard. Its expression was fixedly, even fatally dour. Eventually she decided that it was finished, although she was far from satisfied. Nervously she called Shweizer in to see it. To her surprise, he embraced her. 'Vonderful!' he cried. 'Vot a good joke zat vill be, ja? Ze husband vill not only be shouting at a bust, he vill be yelling at ze venerable head of President Paul Kruger! Ze audience vill love zat.' She had seldom seen him so happy. For a short while, he even forgot to be gloomy.

The strangest aspect of this was that, until she was putting the finishing touches to it, Barbara hadn't realised that she was reproducing the bust of Paul Kruger. When it was done, she saw that that was indeed what it was, that it had been his craggy Biblical head from the start. But there had never been an explicit intention. Her hands, in their making, had known more than she: they had conspired to bring her to acquiescence. She saw at once that, if the fame and freedom she longed for were ever to come to her, they would come through these busy, devious hands. Staring at them, she felt exhilarated by their power, but also a little frightened of what they might do.

She thought again of Pandora and her box, and of the unleashing of powers whose intentions are hidden. She remembered that in some of the accounts of the myth which she had read, the box was described as being made of rich dark wood. A golden cord encircled it and upon it was a finely carved head. Everything in the description suggested design, care and time. The box was a work of art. Pandora could have left it as it was and still found pleasure in the ingenuity that made it. She could have put her curiosity aside in favour of a still and replete craftsmanship. But she had not been able to do so. She had not been able to withstand the beseeching of the creatures trapped within the box. The urgent whisperings of what was hidden had been more persuasive than the declared and evident beauty of what lay revealed.

What, Barbara wondered, would these hands of hers do if she didn't hold them back at all, if she gave them complete freedom? Something would be released, she had no doubt of that; something would come pelting down. But what would it be? And what form would it assume?

The *Promised Land Pleasure Tours* advertising and public relations team suspected that they wouldn't even be discussing the proposal if it weren't for Slush. Whenever Susan put something before them which they didn't like, they tended to attribute it to his influence, which they regarded as invariably sinister. Susan was too brusque to be likable, but she commanded respect, partly because she was such a successful, canny businesswoman. Slush, however, was young, taciturn and haughty. Worst of all, he was the boss's adopted son. They had heard that he came from nothing (although very little was known of his early life, and no one dared ask Susan about it) and now he had everything; but instead of seeming grateful for his good fortune, which might have endeared him to them, he wore an air of cool, slightly sardonic entitlement.

Looking at him across the boardroom table, Susan smiled to herself. He was almost a caricature of a prosperous, trendy young black man: he wore Ray-Ban sunglasses, even when he was indoors, a leather jacket, a gold chain around his neck, an earring in one ear and tight-fitting trousers. He refused to switch off his cellphone, even during meetings. He played with the keys of his BMW convertible, tossing them from one hand to the other. He was so comfortable in his gilded insouciance that he seemed to be one of those who had been lucky enough to slip through the clamping fingers of history, one whose ears had never known how discordant its invective can be. The past seemed entirely silent in him. He was not even born when the Soweto Uprising took place and he was still at school when South Africa held its first democratic elections. In his languid sleekness he looked as if he had bided his time so that he could come into the world only when it was safe to do so, at the very moment when the storm abated.

Such a presumption would not have been correct, for Slush's early years were full of bad weather. He had never known his father, and his mother was killed in a bus accident when he was twelve. He was sent to live with his great-aunt, Evelyn, who was Susan's housekeeper in Johannesburg. Susan remembered the first time she saw the young boy. He had been crying and there were tears on his cheeks and blobs of mucus in both his nostrils. He cast his eyes down when she spoke to him. She had never been a maternal sort of woman and this boy provoked no tender feelings in her. He looked too much like a symbol of commonplace misery. In his sniffling she heard something else – the unassuageable, centuries-old lament of orphanhood and indigence, a sound that can never be stilled. It is so cavernous a cry that compassion shrinks from it as if from a contagion. Susan shuddered. She had little difficulty in hardening her heart.

She didn't have much to do with the boy at first, although she saw to it that he was fed and clothed and she undertook to pay for his schooling. The day after his arrival she asked him what his name was. He muttered something which she couldn't catch. Later she questioned Evelyn about it. 'What's the boy's name?' she asked. 'He told me, but I couldn't hear what he was saying.'

Evelyn, who was bent over the ironing-board, said, 'Nhlanhla. It means good luck. It says he's the lucky one.'

'No evidence of it thus far,' said Susan wryly. She asked Evelyn to repeat the name. Then she tried it herself, but all she could manage was 'shush-la' or 'nsha-sha'. 'I'll never get it right,' she complained. 'What a name! Why can't you people give the children names that can be pronounced?'

'He's got an English name also, Mrs Southern,' Evelyn said. 'You can call him by that name.' She always addressed her employer as 'Mrs Southern'. Susan wouldn't allow anyone to call her 'Miss', and Evelyn couldn't be induced to say 'Ms', so they had settled on 'Mrs Southern' as a compromise.

'What is it?'

'Luxury.'

'You've got to be joking! You're pulling my leg, aren't you?'

'No, I'm not joking. That is his name. Nhlanhla Luxury Gumede.'

'Well, optimism was certainly expressed at his birth,' said Susan, laughing. 'But seriously, Evelyn, there's no way I'm calling him that.' She spoke with her characteristic firmness. 'The child will be a laughing-stock if I call him Luxury. And I can't get my tongue around the other name. I'm going to call him "Slush". That's the nearest I can get to pronouncing it. It will have to do.'

And so Slush he became. Susan hadn't intended it to be anything more than the private name she used for him, but, after a while, she noticed that other people were calling him that too. And eventually, when the boy was asked what his name was, he too said 'Slush'.

Susan regarded him as an ephemeral presence: she expected him to finish his schooling and return to his village or go elsewhere. He was one of those who are destined to move on, who must move on, and there is no point in allowing such people to impinge on one's life more than is necessary. His school reports – which were dutifully presented to Susan at the end of every term – were always favourable and, based on that information, she knew him to be a bright boy. But there was nothing in their everyday interactions which showed her his intelligence, for they exchanged few words.

Then Evelyn suffered a stroke. It left her partially paralysed on her left side. She could walk with difficulty, but was unable to work. She wanted to return to the village where she came from, to be cared for by her family. Susan gave her a generous pension and, as a parting gift, bought several pieces of furniture for the house in Zululand. She assumed that Slush would return with his great-aunt to the village or that other arrangements would be made for his accommodation in Johannesburg. But nothing was done. The day before Evelyn's departure, Susan went to her back-yard room to say goodbye to her. There she found herself confronted by a most unwelcome request: Evelyn begged her to allow Slush to stay on.

'Please, Mrs Southern,' she said. 'He's doing so well. I don't want to take him out of school. And there's nowhere else for him to go. He'll work in the garden for you. He'll work hard. He's a good boy. He won't make trouble. Please. I'm asking nicely.' Evelyn lay in bed, covered by several blankets and a quilt, although it wasn't cold. Suitcases and cardboard boxes were lined up neatly near the door. A cousin, who had been sent to accompany her home, sat silently on a chair next to the bed.

'No,' said Susan. 'Definitely not. I'm sorry. It's too much responsibility.'

There was no hesitation in her voice and no doubt in her mind. The boy was nothing to her. She had done her best for him, but circumstances had changed and she could do no more. The ties that bound them had always been flimsy; now that his great-aunt was leaving her employ, there was no connection between them at all.

Evelyn sighed and said, 'God must help me. I don't know what I can do.'

'You must take him with you tomorrow,' said Susan. 'It's really quite simple.'

That evening, as she prepared fried eggs and mushrooms on toast for her dinner, she thought again about Slush and her resentment towards him and Evelyn deepened. How *could* they even imagine that she would take him in? She had no children of her own, had never wanted any; she certainly was not going to be encumbered with someone else's child! And teenage boys were notoriously difficult. It wasn't as if this were a new-born infant whom she could set on an easeful path from the start. Slush was damaged goods: all the disfigurements of penury and loss were evident in him. Susan had made many difficult decisions in her career, had fired people and not given the matter a further thought; but now, although she knew she was doing the right thing, knew that she had no choice, the dismissal of the laconic boy tugged at her and made her uneasy.

As she was scooping the eggs out of the frying-pan, all the lights went out. She looked out of the window and saw that the neighbouring houses were also in darkness: there was a general power failure. She rummaged through the kitchen cupboards in search of candles or a torch, but found none. Stumbling in the darkness, she made her way to the bathroom and emptied the contents of the bathroom cupboard onto the floor, but there was nothing there either. She was sure she had a torch somewhere, but where was it? She searched for another twenty minutes and then gave up. Evelyn, she felt sure, would have candles. She let herself out of the kitchen door and walked gingerly across the back garden to the housekeeper's quarters. There was no moon and all about her there was the eerie silence that falls when there is a power failure.

A light shone in the first room, which was Slush's. She stopped and looked through the open window. Slush had a candle, which he had lit and placed on a chair in the corner of the room. It cast very little light, but she could see that he had been packing: there was one small cardboard box, already sealed with tape, and a suitcase, which lay open on the bed. In it she saw a small pile of shirts and underpants, a pair of jeans, a pair of tackies and a few cassettes, all neatly packed. Next to the suitcase, on the bed, was a small portable radio. Music was coming from it and Slush, standing in the middle of the room, was dancing. The music sounded strange to Susan's ear: it had a jazzy feel to it, but it wasn't jazz. There was something that reminded her of R&B, but it wasn't that either. It puckered the air with pinching, squeezing notes. A female voice was singing.

Found me a baby
Layin' there all alone
Whatcher doin', baby?
Baby, where's your home?

Found me a baby
Fell from the sky like hail
Whatcher doin', baby?
Baby, tell your tale.

Found me a baby
Sweet as sad can be
Whatcher doin', baby?
Baby, come with me.

She wouldn't have thought that it was the kind of music one could dance to, but Slush was dancing anyway. He swooped and glided, his arms and neck stretched out, his whole body swaying and casting vast, turbulent shadows. There was great energy in his movements, but it was not a joyous dance. The acrid melancholy of the music seemed to be holding the boy and enveloping him as he flung himself about the room. Susan felt that she shouldn't be watching: she knew she was intruding on a very private act. But she couldn't drag herself away. It was an extraordinary sight. Slush had been sent away, he was packing to go, he was leaving early in the morning; yet here he was, dancing all alone in the flickering light of the candle.

The music ended and Slush stood still. 'That was *Bulrush Blues*,' the presenter said. His subsequent words were lost to Susan, for at that moment the boy glanced through the window and saw her. Neither of them moved or spoke. And in that instant everything was decided. If Slush had cast his eyes down as he had on the night Susan first met him, if he had looked embarrassed or sheepish, if he had reminded her in any way of the multitudinous unfortunates of the world and the pity and charity they require, he would have boarded the bus the next morning as planned. But he looked directly at her. If anyone should feel embarrassed, his look seemed to imply, it was she. He had nothing to be ashamed of. As he stood there, in that dark little room, surrounded by his meagre belongings, Susan saw in him something she'd always thought of as an offshoot of privilege, a luxury the needy could not aspire to and would never be able to afford: dignity. Her discovery of it in the place where she least expected to find it moved her greatly. Slush, inexplicably, was dignified. And that was what saved him.

The next morning Susan said to Evelyn, 'I've changed my mind. He can stay for three months – as a trial period. Let's see what happens.'

'God is good,' said Evelyn. 'Oh, God is very good.'

That was more than a decade ago. Slush never left. A year after her first stroke, Evelyn suffered another and died. And then there seemed to be no one in the village who took an interest in the boy, no one who maintained contact with him or Susan. When he was sixteen, she adopted him formally. He took the name Nhlanhla Gumede-Southern (he agreed with Susan that it was time to drop 'Luxury' as a second name). He completed a commerce degree at Wits and then joined the staff of *Promised Land Pleasure Tours*.

The air of self-sufficiency he had shown as a boy remained with him; so did his dignity, although it sometimes seemed to Susan that it had hardened into arrogance, which was a pity. She loved him entirely, loved him in a way that she had never imagined she could love anyone; but when she thought of the boy who was told he had to leave and who responded by dancing, she felt that there had been something delicate in him which the years had coarsened. He had lost the disquieting allure which foundlings always bear with them. Poverty, she knew, would not have preserved in him that delicacy – it never does; but freedom from need hadn't preserved it either. As an adult he was less remarkable than he had been as a child.

Susan knew that he wasn't popular at work, that his special relationship with the boss meant he would always be regarded with suspicion. But Slush, as she had long since discovered, was able to take care of himself. And she used him strategically, sometimes feeding proposals through him so that she could test the responses of others before she declared her own position. She never needed to prepare him for it in advance or explain what she was doing: he understood and always played his part perfectly.

'As you all know,' said Susan, 'we have invested in a major new development, the Apartheid Memory Park, which is to be constructed over the next few years on an open piece of ground on the East Rand.' The advertising and public relations team nodded. 'You've seen the plans,' she went on, 'and you know what it's going to look like.' They nodded again. 'When it's finished, it will become an important part of our clients' itinerary. They'll visit it either at the beginning or at the end of their trip. And, as investors, we'll be entitled to a share of the takings, which we trust will be lucrative.'

The members of the team glanced at one another. They knew all this; the financial commitment had already been made. Why was Susan bringing it up again?

'A new proposal has come forward,' she continued, 'which I need to put before you. It comes from the MM Group, which, as you are aware, is the biggest investor in the scheme and will control 51 percent of the shares.' The MM Group was a large and well-established pharmaceutical company, the chief producer of skin-whitening creams during the apartheid years. The initials stood for Mnyama-Mhlophe: Black-White in Zulu. 'What they propose is as follows: they would like to commission a large sculpture, which will be placed at the entrance to the Park.' Susan's eyes travelled quickly about the room as she glanced at every member of the team.

'A sculpture of what?' someone asked.

'Of a hand,' said Susan. 'A giant hand.'

'A hand?'

'Yes. Nelson Mandela's hand. His fist, to be more accurate. It will be carved in granite and will be six metres high, more than three times taller than the average person. The fist will be depicted as thrusting through bars.'

'Bars?'

'The kind they have on the windows of prisons.'

A long silence followed. Eventually someone said, 'And where did you say this sculpture would be, Ms Southern?'

'In the open veld,' said Susan. 'Outside the entrance to the Memory Park.'

The team did not know how to respond. They couldn't read the tone of Susan's presentation of the proposal. Surely she wasn't in favour of it? How seriously did she wish them to consider it? When no one spoke, Susan said, 'In view of the fact that the MM Group control 51 percent of the shares, they do not, strictly speaking, need our support. They can go ahead even if all the other shareholders vote against it.'

'Then why are we discussing it?' asked an earnest young man.

'Well, if they get a strong message that we don't want it, they may reconsider. But I have to tell you that they're very keen on the idea. They're already talking to sculptors about it. Because of the size, it's going to be extremely costly.'

'It's a dreadful idea.' The earnest young man's voice wavered but he swallowed hard and drummed with his fingers on the table. 'Really, Ms Southern, we must protest as hard as we can.'

'Why?' The question came from Slush, who had not spoken thus far.

'Because it's tacky,' said the young man. 'It's crass. It's over-the-top – to say the least.'

'I see,' said Slush. 'But the Apartheid Memory Park is not?'

'Well…'

'There will be separate entrances for different racial groups,' Slush went on. 'All visitors will have to carry passes, and will be required to produce them when officials demand to see them. There'll be a recreation of Mandela's prison cell on Robben Island and visitors will be locked in there for ten minutes each. There'll be a series of T-shirts for sale called *Madiba Meets the Stars*, which will feature photographs of Mandela with, amongst others, Whitney Houston and David Beckham. And you're worried about good taste?'

'I was never in favour of this theme park in the first place,' said the young man. His voice had a defiant ring to it now. 'Or at least, our participation in it. We were told that it's a fantastic business opportunity, that we're lucky to be offered a chance to come on board, and so on. But I still felt uneasy about it. And now I think we have to draw the line somewhere. This sculpture is going too far. We can't allow ourselves to be associated with it.'

'But maybe it'll become one of the great wonders of the world,' said Slush. He didn't smile and they had no idea if he were serious or not. 'Maybe people will flock to see it. Mount Rushmore, the Statue of Liberty, Big Ben, the Eiffel Tower, the Leaning Tower of Pisa and the Boksburg Freedom Fist. Don't you want us to be part of that?'

Some of the team smiled awkwardly. They all looked at Susan, but her expression didn't change. 'Even if you're right,' the young man persisted, 'is money the only consideration?'

'What else is there?' asked Slush. 'What else does *Promised Land Pleasure Tours* do, except make money?'

'That's true,' said one of the women. 'The financial imperatives come first and foremost.'

The young man did not answer and for several minutes there was silence. Then Susan spoke. 'You're going to have to do a lot better than that,' she said. 'I've never seen such a feeble display. You collapsed like a house of cards. There's a meeting next week with some of the people from the MM Group and, if we're going to fight this thing, we have to have better arguments against it than we've heard today. Otherwise the Boksburg Freedom Fist will become a reality and we'll find ourselves associated with it forever whether we like it or not. It's your job to make sure it doesn't happen. We cannot simply let the MM Group out-vote us on this. I want you to get in touch with the other shareholders and consult with them, and by Friday morning I want to know what our strategy's going to be. If we lose this fight, you will all be held responsible.'

Susan got up and strode out of the room. Slush, tossing the keys of his BMW convertible from one hand to the other, followed her.

The days were still warm, but there was a coolness now in the evening, the first sign that the season was beginning to change. The roses, despite having lost many of their leaves, were flowering again. It was the middle of March and Tessa was in Johannesburg for ten days. Once more she had travelled alone to South Africa. But it was the last time she would be making the journey without

Brian and the children. Her task was to rent a house for the family to live in when they arrived. Their home in Barnet had been sold and when she left the rooms were strewn with boxes, the days jerked here and there by sporadic leave-takings.

Dorothy seemed resigned now to their return and offered no further opposition. She even invited them to stay with her until they found a house. Tessa, thanking her warmly, declined, saying that it would be too disruptive and that they needed to have a place of their own from the start. Her decision was based partly on solicitude for her mother, but it arose also from a powerful impulse to ensure that the house in which her childhood had been spent was left undisturbed. The children – even she had to admit it – were noisy and sometimes destructive, especially Luke, who was hyperactive and on Ritalin. Yet why should the house matter so much to her? Her mother's refusal to countenance change had troubled her for years and the acrimonious exchanges that took place during her last visit had confirmed her in her view that Dorothy, in pursuit of what she mistakenly thought of as steadfastness, had allowed life to congeal about her. It had seemed to Tessa that there was a strong link between her mother's stubborn determination to hold onto the past and her long habitation of the same quiet rooms, where the curtains moved so very slightly and the parvenu sunlight, meeting old solemnity, was daily abashed. But now, faced with the prospect of boisterous children romping through the house, Tessa felt differently. She was excited about showing the children her early life, she wanted to share it with them; but when she thought of how they would rummage through her childhood, of what they would do to her bedroom and Anthony's, she felt she couldn't permit such a desecration to take place. The strength of her resolve astonished her.

Dorothy made no reference to the other part of their dispute, Tessa's declaration that she intended to establish contact with the Slaters, and Tessa too didn't bring it up. Yet she was more determined than ever to get in touch with them. Her homecoming would not be complete without this attempt to confront the most painful aspect of the past. She didn't know what she expected to gain from it, didn't know if it could bring appeasement or peace –

didn't know even if that was what she sought. All she knew was that she did not want a partial return, a soft resumption. She was about to take up residence once more in her former life and she was adamant that she wouldn't enter it through a side door.

Criss-crossing the suburbs, looking at houses that were for rent, it struck her that she was experiencing Johannesburg differently now. She had visited it often over the years, but had seen the fast-changing, febrile city as if from a distance. But now that it was to become her home again, the place in which she was to bring up her children, she felt its familiarity and its strangeness as sensations that stung her with a sudden new pertinence. There were jacaranda-lined streets in which nothing seemed to have changed since she was a child. But there were also parts of the city which bore no resemblance to anything she could recall from the Johannesburg she'd known before her emigration. The proliferation of shopping malls, the American brand names and pseudo-American accents, the number of vehicles on the roads, the almost complete absence of white people from Hillbrow and parts of the inner city, the high walls around the houses, the signs which read *Property Protected by Make-My-Day Security Company* or *Danger: Hijacking Hot Spot* – all these disconcerted, even bewildered her. But then she saw also the mixed-race couples walking hand-in-hand, the children, black and white, at school together, playing and laughing. These made her feel that her return would enable her to participate in a normalising society, a forgetting society, and it thrilled her. Admittedly there was something in the nature of the forgetting that seemed forced, that had a desperate quality to it; but surely it was better than not forgetting at all, not moving forward? That immobility was what she saw in her mother. Dorothy had always been a liberally-minded woman and her antipathy to the Nationalists could not have been stronger, but the zeal with which she now guarded her old grievances seemed to Tessa to be a kind of conservatism that was different in origin and direction from what her mother had abhorred, but not much different in kind.

Three days before she was due to leave she found a pleasant house for rent in a quiet street in Roosevelt Park, paid the deposit and signed a year's lease. It had four bedrooms and a playroom, a big garden and a swimming-pool. How the children would love the space, the light, the sunshine! She couldn't wait to show it to them.

'Does it have good security?' asked Dorothy.

'Well, I noticed that there are bars on the windows,' said Tessa.

'On all of them?'

'I think so. I can't remember.'

'There have to be bars on *all* the windows,' said Dorothy. 'It's very important. And they must be sturdy ones, preferably on the inside of the windows. Like the ones I had put in. Flimsy ones are useless – they can cut through them in a second. And there should be an alarm system too. If there isn't one, you'll have to get one. You must make the landlord pay for it.'

'Is all this really necessary?'

'Yes, absolutely necessary. You can't put your family's lives in danger. This is not Barnet, you know.'

'There's crime in London too,' said Tessa.

'Not like here.'

Tessa said no more. She was not averse to undertaking the precautions Dorothy was urging, but she saw in the exchange the shape of many dispiriting future conversations. Dorothy would invariably assume the role of portentous authority on all matters South African and Tessa would have to play the part of the naïve initiate. She sighed and went to the kitchen to make tea.

Later, while her mother was having her afternoon rest, Tessa looked in the telephone directory for Richard's number. She found his name listed under the 'Medical' section and, with some difficulty, persuaded his receptionist to give her his cellphone number. 'I'm his cousin, visiting from London,' she said. 'I'd very much like to speak to him.' She dialled the number, aware of the quickening of her heartbeat. Richard answered at once.

'Hello,' she said. 'Is that Richard Slater?'

'Yes. Who is this?'

'It's Tessa. Tessa Strauss.' When he didn't respond, she said, 'Your cousin.'

She heard him exhale, a long, slow sound. 'Good heavens,' he said at last. 'I can't believe my ears. Tessa. Is that really you?'

'It's really me.'

'Don't you live in London?'

'I do. But I'm coming back to South Africa – with my husband and children. I came out in advance to find a house for us to rent.'

'Returning after all these years. You're taking a big step.'

'Yes, we are.'

A silence followed. At last Richard said, 'How's Aunt Dorothy?'

'Okay. Getting old. How're your parents?'

'Already old.'

'I heard that Jock had a stroke.'

'Yes, he did.'

'How is he?'

'He's made a pretty good recovery.'

'I'm pleased.'

There was another uncomfortable silence. Then Tessa said, 'Richard, how would you feel about getting together? I want to talk to you. I'd like to get to know you again.'

'I'd like that very much,' he said, and she heard in his voice how sincerely he meant it. 'That would be great.'

'Well, I'm leaving on Saturday. What about tomorrow? Or Friday?'

They arranged to meet for brunch on Friday morning. Tessa felt pleased with herself. Selling their home in London, packing up the furniture, hiring the movers – those had been momentous activities, but they had all been associated with the severing of ties, the termination of her old life. Now she was taking the first steps towards the establishment of a new life. Finding the house in Roosevelt Park had been one such step; getting in touch with Richard was another – a far bigger one. She was building a beginning and defying her mother at the same time.

Two of the nurses were having tea and biscuits. They had the radio on. 'I like this station,' said the red-headed one. 'They play good music.'

'Yes,' said the other, who had short-cropped blond hair. 'Not that terrible noise young people listen to these days. Thump-thump-thump. I don't know how they can bear it.'

The song ended and the presenter said, 'Have you noticed that modern songs have amazing lyrics? Take it from me, you can learn a lot from listening to them. The next one I'm going to play, for example, reminds me of the ideas of Plato, the Greek philosopher. We were lucky enough, when I was at school in Kakamas, to have a teacher who taught us about philosophy. His name was Mr Herman Neutics and he was the most knowledgeable man I ever knew. He explained to us that Plato believed we never really learn anything. Instead, we spend our lives recollecting what we once knew and have forgotten. Everything has already happened. We think we're going into the future but all we're doing is struggling to open the past. Whether we know it or not, we're trying to get back to where we once were, to recover the wholeness of our lost memories.'

'No idea what she's talking about,' said the blond nurse.

'Me neither,' said the red-headed one. 'I wish she'd just get on with it and play the music. Want another tennis biscuit?'

'If you listen carefully to the words of this song,' the presenter went on, 'you'll see quite clearly the influence of Plato. I don't know what happened to Herman Neutics, but, wherever you are, Mr Neutics, this one is for you. Here on Radio Frangipani, 91.8, the Home of Highveld Harmony, is Savage Garden with *I Knew I Loved You.*'

'What names these groups have!' exclaimed the blond nurse. 'Savage Garden! What will they think of next?'

I knew I loved you before I met you
I think I dreamed you into life
I knew I loved you before I met you
I have been waiting all my life

'It's a nice song, though,' said the red-headed nurse. She turned the volume up.

Archie, sitting on the stoep in the early autumn sunlight, heard the music and the nurses' conversation. He did not react in any way. The last few weeks had brought a marked change in him. He was less agitated and less talkative. His appetite was poor. He seemed to be almost devoid of curiosity, to be slipping into an inexorable docility.

But what was going on in his head as he sat there? What did the long, silent hours tell him? And what did he tell them? Was he forsaking companionship, or was he finding another kind, the kind that appears only when all other voices die down? With whom did he now converse? Was he forgetting more and more, forgetting everything, or was he remembering at last? Was he dreaming himself into life or out of it? And if the stuff into which he was sinking was indeed memory, was it its plenitude that he was contemplating or its thinness? Was he discovering a world of essences, a silence that is full of secrets, too rich and suggestive for speech? Or did the silence merely speak of absence, the nothingness that takes over once the synaptic hailstorm comes to an end? Was the mind of Archie drifting into mystery? Or was it coming to rest on that exposed and humdrum rock where all mysteries end?

Tessa looked about the restaurant when she arrived and saw a dark-haired man seated alone at a table, his back to her. She felt anxious as she approached him. The last time she had seen Richard he was a teenager; would she recognise him as an almost middle-aged man? She saw at once that her apprehension was unfounded: there was no doubt that the man at the table, rising to his feet to greet her, was her cousin. The eyes were the same; so was the crinkly smile. 'Hello, Richard,' she said, and leaned forward to kiss him. He avoided the kiss and instead she found herself tightly clasped as he hugged her to him. She raised her arms to embrace him in turn and they stood there, neither moving nor speaking, for quite a while. When he released her at last and they sat down, Tessa found that she had to dab at her eyes with a tissue. And there was a moistness in Richard's eyes too.

They looked at each other, too full of wonderment to speak much at first. 'I feel as if I'm dreaming,' said Tessa. 'After all these years – can it really be happening?'

'You're the one who made it happen,' he said. 'I'm very grateful to you, Tessa. Thank you. You'll never know how much it means to me.'

'He's nice,' Tessa thought to herself. 'He's not afraid to show emotion, he can talk about his feelings. He's not of the old school, like his father.'

A waiter approached and they ordered drinks. Then they sat

silently, not knowing how or where to begin. At last Richard said, 'You haven't changed as much as I expected. I can see the old Tessa quite clearly.'

'And I can see the old Richard.' She reached across and squeezed his hand.

'Does your mother know about this?' asked Richard. 'How does she feel?'

'I told her when I was here at the beginning of the year that I intended to get in touch with you. She was very unhappy about it. We had quite a row, so I haven't mentioned it again. She doesn't know that I phoned you. Or that we're meeting today.'

Richard nodded. 'I thought she wouldn't like the idea. I'm sorry if it's causing tension between you.'

'It's her life,' said Tessa. 'She must do what she likes. But I can't be bound by her decisions. This is something I need to do, especially now that I'm returning to South Africa.'

'Well, I'm glad. I really am.'

'That I contacted you? Or that I'm coming back to South Africa?'

'Both.'

'What about your parents? Will you tell them?'

'I don't know. Do you want me to?'

'Maybe we should keep it to ourselves for the time being,' said Tessa. 'Let's get to know each other first – take things one step at a time.'

'I'm happy with that.'

Their drinks appeared. Were they ready to order food? The waiter stood with his pen and notepad poised. No, no, they said – they hadn't even looked at the menu yet. 'Five more minutes, please,' said Tessa.

'Do Jock and Elaine still live in the same house?' she asked when the waiter had gone.

'No. They're in a retirement village. They moved there after Dad had the stroke.'

'I can't imagine them living anywhere else. That Greenside house was such a big part of my childhood.' She felt a sudden seep of memories: games of hide-and-seek in the thick shrubbery at twilight; a clumsy kind of poker for three that they devised and played in front of the anthracite fire on winter nights; reading *Alice in Wonderland* and *Through the Looking-Glass* out loud as they sprawled in the shade of a tree; sleeping over on weekends and sneaking into one another's bedrooms to whisper and giggle when they were supposed to be asleep. The games and secrets of their childhood had made the dark, forbidding house seem, if not friendly, then at least tolerant. These recollections were her history. And this man whom she hadn't seen for decades, a stranger to her adult life, was the one who could best bear witness to it.

'My father hates the retirement village,' said Richard. 'He's very unhappy there. Mom doesn't seem to mind it, though. What about your mother? Is she still in the same house?'

'Yes. Nothing's changed.'

'Odd that we never bumped into her during all these years.'

'She says she saw you once. It was at the movies. You were with your parents and a young woman – she presumed it was your wife. She watched you go up the escalator but you didn't see her.'

'That's weird,' said Richard.

The waiter re-appeared. 'I'm sorry,' said Tessa. 'We still haven't looked at the menu.'

'We'd better decide what we want to eat,' said Richard. 'We can't keep sending him away.' They studied the menu and made their choices.

'So you became a doctor after all,' said Tessa. 'You never wanted to be anything else.'

'Yes, I did. And I even married one. But we're getting divorced.'

'I'm sorry to hear that,' said Tessa. 'I must say I've been very fortunate in my marriage. I suppose it's the luck of the draw.'

'No,' said Richard. 'I don't think so. In this regard at least I think we make our own luck.'

'So what did you do wrong? You chose badly?'

'Oh, no. I chose very well. Too well.' He paused and seemed reluctant to continue. Picking up his serviette, he rolled it into a tight little ball. 'I'm not trying to avoid the subject,' he said. 'I'd like to talk to you about it. But perhaps not today.'

'He *is* nice,' Tessa thought again. 'Probably very complex. But nice.' She could see them confiding in each other, becoming good friends. She sensed that Richard would be very glad to have a friend. Charming as he was, he was probably quite lonely.

Richard's next words confirmed that impression. His voice a little gruff, he said, 'You know, I have no family except my parents. None. My wife – my soon-to-be ex-wife, I should say – and I are trying to keep a friendship of sorts going, but it's not the same. It would mean so much to me to have you living here. And to have you back in my life.'

'Me too,' she murmured, leaning forward as if to meet his pleasure. Then, sitting back, she said, 'Do you ever think of your biological parents? You never used to speak of them when we were children. Did you never want to find out who they were?'

'It's interesting that you should ask that. In fact, I always thought of them, but never did anything about it. Recently – last year, in fact – I decided to try to find them.'

'And?'

'No luck. A cul-de-sac.'

'That must be a great disappointment.'

'Yes. It is.' He unrolled the serviette and spread it out on the table before him. 'I decided I was ready for what the past had to reveal to me, but the past wasn't ready for me.' The waiter appeared with a basket of sliced health bread, dark brown and covered with seeds. 'I thought I could make it do what I want,' Richard went on. 'But it won't.'

'The question,' said Tessa, remembering something she had once read, but unable to recall the source, 'the question is: who is to be master? That is all.'

'Ah, the wise words of Humpty Dumpty,' said Richard.

'Yes, that's right!' She was delighted. He had instantly found the source of her verbal memory, had located it in their shared past. She felt again the power of what they had in common. No one – not even Brian and the children – would ever be able to offer her this kind of intimacy. There was no one else on earth who could help her to be brave enough to be nostalgic.

But something was not right. Something was missing. There was a voice that hadn't been heard. In the conversation between her and Richard there had been no explicit mention of her brother. Yet in all her memories there was Anthony: she and Anthony, Richard and Anthony, Anthony telling ghost stories, Anthony shrieking because they were tickling him – he was what these recollections could not do without. And suddenly she wanted to reach into them and pluck him out, to rescue him from the danger that, she now saw, had been hovering like a storm cloud over their blithe childhood games. She wanted to remove him from that stern house before it had a chance to harm him. To kill him.

Could she form a friendship with Richard, an invigorating new adult friendship, in which her brother and his death were never mentioned? Could they proceed as if nothing had ever happened? Could they exclude Anthony? No, it was clear to her that they could not. She was delighted that she had met her cousin, proud of herself for being bold enough to make it happen; but, much as she did not want to be locked in the past as her mother was, she knew now that she couldn't simply turn her back on it either. It insinuated itself into the present. It grew again, sprouting in the most inaccessible crevices. There must, she thought, be a position that lies between those who dwell wholly in the past and those who live entirely in the present. It would not be easy to identify it. But perhaps, if there were enough goodwill, she and Richard could help each other to find it.

Tears came to her eyes again. 'Please forgive me,' she said. 'I feel quite emotional.'

'That's okay,' said Richard. 'So do I.' The waiter returned with their food. Richard stood up and introduced her to her meal. 'Tessa – meet Rocquefort Salad,' he said. 'Rocquefort Salad – meet Tessa. Do you remember how we used to do that?'

'Yes. I do! I do!' And then she was laughing and weeping at the same time.

The first person Barbara ever fell in love with was a cattle auctioneer's daughter. The Christiaan Shweizer Players were plying their trade at a dorp in the Eastern Transvaal. They were to remain in the town for five days and then continue eastwards, towards Swaziland. Their repertoire now invariably included *My Vrou, Haar Man en Ek*, which, as Shweizer had morosely predicted, was a resounding success.

The day after their arrival the town was crowded with farmers from the outlying districts and even further afield. It was the first Wednesday of the month, which was the day set aside for the monthly cattle auction. Barbara, who had nothing better to do, wandered over to the clearing on the outskirts of the town to see what was going on. She found that this was one of the few occasions when the platteland cast aside its sloth. All about her there was shouting and bellowing, the crack of whips, swarms of flies and the smell of sweat and dung. People were selling vetkoek and koeksisters and boerewors rolls. The cattle were grouped in wooden enclosures and were moved slowly along until they reached the auctioneer's ring, around which the farmers sat on low wooden benches.

Despite Barbara's lack of interest in cattle or in farming, she too felt the excitement as the beasts were chased into the ring and the auctioneer's voice cracked the air like the sound of hail on a tin roof. He was a thick-set, balding man who looked no different from the phlegmatic farmers gathered about him. But when he began to speak, all the energy and movement of the day were concentrated in the urgent staccato of his voice. The cattle were offered for sale singly, in pairs and in small groups. There were Afrikaner cattle with their long, curved horns, Herefords with their red and white faces, Aberdeen Angus, black and squat with no horns at all, big-boned, black-and-white Friesland cows, their udders swaying as they walked, petite, round-eyed Jerseys. The auctioneer's voice made every beast seem worthy of the same attention, even the gaunt, toothless old cows. He urged the farmers to find merit in whatever was offered, to compete, to buy. He assured them they would regret it if they didn't. Everything was an opportunity not to be missed. Barbara noticed that very few cattle went unsold. It occurred to her that what the auctioneer was doing was not very different from what the Christiaan Shweizer Players did every evening: it was also a performance, and a highly successful one at that.

Seated next to the auctioneer were two young women. One was fair-haired and the other was dark, but they both resembled him: these were evidently his daughters. The fair-haired one was completely absorbed in the auction. Barbara, gazing at her, was fascinated by her fascination. The young woman must have witnessed many auctions, yet her interest was as great as if she had never before been present at one in her life. The dark-haired one, in contrast, looked thoroughly bored. She stared into space or studied her fingernails.

The next day Barbara bumped into the sisters. She went to the corner café to buy supplies for the Christiaan Shweizer Players and, as she was gathering up her purchases, they came in through the door. She smiled at them.

'You must have a big family,' said the fair-haired one. 'What a lot of milk and bread!'

Barbara explained to them whom it was for. 'I suppose they are my family,' she said. 'I never thought of them that way. But they're certainly nicer to me than my family ever were.'

'Lucky fish!' the girl exclaimed. 'Imagine travelling all over the country, doing whatever you like. And you're still so young. We never have *any* adventures.'

Barbara waited for them (they bought Coca-Cola and chewing-gum and XXX Mints), and then they walked down the street together. 'I saw you at the auction yesterday,' Barbara said. 'Is the auctioneer your father?'

They nodded.

Barbara introduced herself and held out her hand. They shook it, awkwardly. 'I'm Erna Louw,' said the dark-haired one. 'And this is my sister, Elna.'

'Are you kidding me?' asked Barbara. 'Erna and Elna?'

'Unfortunately not,' said Erna. 'Pathetic, isn't it?'

'Unimaginative parents,' said Elna. 'And we're not even twins.'

Erna, the elder sister, was twenty. Elna was eighteen. They chatted animatedly until they reached the dorp's only stop street. There Barbara turned left and they turned right. 'We're having a picnic tomorrow by the river,' Elna said. 'Under those trees.' She pointed to a clump of willows in the distance. 'Come and join us.'

'Okay,' said Barbara.

The next day, when she went down to the river, she found only the younger sister. She was sitting in the shade of one of the willow-trees, her blue cotton dress pulled up above her knees, her bare feet hidden by the long kikuyu grass. 'Where's Erna?' Barbara asked.

'She's not coming. She says she's not in the mood.'

Barbara wasn't sorry. Elna was the sister she liked more. She wanted to get to know her better, and it would be easier to do so if they were alone. She lay down next to her under the willow-tree and they listened together to the wind as it moved through the leaves. The light that reached them had a greenish tinge to it. After a while, Barbara began to feel as if they were lying in a sort of cave – not a dark, walled one, but a cavity made out of light and wind and hushed sounds. It reminded her of the secret donga where she had spent so many hours. She had always believed that that was a special place because no one else knew about it. She had been convinced that, if anyone happened upon it, it would be ruined – its specialness lost to her forever. Solitude was the only guarantee of its sweet, clandestine privacy. And yet, lying next to Elna, talking softly or saying nothing at all, she felt for the first time in her life that it might be possible for her to share her secrets with another person and still keep them for herself.

They met every afternoon in the same spot. They confided in each other, hesitantly at first, but then with a rush of confidence. Elna said that she wanted to become an auctioneer, but that her father had scoffed and said there was no such thing as a female auctioneer. Barbara said that if that was what she really wanted, she shouldn't allow anyone to dissuade her.

'But do you *really* think I could become an auctioneer?' asked Elna.

'Yes. I do. I think you can become whatever you want to be.'

Barbara had never come across anyone as easy to talk to as Elna. She told her about the bust of President Kruger and the surprises that her hands sprung on her. She even told her about William Moxley and what he had done to her. And that Barbara Lombard was not her original name. It felt good to unlock her secrets and spread them before her new friend.

Elna gasped when she heard about the name change. 'But you can't just do that!' she said. 'You can't just decide that you don't like your name and make up another one.'

'Why not?'

'I dunno. I'm sure there's a law against it.'

'Well, I don't care if there is. I'm not going to be burdened for the rest of my life with a name like Marie Moxley! And I don't want that man's surname.'

'But where does your new name come from? Where did you find it?'

Barbara told her. Elna was impressed. What a daring creature Barbara was – she left home, travelled around the country, even created a new name for herself by mixing and matching the names of Hollywood stars! 'I don't think I would ever have the guts to change my name,' she said. 'If I did, it would be so that I could have one that's not almost identical to my sister's. People are always getting them mixed up and calling me Erna and her Elna. I hate that.'

They were both subdued when they met for the last time, on the afternoon before the Christiaan Shweizer Players were to leave town. 'I wish you didn't have to go,' said Elna.

'I wish I didn't either,' said Barbara.

'I'll give you my address. Will you write to me?'

'Yes. I promise.'

'But how will I write to you? You'll be moving around the country.'

'When we're not on tour, we stay in a caravan park in Klerksdorp. You can write to me there.'

'Okay,' said Elna, but to both of them it seemed an unsatisfactory arrangement. Barbara's despair was profound. How could you scoop your secrets into someone else's hands and then be separated from that person? She didn't want to leave, but she knew she had no choice.

Elna was leaning against a tree-trunk. Her hair fell forward across her face. It was dappled by the light that sidled through the leaves of the willows. Barbara looked at her and felt that, although she had known this girl for only a few days, there was no one in the world to whom she felt closer. If only they could remain in their cave of soft light and soft breezes forever! The outside world always made everything difficult, but here was ease and simplicity: this was the place of perfect possibility.

A sudden impulse came over her. She couldn't resist. She leaned forward and tried to kiss Elna on the mouth. But Elna put out her arm to block her, pushing her firmly – but not violently – away. Then she leaned forward and kissed Barbara on the cheek, a quick, darting kiss. Neither of them spoke.

Barbara had heard people speak of 'mixed feelings' before, but until that moment she hadn't really known what it meant. Deep within her she felt the pain of what had just happened and she knew that nothing could ever assuage it. Rejection is rejection is rejection. It has no truck with euphemisms. It spares nobody, least of all women and children. But elsewhere, close to that pain and yet removed from it, she could feel the kindness of the refusal, even its tenderness. Where something hard and stinging could so easily have come pelting down, there had been instead a tactfulness as of soft rain. She parted from Elna that afternoon with her heart full of grief and gratitude.

Rejection is rejection is rejection; but gentleness does make a difference.

8   Locusts

AUTUMN, MOST soft-spoken of seasons, could not be heard at all there: the days were still hot and there was no relief from the sharpness of the light. The tiny Northern Cape town baked in the heat of a sprawling Indian summer, which, when it finally ended, would cease abruptly; and then, almost overnight, there would be winter. This was not a place of subtlety.

'I think you'd better wait in the car,' said Susan. 'I'd like you to go in with me, but we don't want to give them too many shocks all at once.'

'Fine,' said Slush. 'I'll wait here.' As she got out of the car, he leaned forward and grasped her hand. 'Good luck,' he said.

'Thank you.' She squeezed his fingers tightly. Then she opened the garden gate, walked to the door of the house and rapped on it with her knuckles. It was a small brick house with a zinc roof, set well back from the road. The garden consisted only of sparse lawn, a privet hedge and a few doleful cannas.

Slush tilted his seat backwards and made himself more comfortable. He switched on his music, but quickly turned it off again. The pounding urban rhythms were incongruous in this eerily silent dorp. He looked about. A man was sweeping the street, mopping his brow as he did so. Further down, another man, wearing a khaki shirt, khaki shorts and boots, climbed into his bakkie and started the engine. Two young boys leaped onto the back of it as he pulled away. In the house next to the one which Susan had entered, a woman sat on her stoep and stared at the car.

It was a placid enough scene and, at first glance, no different from what one would find in any dusty little dorp. But different it was. The bizarreness struck you only when you realised that there were no black people anywhere – even the street-sweeper was white. Rooiwater was the second such town after Orania to be established in the Northern Cape. All these unremarkable people, going about their business on this late April day, were white separatists who had moved to this bare and remote part of the country in order to be alone with their whiteness.

Slush tried to quell the uneasiness which rose up within him. He told himself firmly that these stolid people were the anomalies, not he. His life was in no way aberrant; he wasn't the one who was swimming against the current. It was the residents of Rooiwater – a town inauspiciously named after a bovine disease – who had been left behind, who had chosen to remain behind. They were lumbering dinosaurs, inexplicably and perversely still alive, although it was clear to everyone but them that their time had long since passed. The jaws of history ought by now to have chomped them to bits, there should have been no trace of them; yet here they were, sweeping streets and driving bakkies and staring at passers-by, apparently quite indifferent to their own obsolescence. He had known that such places existed, but had never imagined that he would find himself in one of them. There was, of course, no law preventing black people from entering Rooiwater, but for obvious reasons, very few ever did.

He was here because Susan needed him. It was as simple as that. She had phoned him early that morning, waking him up. He reached over Refilwe's sleeping body to lift the receiver – she stirred when the telephone rang, but didn't wake up – and heard at once that there was something wrong.

'What's happened?' he asked.

'I need you to come with me today,' said Susan. 'I have to go somewhere. And I don't want to go alone.'

'Go where?'

'To a very strange place. In the Northern Cape. We must leave at once.'

'Susan,' he said, 'start again. I don't know what you're talking about.'

'My sister is dying.'

'Your sister? But I thought…'

'Yes, I know. I haven't seen or spoken to her for nearly fifty years. But her family called me to say that she's dying and she wants to see me. It took them over a week to trace me. Eventually they got hold of a cousin I've been in touch with over the years and she told them how to contact me. There's no time to be lost. I must go at once. Please come with me, Slush.'

'Yes, of course.'

'It's asking a lot.'

'Is it?'

'She lives in Rooiwater.'

'What's that?'

'It's a whites-only town. You know, like Orania.'

'And you want *me* to go with you? Won't we be lynched?'

'Maybe. But seriously, I feel very apprehensive about this. Imagine seeing your sister after decades of no contact at all. And when you do, she's on her death-bed! I really need your support.'

'Of course,' said Slush. 'I'll fetch you in twenty minutes. We can go in my car.' It was not often that Susan admitted to needing anything. Invulnerability was her creed. He was the only person who was ever allowed to see what lay behind the carapace.

'Who was that?' Refilwe asked sleepily.

'Susan. Her sister's dying.'

'Shame. That's terrible,' murmured Refilwe and went back to sleep.

On the way to Rooiwater, they spoke little. Susan had a road map on her lap and gave directions. As soon as they were on the open road, Slush put his foot down on the accelerator and the car leaped forward. When they stopped to refuel, he bought sandwiches and cold drinks for them, but Susan wouldn't eat anything.

The landscape became flatter and flatter. Except for an occasional farmhouse, there was no sign of human life. Acacia trees squatted here and there, surrounded by yellow grass. It looked to Slush like a world abandoned rather then merely empty, deemed long ago to be not good enough, not able to compete with the allure of elsewhere. The countryside he had lived in until he was twelve years old had been verdant and full of undulating hills. He couldn't understand what he saw about him now – such a complete capitulation to flatness and drabness. He didn't know how to read it.

When they were about two hours from their destination, he leaned forward and switched on the air-conditioner. 'Can't believe how hot it is here,' he said. 'You'd think it was the middle of summer.'

Susan didn't respond to his comment, but the breaking of the silence seemed to encourage her to speak too. 'I used to think that if my sister died, I wouldn't even be aware of it,' she said. 'Unless my cousin happened to hear and let me know. And now I find myself rushing to Rooiwater to be at her death-bed. Talk about unpredictability!'

Slush's cellphone rang – or sang, rather, since it struck up a tune: *Hey, Big Spender*. He glanced at it, but shook his head when Susan offered it to him.

'Don't you want to answer it?' she asked.

'It's Refilwe. I'll call her back later.'

Something in the tone of his voice made Susan suspect that Refilwe would not be around for much longer, but she made no comment. Young as he was, there had been many women in Slush's life – some black, some white, some young, some not so young. (There had even been a Swedish businesswoman in her mid-forties.) He never discussed his love life with his mother, and she in turn never asked him anything about it. Their loyalty to one another was beyond question, but it didn't include certain kinds of intimacy.

'I wonder why she wants to see you?' he said. 'Your sister, I mean.'

'I really don't know. I suppose that imminent death has a way of concentrating the mind.'

'On what?'

'Unfinished business.'

'Do you think she wants to apologise? For the rift between you, I mean.'

'I doubt it. She doesn't believe she has anything to apologise for. She's merely been true to her beliefs.'

'Odd that two sisters should be so different,' mused Slush.

'Isn't it? One the mother of a black son, the other the widow of J. W. Greyling, a notorious right-winger. One trying to open the country up, encouraging people to visit it, the other living out her days in a whites-only town which was founded by her husband. Is it any wonder we've had nothing to do with each other for years and years? But I don't think our situation is unique – South Africa's full of these kinds of ironies. Someone told me the grandson of a former Nationalist prime minister has become an ANC member of parliament.'

'Is that so?' said Slush, but his response was perfunctory. He knew too little about Nationalist prime ministers to feel the full force of the irony. The silence that followed was interrupted by the cellphone as *Hey, Big Spender* started up again. Once more, Slush refused to answer, but this time he leaned forward and switched the phone off.

Now, as he waited in his car for Susan, he turned it on again, but found that there was no signal. Cellphones didn't work in Rooiwater. He put his head back and closed his eyes, but he wasn't sleepy. He tried to imagine what was going on in the house. Had Susan arrived in time? Was her sister still alive? Were they able to communicate? What do you say to someone you've been estranged from for fifty years? What does it feel like to come face to face with your past?

Where his own attitude to the past was concerned, Slush was not so much ignorant as impatient. What he didn't like about history was that it was beyond repair. He found hopeless causes distasteful and that was what the past was to him. Dwelling on it, as so many did, struck him as an unhealthy obsession; and it was clear to him, especially where apartheid was concerned, that those who couldn't or wouldn't let go of it (for whatever reason) were suffering from a chronic and probably fatal morbidity. His antipathy was visceral: his young flesh shrank from it as if from something mouldy and clammy.

He couldn't understand people's fascination with memory, either. The past is a field which has been laid waste, made bare by time, which is ever-hungry and sets to work on whatever lies before it; and memories are nothing more than what the swarms of time excrete as they move along. All that memory can tell you is that the great devouring has already taken place. He had his memories, of course, and some of them were tender ones: memories of the Zululand village, of his mother, of the rough kindness of his great-aunt, of his astonishment when it dawned on him that he and Susan loved one another and that they had, almost without being aware of it, become a family. But he did not wish to inhabit his memories, as some seemed to do. He was too preoccupied with present and future possibilities to spend much time looking back.

He opened his eyes and looked about with surprise. A small group of people, mostly children, had gathered silently about the car. They were staring at it and at him. Their curiosity was easily explained: they'd probably never seen a BMW convertible before, let alone one that had a black man at the wheel. The children were tanned and barefoot and their clothes were shabby. One little girl was sucking her thumb. When Slush looked at her, she averted her gaze, but as soon as he looked away, she resumed her staring. He felt uncomfortable, but didn't know what to do about it – he couldn't very well order them to vamoose. He closed his eyes again, but could think of nothing except the silent onlookers. He wished Susan would hurry up and return to the car. What was taking so long? Her sister had no right to be so long-winded: death-bed conversations, if they took place at all, should be brief and to the point.

He knew that he ought to despise all the residents of Rooiwater, but this tatty little group, especially the children, provoked in him a reluctant and grudging compassion. Wealthy white people were accustomed to the sight of indigent black kids; it was not often that a well-to-do black person, like Slush, found himself surrounded by a crowd of shabby white children. They were not begging, they didn't even speak to him; but in their silent and unfaltering stares there was something imploring. Their curiosity was of a sort that pained him. Children should not be growing up in such a place and in such a way. If Rooiwater had to exist, it should be reserved for old and dying die-hards, like Susan's sister.

Forty minutes later, the door of the house opened and Susan strode quickly down the path. The crowd of onlookers had by then grown in number. They made way for her as she approached the passenger door and then closed in again.

'Good heavens,' said Susan. 'You seem to have attracted quite a following.'

'I thought you'd never come,' grumbled Slush as he switched on the ignition. 'It's no fun, being stared at like this for an hour. I feel like some sort of freak.'

He expected the spectators to move away as soon as the engine started up, but they didn't. No one stirred. He inched the car forward, but still they did not disperse. 'Do they want me to run them over?' he asked. 'I can just see the headlines now: *White Children Run Over by Racist Black in Boerestaat.*'

'Use the hooter,' said Susan. He was about to do so, but found suddenly that it wasn't necessary. The crowd began to move, as if guided by an invisible force – some to the left and some to the right. They made a narrow pathway. Slush's silver car inched along, the engine whispering, impassive faces on either side. When he was clear of the crowd and moving more quickly down the main street of Rooiwater, he glanced back through the rear-view mirror. The group of onlookers were still standing more or less where he had left them, but they had merged again and there was no sign now of the little human tunnel through which he and Susan had escaped.

The news was told to Hannelie with painful, tender caution, as if they were informing her of a death. But she surprised them by receiving it calmly. 'How proud my father would have been to have had a grandson who is ambassador to the Netherlands,' she said. 'The rift between the two countries always grieved him. To him, Holland was like a mother who has rejected her own child.'

Noldie was surprised by this: Hannelie almost never mentioned her father and, when she did speak of him, it was with bitterness. 'Well, he wouldn't have been so proud if he'd known which political party I belong to!' he said.

'That's true.' She was pensive. And then she smiled, a dreamy, preoccupied smile.

Even when the day of the departure drew nearer, she showed no sign of falling to pieces. Where they had expected self-pity and a rapid descent into depression, they found instead a stoicism which was neither stern nor stiff, but which lay upon her as if it were a garment she had long cherished but had had no occasion to wear. Noldie couldn't hide his relief. He had been spared what he dreaded most. He had got off more lightly than he had dared to hope. Barbara, although pleased, was wary. What would happen when Noldie was gone? Would this resilience endure? And if it did, what price would have to be paid for it?

One Sunday morning, shortly before Noldie and Theresa's departure, they went to Cape Point on a family outing. The weather was good when they left home, but it soon became windy and overcast. Theresa made the children put on their jackets before she allowed them out of the car. Then she set off with them to explore the promontory. Barbara, who had no interest in sea views, accompanied them.

Noldie and Hannelie walked up the hill to stand at the spot from which one was reputed to be able to see the meeting of the two great oceans. Noldie knew that it was a fallacy, for this wasn't really where the chill Atlantic and the warm Indian crashed into each other. That happened elsewhere. But it didn't seem to matter: there was something in the high loneliness of the outcrop, the tumult beneath them, the great rolling entrails of the sea – now grey, now white, now dirty green – that seemed to engender its own conviction.

Noldie's body was tensed to resist the force of the wind, which sliced at him and made his eyes water. It was quite something to know that one was standing on the tip of a continent that began so fatly at the Mediterranean and grew slowly more slender until it dwindled to this almost absurd thinness. Confronted by this clamour of the abrasive seas, he felt that what he saw before him took the shape of a momentous utterance. This, it said, is where everything comes together. This is the realm of collision, of crossing.

Noldie was a devout rationalist and positivist, but on that day he found himself uncharacteristically susceptible to the persuasions of a to-do of wind and wave, a hubbub of encounters and endings. It said something that he could not but hear. Its message had to do with journeys: the old urgency, the old anxious resolve of journeys. And here he was, poised to make a journey, almost on his way to the Netherlands. Centuries ago, people from that country had rounded this very coast on their way to the East, had stopped to plant a few vegetables and forgot to leave. He was descended from one of those errant families. He was, as it were, the son who had been estranged for generations and was at last being welcomed back. He was a segment of a long, convoluted loop.

He looked at his mother. She was wearing a powder-blue anorak and had pushed her hands into its pockets. The wind was blowing wisps of her hair about her cheeks. He saw that the skin on her face was taut and seemed almost too thin to conceal the bones that lay beneath. She didn't seem to be depressed, but she didn't look well either. He had always sympathised with his mother's illness, but it was a remote compassion, such as one feels for a malady that one has never experienced and which is unlikely ever to afflict one. He commiserated without ever expecting or even wishing to understand. It would always, he felt, lie beyond him; and there was something consoling in that, for to understand it better would be to lie within its grasp. His incomprehension was a form of immunity. And so, although he would never admit it to Theresa, although he hated to confess it even to his own staunch and solicitous heart, he knew that when his mother had moved into illness, he had in turn nudged her away from himself and, keeping her within the word and business of love, had estranged her from its close embrace. Although he was not proud of it, ordinarily he would have found ways to justify it to himself: self-destructive people are dangerous; they drown their rescuers along with themselves; nothing is to be gained by coming too close to their lethal self-abasement.

But today the justifications would not do. Today, because he was indeed leaving her, he could not shift her to a convenient distance. Today the lack of love in so dutiful a son couldn't be rationalised away. Love, when it fails in the exertion, is not simply a withdrawal, an absence: it becomes a wasting force. It consumes and strips bare and enervates, turning the fat years into lean. It casts shadows instead of shade. He, the exemplary son, had done terrible harm.

He turned to speak to her. They had to talk loudly to make themselves heard. 'I'll come back to South Africa from time to time,' he said. 'You'll see me often. And it's only for a few years.'

'I'm not worried about it. I know I'll see you.'

'You've been so supportive,' Noldie said. 'I know this isn't easy for you, but you've given us nothing but encouragement. I'm really grateful to you, Mom. Theresa is too.'

'It's about time.' Hannelie turned her face away as she spoke and he had to lean forward to hear what she was saying. 'It's about time,' she repeated.

'What do you mean by that?'

'I mean that it's about time I stopped holding you back.'

'But you've never held me back,' he remonstrated. 'I've done everything I wanted to do – in my career, in my marriage.'

'Yes, I know. But I feel as if I have. I feel I've been a burden to you. I haven't been the kind of mother I wanted to be.' He began to protest again, but she interrupted him. 'Do you know what it's like to live with guilt, Noldie?'

'Guilt?'

'Yes, guilt. Guilt because my father was the prime minister and that's why they tried to kidnap you. Guilt because you were teased at school about it. Guilt because I left your father when I met Barbara. Guilt because again the children ridiculed you and you were forced to defend yourself and me. And, most of all, guilt because I've been so ill for so long.'

'But you didn't choose to be your father's daughter. And Barbara has been a better parent to me than Dad ever was. I'm grateful that you brought her into my life. And you couldn't help being ill. It's not your fault. I have no resentment about any of that.'

'But I have resentment! Don't you understand? I hold it against myself. I condemn myself every day of my life.'

Noldie didn't know how to reply to that. He gazed at his mother, saw her body contending with the wind, and felt that, small as she was, her frailty had suddenly vanished. What she had to say could no more be gainsaid than the sea itself. She was like an Old Testament prophetess, full of the power of prophecy, of implacable words. For years, he and Barbara had been telling Theresa how formidable Hannelie had been; they had defended the myth of her strength in the face of her weakness, her long decline. And now – but Theresa, unfortunately, wasn't present to see it – here was the old power and more. But oh, how sad it was! It was enough to make him weep. The invective was there, the stark denunciations that prophets must utter, but the words were all words of self-accusation.

And in that moment he understood something he'd never been

able to grasp before: *this* was where the key to his mother's illness lay. When she had renounced her father, her husband, her Waterkloof life, she had been powerful. She had been in the ascendant. But her heart had not absorbed the victory; it had not been able to summon the necessary boldness. It was a captive heart, trembling in anticipation of the punishment that would not come. A Calvinist heart. And the illness, the morbidity, had something to do with that, with the turning inwards of astringency. She had fled, but she hadn't escaped. She was a slave who had defied the taskmaster, but had not had the courage to accomplish her own manumission. Hers was not the sorrow of journeys made, but of journeys never undertaken.

Noldie wanted to tell her that just as he was about to leave her, he had come closer than ever before to an understanding of her denuded heart. He wanted to tell her that he was not free of guilt either. But how was he to say it? 'Will you come and visit us, Mom?' he asked. Hannelie looked at him in surprise, hearing the note of desperation in his voice. 'I know you don't like aeroplanes. But will you come and see us and stay with us in our home in The Hague? You and Barbara? Please say you will.'

'My sweet child,' said Hannelie. She beamed at him. 'My wonderful son. How blessed I am.'

Neil decided it was time to see Farrell again. Two days after the incident at Richard's flat, he had phoned the therapist to tell him that he was withdrawing from therapy for a while. Now, three months later, he was ready to return. He was taken aback, however, when Farrell told him his slot had been given to someone else and he had no openings at present. 'But then…what must I do?' Neil asked.

'There may be an opening later this month,' said Farrell. 'Phone me in about two weeks.'

Neil dutifully waited for two weeks and phoned again. A late-afternoon slot was offered to him and he accepted it.

The three-barred electric heater was on and Farrell was wearing corduroys – both infallible signs of the onset of winter. Otherwise, the small room was exactly as it had been when Neil last saw it. Through the one small window he had a glimpse of the mottled trunk of a tree outlined against the twilight. The setting sun was a reddish glimmer at the very edge of the fading afternoon.

Speaking in a flat voice, he tried to describe the encounter with Richard as accurately and dispassionately as possible. He concluded by saying, 'I haven't seen or heard from him since.'

'Have you tried to contact him?'

'No.'

The therapist didn't question him more closely about the incident, as he expected him to do. Instead he surprised him by asking, 'Why did you stop coming to therapy?'

'I'm not sure. I couldn't face the thought of talking about it. I suppose I was too traumatised.'

'Most people,' said Farrell, 'have the notion that therapy is where one deals with trauma. They don't stay away because they have been traumatised.'

'Yes, I know. I realise it sounds odd. But I felt…humiliated. I felt ashamed. I told no one except Helena.'

'You felt it was all right to tell Helena.'

'Yes, because I knew she wouldn't judge me. And she didn't. Not once did she say, "I told you so," although she could easily have done so. She tried several times to warn me. As you know.'

'You seem to be suggesting that you feel judged in here.'

'Maybe. Maybe not. I never know what you really think. So I don't know whether you're judging me or not. It's impossible to say. Helena is like Aunt Maisie – she always says what she thinks. You can agree or disagree, you can choose to take offence or not. It's up to you. But you never have to wonder what their true feelings are.'

'You consider that a good thing.'

'I do. There's something very reassuring about it. You always know where you stand.'

Farrell seemed fidgety, almost restless. 'Yet you've chosen to come back to therapy,' he said. 'You decided, after all, to tell me about it.'

'Well, in the beginning I thought of it as a catastrophe, something that had been visited upon me. All that was left for me to do was to decide whether I was going to survive it or not. And I wasn't sure which way it would go. I thought a lot about suicide.'

Farrell nodded, but – for once – made no allusion to Neil's mother.

'Now I see it differently,' Neil went on. 'It's not a calamity that has happened. It's something that's still going to happen, it's gathering on the horizon, it's happening now, it's not over yet. Either it's going to crush me or I'm going to overcome it. But at least I have a chance to fight back. And I need all the help I can get.'

'I see.' Farrell stroked his chin. 'And what is it that you have to fight? Richard?'

'No.'

'Then what?'

'I don't know. The shame. The guilt.'

'Guilt? Why guilt? Did you do something wrong?'

'I must have done,' said Neil, speaking very softly. 'For someone to treat me like that. To provoke behaviour like that in someone who's supposed to care for me – a person who is not, generally speaking, cruel.'

'You consider all the responsibility to be yours alone.'

'Well, I don't know.' It was now completely dark outside and the bulb above them provided an oval of light, like a large egg, in which they sat. The corners of the room were not lit at all. Neil looked at the therapist and suddenly – so suddenly that it took him by surprise – he felt a great spike of anger rising within him. Raising his voice, he said, 'What do *you* think? Why don't you stop asking me questions for once and tell me what *you* make of it?' He had never spoken to Farrell in that tone of voice before. He realised that he was furious with him, had been so for a long time, but hadn't known it until this moment.

Farrell said, 'It's clear that you're angry.'

'Yes. I am.'

'Can you say why?'

'Because you didn't warn me.'

'Of what?'

'Helena warned me. She said the friendship was dangerous. I even told you that she said that. Why didn't you also warn me?'

'Would you have heeded the warning? You didn't listen to Helena.'

'That doesn't matter. You should have warned me anyway.

Aren't you supposed to be concerned with my welfare? Why didn't you tell me to stay away from him? Didn't you see that I was going to be hurt?'

Farrell crossed and uncrossed his stubby legs. 'It's good that you're able to articulate these thoughts,' he said. 'It's good that…'

'Never mind that!' said Neil, interrupting him. He was almost shouting. 'You should have stuck your neck out. Ventured an opinion, even if it turned out to be wrong. You should have told me that something bad was going to happen. You should have said it's not safe to love a straight man.' His voice began to tail off and he spoke more softly. 'You should…you should have been on my side.'

Farrell glanced at the clock and said, 'Time's up, I'm afraid.' He said it more gently than usual. 'In fact,' he added, 'we've gone over time.' As Neil stood up, he said, 'I think this went very well. I feel we've made real progress.'

'So pleased it was good for you,' said Neil.

The *Promised Land Pleasure Tours* marketing team decided that, as part of their strategy, they would enlist the support of an expert, preferably a practitioner. Susan was asked to attend a meeting in the boardroom. It was chaired by Slush. He introduced her to Barbara Lombard, who had been flown up from Cape Town for the day to give her expert opinion. Susan introduced herself and leaned across the table to shake the sculptor's hand. Then she sat back and listened while members of the team told Barbara about the Boksburg Freedom Fist and described the potential embarrassment.

Barbara listened intently, interrupting them occasionally to ask a question. Her movements were brisk, even a little impatient. She was small and lithe and wore a smart black trouser suit. Spectacles dangled from a chain around her neck. Her hair was black except for a crest of grey which started at the widow's peak and spread outwards. Her mouth was stern, but Susan saw amusement in her eyes.

'It's delightfully garish,' she said. 'It's so grotesque that it almost deserves to come into existence. Maybe the world needs monuments to bad taste?'

'Maybe,' said Slush, giving a dutiful little laugh. 'But I'm sure you can understand that we don't want to be associated with it in any way.'

'Yes, I do see that. But what do you want from me, Mr…?'

'Just call me Slush.'

'What is my part in all this, Mr Slush?'

'We think it would help if we could quote you as an authority on sculpture,' said Slush. 'If we could say that someone who has had a career that has lasted for over forty years, who has exhibited her work around the world…'

'But why would they listen to me? If these people cared about art, they wouldn't have envisaged something like this in the first place.'

'I don't think the MM Group *do* care about art,' replied Slush. 'You're quite right there. But they care a whole lot about what people think. They can't bear bad publicity. If we can make them feel the sculpture's going to be scorned, especially by people in the know, then they may have second thoughts. And it'll be even better if they get the idea that the negative publicity is not going to please the politicians. Needless to say, ingratiating themselves with politicians is what this is all about.'

'But I don't have any political clout.'

'Yes, but you have been commissioned to do statues of well-known people.'

'That was quite a long time ago. I don't do that kind of work any more.'

'I don't think that matters. You can talk with conviction about the politics of monuments, of appropriate and inappropriate ways to commemorate important people. This is Nelson Mandela's fist, after all. Nobody wants to be seen as demeaning Mandela. Your views may make them realise how ill-considered this is.'

'Okay,' said Barbara. 'I'll do my best. How do we go about it?'

'We'll get a journalist who's sympathetic to our point of view to interview you. Ask you a bit about your career and achievements, to establish your credentials. Then lead on to the controversy surrounding the Fist. Get a few good quotes. Take a few pictures. All very professional and respectful. You say only what you truly believe. There'll be no mention of *Promised Land Pleasure Tours* at all. Then we'll use our contacts in the press to make sure that the interview appears in several publications by next week. There's no time to be lost.'

Barbara nodded. The team looked at her approvingly. Working with Susan had made them appreciate decisive people.

'We'll pay you handsomely, of course. For your time and your expertise.'

Barbara gave a dry laugh. 'If you like, Mr Slush,' she said. 'It amuses me that I should be considered an authority on anything at all. All I've done is follow my hands for forty-five years.'

'You're very modest,' said Slush, favouring her with his most lavish smile.

It was a smile few could resist, but Barbara seemed unmoved. 'Not really,' she said. 'By the time you get to my age, you find that you've left modesty and immodesty far behind. They both seem less and less important. So does hot-blooded ambition.'

Slush's smile faded. 'Can we do it this afternoon?' he asked. 'Or tomorrow morning?'

'It must be this afternoon,' said Barbara. 'I can't be away from Cape Town for more than a few hours. I told you that when you contacted me.'

'All right,' he said. 'We'll get hold of the journalist and tell her that it must be done now. Can we take you to lunch in the meantime?'

'Thank you, but I think that would be too time-consuming. Perhaps someone could bring me something to eat?'

'Certainly. What would you like?'

'A toasted sandwich. Or a tramezzini. Chicken mayonnaise. And a cappuccino.'

Slush inclined his head. 'Consider it done,' he said.

He nodded at the team to indicate that the meeting was over. They stood up and began to file out. Susan put her hand on Barbara's arm. 'May I have a word, Ms Lombard?' she asked. Barbara stopped and they waited until everyone else had left. Emptied of energetic young people, the boardroom looked like a shrine to a painfully sensitive god – one who had forbidden noise, dust and rust. The thick carpets ensured that footsteps were never heard. Everything shone, everything gleamed, including the plants: *Leaf It To Us* had been as conscientious as ever.

Susan did not speak and the two women faced each other silently. Barbara wanted to ask where the toilet was, but she waited instead to hear what this rather imposing woman wished to say to her. Finally Susan said, 'You're going to be very surprised by what I have to say, Ms Lombard. I feel I must tell you that we've met before. It was a long, long time ago. A lifetime ago. We were very young then. You may not remember me, but I remember you. I remember you very well.'

Barbara peered at her through her spectacles. 'Did we meet? I'm trying to…'

'You were with the Christiaan Shweizer Players. You came to our town. You knew me then as Elna Louw. We used to meet in the afternoons under a willow-tree. After you left we wrote to each other for a few months and then the letters stopped. I can't recall who stopped writing first.'

Barbara drew in her breath. 'Elna Louw!' she said. 'Elna Louw!' Her first instinct was to disbelieve, to repudiate. She thought of the tawny creature in the blue cotton dress, sitting in the green-dappled light; of the girl who had refused her kiss with such unwonted gentleness, such unbearable kindness. It was a memory that had assumed a mythical status in her life. What had it to do with this sleek, redoubtable denizen of the corporate world? But then she looked more closely and saw that it was true – undoubtedly true. Yet she still couldn't accept it. It was an extraordinarily eerie feeling. She felt as if her young self and her old self were encountering one another. It was not a happy meeting. 'Elna Louw,' she repeated. It was all that she could bring herself to say.

'So you do remember me?' Susan spoke softly, almost timidly.

'Yes. Of course.'

'I thought about you so often over the years.'

'And I of you.'

'You're a famous sculptor.'

'And you're a big shot businesswoman.'

'I learned a tremendous amount from you,' said Susan. 'You inspired me.'

'Did I?' Barbara was genuinely surprised. 'But we spent such a short time together. And our lives have followed such different paths.'

'Yes, I know. But your influence was greater than you realise. You were the one who told me that my father was wrong, that I could become an auctioneer. And so I did.' She pointed to the eastern wall of the boardroom on which an enlarged version of the *Promised Land Pleasure Tours* logo was displayed. The Table Mountain silhouette with the bashful morning sun rising behind it took up most of the wall.

'I don't follow,' said Barbara.

'Well, I don't sell cattle, like my father did. But I sell other things. I sell South Africa itself. Very successfully too, I might tell you. I'm really just a glorified auctioneer. I'm my father's daughter after all.'

Barbara smiled. 'Well, even if you are, I can't accept any credit for it. But I'm very pleased you didn't listen to your father.'

'And my name. I owe that to you too.'

'Your name?'

'Having almost the same name as my sister became more and more of a problem as we got older. There came a time when I wanted to have as little to do with her as possible. I won't bore you with that story. But we broke all ties. And I always remembered that you had changed your name. And I remembered *how* you did it. So I followed your example. I also looked to Hollywood. I took Susan from Susan Hayward and Southern from Ann Sothern – except that I put the 'u' back in Southern. And so I became Susan Southern. It was a very good name to have, especially in the days when my company was called *Southern Adventures and Safaris*. And it has served me well. It has brought me nothing but success and good luck. Now I'm so used to it I can't imagine having any other identity. And it was you who showed me the way.'

'This is all very weird,' said Barbara. She was amazed. How could their brief interaction, so long ago, have had these consequences? How could she have influenced someone to such an extent and not known about it? Elna Louw had stayed with her all these years, although, as time went by, she had faded as a person and became instead a template of lurking dreams. She had never imagined, however, that she had remained with Elna and been so important to her. She believed she knew precisely what the devouring past had consumed and what little it had spared; and yet she saw now that it was not at all as she had thought. And she would never have known about it had she not been asked to pronounce upon a pharmaceutical company's proposal to build an enormous fist in the veld!

Both women were silent. Their discovery overwhelmed them. The long, silent boardroom receded as they returned to what they had once been: Elna and recently-discarded Marie, sitting under the willow-tree and listening to the breeze and the river gushing past. They were scarcely aware of it, but, as they stood there, a gnarled old quarrel made its way into the impeccable boardroom, an antediluvian struggle between possibility and impossibility, between what is and what might have been. They did not recognise it for the ragged clash that it was: they perceived it only as a sound, barely audible at first but growing steadily louder, like the distant beating of thousands of approaching wings.

Barbara felt that she had to say something. 'What happened to Erna?' she asked.

'She's dead. She died just a few weeks ago. As I said, we were estranged for years and years. But I saw her before she died.'

There was another silence. 'I really need to go to the toilet,' Barbara said.

'And here I am bending your ear! I'm so sorry. Let me show you where it is.' As she held the door open for Barbara, a question came to Susan's mind. She wanted very badly to ask it, but decided that it would be too awkward, that it was better to set it aside. But then she found herself uttering it anyway. 'Tell me,' she said, 'did you ever...did you ever find someone?'

'Someone?'

'You know. Someone to love.'

'Yes.'

'I'm pleased. I really am.'

'But she became ill. I'm still with her, but she's not what she was. We're not what we were.'

'I'm sorry to hear it. But it was good when she was well?'

'Yes. It was. But the good days were a long time ago. And what about you?'

'No. I had lovers, but I never found love of that kind. It doesn't worry me any more. It's too late for it now anyway. But I have a son and I love him very much. At least I've had that in my life.'

'That's good.'

'You met him.'

'I did?'

'Yes. He's the one who chaired the meeting. The one called Slush. The young black man.'

'Oh, that one,' said Barbara. 'Is he your son? He's clever.'

'He is. I'm very proud of him.'

She showed Barbara where the toilet was. 'It was good to meet you again,' she said. 'After all these years.'

'After all these years,' repeated Barbara, holding out her hand.

'Slush will make sure you get your lunch.'

'I'm sure he will,' said Barbara. 'Thanks for everything.'

It struck her, as she went into the toilet, that neither of them had suggested another meeting. What they had found in the present had a past, but it didn't seem to have a future. And what was she to make of this extraordinary encounter? Was it indeed good that they had met again, as Susan had said? And if so, why? The discovery of what Elna had become grieved rather than delighted her; it scored the surface of a memory that had lain perfectly preserved for over fifty years and which she had long seen as secure in its purity. Did this mean that there was nothing the past could do to protect itself from the depredations of the present?

And that raised a broader question, which she pondered as she dried her hands (she was pleased to find soft white towels, not those dreadful steel tubes with their grinding hot breath). It all comes down to this: what do we really *want* from the past? Do we wish it to remain in a hermitage, or don't we? Why is it so difficult to decide? These struck her as deeply melancholic questions.

But she smiled to herself later when she reflected that Elna had indeed become an auctioneer (of sorts) and that she too had looked to Hollywood for a new identity. There was something touching, even endearing about the path Elna's life had followed. And what was it that had brought them together, that had made these discoveries possible? The preposterous Boksburg Freedom Fist! Fiction, if it had any self-respect, would have shunned such ostentatious ironies. It would not have dared to be so crass. But Barbara knew – had long sensed – this one thing about life: intrinsically it has no subtlety or proportion or compunction. If we want those, we must fashion them ourselves.

One night, just as he was falling asleep, Neil heard the telephone ringing. It didn't alarm him: he felt certain it was Helena. She had a habit of phoning him late at night. The telephone was on a small table in the entrance-hall. He switched on the light as he stumbled towards it.

'Fired!' said Helena as soon as he lifted the receiver. 'Can you believe it? The fucking bastards!'

'Who?'

'Those jerks who run Frangipani, of course. They've gone and fired me.'

'Are you serious?'

'Of course I'm serious.'

'But that's terrible. How can they do that?'

'Quite easily. They've already done it.'

'But why?' Neil struggled to take in what Helena was telling him and to make his sleepy head formulate the right responses. 'It just doesn't make sense. You had such a loyal following. Was it because of the jokes? Because you were being so tongue-in-cheek?'

'No, of course not. I *told* you they wouldn't be able to recognise irony if it bit them in the arse.'

'But then I don't understand…what could they possibly have to complain about?'

'One of their listeners wrote a letter of complaint. She said I was giving out inaccurate information.'

'I still don't understand.'

'She used to live in Kakamas.'

'Oh.' He sat on the carpet and pulled the telephone towards him. 'Now I see. How unfortunate.'

'She said she knew for a fact that there was never a teacher there called Herman Neutics. She discussed it with other people from the dorp to make certain. And lots of other things that I was telling people were wrong too.'

'But is that so terrible? Is it bad enough to fire you?'

'Apparently it is.'

'But this is awful. What are you going to do?'

'Oh, I've already got another job.'

'*Already*? So quickly?'

'Well, I've got a lot of contacts. And I'm good at what I do – everybody knows that.'

'Yes, you are. Well, I'm relieved that there's something else. I had visions of you having to come and work with me at *Time Immemorial Tombstones*.'

'No fucking chance!'

'So what's the new job?'

'Not very different from what I was doing before. It's for a station called Radio Blue Crane. They play mostly what they call classics and golden oldies.'

'From what period?'

'The 80s and 90s.'

'But….'

'I know, I know,' interrupted Helena. 'Don't even say it. It seems there *are* people who were born yesterday. Anyway, it's not for me to reason why. I just have to do the job.'

'But are you going to be happy there?'

'Probably not. I wasn't happy working for Frangipani. But a girl's gotta eat…'

'Yes, yes, I know. You told me that before. And this girl likes prawns and crayfish.'

'Langoustines. Not crayfish. Langoustines.' Helena sounded quite cheerful now. 'Ciao, Neil,' she said, ending the conversation abruptly. 'Speak to you tomorrow.'

'Bye.' He smiled to himself as he put the phone down. Helena's anger was as short-lived as it was intense. He wished he had that capacity to bounce back, to laugh things off.

As he got up to go back to the bedroom, he noticed something lying on the carpet. It was a plain white envelope. Someone had pushed it under the front door. He picked it up, saw the single word *Neil* written on it, recognised at once the big, sloping letters. He wondered whether he should open it and knew that he would; wondered whether he should toss it aside and leave it unread for several days and knew he must read it this very minute. He tore it open. There was a single page, hand-written.

Neil,

I shouldn't have waited so long to write this. If I had known exactly what to say, I would have written ages ago. It's clear to me that I owe you an apology. That much is easy. What's not so easy is knowing what to apologise for and how.

This much I can say: I am deeply sorry about what happened. You didn't deserve to be treated that way. You didn't deserve to be hurt. I apologise to you for the part I played in it. I say the part I played in it, because you played a part too, Neil. I hope you can see that. I can't apologise for it all, because, to be honest, I didn't do it all. You also need to accept responsibility for what happened that night. Even if it was mostly me, it wasn't all me.

If you can't see that we both did wrong, then it's unlikely that you'll be able to forgive me and I suppose there's nothing more to say. If you can, then perhaps we could try together to rescue something from this awful mess? Is there something left or isn't there? I believe there is, but it's up to you to decide. You know what I can offer you and what I can't. Is it enough for you?

From my side, I can say that I truly miss your friendship.
Richard.

Neil sat down and read it through twice, thrice, four times. He both liked and disliked it. What he liked best was the form in which it had come to him: the fact that Richard had not sent him an e-mail, but had written him a letter in his own hand and had taken the trouble to come and push it under the door. The sentiments that it expressed were less to his taste. There wasn't nearly as much contrition as he would have liked. There was far too much accusation within the apology. He had been prepared to assume responsibility for what happened when he discussed the incident with Farrell, but now he resented Richard's foisting it upon him. It was for him to decide, not Richard. What the letter did do, however, was confer upon him the power to determine what happened now, which was as it should be. But what decision would he make?

Whatever it was, he would not make it now. He wouldn't reply to the letter at once. He would talk to Helena; he would talk to

Farrell. He would take his time. He would keep Richard guessing. He would wait to see what his impulses would disclose to him. He couldn't ascertain yet the extent to which his heart had been made barren. Magnanimity might come; but then again, it might not.

He climbed into bed and switched off the light.

9 Darkness

A GROUP OF FIVE people waited in line at Cinema Nouveau in Rosebank to have their tickets torn. It was Friday afternoon, the five o'clock show, and already it was getting dark outside. The tickets were duly torn, they were advised to 'enjoy the show,' and the quintet moved on to take up their seats.

No one who saw them would have been able even to surmise what they had in common. It was a motley collection: four women and one man; four white and one black; one elderly, one middle-aged, two in their thirties, one in her twenties.

Striding ahead, pausing only to glance impatiently behind her as she waited for the rest of the group to catch up, came the elderly woman. She was tall, straight-backed and grey-haired. She led the others as if into battle. Behind her, walking much more slowly, came the black woman. She was short, dumpy and dressed as if she were going to church. They were followed by the woman in her thirties. She wore a calf-length black coat and was listening to messages on her cellphone. Then came the man. He was thin and walked slightly stooped. He was dressed smartly, in a suit and tie, as if he had come straight from work. At the back slouched the youngest of the group. Her hair was cropped short and she wore tackies, black jeans and a shabby black jacket. She was chewing what seemed to be an enormous wad of gum.

'Miss Bertha likes to sit on the aisle,' said Aunt Maisie as they took their seats. She filed in first, followed by Deanna. Helena and Neil took the next two seats. Bertha dutifully sat on the aisle. Almost immediately the cinema went dark, and, introduced by a blast of sound, advertisements and forthcoming attractions flashed onto the screen. Loud as it all was, no one had any difficulty in hearing Aunt Maisie's voice. She was addressing the person who was seated on her right. 'Young man,' she was saying, 'listen here. I'm giving you five minutes to finish your popcorn. What you haven't eaten by then, you'll have to do without. If you think I'm going to endure that dreadful scratching and crunching for two hours, you've got another think coming!'

'Okay,' said a meek voice, followed by the sound of rapid eating.

'There should be a law against it,' said Aunt Maisie, speaking now to no one in particular.

Getting this party together had entailed numerous logistical problems, not the least of which was the question of which movie to choose. Aunt Maisie wouldn't see anything which was likely to be 'schmaltzy'; she also had an aversion to science fiction, gratuitously violent films and remakes, which she invariably found inferior to the original version. Helena didn't like Merchant-Ivory, or anything that resembled Merchant-Ivory. Neil and Deanna were both opposed to romantic comedies. Deanna disliked animated films too. A sophisticated, keep-you-guessing-to-the-end, not-too-bloody thriller would probably have been the best compromise. But there was still Bertha to please, and she was the biggest problem of all, for she was deeply offended by nudity and four-letter words, and it was almost impossible to find a contemporary thriller that contained neither. 'Honestly,' said Aunt Maisie, 'it's like living with the old Censor Board – you know what I mean? But if we take her to the wrong movie, if there's one swear word or one bare breast – not to mention that floppy appendage that men like to wave around – I'll have her sulking and glowering for a week. It's just not worth it.'

Bertha was also not keen on foreign films with subtitles. This left almost nothing to choose from. After much debate, they settled on an Australian comedy which critics had described as 'quirky' and 'an unpretentious little gem'. It had a PG 13 rating. The first few minutes, however, revealed that it wasn't free of expletives, and Aunt Maisie drew her breath in sharply and groaned, as if suffering already from Bertha's impending disapproval.

Neil found it hard to concentrate on the movie, for he was still feeling unsettled by what had just happened. They had parked on the roof of the shopping mall, got into the lift and were travelling down to the basement, when it stopped and the doors opened. Three people stood there, hesitated as if unsure whether there was enough room for them, and then squeezed in. There was a middle-aged woman, a teenage girl and a short man with a large head. The man was Farrell. He was dressed in his usual winter garb of corduroys and jersey and was talking animatedly to the other two, but fell silent when he saw Neil. He nodded curtly and then looked away. Neil said, 'Oh, hi,' and felt foolish. Bertha chose that very moment to ask Neil a question about the price of tombstones and Aunt Maisie interrupted their conversation to relay something from the *Hatched, Matched and Dispatched* columns. The doors opened and Farrell and his companions vanished.

Neil was mortified. He had often imagined how he would react if he bumped into Farrell somewhere. His fantasies had included a number of scenarios in which he appeared to great advantage. In all of them he showed his therapist how efficacious he really was in contexts other than the quiet darkness of the room in which therapy took place. In one of his fantasies, he found Farrell stranded on the highway with a flat tyre and came to his aid. In another, the therapist was being mugged; Neil turned up unexpectedly and the startled (and heavily armed) muggers ran off. In the wake of this, the fact that he had probably saved Farrell's life brought an entirely new dimension to the therapy. In yet another scenario, they found themselves in the same restaurant, but Farrell was dining alone while he was surrounded by a group of laughing, appreciative friends. What he had never envisaged was that he would meet his therapist in a lift at the Rosebank Mall and that his companions in that encounter – who would insist on speaking to him, so that he could not even pretend that he didn't know them – would include his aunt and her housekeeper!

What would happen now? He hadn't been to therapy since he'd received Richard's letter. He wanted to talk about it and discuss his options. He didn't want to have to confront the awkward meeting in the lift, but he knew it would be difficult to behave as if it hadn't taken place. Would Farrell wait for him to raise it first? Would he have to talk about how it made him feel? And what about the two people who were with Farrell? There had been a time – not very long ago, in fact – when he had not had the slightest curiosity about his therapist. Now there was curiosity in abundance, but he didn't know if there were any way of satisfying it. Was he entitled to ask questions? Probably not. But who was the woman? She seemed much older than Farrell. Was he having a relationship with an older woman? Was he married, even though he didn't wear a wedding-ring? Was that a stepdaughter? Or was he on the wrong track altogether – perhaps they were Farrell's sister and niece? Some of the anger he had felt during the last therapy session returned. He was annoyed with Farrell for turning up so inopportunely, for embarrassing him. And yet he knew it was unreasonable. The therapist had as much right to visit the Rosebank Mall as he did. Or did he? Absorbed in these thoughts, Neil paid scant attention to the movie.

Bertha, seated beside him, was equally inattentive. Had Aunt Maisie known how preoccupied she was, she would have worried less about expletives and their consequences. Bertha had troubles of her own, a great many. Her woes weighed so heavily upon her that she couldn't see how they would be dislodged. God would lift them from her eventually, she knew that; but when would that be? He came to you in His own time; and His time was very, very long. Bertha's problems were of a more immediate kind. There was a good reason why she had asked Neil about tombstones: two more members of her family had recently been buried and their tombstones had to be erected before Christmas. She knew that she would have to make a significant contribution to the expense; in one case, she would probably have to pay the entire sum. And she still owed money for one of the funerals, her niece's husband's, which had taken place in May. Neil had given them a generous discount before, but would he do it again? At what point would he begin to say she must pay full price? Everyone knew that her employer's nephew sold tombstones and they all wanted her to exploit that connection on their behalf, but Bertha refused, saying that, if she did so, she wouldn't be able to get discounts when she needed them most desperately. And, even with the discount, how was she to pay for the next two stones? Miss Maisie had lent her money in the past, but would she be prepared to help her once more? Bertha knew that her employer resented the fact that she had attended so many funerals lately, but what was she supposed to do about it? Whichever way she turned, she was mired in obligation.

And the dead were not her only problem. There were several

family members who were ill. She prayed for their recovery, but in the dark of night, when she lay in her narrow bed in her little room in the servants' quarters at the top of the block of flats in Killarney, she found herself calculating over and over what their funerals and tombstones would cost. And when she got up in the morning, she was ashamed of herself for preparing in her mind (and in her lamentably depleted bank account) the funerals of people who were still alive. But she couldn't help it, for never had she known such a profusion of death.

The afterlife, to her, was a place of light: an orb shone there around the very end of things. But before that there was death, and in the paraphernalia of death, the struggle and the yielding, the wanting and the not-having, the privations that came before and those that crowded upon her afterwards, there was darkness: a terrible darkness. And it had become increasingly difficult for her of late to balance the darkness that was here against the coming of the light. The Lewis family did not believe in God. She didn't think any less of them for it, for she knew they were good people. Their atheism was an eccentricity, like preferring rice to mealie-pap: something to be indulged but not taken seriously. But for her, atheism wasn't an option. She had to find a way to understand why God, who had brought the world out of darkness and into light, sometimes allowed it to slip back into darkness again. Why did He do it? And why was granite so expensive?

Deanna too wrestled with her thoughts in the darkness of the cinema. It was almost a year since Richard had moved out, since the needle-stick injury. Her blood had continued to test negative and she no longer felt anxious about the possibility of having contracted HIV. She had escaped. Her life had been spared. She was relieved, yes. Exultant? No. Her responses to things both good and bad were characterised nowadays by an emotional flatness. The great anger of last August had gone; so had most of the misanthropy. People were not as dangerous as she had believed them to be. But that didn't make them particularly likable.

She knew she had scarcely begun to mourn her failed marriage and the very thought of the emotional labour which still lay ahead exhausted her. It presented itself to her as another Sisyphean struggle, to add to the ones with which she was already contending. She had never been able, for instance, to penetrate the darkness of her mother's suicide. Nothing she had been told about it by way of explanation brought her closer to an understanding. Her father, they said, was much older than her mother; he was staid and prudish where she was fun-loving; they belonged to different generations; they were hopelessly incompatible; her mother felt trapped and lonely; she suffered from post-natal depression at a time when very little was known of the condition; she never recovered from the depression prompted by the birth of her children; she was probably bipolar; she was possibly schizophrenic. All these sounded to her like rough outlines of a plot for a novel or a movie. They did not help her at all to do what she needed to do, which was to stand with her mother on the balcony of that penthouse flat in Sea Point and to see what she had seen.

And what of her father? There was little point now in going to see him, but she still went occasionally; so did Aunt Maisie. Neil refused to visit the Home. Physically, Archie was still quite robust, but he had ceased to speak, had ceased to respond to speech. He stared ahead, starting occasionally as if he saw something that alarmed him. His mind was now in its uttermost darkness.

Her mother and her father: two different kinds of darkness. If Aunt Maisie were right, if your parents do indeed give you whatever they have, whether you want it or not, were hers even now, in their different kinds of death, devising for her what they had encountered in their own lives? Had they prepared it even before she was born? Was darkness their greatest gift to her? Had she escaped one kind of infection only to discover that she had been infected since birth by her own parents? Was it right to be so afraid of one's mother and father, especially when one had already lost them both?

Thoughts of infection led her mind to cholera and bubonic plague and Aunt Maisie's introducing her and Neil to the joys of Yiddish curses. She remembered another word which she and Neil had learned from their aunt: *faribel*. Many Yiddish words and expressions, Aunt Maisie told them, couldn't be translated, or at least not in a way that did justice to their many meanings. *Faribel* was a good example. One could translate it as a grudge or a grievance, but it was much more than that. The best way of communicating what it meant was to describe the scenarios in which it was likely to occur. No Jewish wedding, for instance, is complete without a plethora of *faribels*. You have a *faribel* if you weren't invited to the wedding. Or if you were invited, but your offspring weren't. Or if you weren't seated at the main table. If you were seated too close to the band, too close to the kitchen, too close to the servants' table, too far from the smoked salmon and mock crayfish. If you weren't mentioned in the speeches. Or if you were seated at the same table as people with whom you already had a much-publicised *faribel*.

The thing about a *faribel*, Aunt Maisie explained, is that it's eternal. No reparations or reconciliations can ever really stem its flow. It lives on from decade to decade, even from generation to generation. And the best *faribels* are the ones whose origins are so obscure that no one remembers any more how they started or what they were about. In no way does that diminish the zeal with which they are perpetuated. In the end they are like cycads: among the oldest living creatures on earth, their very antiquity demanding respect.

She and Neil had been delighted by the concept. They enjoyed thoroughly the many examples which Aunt Maisie discovered amongst her acquaintances and with which she regaled them. It seemed you didn't even have to be Jewish to have a *faribel*, although Jewish people had turned it into a fine and nuanced art. 'But isn't it better to make friends with people?' Deanna asked once. Cherishing one's *faribels* contradicted what she had been learning in Bible Class. 'Isn't it better to forgive them?'

Aunt Maisie, who was lowering the back of the front seat of the Beetle so that Neil could clamber out, said, 'You mean like Jesus? Maybe, but it's not as much fun. Much better to wait until it's *your* wedding and then you don't invite *them*. Or you stick *them* as far away as possible from the main table.' Neil hopped out, she returned the seat-back to its upright position and slammed the door. 'Besides,' she said, 'many Christians still blame the Jews for

Jesus' death – and if *that's* not a *faribel*, and a fine old one too, then I don't know what is!'

Deanna found this much more persuasive than anything she'd heard in Bible Class and had no more qualms. But now she wasn't so sure. *Faribels* seemed more troubling than they had when she was a child. What was there between her and Richard if not a tangle of *faribels*? Did she want to live with them and nurture them for the rest of her life? No, she not. She might die with the unrelieved darkness of her parents still about her, but her failed marriage must be countered. Sisyphean struggle or not, it had to be braved.

She thought of the feud with which she was most familiar, the one between Richard's parents and Dorothy and her family. It was decades-old; it would no doubt endure until all the people concerned were dead (the older generation, at least; Richard told her he'd recently been reconciled with his cousin Tessa, who was returning to live in South Africa). The hatred and bitterness had calcified over the years and couldn't now be altered. And yet South Africa was in love with newness: one was bombarded by a rhetoric of newness (in its various manifestations) every day. One could scoff at it, certainly; one was inclined to be suspicious of its glibness. But it seemed to her that it was necessary to embrace it at some level; that to be closed entirely to it was a kind of darkness. It boiled down to this: what was the cost, the spiritual cost, of *faribels*? Did there not come a time when the past must be past?

As soon as the movie was over and the credits began to roll, Aunt Maisie pushed past the others and rushed ahead. 'Desperate for a cigarette?' asked Neil.

'No, I must get to a toilet at once,' said Aunt Maisie. 'I don't know what's happening to me. I used to have a bladder that was envied by everyone. It was as safe as a Swiss bank.'

Neil and Deanna looked at each other. When their aunt was out of earshot, Neil said, 'Not immune to the passing of time after all, it seems.' Deanna laughed.

They caught up with Aunt Maisie in the foyer. 'Feeling better?' asked Deanna.

'The Relief of Ladysmith,' said Aunt Maisie, 'was as nothing compared to the relief I feel.'

At last the children fell asleep. Theresa spread another blanket over each of them. Then she lay back and closed her eyes. She was exhausted, drained more by what had been required of her emotionally than by the last-minute preparations. But now, thank goodness, they were on the plane at last. She shook her head and said, 'No thank you,' without opening her eyes, when a voice asked her if she wanted a drink, and then regretted that she hadn't ordered a tomato juice: she always drank tomato juice on aeroplanes.

Hannelie had insisted on coming to the airport, even though Noldie begged her not to. 'Let's say goodbye at home,' he said. 'Please. An airport is so uncivilised – it's the least suitable place for farewells.' Theresa had the impression that Barbara, too, would have preferred to avoid going to the airport; but Hannelie wouldn't hear of it. And so there the two women had been to see them off. They were dressed in layers of clothing to protect them from the wet and cold of a Cape Town winter's evening. Theresa, watching them, had felt that there was more pathos in the emotions they suppressed than in the ones they couldn't hide; the tears they held back were far more affecting than those they couldn't help shedding. She had looked at Barbara and Hannelie as they hugged Noldie and the children and, for the first time, both women had seemed old to her: not elderly, not getting on a bit, but *old*. And she'd wondered how many years they had left and thought what it must mean for them to spend even a portion of that dwindling time away from Noldie and their grandchildren. But at least they knew their grandchildren – her father had died long before they were born. How he would have loved them! And how proud he would have been to know that his daughter was the wife of the South African ambassador to the Netherlands; that she and Noldie were to represent with pride the country which had made dignity such a struggle, such a pitifully small victory for him.

When Barbara and Hannelie had disentangled themselves from the children and come forward to embrace her too, she'd found, to her consternation, that she was weeping. 'These tears are for my father,' she'd told herself.

She heard Noldie's voice and opened her eyes. He was talking to the man who was seated across the aisle from him. His companion had a very pale skin and an almost bald head, the shiny dome of which stood out in the half-darkness of the aeroplane. 'I stay in hotels when I'm in Jo'burg or Cape Town,' the man was saying.

'But you say you're based in Toronto?' asked Noldie.

'That's my home. But I'm in South Africa at least two weeks of every month.'

'You must spend your life in aeroplanes.'

'I do,' said the man. 'That's the price I have to pay. You get used to it.'

'What work do you do?'

'Investment banker. You know, off-shore funds. That kind of thing.'

Noldie saw Theresa looking at them. 'Excuse my manners,' he said. 'I'm Noldie van Wyk. This is my wife, Theresa Abrahams. And these two little lumps,' he went on, pointing at the blanket-covered children, 'are our kids.'

'Pleased to meet you.' The man got up and shook both their hands. 'My name is Pilkington. James Pilkington.' When he stood before her, Theresa saw that he was quite a young man, perhaps in his early forties. From a distance he had looked much older.

'I'll have a two-hour wait in Amsterdam,' said Mr Pilkington, still standing and facing her. 'And then I catch the flight to Toronto. I'm looking forward to seeing my family, I must say – I saw them last at the end of May.'

'It must be very hard to be parted from them so often,' said Noldie.

'It sure is.'

'But is it really necessary?' asked Theresa. 'Can't you all be together?'

'Unfortunately not. I do a lot of my work in South Africa, but I don't want my family to live here.'

'Why not?' asked Noldie.

'Well, it's not a place to bring up children. Not if you have a choice.'

'I'd be interested to hear why you say that,' said Noldie.

'Oh, all the usual reasons. Crime. Declining educational standards. Poor economic outlook for the country as a whole. You have children too – I'm sure you also worry about these things. Perhaps you've also thought of emigrating?' He sat down again and turned so that he could look directly at Noldie and Theresa.

'Yet you still do business here?' Noldie stretched his legs out before him.

'Sure. There's lots of money to be made. I tell you, there are some very rich people in South Africa and they need someone to look after their money for them. Off-shore investment is what they all want – somewhere safe to stash their cash. And more and more of them these days are black. You see, the government says it wants to create a bigger and more powerful black middle class. But what we're getting instead is a black elite. The rest have had it, of course. They're done for. They're never going to get a foothold. That's why the country can't come right: too great a disparity between the rich and the poor. Doesn't bode well.'

'But aren't you helping to widen that gap?' asked Theresa. 'With the work that you do?'

'Probably. But hell, that's my job. I'm not here to solve the country's problems. In any case, it's not my country any more. I'm a Canadian citizen now.'

'This is most interesting,' murmured Noldie. 'Fascinating.' He sank down in his seat and tried to get comfortable. 'Well, good night, Mr Pilkington. I hope you get some sleep.'

'Say, what line of work are you in?' asked Mr Pilkington. He didn't seem to be sleepy at all.

Theresa spoke before Noldie could answer. She wanted the pleasure of saying it, of watching the man's face. 'My husband,' she said, 'is the new South African ambassador to the Netherlands. We're on our way to take up the post. Until recently, he was part of the government.'

'No kidding!' James Pilkington shook his head in amazement. 'Ambassador, eh? Well, it takes all types. I must say, I sure don't envy you that job.'

He settled back in his seat. Then he turned suddenly to Noldie again. 'Say, Mr Ambassador, what did you say your name was?'

'Noldie van Wyk.'

'Amazing. When I was at school I made a speech about a little boy called Noldie van Wyk. Haven't thought about it for years. He was the prime minister's grandson. They tried to kidnap him. Such a coincidence to come across someone with the same name.'

'The world,' said Noldie, 'is full of coincidences.'

The afternoon retreated swiftly, casting a little silver, a little russet, some smudges of pale yellow. And then the darkness came. It had been stretching and unfolding itself for months and now it was as deep and as long as it could go. Far, far away, in the Arctic, there was the midnight sun. But in this hemisphere it was the winter solstice, the longest night of the year.

For months the darkness had turned its face away, had counted softly, patiently, giving every opportunity to those who wished to hide. Now it said: *here I come, ready or not.* And then there were no fugitives, only those whom the night discloses.

The wooden gate, as one approached, stood ajar, which was unusual, but in the tiny garden there was nothing untoward: the same patch of lawn, the juvenile plants still tagged with their names and prices (the hibiscus already burned by the frost), a hose-pipe wound neatly around the tap, a watering-can, secateurs lying on the patio table.

The front door was open, which was strikingly out of the ordinary for this time of night. Within the little dwelling there was much that was unremarkable. The grandfather clock, ticking ponderously, stood as it always did in the entrance-hall. The same bulky couch divided the lounge and dining area, which were one room. On the sideboard, which took up almost an entire wall, were the familiar framed photographs (one taken during a graduation ceremony, the graduand's head bowed before the chancellor), two mugs (one commemorating the Queen's Silver Jubilee, the other her Golden Jubilee), three Toby Jugs and a porcelain dog. A TV programme, opened to 21 June, lay on the couch. In the kitchen the fridge hummed the same old tune. Two dishes, two knives, two forks and two glasses lay unwashed in the sink.

The further one went in, the more one was struck by what was aberrant. Glass and splinters of wood lay on the carpet near the front door. The television and video recorder were gone, torn out of their places in the wall unit. The safe, which was in the wall next to the toilet, gaped open. One chair was overturned. One vase was broken. In the bedroom the disorder was much greater. Clothes had been dragged out of the cupboards and tossed onto the floor. The dressing-table drawers had also been thrown on the floor; some of them were turned upside down.

There were two figures in the bedroom. Something was wrong with them both. One lay on the floor, next to the bed. It groaned and made a rasping sound as it breathed. The other, which was stretched out on the bed, arms spread open, made no movement or sound at all. It was still with a final stillness.

And so the telephone call that everyone dreads was made. But it didn't come at four in the morning, when one knows it for what it is. It didn't break anyone's sleep. It was 7.45 on the morning of 22 June, a typically crisp winter morning. Where the rays of the sun had fallen, the frost had already melted, but in the shade of the trees and bushes, there lay still a thick crust of ice. Deanna was hastily smearing fish-paste on two slices of toast. She was almost ready to leave for work. She answered the telephone without suspicion, not expecting for a moment that it would be anything out of the ordinary.

She heard the anguish in the voice before she took in what it was telling her.

Deanna sat with Richard outside the operating room. 'I wanted to assist,' he said, 'but they wouldn't hear of it. I begged them to let me.'

'They were right,' she said. 'You're not in a fit state to be operating on anyone.'

His face was ashen, but his eyes burned and glistened. 'This can't be happening,' he said. 'Please tell me this isn't happening.'

Deanna did not reply. Instead she put her arm about him and drew him closely to her. For a moment he lay quietly against her; then he pulled roughly away. 'Oh God,' he said, running his hands through his hair. 'If I'd left them in their house in Greenside, in that unsafe house, they'd still be okay. Instead I forced them to go to that place where they promised security, security and more security, and look what happens!'

The hospital corridor was empty except for a woman who was dipping a mop into a bucket and cleaning the floor with slow, rhythmical movements. Absorbed in her task, her head bent, she moved towards them without seeing them.

'I forced them to move,' repeated Richard. 'To that fucking *Majuba's Haven*. This is all my fault. How am I supposed to live the rest of my life, knowing that? I think I'm going to go out of my mind.'

'It's *not* your fault,' said Deanna firmly. 'You didn't do this, Richard. You didn't. Don't think that way. You had only the best of intentions.'

'Yes,' said Richard bitterly. 'My intentions were good. Oh, they were very good. But intentions are nothing in life. It's results that count. And the result of my actions is that my mother has been raped and murdered and my father is in there fighting for his life.' And then he leaned forward and groaned. His shoulders shook. Deanna held him tightly and made hushing sounds as if he were a baby. But she didn't really want him to stop. He needed to cry. And his tears were easier to cope with than his self-recriminations.

The hospital corridor was stuffy with the crackly thickness of artificial heat. Deanna pulled off her jacket and drew Richard to her again. The floor-cleaner was moving closer and closer to them, the part of the floor that she had already scrubbed extending behind her like a long dark tongue.

Richard blew his nose. 'What did the police say?' asked Deanna.

'They said it must have been an inside job. How else did they get into the complex? The guards must have been in on it.'

'But why your parents? Why not someone else?'

'I don't know. How must I know?' He rubbed his eyes with the back of his hand. 'Sheer bad luck, I suppose.'

'What did they take?'

'Not much. TV, VCR, my father's gun from the safe. Some of his suits. Some money.' He spoke flatly, but then his voice rose as the note of anguish returned. 'But why can't they just *take*? Take what they want and go? Why must they kill and rape? What kind of people are these?'

'I don't know,' said Deanna. 'I really don't know.' She didn't know how to respond to any of his questions. But perhaps it didn't matter. What he needed right now was not to have his questions answered, but to be held tightly. While his mind was lacerating itself with the knowledge of what had been done, of how dangerous people are, of how there is never a refuge, he needed to be reminded, as soon and as often as possible, that there is another side to living as a human being amongst human beings. He needed to be told it, even if it was far too soon to expect him to hear it. The closeness of another body had to find a way to convey to him, as nothing else could, that there is a human gentleness; that it has not been wholly extinguished; that it comes forward when it has a chance, when violence recedes.

The floor-cleaner came up to them and began to clean around their feet, her mop brushing up against their shoes. She was humming to herself, very faintly. She took her time. Eventually she moved on.

One read of incidents such as this almost every day, Deanna reflected. Violence in their society was unremarkable. It was only when you knew the victims that it shocked you. Otherwise it simply passed over you; it looked you over and went elsewhere. And you overlooked it in turn. She knew that if this had happened to strangers, she wouldn't have been perturbed by it. She would have glanced at a brief newspaper report (probably on page four) – *Couple Attacked in High-Security Retirement Village; Wife Raped and Strangled, Husband Stabbed* – and thought nothing of it. It would not have struck her as egregious. Such incidents were commonplace, run-of-the-mill. And even when people bemoaned the banality of violence, their lament itself sounded platitudinous.

She nudged Richard. 'Look who's here,' she said softly. Richard followed her gaze. They saw Neil in the distance, moving slowly, like an astronaut, down the long corridor. Deanna had phoned him before she'd left her house. She knew that the friendship between the two men had soured and that they didn't see each other any more, although neither of them seemed inclined to tell her what had happened. But it didn't matter: at such a time, nothing mattered. Richard needed every friend he had.

She was seated on Richard's left. Neil approached and sat on his right. He hugged Richard, wordlessly.

Hours later, when the surgeon emerged, he found the three of them huddled silently together. He knew Richard and Deanna: they had all been to medical school together. 'I think he'll be all right,' he said. 'He's lost a lot of blood and we had to remove his spleen, but we've managed to stop the internal bleeding. I think he'll pull through. He's a tough old guy.'

'Yes,' said Richard. 'Tough. Yes.' He spoke as if someone were prompting him. Then he got up and shook the surgeon's hand. 'Thank you, Ibrahim,' he said. 'I can't thank you enough.'

'Don't you want these, Miss Maisie?' asked Bertha. A plate of shortbread lay untouched next to the teapot.

'No, not today, Miss Bertha,' said Aunt Maisie. 'I don't feel hungry.'

The two women had returned from attending the memorial service for Elaine and were having their afternoon tea later than usual. The service had been held in the little non-denominational chapel at *Majuba's Haven*. Events involving religion always put Aunt Maisie in a bad mood and this one had a particularly inflammatory effect. She suppressed her annoyance until she had an opportunity to be alone with Deanna and Neil. They were in the parking lot, waiting for Bertha: she had joined a long line of people, mostly residents from the retirement village, who were queuing patiently to offer Richard their condolences and enquire about his father.

'All we heard was God being praised!' said Aunt Maisie, lighting a cigarette. 'I can't understand it. Why does a being who can bring an entire cosmos into existence need to be praised? If I were the creator of the universe, I would find all the praise embarrassing. I'd say, "It was no big deal, really. Please don't mention it. It's just a little something I threw together when I had six days to kill. And as you can see, it's a very amateurish first attempt – full of errors. I hope to do better next time."' She opened her large black handbag and tossed the lighter into it. 'If I'd been responsible for bringing forth something so imperfect,' she went on, puffing savagely, 'I'd be filled with contrition. I tell you, the only God I could ever even begin to accept is a humble one.'

'I'd better go and see if Richard is all right,' said Deanna. 'I'm sure he wants to go back to the hospital.'

'And besides,' said Aunt Maisie, ignoring her, 'to offer praise now is particularly inappropriate – you know what I mean? Elaine had her faults, but she certainly didn't deserve such a terrible death. It's too ghastly to contemplate. Why praise a God who allows things like this to happen?'

'Here comes Bee-Bee,' said Neil. 'You'd better change the subject.'

Bertha clambered into the Beetle and Aunt Maisie drove off. The car announced the change from first gear to second with a loud whine followed by a grunt of appeasement.

Bertha picked up the tray and began to walk to the kitchen. 'I think we should place an insertion in the *Hatched, Matched and Dispatched*,' Aunt Maisie said to her. 'I never had much time for the Slaters and I'm not going to pretend now that I liked them. I can't bear that kind of hypocrisy. But we must acknowledge it in some way. It's the right thing to do. I'll show it to you before I send it in.'

'All right, Miss Maisie,' said Bertha.

A few minutes later, when Aunt Maisie went to look for Bertha, she found her loading the washing-machine. 'Here, this is what I've written,' she said, pushing a square of paper into her hand. Bertha put on her spectacles and read what her employer had penned in her striking copper-plate hand.

SLATER
Elaine. Died tragically 21 June. Deepest sympathy to Jock and Richard. Wishing you strength during this very sad time. From Maisie, Deanna and Neil Lewis and Bertha Nyathi.

'Well, what do you think?' asked Aunt Maisie. 'It's plain and to the point, but at least it's not insincere.'

'It's okay, Miss Maisie,' said Bertha.

'Good,' said Aunt Maisie. 'I'll phone it in at once.'

Although she hadn't said so, the insertion was distasteful to Bertha in every way. She knew, however, that there would be little point in criticising it. She wouldn't be able to make Miss Maisie understand what was wrong with it. She wouldn't see that its terseness was so ungenerous that it would convey no compassion at all. To Bertha, the death notice resembled a room that was almost bare except for an iron bedstead, a chair and a lamp. There was no softness, no embrace in it at all. How could one expect bereaved people to find solace in such a room?

After three days, Jock was moved from Intensive Care to a high-care unit. He was heavily sedated and slept most of the time. When questions were asked of him he seemed to understand, nodding or shaking his head, but he didn't speak. He was being fed clear fluids. Richard never left his bedside, except when he went to the memorial service. He couldn't bear to be parted from his father. He felt as if he needed to be there all the time to protect him, although he didn't know what he was protecting him from. Above all, he wanted to be useful. He took over some of the work of the nurses, changing Jock's drip, checking his blood pressure, filling in the readings on the chart at the foot of the bed. He thought how he had never even hugged his father; and now he touched the old man's body and rubbed it and turned it and stuck needles into it. And it was right that he should, for he had to do what little he could to assuage the contempt that had been visited upon that body.

There were two beds in the ward and the other was empty. He threw himself onto it at night. For hours he lay there, listening to his father's breathing. He had thought he knew what a hospital sounded like at night, but he experienced it now as if for the first time. In its rhythms, there was something reassuring, but also something heedless and remote. They kept him awake. And when he did at last manage to drop off, he was jolted out of his sleep by clanking noises and the sound of breakfast trolleys.

Deanna came to keep him company as often as she could get away from work; so did Neil. Occasionally they would converse in subdued tones, but mostly they sat silently. Jock lay on his back, his chest rising and falling. Richard could not reconcile this long, almost skeletal prostrate form, fed by tubes and drained by a catheter, with the imposing man he'd known all his life. His memories of Jock bypassed the stroke and the cooped-up, peevish man in the retirement village and went back to the house in Greenside. He remembered him in his study, seated behind the desk or pacing to and fro on the carpet, saying, 'Anarchy is the greatest threat.' He looked at his father's straining chest, the yellowish-white of the skin visible between the bandages, the ribs showing through: his old man's chest. What could such a chest withstand? Surely, when every breath seemed so great an effort, it must give up the struggle? But it did not. The sight of the laborious swelling and subsiding, of such a determination of breath in so feeble a chest, filled Richard with a sense of unbearable pathos.

The police said they were following 'certain leads'. They were still convinced that at least one of the guards was in cahoots with the assailants and had helped them to gain entry and to leave again without being detected. There was no doubt in their minds, they told Richard, that their first instinct had been correct and that it was indeed an 'inside job'.

During the long hours of his vigil, Richard pictured again and again what must have happened. He saw the surreptitiousness, the cold, quiet strategy of the violence-makers. And then he saw what was revealed when the stealth was cast aside. He saw the stabbing; he felt it. He saw the throttling; he felt it. He saw the forcing, the cynical violence of the rape. He tried to think of his mother, to find memories of her that were not subsumed and elided by her death, but he couldn't. He recalled her indefatigable loyalty to her husband and son, her love for them that shrank always from judgement, that could not function – could not be what it was – unless it found no fault. Could he not be comforted by those memories, by a love which, however inaccurate, was always tilted in his favour? No, he could not. For those whom she loved had not seen the danger. They had not saved her. They had not been loyal to her loyalty, had not made love efficacious; and when love is not efficacious, it is nothing at all. The men who came under cover of darkness had obliterated her steadfastness, her incorrigible, imprecise fidelity. And Richard felt as if they had made him forever an accomplice.

He would never be free of these faceless men, these murderers and rapists. He knew that he would have to contend with the images they enjoined upon him for as long as he lived. The prospect of having them forever in his head, contaminating everything else that resided there, of being unable for the rest of his days to think an unsullied thought, filled him with a despair that terrified him. For the first time in his life, he began to understand why some people feel they have to sever themselves from themselves, why they embrace grotesque forms of freedom.

He gave Deanna the keys to his flat and asked her to bring him his toiletries and a change of clothes. She brought him his mail too. He flicked through the heap of letters and telegrams, skimming the messages of condolence. They did not move him in the least: they were too formulaic, too constrained by people's evident inability to approach what had happened, to draw close to him, standing as he was both at the centre and in the wake of calamity. They were all intimidated by his grief. The only exception was a letter written on lined paper, of the kind that one finds in exercise books. He saw at once that much time and care had gone into the writing of this message and understood that he in turn needed to respect the effort that had produced it.

Dear Dr Richard,

When I see you at the church, my heart is too full. What can I say to you? I can say nothing. So I must write a letter. To tell you that I pray for you all the time. And for your father. To tell you that God will look after you. He will stand by you. I cry with you, Dr Richard. But I know He will wipe away your tears, slowly, slowly. Your mother will come to peace. He will bring her into a place of light. God bless you.

Yours sincerely,

Busisiwe Bertha Nyathi [Miss Bertha]

Richard read the letter several times. He was greatly moved by it; moved to tears. He didn't share any of Bertha's beliefs: what to her had the status of absolute truth was a thin, even dingy superstition to him. And Bertha herself was not an important person in his life as she was in Deanna's and Neil's. She was merely Aunt Maisie's employee, her devotion to him affording an amusing contrast to Aunt Maisie's grim disapproval. What affected him was the way she had felt the impulse to reach out to him though her letter. He was struck by the boldness of the hope it expressed, the certainty that lay within the diffidence of the language. *He will bring her into a place of light.* He did not believe in an afterlife, didn't think for a moment that Elaine was anywhere, least of all in a place prepared for her by God. But Bertha's saying so, testifying so, seemed to confer in itself a kind of light on Elaine and, indirectly, on him: a light that had nothing to do with the empirical fact of the extinction, the nothingness of his mother. Bertha, in proposing light, was casting some of her own.

He heard a tapping sound in the corridor outside the ward. It came nearer and nearer and then stopped. He looked up. A thick-set elderly woman, leaning heavily on a walking-stick, stood at the door. Richard presumed that she had come to the wrong ward and was about to ask her if he could help her to find her way. But something made him pause and look at the woman more closely.

Slowly he got to his feet; slowly, very slowly, he moved towards her. When he was facing her, he said, with almost no inflection in his voice, 'Aunt Dorothy.'

'Hello, Richard,' said Dorothy.

'Do you remember the Metro-Goldwyn-Meyer lion?' asked Helena. 'You know, the one who roared and rolled his head at the end of the movie?' She and Neil were having coffee in Melville. The winter sun was strong, but in the shade, where they sat, it was cold.

'Of course,' said Neil. He wondered where this was heading. Talking to Helena was a bit like being lead blindfolded: you never knew where you were being taken.

'I really loved that lion,' said Helena.

'So did I. We all did.'

Helena waved her hand in dismissal. 'But not any more. I've

gone right off him. Gone off lions altogether. Can't even look at them.'

'Why? What…?'

'Listen to my show tonight. You'll understand.' She glanced at her watch. 'I'd better go.' She fumbled in her bag.

'Don't worry about the bill,' said Neil. 'This one's on me.'

'Thanks.' She continued to rummage, dug something out and tossed it onto the table. 'Here's a present,' she said.

'A present? What for?'

'Does one have to have a fucking reason to give someone a present?'

'I suppose not. Thank you.' He picked it up. It was a CD. On the cover was a sepia photograph of Helena. She was sitting on a couch, her face cupped in her hands, looking pensively into the distance. Her name appeared at the top of the picture and, at the bottom, the words *Voetstoots: Songs Old, New, Borrowed and Blue.* Neil drew in his breath. 'I don't believe this. But why didn't you *tell* me that you made a CD?'

'I like surprises.'

'This is wonderful!' He stood up and embraced her. 'I'm thrilled for you. And what a great title!'

'I always wanted to use the word *voetstoots,*' said Helena. 'The nightclub has closed, but now the name lives on.'

'I can't wait to listen to it.'

Helena waved good-bye and set off down the street. 'Hey, don't forget to tune in to Blue Crane tonight,' she called out. '8 o'clock.'

'I won't,' Neil shouted back.

'I might find a way to bring back Mr Herman Neutics,' she said.

'Oh God, no. Please don't.'

'I simply can't play it straight any more,' said Helena. 'Try as I might. Can't get my tongue out of my cheek. I've become a serial subversive.'

'But you'll get fired again!'

Helena's response was inaudible. She disappeared from view.

That night, Neil turned his radio on and fiddled with the dial until he found Radio Blue Crane. He endured several advertisements before Helena came on the air. 'I'm Helena Verster and, as always, it's a great pleasure to have your company,' she said. 'Sit back, relax, and enjoy our selection of fine music. This is Radio Blue Crane.' A scampering little melody started up and Helena, speaking against it in slow, sonorous tones, recited what was evidently the station's slogan:

We're proud as the noble lion
Shaking his golden mane
Proud of the Rainbow Nation
We choose Radio Blue Crane

Neil laughed and laughed. He couldn't remember when last he had laughed so much. Was Helena really doomed to utter this little poem at regular intervals? No wonder she had 'gone off lions!'

'Life is full of contrasts,' Helena went on. 'I learned this when I was still at school. I was lucky enough to have a wonderful, inspiring teacher. His name was Mr Harry Clitus. He was a swarthy man who spoke with a thick Greek accent. Opposites, he told us, are always coupled together. We think they are at war, but they're simply conversing. Underlying everything is connection. Take it from me, listeners, we appreciate love only because we know hate and indifference. We value light only because we know darkness. And here is a song that illustrates that perfectly. On Radio Blue Crane, 88.7, the Station for Committed South Africans, we bring you another classic: Celine Dion and Peabo Bryson in their duet from the movie with the same name: *Beauty and the Beast.*'

Neil listened for a little while longer. Then he turned off the radio and switched on the CD-player instead. He played Helena's CD from beginning to end. More than half the songs were her own compositions. Some of them – like *Genetically Modified Lover* and *The Road Never Travelled* – he'd heard before. But there were several that were new to him. One of these, the second-last song on the CD, was called *Plato's Cave.*

All the old haunts
Just didn't feel right

I'd nowhere to go
On a Saturday night

I wanted to jol,
I wanted to rave
And then I heard
About Plato's Cave

Plato's Cave
Small and poky
Plato's Cave
Hot and smoky
Plato's Cave
Dimly-lit
Plato's Cave
Shadows flit

Drove there at once
Pushed through the throng
Thought they'd know me
But I was wrong

Showed them my profile
And my silhouette
Said I'd much to learn
Even more to forget

Plato's Cave
Small and poky
Plato's Cave
Hot and smoky
Plato's Cave
Dimly-lit
Plato's Cave
Shadows flit

They waved me in
Little could I see

Shapes came, shapes went
In thick obscurity

Faces averted
Turned to the wall
Eyes preoccupied
Closed to me, all

Plato's Cave
Small and poky
Plato's Cave
Hot and smoky
Plato's Cave
Dimly-lit
Plato's Cave
Shadows flit

Helena phoned later that night, before he went to sleep. 'I see what you mean about lions,' said Neil.

'To think I saw *Born Free* five times!' said Helena. 'And cried each time. Little did I know what lay in store for me.'

'Your CD is fantastic,' said Neil. 'I'm proud of you.'

'Ciao,' said Helena. 'Speak to you tomorrow.'

Jock was declared out of danger. He began to speak a little, but seemed to have no memory of what had happened, for he made no reference to the events of the night of 21 June. He asked for Elaine. The doctors felt that it was too soon to tell him that she was dead. Richard still spent most of the day with him, but felt that it was no longer necessary to spend the nights at the hospital too.

For the first time in almost two weeks, he returned to his flat. He unlocked the door and stood there in the darkness, which was relieved only by the flashing light of the answering-machine and the tiny lights emitted by the nest of plugs around the television set, VCR and CD-player. Nothing seemed familiar to him. Had he ever lived here? Had he ever lived anywhere, except in the old house in Greenside? He remembered pretending to be sick on the day after the English Orals, lying in bed, listening to the sounds of the house. He could recall every detail of that day, and yet he could scarcely remember the months – was it almost a year? – he had spent in this flat. It was evident to him that the Greenside house was the only home he had ever known, the only one he would ever know.

He switched on the light, walked through the flat to the kitchen and filled the kettle. Then he wandered back to the sitting-room and listened to the messages on the answering-machine. They all said much the same thing and in the same hushed tone: *so sorry; appalling tragedy; thinking of you; hope your father's all right; please let us know if we can do anything.*

And then came a message that was startling in its incongruity: bright words suddenly tumbled towards him, inappropriate as laughter at a funeral. It was the voice of someone who clearly had no idea what had happened. 'Dr Slater,' it said, 'this is Beryl Curtis. I hope you're well. I've been trying to reach you on your cellphone, but it never seems to be switched on. I feel sorry for your patients, if they need to get hold of you! Anyway, please call me as soon as you can. There's good news. I think we have a lead at last.'

10 Death of the First-Born

THE INTERVIEWS with Barbara Lombard appeared as arranged. She gave a very lucid explanation of why she thought the Boksburg Freedom Fist was not a good idea. Her views made an impact and led to articles in several newspapers: *Fist Ill-Considered; An Insult to Madiba, Says Veteran Sculptor*. The *Promised Land Pleasure Tours* team congratulated themselves on their strategy.

But then something happened which made the controversy surrounding the Fist almost irrelevant. The Apartheid Memory Park itself was suddenly in jeopardy. Work had begun on the foundations and huge earth-moving machines began lifting the soil. The driver of one of the machines summoned the foreman: he had found, he said, what seemed to be a cave or hollow area beneath the surface. A rock had cracked open and, lying beside it, was a human skull. The tsotsis, they thought, must have killed someone and buried their victim in the open veld. He showed the foreman the skull, which seemed to be crushed in on one side. The foreman summoned the police, who removed it. They took very little interest in the case. Even if foul play could be proved, it was most unlikely that the tsotis' victim would be identified or that the crime would ever be solved. It was obviously an old murder and they were preoccupied with more recent ones.

But there was something odd about the skull. The police pathologist had never seen anything like it. He sought the advice of others. Experts were called in, and that was when the great revelation was made. If this person had indeed been killed by tsotsis, then there must have been tsotis on the highveld for much longer than anyone imagined, for the skull was thousands and thousands of years old. The earth-moving machines had unearthed a hominid of exceptional antiquity. The open piece of veld on the East Rand was potentially a palaeontological site of unprecedented richness, outstripping even the renowned diggings in the Cradle of Humankind.

A road-house called *Oom Toeka's* (specialising in tripe, pap-en-vleis and morogo) was to have been demolished to make way for the Apartheid Memory Park. It was a landmark; no one could remember a time when it hadn't been there. It was initially called *Van Toeka Se Dae*, but the first owner decided that that was too much of a mouthful and shortened it to *Toeka's*. A subsequent owner was a portly man with a thick white beard. People began to call him Oom Toeka, so he renamed the road-house once more: it became *Oom Toeka's*. In recent years, it had had a succession of black owners and there were few who recalled the portly man, but the name was retained. Someone made a joke and said the hominid that had been unearthed must be the original Oom Toeka. The name stuck and soon everyone knew the newly-discovered progenitor as Oom Toeka.

There was no doubt that he was ancient, extraordinarily ancient. It had not yet been established precisely how old he was, but one famed palaeontologist, when interviewed on TV, said it was quite possible that Oom Toeka was the oldest hominid ever found; he could well be the first-born of our race. Compared to him, he said, Mrs Ples was a parvenu. She was the palaeontological equivalent of a fashionable housewife from Sandton, he quipped. The newspapers made much of his remarks: *Oom Toeka has no rivals; Mrs Ples a 'Sandton Kugel'* ran the headlines.

The MM Group wished at first to go ahead with the project. They announced that they would give the excavators time to go over the site carefully, to see whether any of Oom Toeka's relatives had been interred with him. Then the construction would resume. But there was a public outcry. Letters of protest appeared in the newspapers: *Save Oom Toeka's Tomb*, they urged. The other shareholders, including *Promised Land Pleasure Tours*, very quickly saw that it was in their interest to align themselves with the supporters of Oom Toeka: they declared that they could not, in good conscience, back the major shareholder in its determination to persist with the project. The MM Group, beset from all sides, backed down.

Susan, never one to miss an opportunity for good publicity, arranged to be interviewed on the very spot where the long darkness of Oom Toeka's slumber had been so rudely interrupted. She wished to make it clear that, as soon as the significance of the skull was disclosed, her company had sought to withdraw from the project. *Promised Land Pleasure Tours* had always cherished

South Africa's rich heritage and they would continue to do so. 'They might decide to build the Apartheid Memory Park elsewhere,' she told her staff, 'or they might not. It really doesn't matter. The brownie points we can get out of this will be worth more to us than a dozen theme parks. This is like manna from heaven. Oom Toeka is a great find in more ways than one.'

She and Slush waited for the camera equipment to be set up. The open piece of veld was bordered on three sides by factories. In the northernmost corner were the great mounds of reddish earth which the machines had turned up before their activities were so unexpectedly halted. The highway made an arc as it curved towards and then away from the square of yellow grass where they had assembled. Aeroplanes, taking off or coming in to land, made an intermittent din above them. There was something in the air which told of snow on distant peaks. Susan drew her coat more closely about her.

A more incongruous burial site for Oom Toeka could not have been chosen. He ought to have lain at the foot of a crag or beneath the roots of a vast baobab. Silence and hollowness should have colluded to fashion a place for him which did homage to his hoary old age; which respected his Adamic status. Instead he'd been plonked in a spot which was now right in the middle of factories, highways and an airport, within sight of mine dumps and slimes dams. To be woken ungently from a long, long sleep is bad enough; but to be roused to so extreme a bathos must be intolerable.

Or is it? Maybe they had it all wrong. Everyone presumed that Oom Toeka would be shocked by modernity in all its crassness. But what if he were not? He might have been in his lifetime a progressively-minded antediluvian, who laid himself down to die with the full and confident expectation that unimaginable change would come. He would not then have felt the impulse to be chauvinistic about his own age, would not have regarded eating chunks of raw meat and wearing shaggy animal skins as the last word in sophistication and taking only two hours to make a fire as the apex of ingenuity. Such an Oom Toeka would already have made peace with the archaism of his own life and time and would have been inclined to take the long view. In that case, highways and cars and shopping malls and aeroplanes wouldn't disconcert him in the least. He would expect nothing less. Looking about him now, he would see not the differences between his age and the present one, but the similarities. He would feel dejected to find how small and few are the steps that have been taken. He would dismiss his admirers as troglodytes. How dismaying it must be to rise from a bed of primordial slime, only to be confronted by a fresh and smug atavism!

'Are you ready, Ms Southern?' called one of the technicians. Susan nodded. The interviewer held out her microphone. Slush, who was talking on his cellphone, smiled encouragingly and gave her the thumbs-up.

Susan cleared her throat and spoke the words which she and Slush had prepared. Oom Toeka, she said, deserved to be treated with respect. If, as the evidence increasingly suggested, Africa was indeed humankind's place of origin, then Oom Toeka needed to be greeted by the continent at its best: Africa as the guardian and repository of old traditions and old things. What he should be preserved from was the other Africa: the one in which expedience and exploitation were rife. Oom Toeka was the first to have lived and died; and the first should always be honoured. It was no coincidence that he'd come to light in the very spot where the Apartheid Memory Park was to have been built. Post-apartheid South Africa was a place of new sensibilities and new priorities. Saartjie Baartman had been rescued from ignominy and Oom Toeka should not now be subjected to it. The management and staff of *Promised Land Pleasure Tours* were proud to have intervened on his behalf from the start. Oom Toeka, Susan said, had been displaced; but he had also come home.

'I owe so many people an e-mail or a letter,' said Tessa. 'But I can't bring myself to write to them. I suppose I'll have to reply sooner or later.'

'Why don't you want to write?' Brian, sitting on the carpet, was trying to connect the VCR.

'Well, what am I going to say? Should I send them each a postcard? *Weather unbelievable, even though it's mid-winter. Children settling well. House roomy. Garden sprawling. Please visit soon. P.S.: my aunt was raped and murdered.*'

Brian smiled faintly, then shook his head. 'I still can't believe it,' he said. 'I mean, I never met your aunt. But to think that so soon after our arrival…'

'After we told everyone that we'd be safe – that things weren't as bad as they'd heard. What are we going to say now?'

Brian lifted the VCR, turned it round and studied it gloomily. 'Why do they make these things so damn complicated?' he muttered. 'And the instructions make no sense at all.'

'We had to defend our decision before,' Tessa went on. 'To people in London. To your family. To my mother. Now it's almost impossible to defend. Those who predicted murder and mayhem will say, "You see, we told you so."'

'But why do you feel the need to defend it at all?'

'I don't know. But somehow I'm expected to. People always have to justify their lives to others. Especially when they're seen to be going against the grain.' She moved towards the kitchen. 'Do you want something to drink?'

'Yes,' said Brian. 'Rooibos tea.' He pronounced it *roo-boss*.

'Don't know how you can drink that stuff,' said Tessa, as she switched the kettle on.

'It shows how quickly I've become indigenous,' said Brian. 'The next thing is rugby. Then I'll acquire some road rage. If I weren't a vegetarian, I'd be eating biltong and that long dried sausage – what's it called?'

'Dried wors,' said Tessa, re-entering the sitting-room.

Brian tried to say 'wors', but *vause* was the best he could do. He pushed the VCR aside and threw his hands up in despair. 'I don't think we're ever going to be able to watch videos. I feel defeated by this thing.'

'Let's ask Richard to look at it when he comes round.'

'When's he coming?'

'I don't know. Maybe next weekend.'

Brian stood up. 'How do you think he's coping?' he asked.

'I'm not sure. It's hard to say. On the surface he seems okay, but…'

'I feel for him,' said Brian. 'I really do. No one should have to go through that. Have they arrested anyone yet?'

'No.' The water had boiled. They walked into the kitchen

together. 'He said something very interesting about that the other day,' said Tessa. 'He said he wants the killers to be caught, of course. He wants justice to be done from a legal point of view. They should be locked up for the rest of their lives. But then he said that whether they're caught or not, they'll always remain faceless to him. Even if he stood before them and looked them in the eye, they'd still be faceless. A person who can do something like that, he said, will always be to him a person without a face.'

'Hmm,' said Brian. 'I must think about that. Quite a deep sort of character, your cousin.'

'I suppose so. I don't know him very well. We're rediscovering each other.'

The winter sunlight had motes of dust in it. Tessa looked through the window at the yellow lawn at the back of the house and the bare fruit trees: they would be able to eat plums and yellow-cling peaches in the summer, the landlord had told her – if the birds didn't get to them first. For years she had visited South Africa only in the summer and had forgotten how dry the highveld winter was; how strong the sun, yet how ungenerous in what it would not reach and would not warm. Suddenly she felt cold: cold with an intimation of what regret would do to her if it came.

'Brian,' she said, 'have we made a terrible mistake?'

Brian, handing her a mug – he preferred to drink his tea in a cup – said, 'I don't know. All I know is that it's too soon to say. We have to give it a proper chance. We can't give up so soon. We've made a lot of sacrifices. So have the kids.'

'But I'm not talking about the usual settling-in difficulties. Everyone goes through those. What I mean is: will we ever get past what's happened to the Slaters?'

'I'm sure we will. We're all still in a state of shock…'

'But has it not ruined everything?'

Brian, who had been rummaging in a cupboard, emerged, waving something triumphantly. 'I *thought* there were more of these,' he said. 'Another great South African invention – Tennis Biscuits. What were you saying?'

'Nothing,' said Tessa. 'It doesn't matter.' She couldn't explain why the death of an aunt she hadn't seen in years, who meant very little to her, should threaten their new life. It brought home, of course, the dangers of a society in which everyone seemed to know at least one person who had been murdered; some knew several. In the wake of the attack on the Slaters, they had hastened to install all the security measures Dorothy had insisted on and more, although they all knew that no one could have had more security than Elaine and Jock – and what had it done for them? Security had become an act of faith, an expense you resented and grumbled over and paid for anyway. It loaded the dice a little in your favour, but that was all.

No, it was more than that. Somehow the attack on the Slaters had compromised her homecoming. No matter how successful her family's adjustment, there would always be something that was not right, that had sullied the hope, the conviction to which their return attested. She had been quietly proud of herself for being able to embrace new possibilities in the place of old pain. It hadn't been easy. She had had to do battle with her mother; she had had to contend with the ever-sadness, ever-darkness of Antony. But she had done it. She had said, in effect: *I am coming back in order to move on. I am turning round so that I can go forward.*

And now she felt that something had destroyed her first-born hope. It had vitiated what was most commendable in her desire to come home. There was something that had turned away from the supplication of her return, had hardened its heart. And she didn't know precisely what that something was, but she knew it was inimical to newness. It would not tolerate a transformation of any kind – not even the most modest of miracles.

Maybe, she thought, we're all still on the outside, mistakenly thinking we've entered. Perhaps we're standing on the doorstep, waiting to be admitted, and are persuaded that we're already within. What if there is no hospitality after all, none of the welcome that makes arduous journeys tolerable? If so, we must settle for a glimpse of a land we'll never enter: the land afar off. Vouchsafed a vision of what could have been, we must resign ourselves to the fact that the milk and honey are not for us. We will never be part of an arriving generation. We will remain encumbered by shadows. Our fate is to see what could have been and turn away, stricken with a mortified heart.

She had felt *patriotic* – sheepishly, shyly so, for the stern circumstances of her upbringing had taught her that patriotism is, at best, suspect. But suddenly it had seemed possible. It had been part of the new configuration. And there was no reason, rationally speaking, why what a small group of vicious men had done should have anything to do with her patriotism. But somehow it did. It warned her, it chastened her. Tenuous as the connection was, it reminded her of what she'd known and had chosen to forget: patriotism is always an unrequited affection.

Too soon, Brian had said; too soon to say. He was right, of course. But what if it were also too late?

He was speaking to her. 'I'm sorry,' she said. 'What did you say?'

'Which month?' He sipped his tea appreciatively. 'This *roo-boss* is *good!*' he said, not waiting for her reply. 'Why didn't you introduce me to it before? Dorothy could have sent it to us.'

'I'm quite sure you can buy it in London,' said Tessa, 'if you know where to go. Tennis Biscuits too. What do you mean – which month?'

'Haven't you been listening to *anything* I've been saying? I asked you which month we're supposed to prune roses in this country.' They were at least thirty rose bushes in their garden, including several creepers and about a dozen old, thick-stemmed standards.

'July.'

'It's July now.'

'Well, we'd better do it then, before they start making new leaves.'

The electric gates swung open and Richard drove down a long, winding driveway. A large white house stood at the end of it, a double-storey with a thatched roof. Two gardeners, bent over their work, looked up as he drove past. Not only were the grounds vast, but they were on more than one level: steps led down to a smaller, sunken garden which had a fountain at its centre. In the distance there was a gazebo and, set in a low wall, a gargoyle, water dribbling out of its mouth. The lawns and flowerbeds were being watered by sprinklers. Everything was astonishingly green for a Highveld garden in July.

'What a mansion!' said Neil. 'It looks like your relatives are loaded. And perhaps they're itching to give you vast sums of money, to make up for having given you away.'

Richard laughed. 'I doubt it,' he said. 'People who have that kind of money are very good at hanging onto it.' He glanced at Neil. 'Thanks for coming with me,' he said. 'This may turn out to be a false lead. In fact, it probably is. I'm determined not to get my hopes up. But I wanted you to be part of it, whatever happens.'

'I'm touched,' said Neil. 'I really am. It's a great privilege.'

'Well, you've been in on it from the start. It's only right.'

He parked the car in the driveway and they walked towards the front door. Despite what he'd said, Richard felt nervous and anxious. His heart was beating and his mouth and lips were dry.

A young black man met them at the door. He mumbled something which they couldn't catch and led them down a flight of stairs into a large sitting-room which looked out onto the sunken garden. As they entered the room, a middle-aged white woman came forward to greet them. From a distance she looked as if she were in her fifties, but, as she came nearer, they could see that she was older – maybe even a well-preserved sixty-five, Richard guessed. The young man stood silently next to them as the woman approached. He was oddly dressed for a manservant: he wore a Gucci sweater, stonewashed jeans and short black boots.

Richard held out his hand to the woman. 'I'm Richard Slater,' he said. 'And this is my br...I mean my friend, Neil Lewis.'

She shook their hands. Her grasp was firm and certain. 'Dr Slater,' she said, 'Mr Lewis. So good to meet you. I'm Susan Southern.' The manservant stepped forward too, hand outstretched. 'And this is my son,' Susan went on. 'Nhlanhla Gumede-Southern. We call him Slush.'

The hand-shaking concluded, they sat down. 'May I offer you something to drink?' Susan asked. 'I can ring for tea. Or a soft drink, if you'd prefer.' Neil and Richard declined. 'Maybe later,' said Susan.

There was a brief silence. The swish-swish sound of the sprinklers came through the open window. Susan cleared her throat. 'First of all, Dr Slater,' she said, 'I want to thank you for coming to see me.'

'Not at all,' said Richard. 'I'm the one who should thank you – for getting in touch.'

'Well, I happened to see the advert in the newspaper. And I spoke to that woman – what's her name again?'

'Mrs Curtis,' said Richard.

'Yes, Mrs Curtis. I take it she makes a living out of this – tracing long-lost relatives?'

'That's right. She has a business called *Relative Success.*'

'I told her I would rather communicate directly with you. So I haven't discussed with her what I wish to reveal to you today. But she did give me more information about the circumstances of your adoption.'

'I believe so,' said Richard.

'What she said convinced me that I do indeed have something to tell you.'

It was taking unbearably long to get to the point. Richard struggled to contain himself. He thought of *The Importance of Being Earnest,* of Jack's turning to Lady Bracknell and imploring her: *Lady Bracknell, I hate to seem inquisitive, but would you kindly inform me who I am?* He wished he could come up with something like that, something that would make this woman hurry up and say what she had to say.

They could hear Slush's fingers drumming on the arms of his chair. He crossed and uncrossed his legs. Susan leaned forward and looked directly at Richard. She said, 'The first thing I must tell you, Dr Slater, before there's any misunderstanding, is that I am not your mother.'

'You're not?'

'No. Definitely not. I have never given birth to anyone.'

'But then…'

'If I'm right,' she went on, 'and I'm pretty sure that I am, then – I'm sorry to tell you this – your mother is dead.'

'Oh.'

'She died earlier this year. Her name was Erna Greyling, *nee* Louw. She was my sister. My elder sister and only sibling.'

'But how…'

Susan held up her hand. Speaking calmly, matter-of-factly, she told them about her long estrangement from her sister and about the deathbed meeting a few months earlier in Rooiwater. She explained to them what kind of dorp Rooiwater was. Her sister, she said, had been the wife and then the widow of the town's founder and chief ideologue. 'It was very strange to see her again after so many years,' she said. 'Undoubtedly the oddest experience of my life. The last time I had seen her she was a beautiful young woman, her whole life stretching ahead of her. Now she was in her seventies, riddled with cancer, her life rapidly coming to an end. The people who were looking after her left us alone together. And while I sat there, listening to what she had to say, my son waited outside in the car.' She smiled at Slush and her features softened.

'Don't remind me,' said Slush, shuddering. 'Man, that place was *weird!*'

'Anyway, what was even more curious was that she didn't simply want to see me before she died. She wished to confide in me. She told me, she said, what no other living person knew.'

'But why would she confide in you? Considering that you had had nothing to do with each other for so long?'

'I'm not sure. I've gone over it again and again in my mind. All I can think is that, even though our lives went in such radically different directions, we still had a shared history. Even the fifty years in which we had nothing to do with each other couldn't take that away. It seemed to me that confiding in me was her way of trying to acknowledge that shared history. She couldn't bring herself to apologise for the rift between us – not even on her deathbed – but she was determined to tell me her secret. Perhaps it was her way of making up to me. Of giving me something. I'm not sure. I felt strongly that she was desperate to tell *somebody* before she died. She knew I wouldn't judge her – which is more than one can say for those Neanderthals in Rooiwater. She made her life with them, but I had the impression that dying amongst them was not as gratifying an experience as she'd anticipated, even though she was their queen, so to speak.'

Slush's cellphone burst into a jangling rendition of *Hey, Big Spender*. Richard shifted irritably in his chair. Slush glanced at the phone and switched it off.

'She told me,' Susan went on, 'that she'd been pregnant in the early 1960s, years before she got married. She didn't explain how she managed to conceal her pregnancy.'

'Didn't you ask her?'

'No. She didn't encourage me to ask questions, she wanted me just to listen. Anyway, she said that when the baby was due, she went to Johannesburg and was admitted to a Home for unmarried mothers. She gave birth almost immediately to a little boy and told the staff to put him up for adoption. She had no idea what happened to him afterwards.'

'Did she ask you to try and find her son for her? Before she died?'

'No.' Susan spoke more softly. "I'm sorry. I would be lying to you if I said that. She made no such appeal. You see, I'm convinced that what she told me had more to do with me than with her son. The sharing of the secret was of much greater importance than its content.'

'But when you saw the advertisement in the newspaper, you decided to get in touch?'

'That's correct. She gave me this knowledge, I thought, even though I didn't ask for it; and now here's someone who wants it. Do I give it to him or not? I decided that, in telling me, she had given up control of her secret. It could easily have died with her, but she chose not to let it. And so now it has to make its own way and do what it will, for good or ill. I got in touch with Mrs Curtis. And the more I heard, the more convinced I became that the mysterious woman who disappeared from the Countess of Athlone Home was Erna.'

'What made you so sure?' Richard hadn't moved. His gaze was fixed on Susan as hers was on him. Neil and Slush watched them silently, their eyes moving from one to the other as they spoke.

'Well, she gave the name Rena Niemandt. Rena is an anagram of Erna. And *niemandt*, as you know, means nobody. But there's more to it than that: our best friends when we were growing up were some children called Niemandt. And she said she lived in Low Street – and Louw, as I have told you, was our surname. She went to great lengths to keep her identity a secret from the staff at the Home. But there are just too many coincidences. I was convinced, when Mrs Curtis gave me these details, that it was her. And now I'm absolutely sure that you are her son.'

'Why do you say that?'

'Because you look like her, Dr Slater. It's one face.'

After this, they all sat in silence. In one of the upstairs rooms someone turned on a vacuum-cleaner. Neil, looking at Richard, saw a muscle twitching in his jaw. He wondered what was going through his mind. What must it be like to search for so long and so tenaciously, and then to find that this is how the search ends?

Richard broke the silence. 'And from what you could gather, she didn't tell anybody else about it?'

'That's right. You can imagine how an illegitimate child would go down in the conservative circles in which she moved. And it was the 1960s, after all.'

'But she told you who the father was?'

'No. She didn't. That she refused to divulge.'

'But there must be *someone* who knows?'

'I don't think there is. That part of the secret, at least, died with her. I have a hunch that it was Greyling himself: that she had an affair with him when he was still married to his first wife. His wife died some years later and then he married Erna. But by then she was too old to have more children. I can't be certain, but it seems to me the most likely scenario.'

'How am I going to find out?'

'You're not. As far as getting information, this is where it has to end. You can go to Rooiwater and ask questions, but I assure you that you'll get nowhere. They know less than we do. And even if they knew something, they wouldn't tell you. You can't imagine what an insular lot they are.'

'That's putting it mildly!' interjected Slush.

'I see.' Richard looked down at his shoes. For a long while he said nothing. Then he rose abruptly to his feet. He was breathing hard. 'So that's where it all ends: *nowhere*. I've got to say, this must be the anti-climax to beat all anti-climaxes.' He turned to Susan. 'I'm sorry. I don't mean to be rude. It's very good of you to have gone to this trouble. It's just that it's devastating to look for so long and come up with nothing.'

'Well, I don't know. It depends how you look at it.' Susan stood up and walked towards him.

'I don't understand.'

'We may not always find what we're looking for, but, provided we haven't closed ourselves off to the possibility of it, we may stumble across something else in the course of our search, something we weren't expecting. It all depends on one's attitude.'

'I still don't understand.'

'Richard – may I call you Richard? You didn't find your mother or your father. I know it's a bitter disappointment. That hope is certainly dead. But does everything have to come to an end? Here' – she pointed to Slush and then to herself – 'here, if you'll have us, are a cousin and an aunt.'

Richard looked at her and then at Slush. 'I…I don't know,' he said. 'That's not really…'

She reached over and took his arm. Her movements up to now had been clipped, even brittle. But this gesture, although unexpected, did not seem incongruous. 'Richard,' she said. 'Don't go yet. Come, let's sit down. Let's have some tea. I have a lot to talk to you about. I want to tell you about your mother. About our childhood. About our father. You know, he was a cattle auctioneer, of all things. I want to show you how beautiful Erna was – I've got photographs. I want you to know why we quarrelled. Please don't go.'

Richard hesitated. Susan released his arm. 'All right,' he said at last. 'Thank you.' He sat down again.

At first Slush couldn't see what all the fuss was about. Richard's drive to find his biological parents was unfathomable to him. His mother had not shown the slightest compunction in giving him away; why then bestow so much effort on her? Why chase after those who don't want to be found? Why want those who don't want you? Nothing could be more futile than such a pursuit. And yet time and money and energy had been devoted to this pointless quest. Slush shook his head in amazement. Nonetheless, he remained in the room, watching and listening.

Susan and Richard sat close to one another on a couch, poring over a photograph album. The two heads, one dark and one fair, almost touched as they studied the photographs together. They spoke softly, but Slush could hear every word. He and Neil exchanged an occasional comment, but most of the time they were silent onlookers. From time to time Susan would look up; then she would lower her head again. As she turned each page of the photograph album, she smoothed it down with her hand.

Slush was intrigued to see that all his mother's habitual curtness was gone. She responded to this man whom she'd never met before with a patient, even tender indulgence. She had never been a physically demonstrative person, but he saw her touching Richard's hand, his shoulder, allowing her sleeve to brush against his. He saw how painstaking were her efforts to draw him in, even as she laid before him the early life of one who had pushed him away. She herself had been expunged from that life; it had been lost to her too. But she did all she could to recreate it now, fifty years later.

It was this unwonted behaviour in his mother that moved Slush. Richard's urgency continued to make little impact on him; it was Susan's response to her new nephew's hunger, her scrupulous gentleness, which affected the young man. Despite himself, he grew intrigued.

He saw to what lengths Susan went to flesh out the years she and Erna had shared before the estrangement. She could do nothing to change the subsequent trajectory of her sister's life: there was no way of thwarting its destination. But what she did do, very carefully and astutely, was admit Richard to the early, as-yet-unencumbered days, showing him the sheen of excited possibility that lay upon them. There was a limit to what she could give, but she tried as hard as she could to make the most of what there was. The strenuousness of her attempt was not lost on Slush.

The photographs came to an end. 'That was the last time I saw or heard from her,' Susan said. 'At least, until this year, when she was on her death-bed.' Here they must halt, thought Slush. Now they could go no further. This was the cul-de-sac of Erna. But no – he was wrong. Richard and Susan pressed ahead. They could only speculate as to what came after the parting of the sisters, they could know nothing for certain; but working within the limitations which conjecture necessarily imposes, they began nonetheless to construct a story that gave a shape to the lost years. And as they did so, they ceased to be the one who tells and the one who listens and became partners, helping each other to weave shadows, construing the what-ifs and might-have-beens together.

Slush heard names that had hitherto belonged to what he regarded as the dank and distant past: Herzog, Smuts, Malan, Strijdom, Verwoerd. The Ossewabrandwag was mentioned and he tried to remember what it was, but failed. He had a vague feeling it had something to do with the Great Trek, but that had taken place hundreds of years ago. Surely they weren't going *that* far back? Susan told Richard that Greyling had been a member of the Ossewabrandwag. He was interred by Smuts during the war. Slush presumed they were talking about the Second World War. In that case, the Ossewabrandwag couldn't possibly have had anything to do with the Great Trek. He was obviously wrong about that. But then what *was* it? He wished he could remember. They went on to talk about the election of 1948. Yes, he knew about that. That was when everything went wrong. Smuts was mentioned again; so was a place called Standerton. What had happened at Standerton? He had an idea that it was the scene of a battle from the Boer War. But if so, then they were going back in time again. It was all very confusing.

They spoke about rifts within the Nationalist party, break-away groups and the prominent role that Greyling had played in the politics of the far right. To Slush it was as if the ungainly sparring of extinct creatures were being described. What difference could it make to anyone now whether the sabre-toothed tiger had killed the brontosaurus or the other way around? They were both doomed, in any case. One could not say that one was more defunct than the other. He felt nothing but a sense of relief that these gross beasts no longer roamed the planet. Their internecine quarrels seemed very remote, both in time and in pertinence. And yet Susan and Richard clearly didn't see it that way. He saw that for the two seated on the couch the past had all the immediacy of a tale that was still unfolding. It had scarcely begun to disclose its secrets. But what hope had they of getting it to cough up what it knew? Surely theirs was a misguided, a doomed appeal? You cannot animate the dead, no matter how fervently you wish to do so.

Suddenly the trip to Rooiwater came into his mind. What he remembered most vividly were the children who had gathered around his car and were loath to move away, the little girl sucking her thumb, her faded dress, the silent staring. He had done his best to erase what he had seen that day, but every detail of it came back to him now, including the feeling of uneasiness prompted by the ominous torpor of the dorp. That was the very town which the man who may have been Richard's father had built. Those scruffy children were growing up in a place where the inhabitants revered him still as a founding father. Dead as he was, he was not dead to them.

The winter sun was warm, but Slush shivered a little.

He smiled at Neil, asked him if he wanted more tea or a slice of carrot cake, and then turned to listen to Susan and Richard again. The more he listened, the more engrossing he found their conversation. They were helping each other to transform Erna's life, with all its gaps and secrets – unwholesome secrets, in all probability – into a story that they could live with. It would never contain the untrammelled, first-born words that revelations and prophecies require. Those words were impossible. They were lost forever. What was being composed was something different. It would never be what Richard so clearly longed for: a story that justifies, that completes as it encloses. Instead it sagged; it was patchy and frayed. But still, it *was* a narrative. It would never satisfy Richard's hunger completely. But Slush had the feeling that it wouldn't leave him wholly unnourished either.

What he witnessed that morning as Susan and Richard became accomplices did not convert him. He still believed that it's healthier and more rewarding to dwell on the largesse of the present. He still saw the past as irreparable. But he had to confess that he had never seen so resolute, so valiant an attempt to repair it.

'Well, that was quite a morning,' said Richard suddenly. For a long time he had said nothing, had driven as if he were completely unaware that he was behind the wheel of a car. Neil, seeing how preoccupied he was, had not sought to make conversation.

'Quite a morning,' repeated Neil.

'Of course, what we *didn't* hear,' Richard went on, 'is the story of Slush. I'm curious about that. I mean, how did he and Susan become mother and son?'

'I'd also like to know. But I'm sure they'll tell you next time you see them. You had other things to talk about today.'

'We did indeed.' Richard switched on the indicator and waited to turn onto the highway. 'Well, it looks as if I found me an aunt,' he said, as he swung the wheel round and made the turn. 'And a cousin. I thought so often over the years of what my relatives would turn out to be like if I found them, but the one thing I never imagined was that one of them would be a black yuppie!'

Neil laughed. 'No, nothing could have prepared you for that. Did you hear the tune he's got on his cellphone?'

'What is it? It sounded familiar.'

'*Hey, Big Spender.*'

'Of course!'

'Well,' said Neil, 'however he came to be Susan's son, he certainly landed with his bum in the butter.'

'In the pâté de foie gras, you mean.' Richard slammed on the brakes as a mini-bus taxi, which had been driving in the emergency lane, pushed in front of him. Neither he nor Neil commented on this. 'Very good-looking,' he said, as he moved his foot back to the accelerator.

'Who?'

'Slush.'

'Is he? I didn't really…'

'*Don't* give me that,' said Richard, punching his arm lightly. 'I saw you looking at him.'

'There's nothing wrong with looking,' Neil protested.

'I never said there was. My, what an interesting shade of red. I've never seen you blush before.'

Neil turned his head and gazed out of the window.

'Can I change the subject?' he asked.

'Sure.'

'I haven't had a chance to tell you yet. I've made a big decision. I'm going to sell *Time Immemorial Tombstones.*'

'Why?'

'I just have to make a change. I can't go on selling tombstones forever. My father devoted his life to building up that business, but that's his life, not mine.'

'Have you told the others – Deanna and Aunt Maisie?'

'Yes.'

'And what do they say?'

'They've been very supportive. Archie is the major shareholder, but Deanna has been appointed *curator bonis*, so she can vote on his behalf. Bee-bee is the only one who seems to disapprove: that's because she won't be getting discounts on tombstones any more.'

'She wrote me a letter,' said Richard.

'Who? Bee-Bee?'

'Yes.'

'She always adored you.'

'It was very moving.' The traffic on the highway was congested, even though it wasn't peak hour. They came to a complete stop. A string of mini-bus taxis, hurtling along in the emergency lane, passed them by. This, too, provoked no comment. 'What will you do instead?' asked Richard.

'I'm not sure.'

'Well, whatever you decide, I'll be rooting for you. You've done the right thing.'

'Thank you.'

'We must go out for dinner again,' said Richard.

'Yes. I believe that *Renaissance* has closed down.'

'Really? It was so popular at one stage. Well, where shall we go? What's that place in Westdene?'

'*The Pink Chicken*.' There was an awkward silence as both recalled the failure of their plan to visit it in February. 'I don't think we should go there,' Neil went on. 'Someone told me that it's become very over-priced.'

'Is there somewhere else?'

'There's a new restaurant in Craighall Park which specialises in Korean cuisine. I read a review of it in the paper.'

'Great. Let's give it a try,' said Richard.

The bonhomie pleased Neil, but he was still not sure how he felt about seeing Richard again. The attack on the Slaters had robbed him of the opportunity to respond to the letter that had been pushed under his door. It had taken away from him the power of granting or withholding forgiveness, of setting terms and conditions. He had felt cheated. He knew he couldn't slip back into the same mode of friendship, couldn't behave as if nothing had happened. And yet he could also not insist that his sorrow had to take precedence. What had happened to Richard entitled him to special treatment. How small-spirited it would be to deny him compassion now. Before he had been able to read his own heart, to ascertain whether he wished to be magnanimous or not, the decision had been taken away from him.

He knew that Richard was grateful for everything he had received, from Deanna and from him. It was satisfying to know that he'd been able to help. And it had been very exciting to share in this morning's discovery. But where to from here? He wasn't even sure how he felt about Richard any more. When he thought of that hot February night and of the scene in the flat, he thought of a Richard who had too much power while he had too little. And then he thought of the Richard who had sat outside the operating-room, looking up at him with tears in his eyes. At that moment the power had been his: the power of compassion, of beneficence.

Could there ever be a relationship between them that was free of pain and untarnished by power? And if not, was there any point to it? What did he really want?

He didn't have the answers to those questions, but the meeting that morning with the Southerns had shown him another way of thinking. Something in Susan's freely given solicitude had rebuked him for being so begrudging with his – in the impulse, not in the deed. It was not the same, of course: Susan and Richard had no shared past, there was no scar tissue in their relationship. But he was moved by the adroitness of her tact. And he understood that in inviting Richard into his mother's life, Susan was trying to help him to forgive her. It was a great deal to ask, when one considered Erna's discarding of her son and what she had afterwards become. But it was crucial. Finding his mother was only the first step; Richard had also to learn how best to take leave of her. Susan understood that the search had much more to do with himself than it did with the woman who had so negligently given birth to him.

Neil saw that morning that the question he had asked after receiving the letter was the wrong one. The point was not whether or not he should forgive Richard for what happened that February night, for, even if he forgave him, it would not repair anything; it wouldn't help him to move on with his life. The terms of that decision were far too narrow. There would be no true magnanimity in such an act of forgiveness.

In order to forgive Richard, he had to forgive himself – but for what? For failing to tell Richard how he felt, for bad faith? Yes, but it was more than that. A long time ago he told Farrell that he was suffering from desire. Then he had seen desire as something that came from outside him, as a visitation, a plague. He was its helpless victim. He had not wanted to think that it emanated from him, for then he would have to assume responsibility for it. But Susan had shown him the freedom of making even that which afflicts or distresses you your own. In the assumption of that responsibility lies a kind of freedom.

The truly magnanimous gesture would be to forgive himself for desiring Richard. And to forgive Richard for being desired.

When Deanna was a young girl, in the months after her mother's death, she used to indulge in an elaborate daydream. She had read somewhere that the earth was always in danger of being struck by a meteor. In her waking dream this had come to pass and she found herself the only survivor of the cataclysmic collision. She searched dutifully for signs of life: she went from crèche to school to old-aged home to supermarket to police station to airport and everywhere she found nothing left alive, not even a cockroach. She was the only living creature left on the entire planet, destined to live the rest of her life in absolute and unrelieved solitude. No Man Friday would ever appear suddenly to return her to the pleasures and frustrations of companionship. The meteor had made the earth new again and she was its first-born and only child.

Curiously, in her daydream all the buildings remained undamaged by the meteor. She had access to libraries and shops and private homes (none of which was locked). If she were inclined, she could spend every night of her solitary life in a different house, safe in the knowledge that the owners would never return: a Goldilocks who would never be inconvenienced by proprietary bears. She had no need ever to make a bed again as long as she lived – she merely moved on and slept in another house, in a fresh new bed, in crisp white sheets.

As the years passed, the daydream receded. There were long periods of time in which she didn't even think about it. It was always there, though, beckoning, urging her to enter, to become once more the solitary revenant. She knew that fantasies come from longing, from the womb of wishes. But what yearning could such a vision of solitude have satisfied? Why had the young Deanna wished to be the earth's sole heir, the only witness to its dehabitation?

It had to do, she came to understand, with exemption, with aloneness beyond reprehension. That was why its appeal had been so strong. In the wake of her mother's abandonment of her, it had made sense. But now the emptiness and silence disconcerted her, whereas, as a child, she had delighted in them. She no longer found consolation in a shadowless purity. Her impulse was to contend with misshapen seasons, not escape them.

And that required change. Neil was beginning to make changes in his life – he was even selling *Time Immemorial Tombstones*. It was time for her to do the same. And changes, if they meant anything, had to come from within herself. She had to dream different dreams: variegated dreams. Somewhere there is an isthmus – so narrow that it is scarcely possible to stand squarely upon it – where longing and prophecy meet. Her dreams had to guide her in her search for it.

Changing yourself means surprising yourself. But the difficulty was that she wasn't good at that, had never been good at it. She couldn't see how a life such as hers would ever be cajoled into yielding something unexpected.

And then, to her amazement, she did indeed surprise herself. When Richard phoned to tell her of his meeting with Susan and Slush and what he had discovered about his mother, she listened carefully and was preparing in her mind the appropriate sympathetic comments. But none of them came. When she thought about it later, she couldn't believe that she had reacted the way she did. She, the ever-cautious one, the one who body-searched words before she used them – had that really been her, *laughing*? How *could* one laugh at such a thing? What gross insensitivity! She tried to stifle it, but to no avail. More laughter rose within her. Nor could she suppress the words that came tumbling out. 'Oh, Richard,' she said. 'A white supremacist. And dead. You found your mother at last, after searching for so long, and she's a dead white supremacist. Well, what can I say? Nobody's perfect!'

'I'm pleased you find it so amusing,' was Richard's stiff reply. 'Really, Deanna, this isn't the response I expected from you at all. This is my life, you know, not a scene from *Some Like It Hot.*'

'I'm so sorry,' she tried to say. 'Please forgive me.' But she was laughing too much.

Richard tried to sound angry, but she could hear that he was beginning to laugh too.

Barbara, working in her studio, wiped her hands with a towel and studied them. They were old hands now – there was no denying that. The skin was thin and papery and the knuckles had thickened. What time marks it seems also to chasten, so it was easy to believe that these hands, abashed by age, no longer had the power or the inclination to be unpredictable. But it was not so: they had surprised her yet again.

Theresa, in a moment of rare intimacy, told her once that her father's favourite saying had been, 'Take it from whence it comes.' For some reason it came now into Barbara's mind. Of course, it was sagacious advice. Things don't just happen, it said; consider always the origin, the cause that underlies the effect; never overlook the context of an action or an utterance. Theresa, it was clear to her, had struggled to live according to her father's maxim, had succeeded in some respects and failed in others. In general, people would do well to abide by such a precept. But Barbara knew it was not for her.

For a start, it went against her efforts – her life-long struggle – to remake herself. From whence did she come? She came from Marie Moxley, sitting in a donga and dreaming of escape, reading about myths and legends, listening to the wind and making little figures out of clay. Yes, Marie was her origin. But she was also her greatest enemy. Marie had had to die so that she could live, so that Barbara Lombard could be brought to life. If she were truly to take things from whence they came, she would have to go back, to allow the revivification of Marie. Where would Barbara be then? And it would mean conceding that the beginning and the destination are the same, that we are bound by an unrelenting circle; and that she could not do, for she had striven all her life for the emancipatory possibilities of a line that leads on, that pushes ahead.

Yet Marie was much in her mind these days. So were Christiaan Shweizer and his troupe. So was Elna Louw. Of course, meeting Elna again in Johannesburg had returned her to those days as nothing else could. And, thinking of them, a wistfulness such as she'd never known came upon her. It was the weatherbeaten sadness of a shrinking life. She remembered how intolerant she had been of Christiaan Shweizer's melancholia, how she had shuddered to witness his solitary despondency as he consumed half a bottle of brandy every night. She saw it differently now. The methodical drinking, the bowed head, the shoulders hunched over the bottle and glass: it was a scene of unbearable pathos. Shweizer had been dead, of course, for years and years; yet she pitied him now as she had not done when he was still alive. She felt compassion where newly-minted Barbara had felt only contempt.

That German who had never been to Germany, that glum platteland romantic, was beyond the reach of this late sympathy, this emotional revisionism; but there were others who were not. Hannelie could still be reached. In Shweizer's case, she had been so preoccupied with the implications of his defeat for her own transformation, for her Pegasus dream, that she had not been prepared to consider what his disappointment meant to *him*. And all these years, when she thought ruefully of the waning of Hannelie's power, when she mourned the resolute self that had defied a father and a prime minister, had she not dwelt chiefly upon the loss to her rather than to Hannelie? Had she not, in that part of her heart where unworthy thoughts are hidden, made herself the chief victim?

It was not too late for compassion: the true compassion, which is a transmigration of souls. It was not too late for a different kind of love, a second-born love. But it required sacrifices. The departure of Noldie and his family meant that she was now almost house-bound, as she'd known she would be. She could not travel, could not attend exhibitions, could not leave Hannelie, except for very brief periods. The only trip she made was when she flew to Johannesburg to meet the *Promised Land Pleasure Tours* team and to be interviewed by the journalist; and even then she was back in Cape Town by nightfall.

Her curfew was not because Hannelie was ill again, but because she had to be watched all the time for the first sign of a decline. Barbara had promised Noldie that she would manage without him, and she was determined to keep her promise; but that required constant vigilance. She had to fulfil his obligations as well as her own. It was not easy.

Growing old, suffering the restriction of her movements, seeing how easily love bends to compromise – all these seemed to force upon her the notion that she had never really been free of anything. It had all been an illusion. Life had merely let her out on a leash, so long and loose that, until recently, she was not even aware of its existence. And now the leash was being gathered in.

Yet this was where her hands came up with their surprise. While all her thoughts were of her curtailed life, her hands decided to become expansive in their ambitions. For over sixty years the story of Pandora's Box had been with her. She had inhabited it as only a story from one's childhood can be inhabited. And now – but why *now*? – her hands resolved that the time had come at last to sculpt the story of Pandora.

They decided that it needed to be told by means of a sequence of three sculptures. The first depicted the box itself: ornate, finely wrought, giving no sign of what lay within. Pandora's hands – slender, delicate hands – rested lightly on the top. The second was the box lying open, the plagues released, Pandora's hands clutching one another, stricken with the consequences of their actions.

The third sculpture had not yet been revealed to her. She knew, however, what it had to represent. For after the plagues had all been released, after the malevolent swarm had flown off, something remained behind in the box. That something was hope. It was not the most vigorous child of the gods: it was abandoned, neglected. But still, it was not nothing. It was hope.

Barbara felt that this last image would contain an answer. She didn't know if it would reply only to the questions raised by the work itself, or whether it would stretch further than that to meet a broader enquiry. That would only be divulged when she knew what the final sculpture looked like. And her hands had not shown her that yet. They had not disclosed to her the shape of hope.

'I'm sure you know our slogan by now,' said Helena, 'but, in case you don't, let's run through it again.' The familiar tune started up and she intoned the words which accompanied it.

We're proud as the noble lion
Shaking his golden mane
Proud of the Rainbow Nation
We choose Radio Blue Crane

'For some reason,' she went on, after several advertisements had been aired, 'I find myself thinking a lot about reincarnation. It's very much in vogue again, partly because of all this renewed interest in the Kabbalah. I can see the attraction, of course, but it makes me uneasy. Why should souls be used again? Would anyone want a second-hand soul? Isn't it a bit like retreads on tyres? Do we really want Mahatma Gandhi coming back as a caterer? Or Lady Godiva as a dress-designer? Or Lucrezia Borgia as a social worker? And what about our own Oom Toeka from Boksburg? What should he come back as? Isn't it enough that he was the first of our race?'

She paused and then continued. 'As always,' she said, 'songwriters and lyricists have explored all these issues thoroughly. Here's another lovely golden oldie for you. I'm Helena Verster, enjoying your company on Radio Blue Crane, 88.7, the Station for Committed South Africans, and this is Crowded House with *Don't Dream It's Over*.'

They arrived so quietly that at first there was nothing more to discern than a gathering of small movements and sounds. Many did not even notice this faint clamour. Those who did, however, knew it for what it was.

The winds of August were come again.

Acknowledgements

I have been extraordinarily fortunate in both my publisher and my editor.

Terry Morris and her team at Picador Africa/Pan Macmillan responded warmly to my manuscript from the start, and their enthusiasm never waned. It has been a delight and a privilege to work with them.

I am most grateful to my editor, Alex Dodd, for caring so deeply for *The Shadow Follows*, for her wise counsel and astute recommendations.

Darryl Accone, Shayleen Peeke and I initiated a writing group several years ago. The entire novel was workshopped in the group and benefited immeasurably from the creative, enabling and nurturing environment which it provided. I would like to thank Darryl and Shayleen for their support and loving friendship, as well as all those who, at various times, have participated in the group and helped to make it such a success: Gill Berkowitz, Maren Bodenstein, Emma Chen, Dave Chislett, Susie Dinneen, Damon Garstang, Michael Holm, Kate Hutchings, Jean Isserow, Anton Krueger, Carla Monteiro, Jill Nudelman, Geoff Sifrin, Cecily Singer, Renos Spanoudes and Miriam Stern.

Portions of the novel were also workshopped in a writing group run, since Lionel Abrahams's death, by Jane Fox. My thanks to Jane for her cogent insights, and to all the participants in that group.

I would like, as so many have done, to acknowledge the enormous contribution of the late Lionel Abrahams to South African literature, as well as his importance in my life and to my writing.

A number of other people read the manuscript as it evolved. I would like to thank the following, in particular, for useful suggestions and advice: Brenda Block, Molly Brown, Anthony Chennells, Rose Cohen, Natasha Distiller, Elisa Galgut, Carron Katz, Kathryn Laing, Karen Lazar, Nadine Lemmer, Patrick Lenahan, Melanie Miller, Sharon Seftel, Ann Smith, Elena Thomas, Marijke van Vuuren, Shaun Viljoen, Andries Wessels and Fiona Wicksted.